# BRIDE OF DREAMS

*Recent Titles by Jane Aiken Hodge*

ESCAPADE
FIRST NIGHT
LAST ACT
LEADING LADY
THE LOST GARDEN
POLONAISE
SECRET ISLAND
WHISPERING
WIDE IS THE WATER
WINDOVER

# BRIDE OF DREAMS

Jane Aiken Hodge

This first world edition published in Great Britain 1996 by
SEVERN HOUSE PUBLISHERS LTD of
9–15 High Street, Sutton, Surrey SM1 1DF.
First published in the USA 1996 by
SEVERN HOUSE PUBLISHERS INC. of
595 Madison Avenue, New York, NY 10022.

British Library Cataloguing in Publication Data

Hodge, Jane Aiken, 1917–
  Bride of dreams
  1. English fiction – 20th century
  I. Title
  823.9'14 [F]

  ISBN 0-7278-5102-0

All situations in this publication are fictitious and
any resemblance to living persons is purely coincidental.

Typeset by Palimpsest Book Production Limited,
Polmont, Stirlingshire, Scotland.
Printed and bound in Great Britain by
Hartnolls Ltd, Bodmin, Cornwall.

# Chapter One

Amanda and her mother were early. The fiddlers in the little musicians' gallery that overhung the Assembly Room were still tuning their instruments. Mr Random, the proprietor of the George Inn where Rye's Assemblies were held, was hurrying about with last minute preparations and it was left to his wife, buxom Mrs Random, to make her nervous bob to the first arrivals and guide them through the dance hall and up to the dressing room they had hired for the evening. As always, she talked, lugubriously, all the way. The weather was bad; the attendance at this, the first Assembly of Rye's little season, would be thin; the news was terrible – particularly that from France. In the year 1791, France, with its developing revolution, could be relied on, by pessimists, as a source of bad news.

Equally true to form, Mrs Carteret took not the slightest notice of Mrs Random's flow of nervous talk, and it was left to Amanda to make the rejoinders courtesy demanded. At seventeen, world affairs do not seem vastly important, but the question of the weather struck nearer home. Yes, it had indeed rained all day; their coach had nearly stuck in the mud at the foot of Rye Hill; did Mrs Random really think the attendance would be poor? "For my first ball? I do not believe I could bear it."

Satisfied with having got the reaction she wanted, Mrs Random relented, promised Amanda all the partners her heart could desire, and took her leave.

"Truly, Amanda," said her mother, turning to the long glass as she removed her cloak, "sometimes I despair of your breeding. Must you always be gossiping with the lower orders? I wish you would at least try to remember who your father was."

Amanda made a face. "I wish you would try to forget it, Mama. What is the use of giving ourselves the airs and graces of the nobility when everybody knows we are as poor as church mice?" She stopped and coloured, alarmed at her dangerous plain speaking, but on this important night her mother was determined to be pleasant.

"What a little Jeremiah it is, to be sure." She pinched her daughter's cheek affectionately. "But I tell you, my love, there are those who recognize how infinitely more important blood – and breeding, of course – are than mere money. Who knows, perhaps our troubles are nearly over." It was her turn to pause, colour, and apply herself assiduously to the problems of her toilette.

Though young and full of dreams, Amanda was no fool. She had not failed to notice the steady diminution in the trappings of her mother's widowhood. Tonight, Mrs Carteret's admirably preserved charms were set off by a gown of palest lavender, with faint touches of crêpe surely more for ornament than out of respect for a long dead husband. To Amanda, who had grown used to the widow's cap and the widow's black, she looked, just faintly, ridiculous, but then, to Amanda, Mrs Carteret was a mother and, by definition, old. To a chance observer she was a woman in the ambiguous mid-thirties; to herself, she was in the prime of life.

Amanda, on the other hand, was very young. "Is Lord Meynel to be here tonight?" She knew the question for a mistake as she spoke it.

But once again, almost miraculously, her mother's uncertain temper held. Mrs Carteret had learned, among many bitter lessons of a disappointing life, how fatally anger blotched her pink and white complexion. "How should I know?" she countered mildly. "But come, my love, let me look at you. To think that my little girl is really old enough for her first ball. I can hardly believe it."

Amanda was privately convinced that she had been quite old enough to attend the quiet Rye Assemblies the

2

year before, and knew equally well that she owed this year's unexpected indulgence to a chance remark of Lord Meynel's. It had been at the end of one of the neighbourly morning calls that had become so frequent of late – to Amanda's disgust and her mother's not quite concealed delight. Rising to take his leave, he had paused for a moment to twirl the inevitable cane in his thinning white hand and spare one of his uncomfortably appraising glances for Amanda. "You will be bringing this child to the Assemblies this year?" It was hardly even a question.

Amanda, whose own timid overtures in the same direction had been briskly rebuffed, had looked up with a sudden flaring of hope. Here was an ally indeed, however dislikeable a one.

Mrs Carteret had paused, coloured, seemed to consider, then deferred prettily to her guest's opinion. "Do you truly think her old enough? Is it really my duty to cast off my widow's weeds and bring my baby before the world? Must I – for her sake – give up the retirement that suits me so well?"

"Of course you must, ma'am," her visitor had said roundly. "For her sake, and your own, and the world's, that has missed you too long. There'll be many a hot cheek and anxious brow, I warrant, when the belles of Rye hear Mrs Carteret is coming among them again. You'll put them all in the shade, and they know it."

Already on her feet to wish her visitor good day, Mrs Carteret had curtsied and coloured prettily for the compliment, and Amanda, while wondering how her mother – that dragon of good taste – could overlook its vulgarity, had known her point gained. There could be no doubt now: she would go to the Assemblies this year.

And here she was, obediently standing and twirling for her mother's inspection, while downstairs the fiddles were warming to their work and a rising hum of talk suggested that the world was beginning to arrive. "Will I do?" she asked anxiously. Impossible, now, with the sounds of music and talk coming up from below, to trouble herself too much about the unwelcome likelihood that Lord Meynel would

3

soon be her stepfather. She had other things to think about.
She was at her first ball at last. Her dress of finest pale blue
sprigged muslin was almost exactly what she had wished.
Her mother's judgement of people might leave something
to be desired, but on clothes, she was superb.

Mrs Carteret was nodding critical approval. "Yes," she
said at last, "you will do admirably, my love. The dress is
just as I wished it, modest but," she paused, "becoming. I do
not think you will lack for partners, and if, by any unhappy
chance you should, I am sure Lord Meynel will have an eye
to you."

That was just what Amanda was afraid of. She knew, she
sometimes thought, rather more about Lord Meynel's eye
than her mother did. It was apt to lead him into dark corridors
or shady paths among the shrubbery where he would linger
to await a chance encounter with any personable young
female. After the first of these meetings, Amanda had
hurried for counsel to her friend and comforter, Phoebe,
her mother's maid. It was characteristic of her relationship
with her mother that it had never occurred to her to go to her.
But Phoebe had been robustly comforting. "Think nothing
of it, love," she said. "He does it to all us girls and we just
laugh at him for his pains."

Amanda, who had never expected that her first kiss would
be from elderly, snuffy Lord Meynel, had almost managed
the laugh, and had become expert in avoiding dark corridors
and shady paths when he was about. But it was certainly not
to dance with him that she had dressed so carefully for her
first ball, while the idea of his sharp little eyes upon her made
her dress seem suddenly far too low cut. She had protested
about this when she had first tried it on, but her mother had
been firm: "You should see how the Duchess of Devonshire
wears hers." Amanda had not thought the argument exactly
to the point, but she had bowed, as, in the end, she usually
did, to her mother's superior judgement. Now all the old
qualms returned with a rush and she turned for an anxious
and appraising glance at herself in the long glass. It was
very well as long as she carried herself strictly upright, but
suppose she should chance to bend forward? Worse still,

4

imagine dancing with a partner taller than herself. And John Purvis was taller – taller by half a head. Suddenly, she was overwhelmed by confusion.

"Mother," she turned from the glass, "I have the headache. Could I not stay here and wait for you?"

"Nonsense," said her mother robustly. "It is nothing but a spasm of the nerves; you will feel better directly you have got your first partner. Come, my love, you will only make yourself worse if you stay lingering here."

For once in her life, Amanda had to admit the justice of her worldly mother's opinion. If the ballroom must be faced, the sooner the better. Besides, John had promised to watch for her and take her out for her first dance, and John did not like to be kept waiting. She spared one last quick glance, half fright, half satisfaction, at the unfamiliar and undeniably elegant reflection in the glass, then followed her mother down the long corridor to the ballroom. To her deep, delighted relief, John was indeed waiting close to the door and came up at once to greet them and ask for her hand for the next dance. Amanda had never seen him in evening dress before, and forgot her qualms about her own appearance in admiration of his. Even her mother, who habitually, and infuriatingly, referred to him as "poor Mr Purvis," treated him, tonight, with something like respect, made no objection to his claiming Amanda's hand for the dance, and even went so far as to enquire, almost archly, what he was doing so far from the fleet.

"Wishing for war, ma'am," was his forthright reply. "God knows how we poor sailors are to earn our living else."

Mrs Carteret flirted her fan at him in pretended horror. "La, Mr Purvis, how can you be so callous. To want a bloody war, merely for your own advancement! I am shocked at you, and so, I wager, is Amanda."

"Indeed, Mrs Carteret," he protested, "you do me less than justice. If I did not think the declaration of war in the country's best interests, I would starve gladly on half pay for the rest of my days. But, I tell you, if those madmen in France are not taught a sharp lesson, and quickly too, the whole world will rue it. And of course," he added, with the engaging frankness Amanda had always loved in him, "there is no question but the sooner war is declared, the sooner I shall be at sea again, where, but for one thing, all my happiness lies. But, come, Miss Carteret, the set is forming, shall we go?"

He held out his hand, and Amanda took it, blushing. How odd it seemed, after all their childhood years together, to have him calling her "Miss Carteret". In the good old days – how long ago they seemed – the Purvis estates had marched with the Carterets' and Amanda, five years the younger, and a lonely, fatherless child, had been John Purvis's willing slave. Then, it had been "Mandy, come here," or "Mandy, hold this . . . mind my dog . . . see how far I can jump. . . ."

Overnight, the long, happy companionship of childhood had ended. Mr Purvis, who, it seemed, had been speculating wildly in the East Indian market, shot himself to avoid the disgrace of bankruptcy and his wife followed his example in a timely decline and graceful death. Lord Meynel, the chief of Mr Purvis's creditors, had taken over the house on Leasam Hill and John, after one last wretched scene with Amanda in the course of which, to her amazement and his fury, he had actually shed tears, had left the district. Taken in hand by his mother's brother, he had been sent to sea, almost at once, as a midshipman, and from then on Amanda had seen him only occasionally, on his brief visits to his father's sister, who still lived in a dark little highly polished house near Rye church. Like him, an only child, Amanda had lavished on his career all the affectionate interest her mother rebuffed, and while Mrs Carteret set her widow's cap now at this eligible bachelor and then at that prosperous widower, Amanda's main interest in life had continued to be John's progress from one of His Majesty's ships to another. Her somewhat randomly selected governesses might lament over the lapses in Amanda's arithmetic, but of her geography and her spelling they could never complain; these were necessary to her, the magic by which she followed John round the world.

6

It had been disconcerting, the other day, to drop in, oh so casually, on Miss Purvis, find John there – with the proper protestations of surprise – and have him great her, with total seriousness, as "Miss Carteret". He was handsomer than ever, too, a man full-grown, his shoulders broad, his skin brown from the weather (terrible, he told them) around the Cape of Good Hope. But he had treated her, throughout a much shorter visit than she had intended, with all the formal courtesy due to a young lady, and that night, in bed, she had wept bitter tears for Mandy and John. At least, however, he had promised to come to the Assembly tonight – but then, how could he help himself when she, still half in, half out of the old casual relationship, had begged him to come and 'see her through'. Well, he was here, her hand was on his arm, the musicians were tuning up for her first public dance – surely, it should be happiness enough?

As soon as it was threatened, she chid herself for a fool to have admitted any qualification in her bliss. For here, now, at the last moment, when the set was forming and the music rising to its preliminary climax, came Lord Meynel, all smiles, all eagerness – and it was just as she had sometimes feared. It was not to her mother that his soft white hand was held out, but to her. "I must have the privilege of taking my dear Miss Amanda down her first dance."

Mrs Carteret had not expected this. Despite herself, perceptibly, she bristled. Amanda blushed crimson, and her little hand clung more tightly, with a desperate silent appeal to John Purvis's arm.

He did not fail her. "I cry your pardon." How completely a man he was. "But Miss Carteret has done me the honour of accepting my hand for this dance."

"Oh," Lord Meynel was only taken aback for an instant. "Young Purvis, eh? And how goes the world for midshipmen these peaceful days?"

"Well enough, I thank you." John had been a lieutenant for several years, but refused to be drawn. "Come, Amanda, we shall lose our place."

He had called her by her first name. In silent happiness, she let him lead her out to the line of couples now forming up in the centre of the room, hardly caring that they left Lord Meynel and Mama equally bristling. In a moment, however, the older couple joined them in the set. Mrs Carteret was all smiles now, and Lord Meynel gave every appearance of complete satisfaction as he made his dignified way down the hall. Only once, joining hands with Amanda, he held her more tightly than necessary and called her, in passing, "Little rogue". And then, as he reluctantly let her go, "The next one, then." She pretended not to hear him.

But John had. "He is a trouble to you?" It was their turn now to meet in the figure of the dance.

"Sometimes – a little." She had to leave him again, and then, as they reached the head of the set, was too busy remembering her steps to be troubled about Lord Meynel or anything else. It was her first ball; she was dancing with John; what else could she do but be happy?

When the dance ended and the couples began the usual parade about the room, John had her arm firmly in his. They were near the little side door opening onto the inn's garden. "Come," he said.

It did not occur to her to resist him. After all, she had obeyed his every command since she had been five years old. The door shut with a little sigh behind them and they were away from the lights, the smell of tallow and the sounds of music and laughter, in a quiet world of moonlight and shadows. They had played here often enough as children under the tolerant eye of Mrs Random while their mothers busied themselves with the eternal female preoccupation of ribbons and gauzes. Now, without thinking, she let John guide her to their favourite seat under the arbour of honeysuckle. The bench was rickety now, with age, and the honeysuckle untrained and shaggy but fragrant as ever.

Seating her, John looked, for a moment, anxiously down at her. "I wish I had a cloak to wrap you in. Will you be warm enough?"

"Of course." She coloured, grateful for the neutrality of moonlight. "I thought it was too low cut. Do you . . . do you mind?"

There was infinite comfort in his well-known laugh.

"Mind? Absurd Amanda, why should I mind that you are beautiful tonight? Or at least," he did not pretend not to understand her, "to be honest, I do not mind when we are out here together, but when I see you with Lord Meynel – then I do. Tell me of him, Amanda."

She folded and unfolded her fan. "I . . . I do not know what to say. He is – always – most attentive to Mama – and to me. I had thought – I had wondered . . ." she dwindled to a pause.

"Whether you might not find him, one fine day, your step-papa?"

"Yes," she breathed it gratefully. "Oh, John – Mr Purvis, do you think it very wicked of me not to like him?"

"Like him? I'd never forgive you if you did. I only hope your mother knows what she is doing; his reputation is – not of the most savoury."

"He is very rich," said Amanda apologetically.

"What's that to the purpose? I tell you, Amanda, I do not like to think of you in the same house as him. Nor," she sensed his frown in the darkness, "nor do I quite understand it. Your mother is a fine woman, it is true, but," he broke off for a moment, then took another tack. "I collect she has not had some unexpected acquisition of riches since I last saw you?"

Amanda laughed. "I only wish she had. You know perfectly well that we are poor as curates."

"Not so poor as I am, Amanda. If only I had something – anything to offer! But a half-pay lieutenant in time of peace is about the lowest of God's creatures. Your mother thought me heartless, I know, to talk of wanting war, but how can I help it? What chance of promotion have I otherwise? And, without that, what hope of happiness?"

His intensity almost frightened her and she answered out of embarrassment: "I had not thought you mercenary."

"Mercenary? I? Oh, Amanda, do you not understand?" He caught the hand that was still playing, nervously, with her fan. "How can you imagine that I want money for my own sake? Surely you know me better than that. But when I see you surrounded by creatures like Meynel, and your

9

mother, Amanda – forgive me for saying it – not the wisest of guides or counsellors. . . . Then I cannot bear my penury, my absolute lack of prospects."

"But you say there will be war." She would not let him stop there.

"I think so. I hope so, for truly, Amanda, I believe the French to be a danger to the world. They must be stopped. But who knows when it will come, or, when it does, how long it will take me to make my mark – and the fortune I need."

"But you just said you did not care for fortune."

"Amanda, you are being stupid on purpose!" And then, when she did not deny it, "You must know my only wish for a fortune is so that I may ask you to be my wife. There: I have said it, and I promised myself I would not. I should not have done so, but you teased me into it. Amanda, forgive me."

"Forgive you? Why? What is there to forgive? I am glad you want to marry me," she said simply.

"Oh, Mandy, you are an angel." He lifted her hand to his lips. "But I shall not easily forgive myself. I have no right to speak to you, circumstanced as I am. You must forget that I have done so. I shall always consider myself bound to you – nor could I wish myself otherwise, but you are to be free as air, Amanda."

"But suppose I do not want to be free," she said a little petulantly. "You are really most unreasonable, John. Why should you be bound, and I free? Perhaps I want to be bound."

"Oh, Amanda," he said again. And then, briskly, "But we shall be missed; I am twice ashamed, for keeping you here so long, and for speaking to you so, when, on my honour, I had vowed no word of love should cross my lips."

"Nor has it," she said crossly. "And if you think, after all that has passed, that I will consent to be taken tamely back indoors like a good little girl, without so much as one kiss, you are gravely mistaken."

It was too much for the self-control he had promised himself. He had risen, to lead her back to the ballroom; now the hand that held hers turned suddenly to iron.

Breathless, laughing, trying to protest, she found herself in his arms. His lips on hers stopped her laughter, and she submitted to their fierce demand in a sudden ecstasy, aware, in every fibre of her, of the controlled strength of his body against hers.

If it would only go on for ever. But as suddenly as he had seized her, he let her go. "Amanda, forgive me. Forget that happened. Only remember, that, always, I am yours."

As he turned to lead her back through the moonlit garden, a door opened ahead of them and a gust of music and laughter blew out to shatter the still ecstasy of the garden. Two figures were outlined against the light from within.

"There," it was Lord Meynel's voice. "What did I tell you? She is stolen away into the garden, the little minx."

"Amanda," said Mrs Carteret. "I blush for you."

"No, no, ma'am, never put her to the blush," said Meynel. "I wager you stole away often enough in your day." And then, as Mrs Carteret digested this reminder of advancing years in silence, he held out his hand to Amanda. "My dance, I believe, my dear Miss Amanda."

She curtsied, blushing. "I cry your pardon, my lord. I . . . I had quite forgot."

"I see you had." A knowing glance passed from Amanda to John, and back again. Then, "My dear Mrs Carteret," he said, "I congratulate you. Your Amanda is grown up."

For Amanda, the rest of the evening passed like a dream that is nearly nightmare. More than anything, she wanted a few minutes of quiet talk with John, simply to reassure herself that those moments of brilliant happiness had been real. But fate – or was it fate? – was against her. Lord Meynel, having teased her unmercifully for forgetting her dance with him, had claimed, as his recompense, the two next ones, the second of which turned out to be the supper dance. So, to her bitter disappointment, it was from him, not, as she had hoped, from John Purvis, that she accepted her cold chicken and lemonade. But there was still hope; the evening was young and John, somehow, always near her in the crowd. But hope was soon dashed. No sooner had she swallowed the last crumb of chicken and sip of warm

11

lemonade than she felt Lord Meynel's hot, unwelcome hand on her shoulder. "The child is exhausted," he said to her mother, who had shared his attentions through the supper hour. "And you, my dearest Mrs Carteret, look, if I may say so, a trifle fatigued. Let me claim the privilege of an old friend and take you home."

Amanda protested, but, she knew, vainly. Her mother had angled so often, so unsuccessfully, for the loan of Lord Meynel's carriage and his four exquisitely-matched bays that it was idle to hope she would do anything but jump at his offer now. Besides, there was economy to be considered. Their hired carriage must be paid by the hour. . . The outcome was inevitable. Mrs Carteret had the headache at once – "So like you to have perceived it, my lord . . . and to tell truth this child was so afflicted when we arrived that she begged to wait out the ball above stairs."

"I am glad you persuaded her not to do so," said Lord Meynel, with the detested, familiar gallantry, as he took an arm of each to lead them back through the ballroom. And now, when Amanda particularly wanted to see him, there was no sign of John. No doubt he was still in the supper room . . . But there was always, Amanda consoled herself, tomorrow. She would call on his aunt betimes in the morning.

As Amanda had hoped, her mother slept late next day, and she was able to escape from the house without the usual tirade against her "hoydenish rambling about the country-side". It was a fine, sun-washed morning and Amanda's heart was as light as her tread as she walked the familiar downhill path to Rye and paused, as she always did, at her favourite corner, to admire the spreading prospect of marsh and sea. Today, the future was as bright as the world below her; John had spoken at last; he loved her. She had always, in her heart, been sure of it, but now her head too could revel in the prospect of happiness. War would be declared. . . . Recalled to active service, John would distinguish himself, of course, at once. Soon he would be commanding his own sloop . . . Negotiating a stile with a whisk of muslin skirts, Amanda built herself a golden castle in the air. The prize money would flow in; her mother would yield to the over-whelming argument of affluence. . . As she crossed the river and entered the little town, Amanda settled the design of her wedding dress (white satin and silver gauze) and started down the aisle of Rye Church. . . Soon she would be the youngest captain's wife in the fleet and John's ship the smartest . . . At this point she was nearly run down by a brewer's dray and interrupted her dream to smile an apology at its driver, whose first outburst of frightened anger had turned to an appreciative whistle at sight of her small pointed face, flushed at once with happiness and alarm. It was time to pay attention to her footing as she made her way on light, slippered feet over the cobbles of East Street and around to Miss Purvis's little house by the church.

As she approached it, she heard the quarters chime out from the church tower, and congratulated herself on having timed her visit just right. Miss Purvis would have returned from her bustling morning round of the shops and John could not possibly be gone out yet. Thinking of him, a belated qualm chilled her happiness. Would he think her forward to call on him like this? Ridiculous, she told herself; she had called on his aunt at least once a week for years . . . But her lagging feet told another story.

Somehow, instead of turning the last corner, she found herself crossing the little grass-grown street and pausing irresolutely at the entrance of the churchyard. She could not turn back, having come so far, and yet, how could she go on? It had seemed entirely natural to plan this visit last night, and she had been too busy with her day-dreaming to think about it on the walk into town, but now – what should she do? Of course, she should have waited at home for John to pay her the formal call he owed her after last night . . . but then, for years now, it had been tacitly agreed between them that he would not call on her, since Mrs Carteret always contrived to make such visits unpleasant to all of them. Kind Miss Purvis's house had always been their meeting ground; why then did everything seem so different today?

But she could not stand here, the target of goodness knows how many curtain-screened, knowing eyes. Suddenly determined, she left the churchyard, crossed the street again, turned the last corner and rang a louder peal than she had intended on Miss Purvis's front door bell.

The door was opened instantly by Miss Purvis herself. In street dress, her capacious shopping basket on her arm, she was obviously just going out. A grave breach of routine this. What could be the matter?

"My dearest child," Miss Purvis's colour was high, her manner even more flustered than usual, "you are come in the nick of time; I was just casting about in my mind for a messenger I could send to you."

"A messenger? What can be the matter? John – Mr Purvis is not ill, I trust?" Aware at once of indiscretion, Amanda blushed scarlet but saw with relief that Miss Purvis was much too discomposed herself to notice anything out of the usual. "Ill?" she said. "Of course not. You know he has never been ill in his life, the dear boy, at least not since he had the measles and that, you know, was ten years ago, as you must well remember, since you gave them to him. But what am I doing keeping you standing here. Come in, my love, we are all at sixes and sevens this morning, with dear John going off so suddenly. Why, I have not even been down to the fishmonger's for poor Midge's bit of fish, but he'll have to wait now, won't you my Midge?" And she picked up the vast ginger cat that had been twining itself lovingly round her ankles and led the way into her dark little living room where the parrot mourned eternally for sunny Spain.

Settling herself in the usual faded rocking chair, Amanda seized at once upon the important point. "Mr Purvis is gone?"

"Yes; poor dear John. I hope he has done the wise thing, but he said he had no alternative, and you know the days are past when I could sway his opinions – and quite right too, a poor scatterbrained old maid like me. But to be travelling

14

all day, and without a wink of sleep last night is not at all what I can like."

"No sleep last night? What can you mean, Miss Purvis?"

"Why? Did you not know? I quite took it for granted you would, since Lord Meynel is such a friend of your mother's. But, here, what am I thinking of?" She fumbled in her shopping basket and produced a note. "Let John explain; he will do it much better than I ever could."

John's note was brief and to the point. Lord Meynel, it seemed, had returned to the Assembly rooms the night before, sought him out, and offered his assistance in getting him a place on the *Phoenix* Indiaman presently fitting out for the long voyage to India. It was a chance that must be taken on the instant; John intended to catch the morning mail coach to London; he would write to her again as soon as anything was settled. '*In the meantime,*' he concluded, '*we must hope that this is the first step on the way to success – and happiness.*' He had filled the page by now, only down at the bottom, in the finest of fine print, was a last, heart-warming message: '*Amanda, it cuts me to the heart not to see you again. Do not forget. I never shall.*'

Blushing and smiling, Amanda put up the note and joined Miss Purvis in her exclamations at this piece of amazing good fortune. "Of course," as Miss Purvis said, "India is a long way off, but he will be back soon enough, I am sure, and with a nabob's fortune, I have no doubt. But had you truly known nothing of this plan of Lord Meynel's? To tell truth, I had been convinced we had you to thank for his goodness; can it be your Mama who has spoken for dear John?"

This seemed more than improbable to Amanda, but she hardly liked to say so, and they passed the morning in an orgy of hopeful if unprofitable speculation. For Amanda, the immediate disappointment of having missed John was lost in the widening dream of hope before her. As he said, this was the beginning; now it was but to wait. . . . Walking home up Rye hill a few hours later she re-designed her wedding: John was in captain's uniform now and her wedding dress was of India silk.

15

# Chapter Two

"So you have deigned to come home at last." Her mother's angry greeting put an end to Amanda's dream of happiness. "Who gave you permission, I should like to know, to be running off to Rye like a serving maid after her trooper? And draggling your petticoats through all the mud you could find, too? I am only grateful Lord Meynel did not stay to give you the meeting as he at first intended. He was not best pleased, I can tell you, that you had not the common civility to await his visit after the great – and undeserved – attention that he paid you last night." And then, in one of her sudden spurts of rage: "Well, child, what do you think you are doing, standing there gawping? Run upstairs and change your dress and try at least to look like a lady, if you cannot conduct yourself like one."

Something of a termagant at the best of times, Mrs Carteret outdid herself that week. The servants trembled; Amanda kept out of her way. So, she noticed with pleasure, did Lord Meynel, and this, though good in itself, was doubtless the reason for her mother's rages. Despite his assiduous attentions on the night of the ball, he had not, after all, proposed to Mrs Carteret, and each day that he stayed away made it seem less likely that he would. He was busy, it seemed, supervising the hay harvest on his extensive estates. As these almost entirely surrounded the small garden to which the Carteret property was reduced, Amanda had to exercise a good deal of ingenuity in taking her walks so as to avoid the 'chance' encounters with him that she had learned to dread. Luckily, her mother's maid Phoebe was being courted by one of the labourers who were getting in Lord Meynel's hay, and usually contrived

16

to get advance knowledge of where they would be working. By taking her walks in the opposite direction, Amanda contrived to pass a peaceful week of dreamy solitude. Any day now, she must hear from John.

The London mail coach reached Hastings at eight o'clock in the morning, but it was nearer eleven before the mail reached Rye, and Amanda often made enquiring for letters her excuse to walk into town and visit Miss Purvis. Unluckily for her, on the morning when John's letter arrived, she was reluctantly closeted with her mother, who was trying to improve her spirits by a root and branch inquisition into her daughter's scanty wardrobe. She had just reached the category of neck handkerchiefs and was exclaiming in inevitable horror at the discovery that Amanda had only four – and one of those badly stained with blackberry juice from an autumn escapade – when Phoebe tapped at the door to announce that Robert was "back with the mail, ma'am." An expressive glance for Amanda announced that the longed-for letter had come. But what was the good of that when Phoebe was forced to put all the letters into her mistress's eagerly outstretched hand?

Mrs Carteret was an extensive correspondent, and there were letters from dearest friends in Bath, Scarborough and Brighthelmstone to be exclaimed over before she came to John's letter. "What is this? For you Amanda? I do not think I know the hand."

"I collect it will be from John, Mama." She saw her mistake the moment she had finished speaking.

"From John? From Mr Purvis, you must mean. And by what right, pray, does he take the liberty of addressing you? It was well enough when you were a child, but it will not do to be encouraging the attentions of a half-pay lieutenant now, when you have the world before you, Amanda, and so I warn you. I have been intending to speak to you on this very subject since the night of the Assembly when you made such an exhibition of yourself with him." As she spoke, she had torn open the letter, despite a strangled protest from Amanda, and was glancing rapidly through its contents. "Well, that is something," she went on, "he sails for India today. How *good* of dear Lord Meynel, and only think of his not so much as having mentioned it to me the other day. No doubt he has been awaiting the success of his recommendation before he visited us again. Naturally, his kindness to John Purvis is a compliment to us, his old friends and neighbours. But what is this? 'Always yours' and 'Amanda, do not forget me'. Amanda, I demand an explanation."

"I am engaged to John Purvis." Chalk white, Amanda still managed to speak steadily enough.

"Engaged! To John Purvis!" After the tirade that followed, it was almost a relief to Amanda when her mother went off, at last, into the inevitable strong hysterics. She was busy ministering to these with hartshorn and sal volatile when Phoebe knocked timidly at the door to announce that Lord Meynel was below. This news effected an instant cure, and Amanda was amazed as usual by the speed of her mother's transition from hysterics to coquetry. She was busy at once at her glass, removing all traces of the crisis through which she had just passed, discussing, as she did so, rather with herself than with Amanda, whether it would be better to receive Lord Meynel alone or accompanied by her daughter. To Amanda's great relief, she decided on the former course, and hurried downstairs after one last admonition to Amanda to "forget all that nonsense about John Purvis".

Left alone, Amanda's first thought was for John's letter, which her mother had luckily forgotten in the excitement of Lord Meynel's visit. He wrote with controlled enthusiasm. He had indeed been taken on as lieutenant on the *Phoenix* which sailed that very day for Calcutta. The improvement in his prospects was enormous, but, '*I could wish that I was not going so far away from all that I hold dear.*' This, and the phrases that her mother had picked out, were, disappointingly, all the positive expressions of love that the letter contained, but as she read it for the second and third time, Amanda was increasingly warmed by its tone. He wrote as if there was no need for protestations between them. He hoped to return, he said, within the year. Meanwhile, '*Amanda, do not forget me.*'

How could she? Carefully folding the letter, she tucked it, like a talisman, into the corsage of her dress. She had just done so when the door of the room flung open and her mother appeared. One glance told Amanda that the storm she had just gone through was as nothing compared to the one to come. What could be the matter? Mrs Carteret was yellow-white and the rouge she had applied before going downstairs stood out pitifully on her cheekbones. Her eyes sparkled with rage and unshed tears.

"Well, Amanda," she said, "it seems you are in great demand today. I have just received a proposal for your hand."

"A proposal?" Amanda hoped she could not believe her ears. "But . . ."

"Precisely so." Never, in the rest of her life, would Mrs Carteret allude to or even let herself remember the humiliating misunderstandings of the interview she had just endured. "Lord Meynel does you the honour of wishing you to be his wife. I only hope you will contrive at least to *seem* worthy of him."

"Lord Meynel? Me?" It was what, in her heart of hearts, Amanda had sometimes, secretly, dreaded. It was the threat against which John's love had seemed so sure a defence. And John had sailed, today, for India. Cold terror seized her. He had sailed because Lord Meynel had arranged it. Lord Meynel, in fact, was no fool. Her hand on her heart, Amanda felt John's letter there: '*Amanda, do not forget.*' She mustered her defences. "Mother, there must be some mistake. It is you, surely, Lord Meynel has been courting?"

"Apparently not." Now Mrs Carteret's colour came flooding back. At this moment, remembering his careful pretence that he did not understand her, she almost hated Lord Meynel. And yet, perhaps, she should be grateful for that very pretence. The connection was too profitable a one to be lost. If it was Amanda he wanted, Amanda he must have. He had made it clear – almost brutally clear – that

Mrs Carteret stood greatly to gain by the transaction. "I could not allow my mama-in-law to live so pinched a life as you do now. A house in town perhaps? A carriage?" He had not tried to be graceful about his bribery. Why should he? He knew Mrs Carteret.

Just for a moment, now, looking at her daughter's white and stricken face, Mrs Carteret had a qualm about what she was doing. Amanda was seventeen, a child still; nobody knew Lord Meynel's age, everyone his reputation. But he was rich, much richer than Mrs Carteret had even hoped her dead husband would be – if he had not died so inconsiderately before inheriting the title and estates. Somehow, her very fury of disappointment because it was not herself, but Amanda, that Meynel wanted turned into a determination that Amanda must have him. Unacknowledged, bitter jealousy wanted Amanda punished. Well, one look at her distraught face showed that marriage to Lord Meynel would be punishment enough. The moment of doubt was over: Mrs Carteret's mind was made up.

"Well," she said, "why are you standing there, gawping, child? Tidy your hair, and come down with me to thank Lord Meynel for the great honour he has done you. We have kept him waiting quite long enough."

"Mother! You cannot mean it." Frenzied appeal shook Amanda's voice.

"Cannot mean it? What absurdity is this? A man of rank and fortune wants to marry you – I cannot imagine why – and you think 'I do not mean it.' Well; I'll show you soon enough that I do." The battle was short and bitter; its conclusion inevitable. Gentle Amanda had never been any match for her mother. If John had been nearer; if Miss Purvis had been a more possible ally . . . But John had sailed for India; Miss Purvis was the mildest of ineffective old maids; Amanda was alone before her mother's rage. She went down, at last, alone, on her mother's orders, to face Lord Meynel.

A clever man in his way, he had a pretty good idea of what must have been happening upstairs and Amanda's white face and shaking hand as she greeted him confirmed his suspicions. He was gentleness itself with her, all courtesy, all respect. She had had some wild idea, when she agreed to see him, that she might, somehow, get him on to her side. Now, finding him so unexpectedly gentle and kind, she began to feel there might be something in this forlorn hope. He had led her to a seat and now settled himself at a respectful distance from her. "My dear Miss Carteret, you must not look so frightened. Do I seem such an ogre to you?"

She stammered something, she did not quite know what, but his gentle tone, calm manner and formal address were beginning to have their effect. She listened passively as he apologized for having spoken so soon, so suddenly, but, "Truly, Miss Carteret, I thought you in need of a protector. You must give me that right, that privilege . . ."

Now was the moment for her appeal. She made it, with sinking heart. In response, he was all that was kind, was considerate. He had been, he admitted it, precipitate. She was so young; a child still . . . she must think of his offer; he would rather die than hurry her, but . . . There were a great many buts, most of them financial ones. By the time he had finished he had made it amply clear how great, both for her and for her mother, would be the advantages of the match. But again . . . his speech was reassuringly full of qualifications . . . he would not dream of expecting an answer from her today. Let her but think of him, as kindly as possible . . . He had her hand now, and pressed it to his lips. Her wish should be his law; she had no idea, he was convinced, how deeply, how truly he loved her.

He let her go. Amanda, who had expected, had feared a much more passionate outcome to this scene found herself at once relieved and faintly, ridiculously, disappointed. Lord Meynel was a very clever man. After this, he left Amanda strictly alone for three days, days in which he knew she would be the target of her mother's furious pressure. Then he called and was once more the kind friend, the devotedly respectful suitor. Amanda was very young; she began to forget the meetings in the shrubbery and to see him, as he intended her to, as a protection

21

against her mother. And all the time, John's ship was drawing further and further away into the mysterious Indian distance. There was no one Amanda could talk to. She called on Miss Purvis several times, hoping for she knew not exactly what in the way of aid and comfort. But Miss Purvis knew nothing of the engagement with John – and John himself had said that only he was to be bound. As for Mrs Carteret, she would not discuss John at all; that was a childish, shameful escapade, best forgotten.

The slow weeks passed. The hay was all in and Lord Meynel, who was usually at Brighthelmstone at this time of year, was still playing the perfect landlord and assiduous suitor. Amanda had got quite used to his visits by now, and did not realize to what an extent she was letting him treat her as if they were indeed engaged. As long as he did not touch her, she found it easy enough to be friendly with him these days, and – an observant man as well as a clever one – he was careful never to touch her except when he arrived or took his leave.

Then, one morning, Mrs Carteret received a letter that threw her into hysterics so genuine that even Amanda was frightened. When, at last, the sal volatile had had its effect, and Mrs Carteret was able to speak again she threw it to Amanda. "We are ruined," she said. "Read that."

Amanda read with a sinking heart. For once, her mother did not exaggerate. The letter was from the lawyers who had handled her late husband's affairs. They reported, with deepest regret, that his family would no longer be able to permit Mrs Carteret to live in the Dower House. A long and apologetic explanation followed. It was beside the point, which was simple. Ever since her husband's death, Mrs Carteret had lived, rent free, in the Dower House. Now she must go, and as soon as possible. It was as simple as that.

They looked at each other. There did not seem even to be anything to say. Both of them knew that Mrs Carteret's tiny income only just met their expenses, without rent. Where could they go? What could they do?

"They cannot mean it," Amanda began.

"But they do," her mother interrupted, and was, herself, interrupted by Phoebe, who announced that Lord Meynel was below. A silent, speaking glance passed between Amanda and her mother. For once, Mrs Carteret had the wisdom to say nothing. She and Amanda went downstairs together and after the usual greetings she lost no time in pouring out the whole story. Lord Meynel was everything that was sympathetic. It was only long afterwards that it occurred to Amanda that he had not seemed particularly surprised. He was not only sympathetic, he was practically helpful. He had been intending, he said, for some time, to pay a visit to his estates in Suffolk, but had delayed going, partly (here a look for Amanda) because he could not tear himself away, partly, he must confess, because he had ordered certain alterations to his house here and wished to stay and supervise the workmen. Now he appealed to Mrs Carteret. If she would do him the honour of using his house as her own – and at the same time have an eye to the decorations that were in progress – she would be doing him a real kindness.

Mrs Carteret protested, doubted, exclaimed and finally, to Amanda's dismay, agreed. Alone at last with her, Amanda in her turn protested, but her mother was adamant. "What else can we do?" she asked reasonably.

And still Lord Meynel behaved like a perfect gentleman. He stayed in his house to welcome Mrs Carteret and Amanda, and then, after commending their comfort with every solicitude to his highly respectable housekeeper, called for his carriage and left for his estates in Suffolk. If they needed him for any reason, he said, they had only to send for him. Driving away, he congratulated himself. He had left Amanda, he knew, in the hands of his best possible ally. One way or another, Mrs Carteret would do his business for him; it was but to apply a little more pressure in his own good time.

He was saved the trouble. The Rye tradesmen, alarmed by Mrs Carteret's move, became clamorous for the payment of their outstanding accounts. Amanda, returning from one of her frequent visits to Miss Purvis, found her mother in tears over a pile of papers. She had always known her to be extravagant, but had never dreamed her to be so deeply in debt as a little simple arithmetic now proved her. So long as she continued mistress of the Dower House, with the Carteret family behind her, the Rye tradesmen had been content to let her bills run on, but now, it was clear, she must be out of favour with the family. Nobody could tell where she might go next. They had all sent in their bills at once. The result was disaster – and tears. "I cannot possibly pay them," she sobbed. "Even if we bought nothing for a year I could not pay them. Oh, Amanda, what are we to do?" From behind the handkerchief, her sharp eyes were watching Amanda.

"What can we do?" asked Amanda.

"Well," her mother began doubtfully. "We could send for Lord Meynel, I collect."

"Send for Lord Meynel." Amanda's heart sank. "But what's that to the purpose?"

"Why, everything, my dearest love, if you would but write him."

"I?"

"Yes, you. This is no time for shilly-shallying, Amanda. It is that, or ruin for both of us. For you, he will do anything. Amanda, you must save us."

It was three months now since the *Phoenix* had sailed and still there had been no word from John. Lord Meynel, considerate as always, had given Amanda news of the ship. She had been spoken with off the Cape of Good Hope by a merchantman on the way back to England. This ship – the *Panther* – had brought back mail from the *Phoenix*. "I had thought," Lord Meynel had said, "that you and your mother might have heard from young Purvis, but doubtless he was too busy with plans for his career in India. That he was in the best of health and spirits I have from the captain of the *Panther*, to whom he handed the mail from the *Phoenix!*"

Amanda was young and unsuspicious. Though she had always disliked Lord Meynel, it had never occurred to her that she should distrust him too. John was well – and had not troubled to write to her. He had not, it seemed, written to his aunt either . . . A thorough man, Lord Meynel, had simply arranged for all John's letters to be suppressed.

Now, the seed of doubt he had sowed so skilfully was ready to bear fruit. Three months had passed, and Amanda had had no word from John. He had forgotten her, it seemed . . . And she and her mother were alone, facing crisis and ruin. Quietly, desperately, she sat down to write the letter her mother suggested. It took her hours of anguished copying and recopying, but the result was short and to the point: *'Dear Lord Meynel,'* she wrote at last. *'My mother and I would be most grateful if you would come to us on a matter of some importance.'* And, then, without preamble, the signature in her neat, schoolgirl's handwriting. *'Amanda Carteret'.*

Her mother was looking over her shoulder. "What, nothing more?" she asked.

"No," said Amanda. "Nothing more. It is enough, is it not?"

They both knew that it was, and so did Lord Meynel. He returned at once, learned the whole story from Mrs Carteret, who thought Amanda best absent from this particular interview, and spent the following day settling her debts, which seemed to him almost ludicrously small, considering the prize they brought him. He would have been hard put to it to say why he was so determined to have Amanda. Young, slender and half-formed, she hovered, these days, between a child's awkwardness and a woman's moments of sudden grace. When she was happy, and forgot herself, her wide-eyed, heart-shaped face might flash into an instant beauty, but in the main Lord Meynel would have agreed with the view of Rye society that Miss Carteret was not a patch on her handsome mother. But it was the child, not the buxom mother, that he wanted. He had had spirited and beautiful mistresses in plenty, but never anything like this slender, quiet girl who paid him so little attention. Sometimes he asked himself why after all his years of freedom he was going to so much trouble to saddle himself with a wife. The answer was simply that he wanted her. She was his last fling, his assertion of youth in the face of encroaching age.

And now, he had got her. Amanda had known it when she wrote to him, and he knew it when he arrived and, so gracefully, kissed her hand. But he intended to play safe still. There should be no passionate demonstration to frighten her off at the last moment. Indeed he went further than that. Finding himself, for the first time, alone with Amanda on the evening of the day he had spent in settling her mother's debts, he took her hand and pressed it to his lips. "May I," he asked, "dare, at last, to hope?"

She had known that this moment must come, but had still not contrived to prepare herself for it. Now, she looked down, crimson and, quietly, trembling. "I . . . I suppose so," she said.

It was hardly an encouraging acceptance, but he took it as warmly as if it had had her whole heart in it. "You make me," he kissed her hand once more, then made himself let it go, "the happiest of men. May I hope that you will name an early day for the completion of my good fortune?" And then, seeing her look of sudden fright, he continued, on the inspiration of the moment: "You are but a child, I know, but I long to have the right to protect you, to care for you as you should be cared for. Let me but have the right to call you mine, and you shall have nothing from me but the affection I would show to a dearly loved sister or friend, until, as I must hope you soon will, you shall wish it otherwise." As he spoke, he laughed to himself. A sister or friend, indeed – let her but be his . . . But this was a shy bird, and must be caught with the very best chaff. "If you will but give me your permission to ask your mother for an early day," he said again, schooling himself not to touch her.

"If you wish it." The die was cast; what was the use of drawing out the agony? She looked up at him, her grey eyes wide with tears, and he longed to take her in his arms, crush her to him, show her what it was to be his. But he had himself well in hand. "Then I have your permission to go to your mother?" he asked.

"Yes. You have been very good to us," she said.

"I would do anything for you." At the moment, he meant it.

Between Lord Meynel and Mrs Carteret, matters were soon and most amicably settled. Resigned by now to her position as pampered mother-in-law, she did not attempt to conceal her delighted relief when he came to her with the news that Amanda had accepted him, and was all acquiescence when he urged the earliest possible day for the wedding. She knew as well as he the dangers of delay. She was, of course, ignorant of his arrangements about John Purvis's letters and thought one might arrive any day, as she told herself, "to upset Amanda". Oh yes, the sooner, the better, particularly as Lord Meynel had ingeniously intermingled bribery with his planning. Always a realist, Mrs Carteret had taught herself from the moment of his first proposal for Amanda to give up all hope of being Lady Meynel. She merely intended to make the best possible thing out of being Lady Meynel's mother-in-law, and with so much to gain he was generosity itself – at least, in his promises. The house in which they were now living was to become hers on the day of the wedding, and here, her prospective son-in-law made it clear to her, he expected her to live while he and Amanda divided their time between his Suffolk estates and the house he proposed to take in London. A handsome income would make life pleasant for her as it had never been before. She would be able to visit Bath . . . Cheltenham . . . her friends and correspondents wherever they were. The only thing he did not, she noticed, suggest was that she should visit her daughter and son-in-law. It was a blow to her; she had counted on tasting once more the almost forgotten delights of London life, and enjoying the fame of her titled daughter. But, clearly, it was not to be. Once or twice, she was tempted to suggest what a pleasure, both for her and for Amanda, such a visit would be, but there was something in his tone to her, since the day when he had paid her debts, that made her instinctively refrain.

Instead, she threw herself, heart and soul, into the

delightful business of assembling Amanda's trousseau – and her own. For Lord Meynel's generosity matched his firmness. His bride and his bride's mother must have every fashionable appurtenance that imagination could conceive of – and Mrs Carteret's imagination could conceive of plenty.

Lord Meynel was far too punctilious to spend the night under the same roof as his prospective bride and mother-in-law and for the two or three days it took to make the arrangements for the wedding he stayed at the George in Rye, riding out every morning for the necessary discussions with Mrs Carteret. He was never alone with Amanda, nor seemed to wish to be, and contented himself with kissing her hand devotedly when he came and went. As he also brought her a series of magnificent presents, she found it impossible not, a little, to enjoy the distinction of being an engaged young lady. Everyone was kind to her and she found herself treated with a new respect by both her mother and the servants. Perhaps marriage would not be so bad after all . . . At night, in the strange bed, she cried herself to sleep over thoughts of John, who had forgotten her, but in the daytime she contrived to seem happy and busy enough.

It was a relief, of course, when Lord Meynel announced his intention of spending the rest of the time before their rapidly approaching wedding day between his house in Suffolk, and London, where he proposed to take one. Everything, he said, with a smile for Amanda, must be in perfect order for his bride. He left the arrangements for the wedding, which was to take place as quietly as possible in Rye church, to Mrs Carteret. His part would be to pay the bills.

The last weeks passed in a flurry of preparations and congratulations. Miss Purvis, it was true, seemed quiet and a little sad, but most of Amanda's friends were worldly enough to think her a lucky girl, and say so. There was hardly time for a last visit to her favourite places, to Camber, where the sea washed peacefully along the edge of the dunes, and to Winchelsea where her father was buried. At his grave, her heart suddenly failed her, and Lord Meynel's coachman, who had strict orders from his master to keep a close eye on her, led her back to the carriage in floods of tears. But that afternoon her wedding dress arrived and was declared by Mrs Carteret to need major alterations. Amanda had grown so thin that it needed taking in all over. There was no time for tears.

Amanda woke on her wedding morning to see an autumn tide of mist washing across Romney Marsh. It was going to be a fine day. "Happy the bride the sun shines on," said Mrs Carteret. If she saw the traces of tears on her daughter's pale face, she did not choose to mention them but applied herself busily to last minute preparations. Once again, Lord Meynel had stayed at the George, and Amanda was not to see him until they met in church. It was a wise move on his part. She was in a panic now and the sight of him might well have precipitated rebellion. As it was, there seemed no time for discussion, let alone revolt. She played with her breakfast under her mother's watchful eye and then yielded herself passively to the hands of the hairdresser and modiste who had come out from Rye. She looked, they said when they had finished, exquisite. They did not add that they were both afraid she would collapse before she reached the church.

Secretly, Amanda rather hoped that she would do so. Somehow, she had never believed she would actually find herself marrying Lord Meynel. Something surely would happen to prevent it. John would return and forbid the bans; Lord Meynel would change his mind; at the very worst she would be stricken with some romantic affliction like brain fever, and so gain a reprieve. It had never, somehow, occurred to her that the only person who could save her was herself. And now it was too late. She and her mother were actually in the carriage driving down the steep hill towards Rye. White as her dress, she held out an appealing hand.

"Mother," she began, "I . . . I can't . . ."

"Nor can I," Mrs Carteret interrupted her briskly. "I simply cannot imagine how we have contrived to get so much done in the course of one morning. No wonder you are exhausted, my love, but it will all be over soon and you will have the whole of your honeymoon to rest in. All brides come to the altar exhausted," she went on. "It is in the nature of the business. Why, I remember when I married your father . . ." She was safely launched on a narrative that carried them through the Land Gate and up the hill towards the church.

Amanda gave up. What she could not do, it seemed, was cry off at this last moment. And yet still, child that she was, she could not help believing that something would happen to save her.

Nothing did. The church bells pealed; children threw flowers; she had a glimpse of Miss Purvis, very white, in the congregation; then she was standing beside Lord Meynel and felt his hand, hot and rather damp, on hers as he slid on the ring. In no time, it seemed, they were in the vestry and her mother was kissing her, crying, and calling her "my love" and "Lady Meynel" by turns. It was all over. She was walking down the hill to the George, where the wedding breakfast was to be held, on her husband's arm. Glad of its support, she was nevertheless aware of something new and strange in his touch that sent a thrill of apprehension through her. And his eyes, when he looked down at her, had a spark she had not seen before. "Mine," he pressed her arm suddenly, "my wife."

But the landlord of the George had hurried out to greet them and it was all turmoil, jollification and toasts. Her mother was making her eat some cold chicken; she drank a little champagne; people kept shaking her hand and telling her she looked exquisite. Somebody, somewhere, was crying, but she could not see who it was. Anyway, it was time to go upstairs and change into her travelling dress. It was the same room she and her mother had used – how long ago it seemed – to prepare for the Assembly. John had been there; he had kissed her in the moonlight; she had been happy. Now, she could not remember what happiness was like. And it was all John's fault. If he had only written to her, none of this nightmare would have happened.

"Come, my love," her mother's voice was impatient. "This is no time to be day-dreaming. The coach is ordered for the hour and Lord Meynel does not like to be kept waiting." And then, in a sudden fury, "If you cry now, Amanda, I shall slap you."

Amanda did not cry. What was the use? She stood, mute and white, and let her mother help her out of white lace and into her travelling dress of red sarsenet with its becoming fur trim. Only, when she was ready and her mother had adjusted her bonnet and handed her gloves of york tan did she raise huge appealing eyes. "Mother, I am afraid."

"Tush, child. Of course you are. All brides are frightened. Why, I remember . . ."

But Amanda could not face another of her mother's reminiscence just then. Better, even to face the unknown. "Come," she said, with a firmness that startled her mother. "Shall we go?"

That little spasm of rage with her mother had put a sparkle in her eye and a sudden becoming flash to her cheek. When she joined him, Lord Meynel noticed it at once, and so did the group of hunting acquaintances who surrounded him. There was a little murmur of appreciation, and her husband's hand, grasping Amanda's was hotter and damper than ever. He made short work of their leave-takings. After all, as he said, the day was well advanced, and they must reach the Chequers at Lamberhurst betimes, and make an early start next morning for his Suffolk estates, where they were to spend their honeymoon.

"An early start?" said one of the hunting men. And, "What will you bet?" said another.

But Lord Meynel was already leading Amanda out of the room and, if she heard, she did not understand them. The coach was waiting for them in the High Street, with Lord Meynel's four high-bred bays snorting and tossing their heads at the delay. "We must not keep the horses standing." He made the farewells almost brutally brief, but Amanda was glad. She had nothing, now, to say to her mother, who was, she noticed with surprise, actually crying.

Amanda did not cry. She sat, still as a statue, in her

corner of the luxurious carriage and looked out of the window as the familiar scenes were snatched away one after another. They were out of the town now and the horses had slowed for the steep climb up the hill. She turned back for a last glimpse of Rye, sitting so snug on its little hill, and the marsh beyond, and Winchelsea, where her father lay buried. And still she did not cry, though there was something behind her eyes more painful than tears. To her deep, surprised relief Lord Meynel had said nothing since he had settled himself, with a little grunt, in his corner of the carriage. Now, glancing towards him under lowered eyelashes, she realized why. Her new husband had been lavishly dined and wined by his friends the night before, and night had somehow mixed itself up with morning. The bridal champagne had been his breakfast. Now, safely married, and with his bride beside him, Lord Meynel was fast asleep. Amanda had never seen a man asleep before and found the spectacle disconcerting. In sleep, the control that usually held Lord Meynel's ageing face together relaxed, and he looked what he was, an elderly dissolute man whose flushed cheeks were marked with little broken veins. As she watched, his mouth fell loosely open and he began to snore.

Amanda shuddered a little and looked away from him and out of the window again. Her thoughts were in a turmoil. Mrs Carteret had been far too well-bred to talk to her about the realities of the married state and her ideas of it were vague in the extreme. Her only clue in this strange world she had entered was the remembered ecstasy of John's one kiss. Now, inevitably, this must be contrasted with the hot unwelcome pressure of Lord Meynel's lips upon her hand. Her mouth, wisely, he had never attempted to kiss. His snore began to bubble more regularly, and she reminded herself, with relief, of his promise that she should be merely a sister or dear friend to him. Why, she asked herself, should he want more of her, an old man like him? And soon, incorrigibly, she was dreaming again: she would be a daughter to him. Under his loving protection she would taste the delights of London society – for Amanda had never been to London. And, somehow, in the end, John would reappear, an Admiral, perhaps – anyway, rich and successful, and . . . Amanda could not bring herself actually to kill off Lord Meynel even in a day-dream, so the picture became vague at this point, and she concentrated once more on looking out of the carriage window at the now unfamiliar landscape. The autumn evening was drawing in and shadows lengthened across the harvested fields. The air, too, was turning colder and she pulled her light pelisse more closely round her, wishing, as she did so, that her mother had not insisted on having her travelling dress made with such a low décolletage, and so insubstantial a muslin fichu.

Something – her movement, perhaps, or the chill in the air – roused Lord Meynel, who gave one last staccato snore, sat bolt upright and looked about him. "My dearest love," he had her hand in an instant, "I cry you ten thousand pardons. You must have thought me the most unfeeling dolt of a bridegroom that ever lived, but to tell truth we kept it up something of the latest last night. But now I am myself again." He proved it by pulling her closer to him. "What, in the sullens?" he asked, feeling her instinctive resistance, "well, I don't blame you; it was scarce flattering, I admit, but we'll make up for it soon enough. What?" He was bending over her now, his breath wine-flavoured on her face. "Not a kiss for your new husband? And I who have been patient as – as Jeremiah, or whoever it was, or what d'ye call 'em who served the seven years, but there's an end of that now, and not before it was time. I tell you truly, I did not know I had it in me. But you are mine now, my pretty, all mine." He had expected, and rather enjoyed her resistance as he forced his mouth down on her reluctant lips and then, not content with this, began to push them open with his rough, exploring tongue.

It was too much. She had resisted from the first, in a child's panic, but now she fought him with all her young woman's strength. The feel of him, the taste of him was intolerable to her. One of her hands was still fast in his, but the other went up, instinctively, to strike him in the

33

face. This was more than he had bargained for, and the pressure eased on her mouth as he let out a ringing oath. She saw his eyes, steel-bright with anger and desire, and felt his hands at her throat. For a moment, she thought he was going to strangle her, and almost hoped he would, but what he did, was worse. With one furious movement he tore the muslin fichu from her breast. Her hands were in his hair now, wildly pulling, but, much practised in this business, he caught them both in one of his, and with the other pushed down the warm cloth of her bodice. "Ah," it was the satisfied growl of an animal as his hand cupped one tiny breast after the other and played with the still childish nipples. Then he let out another exclamation, this time of purest rage. The carriage was slowing down.

He let her go. "Lamberhurst, by all that's damnable." And then, suddenly, amazingly, calm, he drew a comb from his pocket and began to tidy his disordered hair. "If you'd marked me," he said, feeling his cheek, "you would suffer for it. I'll not be a laughing-stock for all the unbroken brides in christendom, but never mind, I like a girl with spirit. We will do admirably together, you and I."

Speechless, she stared at him with huge grey eyes as she tried, with shaking hands, to repair the disorder of her dress. She was almost beyond even relief that the strong red sarsenet had stood the strain without tearing, but her muslin fichu was beyond repair.

"Never mind that." He watched her with a chuckle as the carriage drew up in the inn yard. "They know you're a new bride; they'd think the less of me if you were not something tousled. Come." An ostler had run to throw open the carriage door and now he jumped down and turned to give her his hand to alight. Trembling, cold with terror, clutching her pelisse around her with one hand, she followed him silently into the inn.

Lord Meynel had reserved the landlord's entire accommodation for that night and they were greeted with consequent obsequiousness. The inn's best of capons and boiled and roast mutton was soon steaming on the table in the little parlour and Lord Meynel fell to with a will.

Urging Amanda to join him: "My little bride must keep up her strength," he carved her the most delicate morsels and made her drink a glass of wine with him.

She watched him, over the shaking glass, as one might watch an ogre or some strange prehistoric beast. Was this what marriage meant? And what of that promise about the sister and friend? Dared she remind him of it? No. She did not even dare speak to him. He had seemed, back in the carriage, a madman. How could she know what he might do next? She watched him, silently, timidly, relieved at his joviality – for after all, she had struck his face and pulled his hair. But perhaps it had all been a nightmare. She drank a little more wine and pretended to herself that it had.

She had never had a maid, and Lord Meynel, though he had promised her one, had arranged that this essential abigail should join them in Suffolk. No one, he had promised himself, was going to come between him and his hard-won bride on their wedding night. He persuaded her, at last, to eat a little chicken and drink a glass of ratafia while he killed the last of his hangover with liberal doses of port. She had never had more than tastes from her mother's wine glass before, and the unaccustomed drink combined with fright and fatigue to make her sway where she sat. Lord Meynel saw it and rose. "Come, my dearest life," he said. "You are exhausted, and no wonder. Let us to bed." It was what she dearly wished, but as he led her upstairs past the curtseying maid and smirking landlord, a horrid doubt niggled at her mind. Her father had died when she was a baby . . . but she had visited friends whose parents seemed to share a room. Surely she could not be expected . . .

The landlady had ushered them upstairs to a room where flickering firelight revealed a perfect monster of a four-poster bed. Now she was pouring out voluble wishes for a good night's sleep combined with offers to help the young lady out of her things. For a moment, Amanda's heart leaped . . . could she perhaps persuade the landlady to stay with her? But Lord Meynel was dismissing the woman. The door shut behind her with a soft click of the latch and this hideous stranger who was her husband advanced upon her. "Well, my love," he said, "shall I, this once, act as your maid?"

When she was an old lady, and Victoria was Queen, Amanda still, sometimes, woke sweating from dreams of that night. She never spoke of it to anyone, but in later years her husband knew when she dreamed that dream and would lie, silently holding her hand, until the terror of it had passed. But that was fifty years off. When she woke, that first morning, and saw autumn sunshine behind the heavy curtains, and heard her husband snoring beside her, she prayed, passionately, for a few minutes, that she might die before he waked, might never again have to suffer the things he had done to her. Even as she prayed, his eyes opened and he saw her sitting up in bed, her nightgown half off one shoulder. Once again, she heard that curiously animal grunt of satisfaction, felt his arms pull her down, his breath on her face, fought him until she could fight no more.

"Well, well," he said at last, getting briskly out of bed and pulling the heavy bell rope, "this is better than I had hoped. Who would have thought you would prove such a fine little vixen. But I collect I should have expected it in your mother's daughter." And he turned away to order shaving water and a hearty breakfast from the maid.

# Chapter Three

During the slow, despairing year that followed, Amanda learned that even a nightmare can become routine. Arriving, white and quiet with shock, at Lord Meynel's house in Suffolk, she had found it standing large and lonely on a windswept hill. The servants greeted her with deference and whispered about her in corners. "Not long for this world," she heard once. She only wished she thought it true. But she was strong, healthy and young. Her nights continued a torment and humiliation, since it never occurred to her husband that some thought for her pleasure might possibly even increase his own. Submitting to him, passively, for after all she had sold herself into this misery, she thought, so far as she could, about something else.

In the daytime, Lord Meynel was kind to her, in a careless sort of a way and when he was at home, but most of the time he spent out of doors, killing things. Amanda, schooled at least by her mother about a wife's daytime duties, began by attempting to take over the running of the big house, but soon met her match in the housekeeper, who had held undisputed away since Lord Meynel's mother had died many years before and did not intend to give up what had become an extremely profitable situation to a mere girl. Amanda was housewife enough to realize almost at once that Mr Ffanshawe's housekeeping books bore only the most superficial relationship to the actual expenses of the house, but when she mentioned this, tentatively to her husband, he shrugged it off. Mrs Ffanshawe saw to it that the house was run entirely according to his convenience: that was good enough for him. Amanda yielded the point. If she had loved him, she might have enjoyed taking care of his comfort, but as it was, duty done, she was glad enough to surrender to Mrs Ffanshawe the doubtful privilege of making sure he had a glass of wine the moment he entered the house, and coffee as soon as he waked in the morning.

As a result, she found herself with nothing to do. There seemed to be no neighbours, or at least no female ones. Plenty of hard-riding, red-faced sportsman were happy to hang about Lord Meynel, shooting his coverts and riding his horses through the changing seasons, but their wives stayed at home. Amanda did not greatly care. She was too unhappy to be able to face the idea of strangers. Besides, she had discovered the library Lord Meynel's mother had collected. She had come upon the shuttered room by chance in one of her first lonely explorations of the big house. It was in a wing that was not now in use and the fact that it was at the farthest possible point from the rooms occupied by Lord Meynel made her wonder a good deal about his relationship with his dead mother. She wondered more as she pushed open the shutters to let in the light and began to dust and browse among the books. Lord Meynel never read anything but the sporting papers; his mother had made an extensive collection of English poetry and drama. She seemed to have bought Dr Johnson's *Rambler* as it came out, and had read it, too, for Amanda could follow her progress in marginal notes in a tiny, cultivated hand. The notes led her here and there to other books. Amanda had a lively if uneducated mind, and nothing to do. Gradually, as Lord Meynel fell into his old habits and spent more and more time away from home, she began to read. Greatly daring, she ordered Mrs Ffanshawe to have the library cleaned and aired and a fire lighted there every day. Watching, with the new quietness she had developed since her marriage, she saw the older woman meditate defiance – and think better of it.

The hunting season began and Lord Meynel was sometimes away for as much as a week, hunting with distant packs. Though she knew that she would pay dearly for the bliss of her solitary bed when he returned, Amanda enjoyed it just the same. Reading hungrily for hours on end curled up in the big chair that must have been her mother-in-law's, she worked her way through Pope and Dryden and began teaching herself Italian so as to read Dante as, apparently, the dead woman had done before her. She felt as if they were friends by now and found herself increasingly guided, in such crises as her quiet life produced, by her idea of what the previous Lady Meynel would have done. She was unaware of the new dignity and certainty this gave to her behaviour, but noticed, with pleasure, an increase of respect in the servants' behaviour. Mrs Ffanshawe no longer hinted at insolence and Amanda found her own comfort being considered almost as much as her husband's.

Emboldened by this, she took a step she had been considering for some time. When they first arrived, Lord Meynel had made some careless remark about helping herself to anything she found to ride in the stables. So, one fine November afternoon, she put down *Romeo and Juliet* which she had just read for the first time, dried her tears and rang for her maid. Soon, dressed in the scarlet riding habit her mother had bought her, she descended upon the stables, demanded a horse and got one. She also got a look of grudging approval from the old groom when he saw how straight she sat, and was grateful, for once, to her mother for the riding lessons she had insisted on her having.

After that, she rode out about the windswept countryside every afternoon, dividing her attention between the long prospects of field and sea and a slow satisfied meditation of whatever book she was reading. She had always been prone to day-dreaming, now, with any dream of happiness for herself out of the question, she made a natural and comforting transition to the lives of the people she read about. A lonely figure on the big black horse, she never, in fact, lacked for company. Romeo and Juliet rode with her, or Pamela, or Clarissa Harlowe whose misfortunes seemed so much more agreeable than her own.

Insofar as he had time to notice her at all in the daytime, Lord Meynel began to find a change in her. The daily fresh air and exercise – for she rode in all weathers – were having a remarkable effect on her appearance. Little more than a slim, pale child at the time of her wedding, she was now developing, he saw with pleasure, into an elegantly rounded woman. Her pale cheek had taken on a new brown glow of health and her dark hair seemed to curl more freely. The quiet, mouse-like girl he had married, was turning, under his eyes, into a beauty. It was highly satisfactory to receive the bawdy congratulations of his friends, but there was another side to the picture. Amanda was no longer the timid girl he had married. Sometimes he would find the grey eyes that had once fallen so bashfully before his, fixed on him with a steady, thoughtful stare he found disconcerting. When his friends came home for a meal with him after they had done their stint of killing for the day, she received them with invariable courtesy, but as the bottle passed and their conversation grew freer and, in their opinion, more entertaining, she would quietly withdraw into her own thoughts leaving them as effectively to their own devices as she actually did as soon as good manners permitted.

This was bad enough. Her stoic detachment in his bed was worse. She never refused his advances now, but equally she never responded to them. Her mute acceptance of the inevitable was a sad comedown after the biting, scratching resistance he had so much enjoyed during the first few weeks of their marriage. He was not a man given to introspection or, indeed, to thought of any kind if he could help it, but he thought a good deal about this and finally came to the conclusion that it was the books she read that had wrought this undesirable change in her. He remembered, only too well, how, when he was a little boy, his mother had withdrawn for hours at a time to the library. That had been bad enough, but to have his wife falling under the same pernicious spell was too much. He must take her away before it was too late.

It was spring by now, and the London season was beginning, but despite the many promises he had made her he had no intention of taking her there. She had grown far too beautiful to be risked in society, and, besides, it bored him. He announced instead that they would be leaving, the following week, for Rye.

"For Rye?" The wide grey eyes showed amazement.

"Why not? You will be glad to see your mother, I know, and I have business to attend to there. You had best write to Mrs Carteret today and tell her to expect us next week."

"But I thought . . ." She stammered to a stop. Impossible to remind him that he had told her mother the house outside Rye was to be her own. Now, it seemed, she was to be treated simply as a housekeeper. Oh well, she thought to herself, still considering him out of level, thoughtful eyes, it was all of a piece with the rest of his behaviour. He had kept none of his promises to her; why should he those to her mother? Nor, indeed, could she bring herself to care very much about her mother's position. The tolerant affection she had always felt for her had changed into something dangerously close to hatred since she had realized just what kind of a slavery her mother had sold her into.

She almost began a protest against the proposed visit simply because she could not face the meeting with the woman who had betrayed her, but then thought better of it. For one thing, she knew perfectly well that it would be useless; for another, she had thought of Miss Purvis. There might be news of John. She had scanned the newspapers in vain for news of the *Phoenix* Indiaman, and had watched with an obstinate hope that turned slowly to despair for a letter from John, but surely Miss Purvis would have heard?

So she listened acquiescently enough while her husband outlined his plans for their journey, and gave his orders as to the rooms her mother must have prepared for them. "And while we are away," he concluded, "I propose to have some alterations made to this house."

"More alterations?"

"Yes. It is time to be thinking about a nursery."

"A nursery? But why?" One of the small consolations of her life was that despite her husband's assiduous attentions, she showed no sign of starting a baby.

"Because we shall need one soon, I hope. This and the Sussex estates are both entailed, you know. I must have an heir." He looked at her accusingly.

"I see." She saw a great deal, and liked nothing of what she saw.

"So I intend to have the whole East wing remodelled," he went on. "There will be ample space there for my son and his nurses – and we need not be disturbed by his crying, either."

"The East wing?" Her beloved library was there.

"Yes. You will find some changes when we return from Rye."

He said no more, but she knew what he meant. The books were to go. When she returned she would be alone indeed. But what was the use of protesting? He was the master; he could do what he liked. She just sat there and looked at him.

The journey to Rye was at least a change from the quiet monotony of her days, and Amanda was able to enjoy it with a comparatively free mind, since she had arranged, before she left, with her friend the head groom, that a small nucleus of her favourite books should be moved to a little unused attic above the stables. She was far indeed, now, from the biddable schoolgirl Lord Meynel had married.

He realized this with a reaction of mixed pleasure and alarm, when they broke their journey for a couple of nights in London. He had had his doubts about the wisdom of this, but an old favourite of his was appearing, the night they arrived, at Covent Garden. The temptation was too great. He considered leaving Amanda behind at Grillon's Hotel, where they were staying, but he was not really an unkind man, except when crossed, and thought better of it. Besides, he expected to enjoy the sensation she created.

He did, but Amanda enjoyed it more. The personable young men who thronged their box were a far cry from Lord Meynel's hunting friends in Suffolk. And the play preceding the farce that had drawn her husband was *Jane Shore* with Mrs Siddons. So long as it lasted, she did not care how many men were eyeing her through their glasses, and ignored the attempts at conversation made by those who had contrived to penetrate their box. Afterwards, she rather enjoyed it all.

Alarmed at the sensation she created, Lord Meynel changed his mind about staying two days, and they left next morning for Sussex, before any of the men who had promised themselves the pleasure of calling upon Lady Meynel had arrived to do so. They spent that night at the inn at Lamberhurst that Amanda remembered with such appalling clarity. Everything was the same; the capons, the roast and boiled mutton, the landlord's considering lascivious glances, the landlady's measuring looks. Only, when her husband came to her as she lay, shivering with remembrance, in the huge four-poster bed, she was aware of a new fierceness in him. He had hurt her often enough before, but never so badly as he did that night. Finally it was too much; she screamed, and he relaxed at once, satisfied, it seemed, at last.

In their room under the caves, the landlord and landlady heard the scream. Half asleep, she murmured to herself, thinking of the young creature downstairs, but her husband let out a chuckle of satisfied complicity and turned, fiercely, in the darkness, to take her as he had not done for years.

Mrs Carteret had written that she would expect them for dinner, which, country-fashion, she had at the unfashionable hour of three. Characteristically, Lord Meynel delayed their morning start so that they could not possibly arrive in time for the elaborate meal Amanda knew her mother would be preparing for them. When the heavy travelling carriage finally lumbered up to the house it was past five o'clock and Amanda could well imagine what culinary despairs Mrs Carteret and her cook must have suffered together. She could not help admiring her mother for the warm and unreproachful greeting she extended to them, and was sorry for her when Lord Meynel, throwing himself into his favourite lounging chair, said casually, "And now, my dear Mrs Carteret, I have no doubt you have a delicious dinner ready for us."

"I had at three o'clock," said Mrs Carteret with remembered tartness.

"Three o'clock?" Lord Meynel raised his eyebrows in affected astonishment. "I never dine till six."

That was an end of the pretence that Mrs Carteret was anything more than a housekeeper in the house he had promised would be her own. Watching, with amazement, as her mother submitted not only to this, but to the added indignity of Lord Meynel's sneering comments on the meal the harassed cook finally contrived to serve, Amanda was surprised how much it pained her to see her once formidable mother so worsted. If she had had any lingering, impossible hopes that she might prove an ally, or even a comforter, in the daily battle of her wretched marriage, this put an end to them, once and for all. Money, for Mrs Carteret, was everything. Lord Meynel controlled the purse strings: he might do as he pleased.

Mrs Carteret lost no time in making it clear where her sympathies lay. The second morning of their stay, when Lord Meynel had ridden out to join the bailiff for a tour of his property, she knocked on the door of Amanda's bedroom. "What, still in bed?" For Amanda was enjoying the luxury of breakfast there. "I vow, I'm shocked at you, child. I warrant your husband would rather have your hands than mine pouring his coffee before he rode out."

"I expect he would," said Amanda calmly. "But he should not have kept me awake so late, in that case."

Mrs Carteret who preferred not even to think of the realities of her daughter's married life, coloured angrily at this. "Tush, my love," she said. "That is no way to speak of your husband – or to your mother." She pulled up a chair and settled herself comfortably by the bed. "Indeed, I am sorry to say it, but I am come on purpose to give you a scold. Your behaviour to Lord Meynel, Amanda, is not at all the thing."

"Oh?" said Amanda. "And what about his behaviour to me?"

Mrs Carteret coloured more fiery red than ever. "How can you speak so," she said angrily. "You sit there, in the luxury your husband has provided for you, and make bold to carp at him. I am ashamed for you, Amanda."

"Are you?" Amanda nibbled at a piece of toast. "And what if I told you I would rather be dead than living in this luxury?"

"I should not listen," said her mother firmly. "You shock me more and more. I have been troubled ever since you arrived by the cavalier way you treat your husband, but this passes everything."

"Does it?" said Amanda. "You have not, I collect, paused to wonder how he treats me."

"How he treats you? When I see you surrounded with every luxury imaginable? When do you think I last had my breakfast brought up to me in bed? Or wore a négligé like that one, either? Or a dress like that?" She pointed angrily to Amanda's sable-trimmed travelling dress where it lay tossed aside across a chair. "And if I had," she went on, "I can tell you I would treat it better – and the giver."

"Yes," said Amanda thinking about the destruction of her library, "he gives me things, when it suits him."

"Amanda!" It was almost a screech. "I'll not have you speak so. We owe Lord Meynel everything, you and I. It is true, I have thought, since I saw how amazingly you have come on – For I tell you, my love, I find you vastly improved, and, indeed," she added grudgingly, "quite a beauty. If I had known that . . ." she paused, thought better of it, and went on. "But never mind that; we have taken our goods to market, and must not repine at our bargain."

"You mean," Amanda said, "that I must not grumble at your bargain."

This was too much. Worsted, like Lord Meynel, by something cold and strange in her daughter, Mrs Carteret flounced out of the room. Amanda sighed, put away her breakfast tray and rang for her maid. But while she was being dressed, she gradually regained her spirits. She had half promised herself a treat for today, and her husband's early departure had made it possible. As soon as she was dressed, she descended on the stables, looked over the horses her husband kept there, chose one, and ordered it side-saddled at once. Her mother appeared just as she was mounting.

"Amanda, what are you doing?"

Lady Meynel looked down at her coolly from the saddle. "I am going to ride into Rye, Mama."

"By yourself?"

"Why not? I have walked there alone often enough." And without waiting for further argument, she urged her horse forward and was gone.

It was further to Rye from Lord Meynel's house than it had been from her mother's, and she was becomingly flushed with exercise when she turned her horse into the stable yard of the George. An ostler came respectfully forward at once, and she confided the animal to his care, thinking, with wry amusement, as she did so, that Lady Meynel commanded this as a certainty, where Amanda Carteret would have begged it as a favour. The landlord, hurrying obsequiously out to greet her, confirmed the change in her status. He had never bowed and scraped like this to Amanda Carteret, in her faded riding habit.

Miss Purvis, on the other hand, was just the same as ever. She cried a little, with pleasure, she said, at the sight of Amanda, and bustled about her little house to produce the greatest treat she could afford, Amanda's favourite wafer thin biscuits and a glass of ratafia for each of them. As she trotted about, throwing off exclamatory, affectionate remarks to her cat and her parrot as she passed them, she paused from time to time to gaze once more at Amanda and exclaim at the improvement in her looks. "Quite a beauty," she exclaimed in her breathless little voice. And then, with the friendly frankness that Amanda had somehow never minded, "I would never have thought it! Is not your mother delighted with you?"

Amanda did not want to talk about herself, still less about her mother. And yet, how could she introduce the subject that had really brought her here? She did her best, after her enquiries as to Miss Purvis's health, by turning the conversation to the news of the day. What did Miss Purvis think of the desperate turn of events in

France? Miss Purvis exclaimed suitably and agreed that the chances of war seemed greater every day. "They have declared war on Austria. What is to stop them attacking us?" And then, at last, she came to the subject closest to Amanda's heart. "If only my dear John were at home," she said, "what a chance of promotion would open before him." She hesitated, glancing uncertainly at Amanda.

"Oh, yes," Amanda was proud of her casual tone. "What is the news of Mr Purvis? Did you hear from him at last?"

"Oh, my dear, yes. He has been the most admirable of correspondents, and indeed, I cannot understand how all his first letters came to go astray. You know he promised me he would number them? Well, the first I had was number ten, dated from Calcutta. It was written in answer to mine with the news of your wedding." Aware that this was dangerous ground, Miss Purvis hurried on before Amanda could ask the question that burned in her brain. "But I must tell you, my love, how he has distinguished himself. Only think of him being engaged in an action against the French!"

"Against the French? But we are not at war with them – yet."

"I know. That is what made it such a shocking business when one of their ships of the line opened fire on the *Phoenix* – and all because Sir Richard Strachan insisted on his right to search neutral merchantmen. They had a hot time of it for a while, John says, with six killed on the *Phoenix*, and twenty-five on the *Resolute*. Of course, dear boy, he does not tell me what he did, only that he is promoted as a result – and, what is better still, on his way home."

"Coming home?" This was news indeed.

"Yes, is it not capital? He has contrived a transfer back to the regular Navy, which was, as you know, always the service he wanted, and with a step up, too. He is second lieutenant, now on the *Somerset*. I hope to see him home daily, for he said he should not be long after his letter and lord knows that took long enough to get here."

"He has not made his fortune then?"

"No, dear boy, nor did I expect him to. But he has made a name for himself, it seems, which I like much better."

"So do I," said Amanda, and turned the subject to generalities. She made her escape as soon afterwards as she could politely contrive. She had much to think about, and, besides, Miss Purvis's affectionate enquiries as to her happiness in marriage were coming uncomfortably near the bone. "So glad to see you looking so well, my love," Miss Purvis said at last. "I confess I have been a trifle anxious about you. Do you know, my love, I once hoped . . . but we'll not talk of that now."

"No." Amanda rose to take her leave. Riding home up Rye hill in bright June sunshine, she found her mind full of dark fancies. All John's first letters to his aunt had gone astray. Could he have written to her too? It did not bear thinking of. If she had only heard from him, she knew, nothing could have forced her into marriage with Lord Meynel. But it was too late to be thinking of that now, and she must get what comfort she could out of the thought that John was on his way home. But suppose he had indeed written to her? What could he think of her sudden marriage? If only she had dared ask Miss Purvis what he had said about it, but how could she have? She spent the rest of the ride home wondering how they would meet: as friends, as casual acquaintances, even perhaps, as enemies? But that was impossible. She could not imagine John her enemy.

Coming into the house from the stable yard, she found it in a state of turmoil. Maids were running about, a footman was dragging a heavy trunk through the green baize door that led to the back corridor and her mother stood in the front hall frantically directing operations. "Ah, there you are at last, Amanda," she said. "Trust you to be out of the way when there is work to be done. Come quick and help me pack."

"Pack?" said Amanda. "But what for?"

"We are all going to London tomorrow. Is it not famous? And as for you, lucky child, you are going further than that."

"Back to Suffolk, you mean?" Amanda shrugged. "I do not see anything so wonderful in that."

"Who said anything about Suffolk? You are going on a continental tour and I am to come to London and help with your preparations. You will need to have everything new, Lord Meynel says, since he does not know how long you will stay. I have not been so busy since your wedding. But, come, child, do not stand gawping there; we must be packing."

"Where is Lord Meynel?" Amanda was trying to get her bearings.

"He is gone out again to settle his business about the estate. He will be back soon enough and will explain to you then, no doubt, why he has taken this sudden decision to go abroad. I only know that he decided it soon after he received his London mail. No doubt it was one of his letters put him in mind to go."

The rest of the day passed in a whirl of packing and arrangements and as Lord Meynel only returned home just in time to change for dinner, Amanda began to fear she would have no chance to speak to him alone until late in the evening when he would almost certainly be so fuddled by his nightly intake of port that protest or even any attempt at discussion of his sudden plan would be useless. She found herself coldly terrified at the idea of going abroad alone with him. For a few minutes, when her mother told her of the scheme, she had hoped that she was to be of the party, too, and it was a measure of her distrust of her husband that she should have felt such despair at the discovery that she was not to have even the dubious comfort of her mother's company.

Chilled with apprehension, she tried to raise her spirits by having her maid put her into a highly becoming new dress of red velvet, and was seated at her glass, consoling herself with the gloss it threw up on her dark hair when her husband entered the room. "Good," he said, "you are nearly ready." And then, to the maid, "You may go, Beth."

At another time, she might have resented this assumption of authority over her maid, but now she was glad of the

49

chance to speak to him. She turned from the glass to face him. "I am glad you are come, my lord. I have wanted, all day, to ask you what is the meaning of this sudden departure."

"I thought you would be." He swaggered across the room to her. "I am sorry I have been too busy to enlighten you." It was obvious that he had been enjoying the thought of her puzzlement. "Am I not an admirable husband," he went on, "to go to so much trouble – and expense – to surprise my wife? I expect to be prettily thanked indeed for this treat I am planning for you." He put his hands on her bare shoulders and bent over her to suggest the form the thanks should take.

She looked up at him, as coolly as she could. "But what if I do not want to go?"

"Not want to go? For a last look at France, before the war begins? And perhaps a jaunt into Italy, too; down to Naples, perhaps, to visit my friend Sir William Hamilton and that surprising new wife of his? What girl in her senses could fail to jump for joy at so kind an offer – and the pleasure of a solitary journey with her doting husband. I promise you, we shall be happy as a honeymoon, you and I." His hands were moving down, now, from her cold shoulders to push the warm red velvet away from her breast. He bent for one of the kisses he liked to hurt her with, but she whisked herself out of his hands, and stood, quick breathing, to face him. There had been something she had wanted to ask him all day.

"My lord," she bolted into it without preamble. "When you found a place on the *Phoenix* Indiaman for John Purvis, what did you . . . what were you . . .?" After all, how could she ask it?

"What was I thinking of? Well, what do you think, my dearest life?"

"You mean – you got him out of the way on purpose?"

"Precisely. What a clever child it is, to be sure. And, have you heard? Young John Purvis is coming home now, quite covered in glory, they tell me – and you and I are for a second honeymoon in Naples. And now, I will have my thanks." But as he pulled her into his arms, the door opened behind him. "Where are you, child?" said Mrs Carteret, "the gong is sounding this instant," and then, "Oh, I cry your pardon, my lord."

"No need, no need." Lord Meynel was all *bonhomie.* "We were but anticipating the pleasures of our continental tour. And," his hand was still heavy on Amanda's shoulder, "there will be time enough for that."

# Chapter Four

In London, they stayed once more at Grillon's Hotel in Albemarle Street and Mrs Carteret plunged into an orgy of shopping, dragging her reluctant daughter along with her. Lord Meynel had given no hint as to how long they would be staying abroad, but as Mrs Carteret said, in the troubled state of Europe anything might happen. Austria, Russia and Prussia were united against France now, and the Duke of Brunswick, who commanded their armies, had issued a manifesto, which, Amanda privately thought, was bound to do more harm than good. She was no politician, but her common sense told her that the Duke of Brunswick's avowed intention 'to lay Paris in the dust (and) crush the republican vipers under his heel,' must inevitably stiffen the resistance of the French.

Mrs Carteret's characteristic reaction to this flamboyant pronouncement was to insist that Amanda must have everything new, from pillow-shifts to pelisses. At once unimaginative and sensation-loving, she rather enjoyed the idea of her daughter's being stranded in a hostile country – always provided, of course, that she had enough India satin ball gowns for evening wear and sprigged muslins for the day. As for Amanda, her state of silent hopelessness was only enlivened by the eagerness with which she daily scanned the shipping news. This had, of course, to be done when Lord Meynel was not nearby, and many were the expedients she had to resort to in order to get at his copy of *The Times*. But the days passed; her new dresses, with their complement of matching kid slippers, gloves, pelisses and so forth had all come home, and the elegant new travelling carriage Lord Meynel had

52

commissioned was also ready. They had sheets for the journey and for the furnished house Lord Meynel intended to take when they reached Naples, they had arms for the servants, and a supply of Dr James's powder, laudanum and other medicaments that would, Amanda privately thought, have sufficed for a whole army. In short, they were ready to go, but still Lord Meynel lingered, and Amanda, free of his attentions as she had not been since her marriage, began to suspect that some amorous interlude was keeping him in London. Mrs Carteret, too, was suspicious, tut-tutted to Amanda, and said, "I told you so," in many different ways. Amanda did her best at once to pretend shock, and to conceal the heart-singing relief she really felt. If her husband would only set himself up a mistress and leave her alone, she might yet achieve some kind of a twilight happiness in her married life. Unfortunately for her, this very kindling of hope lent a new spring to her step and bloom to her complexion. When they went to the theatre, the box Lord Meynel had taken was always crowded, when she rode in the park, she was surrounded by cavaliers. Lord Queensberry, sitting on his balcony above Piccadilly, had called her a damned fine young woman, and they were betting on her faithfulness to her husband at White's. Aware of all this, Lord Meynel enjoyed it at second-hand, since he was now comfortably certain that Amanda would never betray him for anyone but John Purvis. He, too, kept his eye on the shipping news. A second copy of *The Times* was delivered, much to her amazement, to the little house in Bayswater where his mistress lived. Since he was paying the rent, she made no objections to this, but was somewhat taken aback by his habit of reading it in bed. One morning (their hours were irregular), he swore, jumped out of bed, then, on second thoughts, got back again for a last passionate five minutes before he dressed, kissed her robustly, gave her ten pounds, and left.

As for Amanda, she had gone out riding before the morning paper arrived, and had therefore not seen the brief announcement that His Majesty's ship *Somerset* had arrived at Falmouth with despatches on the progress of Lord Cornwallis's Indian war. It was accordingly with purest, most exquisite amazement, that she heard herself greeted, as she turned to leave the Park, by a voice she had hardly hoped to hear again.

"Amanda!" John Purvis was immaculate in the uniform of a lieutenant in His Majesty's Navy. His face, looking up at her as she sat, silent with shock, on her quiet horse, was drawn with fatigue – and with something else. The new lines about mouth and eyes deepened as he corrected himself: "I cry your pardon: Lady Meynel, I should say."

"John!" Her hands, on the reins, shook so that her horse turned a wise, considering eye round to her.

"It seems I must give you joy—" And then, with a sudden, heart-rending return to his old, boyish manner, "Oh, Amanda, how *could* you?"

Looking down at him, at the well-known, dearly-loved face, now so grievously altered she found the question unanswerable. She could not explain to herself, still less to him. And yet, she must try. "What else could I do?" she asked pitifully.

"What else? Why, not, apparently, wait even so long as twelve months for one who loved you – was working for you – had dreamed of giving you, at last, some happiness, some certainty, in your life. I only went to India for your sake, in the hopes of advancing myself in my profession and making myself, more quickly, fit to ask for your hand. I might have spared myself the pains, it seems. How long, tell me, how long did you remember me when I was gone? Was it the next day that my Lord Meynel came to you with his offer of wealth? Or the day after? Or did you, perhaps, think of me for as much as a week? And did you, in that time, realize how foolish you had been to engage yourself to a young man of such unlikely prospects? Oh, I know, I told you that you must not consider yourself bound to me, and I meant it . . . If I had come back and found you married to someone worthy of you, who might, perhaps, be able to make you happy, I would have said nothing, Amanda, ever, but worn out my heart, silently, at my disappointment. But to find that you had sold yourself for money – Amanda, can I ever have known you?"

"Perhaps not," almost to her relief, she found herself angry, "since you believe, so easily, the worst of me. So I have sold myself, have I? And what is my gain? This horse? These clothes? The daily misery I suffer . . . But what is the use of talking? Oh, John," now her voice shook with unshed tears, "I have longed so long to see you, to try and explain, to know you understood . . . But what is the use of talking? You have condemned me unheard. Well, comfort yourself with this: no punishment you could wish or imagine for me is one half of what I suffer. But, one thing, before we part, for ever," she leaned forward in the saddle to look down at him, her big grey eyes aswim with tears, "John, why did you not write to me? If you had only written . . ."

His blue eyes met hers in amazement. "Not write? But, Amanda—"

A horse had stopped beside hers. "My dearest life," said Lord Meynel. "I have found you at last. What? And Mr Purvis, too, of whom I have heard so much good. Congratulations on your promotion, Mr Purvis; it is a fine thing, is it not, to be young, and free, and on the way to glory? I only wish we had time to celebrate with you, as old friends should, but we are off on our travels, as my wife has doubtless told you. I have news for you, my love, the tedious delay you have borne so patiently is over: we leave tomorrow. Mr Purvis, I know, will forgive us if we take a somewhat unceremonious leave of him: there is much to be done between now and then. I doubt we shall not go to bed tonight, and that, I am sure Mr Purvis will agree, must be a real hardship." The squeeze of the waist, and grin of complicity with which he accompanied this statement reduced Amanda to such an agony of mortification that she was hardly able to murmur her incoherent answer to John Purvis's speech of leave-taking. At the last moment, he pressed her hand. "Lady Meynel – Amanda, if I have said anything to offend you – forgive me, forget it."

He was gone. Lord Meynel's hand was hard on

Amanda's waist as he turned their horses towards their hotel. "So," he said, "I rather thought I had interrupted a scene of petty tragedy. I had meant to spare you that, my love, but never mind. From his expression that young man will not be troubling you again. If he had really said something to affront you, I trust you gave him the set-down he deserved. My wife is not to be bandying words with young puppies on their promotion."

Amanda was too angry to speak. All that long day she hoped, absurdly, against hope, that John might come to her again, might write, might do something to prevent the exile that loomed ahead of her. And all day she knew her hopes for nonsense. Vain, too, to dream that their departure night once more be delayed. Playing the devoted husband all day, Lord Meynel hardly left her side as she and her mother directed the servants in the final packing of their mountain of baggage. There was hardly time to think, still less to hope, or to wonder what John had been going to say when her husband interrupted them. "Not write?" he had begun, in tones of amazed question. Was it possible that he had written to her and that these letters like those to his aunt had failed to reach her?

Her husband's hot hand on her bare shoulder interrupted her thoughts. "Well, my love," he had dined well and his speech was beginning to slur, "we have been more industrious than I thought possible, and our reward is a night's sleep. Come, you look fagged out, and your mother, I know, will excuse us." And then, as he led her, cold and unresisting, to their bedroom: "I have to make my peace with you; I have neglected you, I know, shamefully these last few weeks and you have borne it like the angel you are, but that is all over now, and our second honeymoon beginning. Come, ring for your maid." His impatient fingers were already fumbling at the fastening of her dress. "I want my wife."

Her last thought, as she finally fell into exhausted sleep much later was that surely he would never wake in time for the early start he had planned. But he had given his orders. They were roused sharp at eight and he rolled, grumbling and haggard, out of her bed, reminding her, from the door of his dressing room, that they would leave on the stroke of nine.

Suddenly lachrymose at the reality of this parting Mrs Carteret delayed them for a few minutes, but Amanda would not join in her tears. What was the use of crying? She lay back at last, white and silent in her corner of the brand new travelling carriage, and thought that the despair of her honeymoon had been nothing to this. Then, she had been terrified of the unknown, now, far worse, it was the known that she feared. And, even in Suffolk, far from her home and friends, there had always been the possibility of help; friendly faces had smiled at her in the lanes, friendly voices bidden her good day. How had she thought herself quite alone when at least, around her, were people who spoke her own language?

But still, of many miseries, the worst of all was the recollection of John Purvis's angry words the day before, and the thought that he might, even now, be calling at the Grillon to apologize for them. Of course he had been angry yesterday; she could hardly blame him. But, today, she was sure, he would have forgiven her – have begun to understand, and have come to her to forgive and be forgiven. Somehow, in those incorrigible day-dreams of hers, she had always imagined that John, when he returned, would find some solution for the disaster in which she had involved herself. And yet – how could he? She was married to this elderly beast, who had fallen, now, into a light, snuffling sleep in his corner of the carriage. She must apply herself to making the best of him – if best there was.

The day was fine. The new carriage moved easily along the road between apple orchards and Kentish fields of burgeoning hops. It was impossible entirely to despair. She was going away from all her friends, it was true, but then they had not been much use to her when she was in England. If she could only have seen John once more, she told herself, she could have faced this exile more cheerfully. But, then, how sorry he would be when he called at the Grillon and found her gone. Perhaps there was no need, after all, to despair. And, besides, the idea of 'abroad' could not help but be entrancing to a girl of eighteen who had hardly had more than a taste even of London. Now she was going to France, where they were all arrant republicans, to Paris, where they had put their king in prison, and then to Naples, where, she had been told, existed the most frivolous court in Europe. She would not have been human if she had failed to find the prospect a little exciting. And Amanda was thoroughly human. Soon she was dreaming again. In Paris, she would contrive to liberate the King and Queen and smuggle them down to Naples, where, of course, she would be welcomed with open arms by Queen Maria Carolina, the French Queen's sister. Waking, with a jerk, around midday, Lord Meynel was surprised to find his wife so cheerful.

When they reached Dover they learned that the wind was against them and had to spend two days in the expensive discomfort of the Ship Inn before they were able to sail. They were two days of anguished hope for Amanda and gloomy anticipation for Lord Meynel, who was, he told her, a damned bad sailor, but hoped he would suffer less this time than last. Both of them were doomed to disappointment. None of the travellers who arrived at the inn was John Purvis with a solution of all Amanda's problems, and when they finally sailed, the crossing took a day and a half and Lord Meynel was quite as sick as he had ever been. Amanda, on the other hand, had never felt better in her life and won golden opinions of captain and crew by the way she enjoyed the stormy weather.

In France at last, Lord Meynel recovered slowly, lying back pale and quiet in his corner of the carriage, and Amanda was free to find everything quite as strange as she had expected. The postilions in their greasy nightcaps and vast jackboots really did call each other *citoyen*, though not very often; she saw the famous tricolour and marvelled at the squalid poverty of the villages through which they passed. Her hope that they might stay a while in Paris and shop in the Palais Royale, if they did not actually succeed in releasing the King and Queen, was dashed by the English Ambassador, Lord Gower, who strongly urged them to continue their journey at once. The mob violence of August 10th might be repeated any day, he said, and relations between France and England were going from bad to worse. He himself expected to be recalled momently, and for them delay might well be dangerous or even fatal. On his advice, Lord Meynel also reluctantly changed his plans for the rest of the journey. He had intended crossing to Italy by Monte Cenis, but Lord Gower courteously pointed out that this would be folly, if not suicidal, since the French and Austrians were already fighting in Northern Italy. Instead, they must drive down to Marseilles and take ship there for Leghorn. For the first time in their marriage, Amanda found herself positively sorry for her husband when she saw him confronted with the prospect of another sea voyage and one of highly uncertain duration. Anxiously enquiring, he had learned that the passage might take them as much as a month. But anything, he said, was better than to get involved in the campaign that was now opening in Northern Italy. Not for the first time, Amanda was made aware that like most bullies her husband was very far from being a brave man.

As it turned out, they were lucky in their winds, and Amanda could have wished the voyage to Leghorn twice as long, and, indeed, nourished a few unquenchable dreams of an attack by the pirates her husband feared. Naturally, the dream ended with her rescue from the pirates by a British frigate commanded by John Purvis. She was angry with herself, pacing about the little ship in unfamiliar fierce Mediterranean sunshine, but how could she help this dreaming? It was all the happiness she had. Though, indeed, the weather itself was almost happiness enough for a healthy girl who had been used, all her life, to English cloud and English rain. Through day after day of brilliant sunshine, she walked the deck and watched the varying prospect of cliff and mountain along the shore, to which their boat was keeping cautiously close. Lord Meynel, retching his heart out in a stuffy cabin found the hot days and airless nights almost unbearable, but Amanda had never imagined such content. They reached Leghorn all too soon for her, and after two days spent prostrate on his bed in the town's best inn, Lord Meynel proclaimed himself fit to travel. He was eager for the end of the journey now and would not even let her pause for a day of sightseeing in Rome. Through long scorching days their little cortège (for the servants rode behind in Lord Meynel's old carriage) rumbled over the rough Italian roads. At night, the inns varied from the dirty to the infested and Amanda was sometimes forced to sit up all night in a chair, for fear of being eaten to pieces, but she did not care, it was all too beautiful, too strange . . . Lord Meynel, of course, who had made the Grand Tour as a young man, had seen it all before and infuriated her with his blasé comments. Oh (she was dreaming again) what ecstasy it would be to drive through these splendid prospects with a sympathetic companion.

It was a fine September morning when they rattled through the main gate of Naples and down the Via Tribunati to the Inn of the Tre Re where they were to stay until they could find a house. To Amanda's delight, their suite in the inn opened onto a balcony from which she could look to her heart's content at the brilliant blue water of the famous bay, from which the city's peach-coloured houses rose in tiers up the hillside. From this sun-drenched privacy, she could watch the fishermen in their striped trousers and listen to their songs and the shouts of crowds of picturesque, half-clad beggars who lounged along the harbour edge while their children played naked in the hot dust. She could have happily spent all evening there, watching the light change on the harbour and the islands beyond, and recovering from the exhaustion of the journey, but her husband soon roused her from a dream in which a British warship sailed into the bay with John Purvis on board.

Lord Meynel had been, already, to write his name at the British Ambassador's residence nearby and had had the good fortune to encounter the ambassador himself. Sir William Hamilton had represented England at the

Court of Naples for almost thirty years, and Lord Meynel had often boasted, on their journey, of ambassadorial kindnesses when he had first visited Naples as a young man. Now, he had successfully renewed what Amanda suspected of having been the slightest of acquaintances, and had been invited by Sir William to join him and his wife for the evening promenade along the seashore. There was, he explained, no performance at the San Carlo Opera House, and therefore the world of fashion would seize the opportunity to meet out of doors in the cool of the evening and enjoy the harbour breeze.

Tired and jaded, Amanda protested that she could not possibly be unpacked and ready in time, but he only laughed at her. The orchestral concert that provided the pretext for this gathering did not begin till midnight. She would have plenty of time to rest and recover herself from the journey while her maid unpacked for her. "It will be an admirable opportunity for you to make your first appearance in Neapolitan society."

She interpreted this, correctly, as meaning that he wished to lose no time, himself, in plunging into the social vortex, and gave up her private dream of an early and peaceful night. It seemed odd to put on full evening dress for a carriage drive along the seashore, but Lord Meynel insisted that this was the thing to do, and the air, still stifling hot at ten o'clock, made her grateful for the deep décolletage and scanty sleeves of her favourite gown of midnight blue silk.

Her husband looked at her with rare approval as he led her out to the carriage. "Travelling suits you," he said. "I have never seen you in better looks. I hope Lady Hamilton will forgive you for being a beauty." And then, returning to his usual bullying tone. "You will treat her, mind, with the deepest respect. You are not to be remembering the stories about her now. When she was merely Amy Lyon, the case was quite other. I remember taking tea with her myself, once, when she was living with Charles Greville, lucky dog – how she adored him. And Romney and the other painters at her feet, and several good offers of marriage, I believe, but she'd have none of them. But she's taken her goods to the right market at last; I'll never believe Charles Greville sold her to his uncle; I have no doubt she had it all planned out from the first time of seeing him. At all events, she is Lady Hamilton now, and the Queen of Naples' dear friend. What is more to the purpose, she is our Ambassador's wife and I'll not have you spoiling my chances here with your prudish airs."

Amanda took her seat in the carriage in silence. What was the use of pointing out to her husband that she would have known nothing about Lady Hamilton's sordid history if he had not thought fit to tell her of it. But it was characteristic of him to spoil her anticipation of an outing of pleasure with this kind of uncalled-for setdown, and she had trained herself to take as little notice as possible. Instead, she looked out of the carriage window at the crowds which still, to her amazement, thronged the streets. It seemed to her that there was a new stridency, now, about their shouts, a new eagerness in their movements. But Lord Meynel, when she remarked on this, merely shrugged his shoulders. "It is just like these idle rascals of *lazzaroni* to turn night into day," he said, "and grow noisier in the process."

With the wisdom of much experience, Amanda forebore to point out that they, too, were turning night into day, and for no more laudable a reason. Instead, she exclaimed with surprised pleasure. Their carriage had turned into the shadowy gardens of the Villa Reale and she forgot her irritation in enjoyment of the animated scene before her. The fountains and cypresses of the garden were illuminated by the flambeaux of the carriages that thronged the walks; behind them glimmered the still waters of the bay, and over all, from a dimly discerned building in the centre of the garden, floated the music of one of her favourite Haydn airs.

She would have liked to sit there, enraptured, to look and listen till morning, but her husband was already urging the coachman forward. Sir William and Lady Hamilton would be in the centre of the garden; they must lose no time

62

in joining them there. But when they reached the central square, they found it so thronged with people that Lord Meynel decided they would have to leave their carriage and take the unfashionable measure of finding their way through the crowds on foot. As they did so, Amanda was again aware of what seemed to her an almost hysterical note in many a half-heard conversation. Odd phrases caught her ear as her husband urged her forward. The talk, she was sure, was all of France: she heard the King's name, and that of the Princesse de Lamballe. There were exclamations of horror, and hands upraised to heaven in pantomimed despair. But they had reached the centre of the square at last, and her husband, who had not troubled to before, now took her arm protectively and led her up to an open carriage surrounded by a group of people talking agitatedly in English. The animated centre of this little circle was the buxom beauty in the carriage, whose blue eyes and luxurious dark curls were set off by a simple gown of white muslin, with blue sash and ribbons. Realizing that this must be the notorious Lady Hamilton, Amanda experienced a little shock of surprise. It was hard to imagine that this young girl, with the entrancing smile and the ringing, carefree laugh, was the heroine of the shabby episodes her husband had warned her to forget. Then, as she drew nearer to the carriage, she saw that the beauty was not, in fact, quite the young girl she had seemed from the distance. The beautiful face was just beginning to sag towards plumpness, the colour, Amanda told herself was a little too good to be true. But there was no doubt about the warmth of her welcoming smile as the Ambassadress greeted Amanda, and Amanda smiled back, instantly conquered by its kindness.

Beside the gay enchantress sat her husband, Sir William Hamilton, the Ambassador, who had added this beauty to his collection of precious rarities. Much older than his wife, and quietly elegant in contrast to her ebullience and diamonds, he greeted the new arrivals with a grave face. "Have you heard the news?" he asked as soon as the presentations had been made.

"No." Lord Meynel had been kissing Lady Hamilton's hand with prolonged enthusiasm and now released it reluctantly. "What is it?"

"The worst possible. Those madmen in France have declared a republic and are baptizing it in a sea of blood. The Princesse de Lamballe is murdered, and scores of others, with barely the mockery of a trial. The King himself, they say, is in danger of his life. I wish I knew where it would all end. For the present, I fear I have to disappoint you, my lord. Their Majesties, to whom I had engaged to present you tonight, stay at home out of deference to the sufferings of their brother of France and his family. We must hope for an opportunity of making you known to them soon, but tonight, as you will imagine, Her Majesty's anxiety for her sister, Marie Antoinette, is too acute to allow of her appearing in public. But for your part, I hope that you will find this scene to be not without its interest."

"The music is exquisite," said Amanda, forgetting shyness in delight as Mr Haydn's symphony wound to its close.

"You like music? That is excellent. You will find Naples a place after your own heart and must honour us with your company at our next concert."

Lord Meynel never liked to see his wife the centre of attention, and now pushed in front of her. "You are kindness itself, my lord. And may we also hope to be honoured with a display of Lady Hamilton's famous attitudes?"

But he had lost the Ambassader's attention. Sir William had turned away to the far side of his carriage where a tall figure had leaned over to clap him unceremoniously on the shoulder. As this newcomer moved forward into the light, Amanda could hardly restrain a gasp of amazement at his bizarre appearance. In contrast to the satin and velvet splendour of the rest of the crowd, this brown-faced big-nosed intruder wore an enormous, battered hat drooping over the shoulders of his shaggy grey coat from the pockets of which he was now producing a handful of dead birds. He held them out to Sir William, who was now, to Amanda's further amazement in fits of apparent laughter.

"Buy my beautiful birds," wailed the stranger in the coarse dialect of the *lazzaroni*, "in Christian charity buy my birds and save a poor man from starvation." And then, he, too, burst into a fit of noisy laughter and clapped Sir William once more on the shoulder. "No need to look so astonished, man," his speech was as broad as ever. "I'm here incognito. The King is at home, in mourning, and shocking bored with it I can tell you, but here is Ferdinand, a poor peasant, and entirely at your service – and that of beauty." He took off the ridiculous hat and made a low and courtly bow, first to Lady Hamilton and then to Amanda. "But what is this? A new beauty? Make me known to her, Sir William, I beg."

Urbane as ever, Sir William lost no time in introducing Amanda and her husband to "Ferdinand, the huntsman". Then, in an aside that made little pretence at secrecy: "It is the King, but he does not choose to be recognized."

Finding this advice somewhat confusing, Amanda contented herself with a low curtsey and was deeply grateful when Lady Hamilton engaged her in conversation about their journey, leaving their two husbands to entertain the King. Answering her frank and kindly questions and listening to her loud, melodious laugh, Amanda was charmed despite herself. It was impossible not to like this friendly beauty who seemed to take such a genuine interest in her concerns. And how beautiful she was. When she spoke and laughed, one forget the slight coarsening of the famous features and saw only the deep blue eyes that formed so striking a contrast with luxurious auburn hair, the beautiful mouth, the classic poise of the head. No wonder Romney and his friends had been charmed by her and had asked nothing better than to paint her over and over again. Charmed herself, Amanda was convinced, already, that much of what her husband had told her must be untrue. This delightful girl who had greeted her so kindly was no sordid and scheming adventuress. Whatever misfortunes had befallen her, she must, surely, have been more sinned against than sinning. And how charming, too, was the pretty deference with which she turned away now to answer a question from her husband.

It was a pleasure, Amanda thought, to see on what terms of easy affection the beauty dealt with her elderly husband. Or – it would have been a pleasure if it had not suddenly brought home to her the miserable contrast of her own position. Characteristically, Lord Meynel had forgotten all about her and had got himself around to the far side of the Hamiltons' carriage, where he had contrived to engage the King in an animated conversation about hunting. Since the Ambassador and his wife were now deep in private conversation, Amanda found herself totally at a loss, alone in the middle of the crowd, and, she felt, appallingly conspicuous, despite the semi-darkness.

She was wishing herself a thousand miles away – home in England for choice – when a girl spoke from beside her. "You must be Lady Meynel, the new arrival," she said, in excellent English. "Allow me to introduce myself, since we do not stand on ceremony at these meetings. I am Julia," she said, "Countess Vespucci. May I be the first to bid you welcome to Naples?"

"Why, thank you, Countess." Amanda was puzzled. "But, surely, you must be English?"

The girl – she was hardly more – shook dark curls away from her face and laughed. "You delight me by saying so," she said, "but in truth I am Neapolitan. My mother, though, was English, and taught me to love that country as my own. But I am forgetting my manners. May I introduce my cousin, Antonio Vespucci?"

Slim and darkly handsome, Antonio Vespucci was a few years older than his cousin and very much the man of the world. He was soon cross-examining Amanda about conditions in the countries through which they had passed on their journey and surprising her more and more by what seemed almost a sympathy with revolutionary France. The countess, too, was beginning to look anxious. "Hush cousin," she said at last. "This is no night – and no place – to be talking of your dreams." And then, to

Amanda. "Do not take him seriously, Lady Meynel. He and his friends at the university have dreamed for years of an ideal state, somewhat on the lines of your England. They are slow to realize, despite the dreadful news, that France is something quite other."

Watching young Vespucci's impatient expression as he listened to his cousin's apologies on his behalf, Amanda felt herself, suddenly, in deep waters, and was relieved at a summons from Lady Hamilton that enabled her to make her excuses and farewells to the countess.

Lady Hamilton leaned forward in the carriage to greet her playfully. "Am I to be scolding you already?" she asked, her smile belying her words. "But never look so perplexed, I'll forgive you this time, since, truly, you could not know that that young Vespucci you were talking to is a dangerous revolutionary and no friend of our beloved Queen."

"And his cousin?" Amanda, who had liked what she had seen of the young countess, could not help asking.

Lady Hamilton shrugged. "Oh, as to her, who can tell?" And went on to explain that Julia Vespucci's mother had been cut off by her English family for marrying Count Vespucci and had died of grief when he was killed in a hunting accident. Still a child, Julia had succeeded to the title and to extensive estates near Syracuse in Sicily, but had never, Lady Hamilton said, been recognized by her mother's family. To Amanda's relief, she then announced that it was time to be thinking of going home and offered to take her up in her own carriage. "Your husband and mine are gone, who knows where, with His Majesty. We had best not look for them till morning."

In fact, Lord Meynel did not get home until Amanda was eating a late breakfast of coffee and rolls on the balcony of her room. She had been afraid he might be angry with her for leaving him and going home with Lady Hamilton, and was relieved to find him in high good humour. He had been, he said, on an early morning fishing expedition with His Majesty. "I have spoiled my brocade, but who cares?" And he proceeded to hold forth at length in enthusiastic description of his adventures with his new – and royal – friend. Not only had Ferdinand spent the early hours of the morning in fishing and swearing oath for oath with his illiterate companions, he had then taken his catch to market and sold it to the highest bidder. "He's a card, this King of Naples, I can tell you," concluded Lord Meynel, before reporting with unfeigned glee that His Majesty had invited him to go pheasant shooting with him on the island of Procida next day.

From then on, hunting monarch and hunting lord were constant companions, and as a result Amanda was left delightfully to her own devices. It was she who found them a handsome suite of apartments on the Chiaia, with balconies giving on her favourite view of the bay, hired servants and generally organized their establishement. Her husband, returning to eat and sleep, complimented her on her arrangements with unflattering surprise. He had not, he said, expected to have her turn out so capital a housewife.

The ladies of the English colony, who lost no time in following the Hamiltons' lead and calling on her, equally exclaimed at such competence in one so young. For they were all established matrons and seemed incapable of talking about anything except the weather, their servants and, if they had any, their children. Amanda soon despaired of finding a friend among them and was therefore delighted when Julia Vespucci called some weeks after they had moved into their apartment, explaining that she had been away visiting her estates in Syracuse. Here at last was someone she could question about all that she found strange in Neapolitan society. In answer to her eager questions, Julia Vespucci explained that the pleasure-loving King ruled in name only. Behind him, an infinitely more formidable figure, stood his wife, Queen Maria Carolina, daughter of the Empress Maria Theresa and sister of the unhappy Marie Antoinette. While the King hunted and fished, she and her minister, the English Lord Acton, really ran the country. "And of course," concluded Julia, "since they have imprisoned her sister and her husband, she hates the French and, because of them, all radical ideas. My cousin says it is but a matter of time before we are at war with France."

"And what does he think of that?" asked Amanda, who had already noticed how frequently Julia referred to this obviously adored cousin of hers.

"Oh, he and his friends pretend to lament it," said Julia. "They like to talk equality and fraternity, you know. But there's no harm in them. It is but play, like their freemasonry."

Remembering Lady Hamilton's warning, Amanda wondered if her new friend was right. It was all too evident that, for Julia, her cousin could do no wrong.

She wondered still more about young Vespucci and his friends when the gay round of Neapolitan social life was rudely interrupted by the arrival, in the beautiful bay, of a French fleet, equipped for war. With his guns trained on the Castle dell'Ovo the commander, Admiral Latouche, sent ashore for an instant apology for various slights the new French Republic considered itself to have received from the Neapolitan Court. A day of panic followed in the city which lay helplessly exposed to French fire. In the evening, even Amanda, who had kept her head better than most, was relieved to learn that the court had given way to all the French demands. There would be no bombardment of the defenceless city. Characteristically, the lighthearted Neapolitans celebrated the departure of the hostile fleet with as much enthusiasm as if they had just won a signal victory instead of being publicly humiliated.

A few days later they had more cause for celebration. The French fleet, which had sailed away in triumph, was scattered by one of the Mediterranean's fierce, sudden storms and came limping back to ask leave to refit in Naples harbour. This permission was reluctantly granted and soon the swaggering revolutionary sailors with their shiny black hats and tricolour striped trousers became a common sight in the streets of Naples. Amanda had never been able to dislike the French as people, but was sorry to see Julia looking increasingly anxious. She soon learned the reason.

Lord Meynel, who had come home for the celebrations of the King's birthday on 12 January, returned big with news from a courtesy visit to the Hamiltons. He began by taking Amanda roundly to task for not having accompanied him. Since he had not thought fit to mention to her that he was going there, she let this pass in accustomed silence.

"Yes, yes," he said, "that's always your way. You sit there looking injured innocence when you know as well as I do you are going roundly about to disgrace me."

"I? Disgrace you? What can you mean?"

"Why, by avoiding our Ambassador and his wife, who have gone out of their way to show you kindness, and associating, instead, with a parcel of revolutionary riff-raff. I tell you, miss, this is the end of it. You are not to see those Vespuccis again."

"Not see Julia? But why not?"

"Because that cousin of hers is a revolutionary – a traitor – worse, if worse is possible. What do you think of him and his friends dining, last night, on their king's birthday, with Admiral Latouche on the *La Flotte*. And as if this in itself was not bad enough they must, forsooth, wear the red cap and make speeches about the beauty of republican principles. I tell you, if King Ferdinand were not the most long-suffering of monarchs, they would all be in prison today, as they richly deserve. And as for you, I have sat, this morning, through a long lecture from Lady Hamilton (who speaks, as you must know, almost as the mouthpiece of her friend, the Queen) about your association with Julia Vespucci. And I tell you," he struck his fist on the desk at which she was writing so that the inkwell overset, "once and for all; it must stop."

"Julia is my friend." Amanda made a great business of cleaning up the ink. "As for her cousin, if you desire it, I will take means not to encounter him. But," she had made up her mind now, "Julia is my friend, and, if this story is true, will be badly in need of a friend herself. I will not abandon her."

The appalling scene that followed ended with Lord Meynel slamming his way out of the house. Amanda

70

had suspected for some time that he had found himself a Neapolitan mistress and this suspicion was confirmed by his prolonged absence on this occasion, when the king, she knew, was actually attending to affairs of state at his palace of Caserta. Somewhat to her relief – for despite her firm stand, she felt she needed time to think – Julia too was absent. She and her cousin had left on the day after the disastrous banquet for her estates at Syracuse, where, she wrote to Amanda, she intended to remain for some time.

Amanda thought her wise. The town was tense; the news went from bad to worse. The usual carnival gaiety that preceded the beginning of Lent was quenched overnight by the news that Louis XVI had been guillotined. It was lucky for the French Admiral, Latouche, that he and his fleet had already left Naples when this black news plunged the whole town into mourning. It was soon followed by the report that France had declared war on England. For Amanda, this had its cheering aspect. She remembered – how could she forget – John Purvis and his hope for war and the chances it must bring for a naval officer. Now he had them . . . And, if the alliance that was talked of between Naples and England should become a fact, surely, one day, her dream might come true and a British warship, instead of a French one, might sail, as a friend, into Naples harbour – with John on board.

Her other hope, that the news of war might drive her husband home and end her exile, was quickly shattered. Lord Meynel's reaction to the news was instant and decided. It was impossible now to go home by land without risking capture in Northern Italy, and at the very least of it making an enormous detour through Germany. And as for going all the way by sea, that was out of the question; it would kill him. Remembering their previous sea voyages, Amanda had to admit that it very well might, but could not bring herself to think this a matter for great regret. But Lord Meynel's mind was made up. "We are very well here, my love." In words, he was more affectionate to her than ever these days. "What say you that we stay out this damned inconvenient war here, where we are well off?"

71

# Chapter Five

With the outbreak of war, the exchange of news from home became almost a mania with the now sadly-shrunken English colony in Naples. They met, more assiduously than ever, at the daily promenade along the shore, or in Lady Hamilton's box at the San Carlo Opera, to compare rumour with rumour, or try and piece together some idea of the real state of things at home from the scanty information at their disposal. Amanda was as bad – her husband said – as the rest of them. He, frankly, did not care. The French were a dead bore, of course, and the war a lot of nonsense which only affected him when one of his hunting expeditions with King Ferdinand was interrupted by a summons from his masterful Queen. For Queen Maria Carolina and her minister, Lord Acton, were bent on joining the fight – which the Queen at least looked on as in the nature of a crusade – against the French. An attempt to unite the various states of Italy against the common enemy had failed, now the Queen's hope lay in England.

At first, the news from England was uniformly good. The country had plunged with enthusiasm into this new war against the old enemy, France. Regiments were being raised; ships recommissioned, even Manchester was reported to have voted bounty money for 3,000 sailers. For Amanda, of course, news of the Navy was of paramount importance. She longed to know what had happened to John Purvis, but his aunt's last letter, written before the declaration of war, had been maddeningly allusive. She had mentioned, in passing, that John had spent Christmas with her: '*Poor boy, he chafes so at inactivity.*' Now, reading eagerly the names of the ships that were being returned to active service, and gathering what information she could about their captains and crews, Amanda tormented herself with wondering whether John would be lucky and secure a position, perhaps even promotion, on one of them.

But the news did not continue good for long. There was dissension, it seemed, at home. Fox had put forward a motion in the House of Commons against the war with France, and though this was defeated, Amanda found it a discouraging portent. And the expedition under the Duke of York that had sailed so gaily for Flanders seemed to have run into difficulties there. Worse still, from Amanda's point of view, was the news that trickled through about naval disorganisation. Manned by pressed, reluctant and half-trained crews, the ships put to sea in no state to cover themselves with glory. The *Bellerephon* collided with another man-of-war on a fine day in the channel for no reason whatever and had to limp back into Plymouth with foremast and bowsprit gone. The pro-French party in Naples rubbed their hands at this news, cut their hair shorter than ever and dared to appear at the opera in the trousers that were republican anathema to the Queen.

Although she missed Julia Vespucci increasingly these anxious days, Amanda could not help thinking it wise of her to stay at Syracuse, and, more important, to keep her cousin with her. This was no time to be talking revolution in Naples. The streets of the city bred rumours as they did flies, these sultry summer days, and even the jovial *lazzaroni* seemed to Amanda dangerously near to riot. Anything might touch it off. Julia and her explosive cousin were much better out of the city.

For Amanda, it was a surprisingly peaceful summer. As before, in London, Lord Meynel had tired of trying to wring a reaction out of her and was carrying on an outrageously public affair with a buxom, notorious Signora Grassi, one of the singers of the San Carlo Opera Company. When the married women of her acquaintance made it their painfully pleasant duty to tell Amanda about the complaisant Grassi, they found her reaction disappointing. She did not scream, or go white, or faint. She did not even pay homage to the conventions by pretending surprise. Shocked by her very refusal to be shocked, they told each other that Lady Meynel was being infected by the low tone of Neapolitan society, and told their husbands that she was a dangerous young woman.

As a result, Amanda found herself pestered with propositions by the more personable of the married Englishmen, who soon, however, admitted to themselves, and to each other, that the new beauty was cold as ice, caring, it seemed, more for the books she was always reading than for masculine admiration. They were not to know that the image of John Purvis stood always between them and the light.

But Amanda's summer holiday was not to last for long. The Grassi became extortionate and Lord Meynel's friends began to tease him about the ice-maiden he had married. Worse still, the King, whose wife, as usual, was pregnant, had taken to twitting his friends Lord Meynel and Sir William Hamilton about their childlessness. Sir William took this with his usual worldly courtesy, but Lord Meynel found Ferdinand's succession of coarse jests increasingly hard to bear. Besides, a cousin of his had recently died in England leaving him next heir, after an old man and an ailing child to the senior title of the family . . . and to an enormous, but entailed estate. He returned home in September with one fixed idea. He must have an heir. Explaining this in terms of brutal frankness to Amanda, he announced that the King had offered him the loan of a small hunting lodge near Torre del Greco. "We go there tomorrow, and stay till you have news for me."

He had convinced himself that the passivity with which Amanda now yielded to him was to blame for her failure to conceive. At whatever cost, he had decided, he must make her react to him. The cost, for Amanda, was great. Since she had married him – however insanely – she admitted it to be her duty to yield to her husband when he wished it. But, lacking the broad training of someone like Emma Hamilton, she did not recognize that it was equally necessary to pretend pleasure, or at least satisfaction. Fresh from the dinner-time teasing of his cronies, and the enthusiastic groans of his mistress, Lord Meynel found her cold and inadequate. And he was beginning to feel his age now, and the results of years of dissipation. Chilled by the coldness he himself had induced in her, he found it increasingly necessary to hurt her in order to obtain a reaction even in himself. Naples had always been the home of every variety of love-making and he did not lack for hints at expedients. The result, for Amanda, was misery indeed. She thought she had been wretched before, but in these lonely weeks at Torre del Greco she plumbed depths of which she should not even have been aware. If she had been in England, she would have run away. If Julia had been in Naples, she would have gone to her. As it was, she hit finally, on a desperate expedient and told her husband the news he wanted to hear.

The result was all she had hoped. He left, at once, for Naples, to boast, she had no doubt, of his approaching fatherhood to the King and his friends. Suspecting this, she felt almost sorry for her deluded husband – and frightened for herself. When she was forced, at length, to tell him that she had been mistaken, he would be more than ever the butt of his 'friends'. Of what would happen to her then, it was best not to think. For the moment, it was enough to be alone, untouched, to let bruised body and bruised spirit make a start at healing.

It was September now and when her husband visited her, briefly, a few days later it was with stirring news. A British man-of-war had sailed into Naples harbour. The *Agamemnon*, Captain Horatio Nelson, had come with a request from Lord Hood for Neapolitan reinforcements to help in the defence of Toulon which had recently surrendered to the British fleet.

"An English ship at last?" Amanda jumped up from her embroidery frame. "Were there letters for us? What is the news from home?" And then, greatly daring. "There is not, I suppose, anyone we know on board?"

"Anyone we know?" He raised heavy eyebrows. "I should hardly think it probable, since our acquaintance among the Navy is of the slightest. And Captain Nelson, I understand, is the veriest nobody; the jumped-up son of a Norfolk parson, and proud as the devil with it all. Still, I owe it him, I collect, to give him the meeting at Sir William's today, and will bring you the latest news from England when I return tonight."

"When you return? But surely I shall come with you? Lady Hamilton, I am sure, will expect me to be present."

"Nonsense," he said roundly. "I have already presented your compliments to Lady Hamilton and explained to her why you think it best to remain here, quietly, for the moment. She sends her kindest congratulations on the expected event, and urges that you take every care of yourself. And as for these rumours about Vesuvius," he looked up for a moment at the lowering sky, "pay no attention to them. They are nothing but servants' gossip and should be treated as such."

"I would still feel safer in Naples," she said, "rather than here, under the very shadow of the volcano. And, besides, you know how I have longed for news from home; you cannot seriously be suggesting that I should stay here when it is to be had, fresh from England."

"Nothing of the kind. What a scatterbrain you are, to be sure. Did you not hear me tell you that Captain Nelson is come from Toulon? News of those madmen in Frnace he might bring you – if you cared to hear it – but as for England, he knows no more about matters there than I do. Less, no doubt, since Sir William keeps me regularly informed. No, no, my mind is made up. You are to remain here, free of the heat and bustle of Naples."

"But I want to come with you." She had never before argued a point so hard with him.

He sighed and shrugged. "They told me I should soon be sick of your megrims," he said. "Am I to endure these fidgets for nine whole months? If you wish me to bring you the news, tonight, you had best leave off quarrelling with me and make yourself a little agreeable, for a change. I am not the man to bear with a parcel of ill humours merely because you are breeding. And do not put yourself into a fret after I leave, either, or you may harm my heir." And without more ado he rang for a servant and ordered the carriage to be brought round.

Perhaps luckily, she was too angry for speech. If she had said anything, she would probably have thrown in his face the falsehood of her claim to be pregnant, of which he had made such use against her. But this would merely be to draw down disaster on herself before it was necessary. And the more he talked of her pregnancy, the more she recognized just what the inevitable day of reckoning would be like. If he should ever imagine that she had deceived him on purpose . . . It did not bear thinking of.

"In the sullens now?" He bent, carelessly to kiss her cheek. "You had best have a more loving greeting for me when I return."

Left alone, she sat, for a long time, gazing tearlessly out across their terraced garden. She was frightened, she admitted to herself at last, horribly frightened. What would this brutal stranger she had married do to her when he discovered she had made a fool of him? A darkening of the air aroused her from this miserable reverie and she heard, suddenly, an outbreak of terrified speech from the servants' quarters, which looked out the other way, towards Vesuvius.

She had hardly paid attention when her husband dismissed the rumours about the volcano so casually, but now she began to wonder if he had been right, or merely, as usual, convinced of what suited him. She had got used, by now, to the white plume of smoke that always hung over the beautiful, dangerous mountain, and even to the occasional showers of red hot stones that rose from its crater. But surely today's smoke was heavier, and there was something strange, too, about the atmosphere. For days now, the air had been heavy and both the sun and moon had had a curious reddish look. The servants had made no secret of their fright, and had only stayed because they were more frightened still of their master.

As the day wore on, heavy clouds gathered on the horizon, but were soon illuminated by the flickering of

77

multi-coloured lightning. It grew dark unnaturally early and the first of a series of mild earthquakes sent the servants panicking from the house. Ignoring them, Amanda stayed on a verandah that looked out towards the mountain and watched with awed fascination as the gathering darkness showed up a cloud of fire above its crater. There was a continual rumbling now, as of thunder, and from time to time another slight tremor shook the earth beneath her. But she found it impossible to care what happened to her, and watched with a curious detachment as a new crater opened on the side of the mountain and a stream of red-hot lava poured slowly down from it. Behind her, the house was quiet now, but she could hear, from the road beyond, the sound of hysterical talk, the screams of frightened horses and the crying of babies, as more and more of the inhabitants of the village fled for their lives. Listelessly, she thought that perhaps she ought to join them, but did nothing, merely sitting there and gazing at the red cloud above the mountain. She had often been tempted, since her marriage, with ideas of suicide, but strong religious principle had always held her back. Now, with fresh disaster ahead she found it impossible to care whether she lived or died. She would never kill herself, she knew, but must she struggle to remain alive?

She was still sitting there, looking out into the gathering darkness, when a terrified servant rode up with a note from Lord Meynel. He had been, he wrote, unavoidably detained in Naples, and would spend the night at their town house. A postscript referred casually to the talk of a possible eruption; Sir William, who was known for an expert in the volcano's behaviour, said there was nothing to fear. She might rest easy and he would join her in the morning.

Glancing sardonically from his letter to the lurid spectacle of the volcano, Amanda became aware that the servant was still standing in front of her, his teeth actually chattering with fright. He was urging her, she realized, to make her escape with him. Lord Meynel had taken the carriage, but his horse was strong. He had no doubt that he could take her up behind him as far at least as the outskirts of Naples.

She thanked the man and dismissed him: "Milord says there is nothing to fear."

All the servants went in dread of their irascible master, and this was an unanswerable argument. Still the man hovered, longing to be gone yet not liking to leave her. She took pity on him. "You will carry an answer to milord for me," she said, and wrote rapidly. *'I am glad you tell me there is no danger.'* she said, *'For, truly, otherwise, I might have been afraid for my life. I shall hope to see you tomorrow.'* As she sanded and sealed the note, she was aware of a soft dust in the air, and the man, hysterically pointing, showed her how close the stream of molten lava had come to the house. She laughed at his fears. "Do you not see," she said, "that the house is on a hill? The lava will flow harmlessly around me and down into the sea. But do be gone and tell my lord how you left me. If he thinks it necessary, he can send a boat for me." In her heart of hearts she hoped her husband would be too busy with his drinking and his friends to take this precaution.

The man left at last, with many protestations of reluctance, and Amanda prowled about the house, wondering at what she had done. The die was cast now and she was convinced that unless her husband was sober enough to arrange for her rescue, she would certainly perish that night. For some time, there had been no more sounds of life from the road that ran below the house; the fugitives from the village must be well on their way to Naples. Instead, the thunderous noise from the volcano had redoubled in volume and the earth shook almost continuously. Amanda noticed that her hands were shaking, it seemed, in sympathy. She was actually hungry. She had not eaten all day and found a curious meal of cold macaroni, fruit and wine in the dank and deserted kitchen. The food and drink revived her and, suddenly, she found herself anxious to live. Death was so absolute. Suppose . . . there were so many things she might suppose. Faced with her own death, she was able to contemplate the possibility of her husband's. How foolish to die unnecessarily here when a few years might see her a widow, free . . . In the past, she had always shrunk from this idea as heartless, but now, condemned to death by her husband's carelessness, she faced the possibility, and found it – possible. Her hand had stopped shaking. She finished her glass of wine, left the kitchen and hurried back to the verandah. A terrifying sight met her eyes. A stream of molten lava was flowing down the road past the house; the whole verandah was inches deep in soft ash, and from time to time the more distant rumbling of the volcano was accented by the crash of a red hot stone falling nearby. The wooden stables at the far side of the garden were burning already. It was only a matter of time before the house, too, must go up in flames. It was an end to detachment. Suddenly, passionately, she wanted to live. It was one thing to have sat safe indoors and dreamed of romantic extinction by a volcano: nobody likes the immediate prospect of being burned to death.

There was no time to be lost. She hurried round to the other side of the house, only to discover that the stream of lava split at the hillock on which it was built and flowed past on either side. No escape that way. Her only hope lay in the cliffs and the sea. The servant she had sent could not possibly have reached Naples yet, or sent help, but she might be able to get away in the little boat Lord Meynel kept in the cove below the house. She breathed a quick prayer, left the shelter of the verandah, and ran for her life.

Luckily for her, she knew the little path well and her feet found their way almost automatically, leaving her free to watch for and dodge the red hot stones that were falling more thickly now. As for the ash, she was covered in it at once, but to her relief it had cooled as it fell and was only pleasantly warm on her face and hands. She pulled her scarf more tightly round her hair and hurried forward.

Reaching the top of the cliff at last, she gazed down the steep path to the little cover. Blank disappointment whitened her face. She had been so sure that the boat would be there, but some other fugitive must have thought of it first. The cove was empty. For a moment she gave way to despair, but the very fact of trying to escape had strengthened her will to live. She turned and walked doggedly forward along the cliff. She did not believe in rescue by her husband. He was doubtless drinking deep with Nelson and the other British officers. Help, if it came, would come by accident. She shook a cloud of ash off her scarf, tied it more tightly over her hair for fear of cinders, and set forward resolutely along the rocky path. She had never been this way before and her progress was slow and uncertain in the half light. At last, turning a corner, she stopped with a gasp. She had forgotten that a small stream ran out to sea here through a volcanic fissure in the cliffs; now, below her, she could see its course outlined in molten lava. There was no hope of passage this way. In order to get to the further cove, she would have to go back to the house and start again down the path along the next spit of high land.

She had been frightened before, now she was desperate. But there was nothing else for it. She turned at a gasping run, back along the path to the house. Going this way, she was more aware than ever of the increasing hail of hot stones and warm ash. She had been hit one or two glancing blows already but was too frantic to notice the pain of her burns. Reaching the house once more after what seemed an eternity of desperate struggle, she was amazed to find it still standing and not, miraculously, yet on fire. An overwhelming temptation seized her. Here was shelter, however temporary. Why not go in, lie down on her own comfortable bed, and sleep. In the morning, she might be safe – or dead. She hardly cared which.

She was standing there, torn between her longing for rest and the unwelcome duty of living, when she saw a light flickering in one of the downstairs windows of the house. Someone must be there, risking his life to look for her. She ran towards the house, then stopped. It might be a looter. She had heard plenty of stories about the criminals who took advantage of these times of chaos and disorder to line their pockets and who would think nothing of disposing of anyone who interrupted them. Still, whoever it was must have some idea of the best way to escape . . . besides, after the past hours of lonely terror, the idea of human company was irresistible. She ran towards the house.

As she approached, a man's figure appeared in the dark doorway onto the verandah. A candle in his hand, he looked anxiously out into the darkness. Flickered in the draught the flame made strange shadows on his face. Certain that he could not see her, Amanda drew a few cautious steps nearer. From his silhouette, it looked as if he was in coat and knee breeches, the garb of a gentleman, and spelling safety. But it was hard to be sure. Then, as she watched, he shrugged, apparently deciding that what he had heard had been mere imagination, and turned back into the house. "Mandy," she heard him calling softly in English, "Amanda, are you there?"

"John!" She broke into a sobbing run. This time he had heard her and met her, open-armed, in the doorway.

"Mandy!" For an exquisite, timeless moment she was in his arms. Then he held her off, to look at her. "You are not hurt? Where have you *been*, Amanda? I was nearly giving up in despair. But are you hurt?" he asked again anxiously.

"Nothing to signify. Nothing matters any more, now you are here. Oh, John," for one more moment she let her head rest on his shoulder. "Is it a miracle, or is it really you?"

She heard him laugh in the darkness. "Something of both, I think. I collect you did not know that I am Second Lieutenant on the *Agamemnon* now. I was dining with Captain Nelson and the other officers at the Ambassador's, met your husband, heard you were here – and here I am."

"And Lord Meynel?"

"Too far gone with drinking your health to care for your safety." He did not try to disguise the scorn in his voice. "Oh, Amanda—" He broke off, then continued in a different tone: "The question now is what is best for us to do." His arm was still supporting her as he turned a little away to look out into the gathering darkness. "No hope of finding our way now. I have a boat in the cove beyond there," he

82

pointed to the cliffs to the north of the path along which Amanda had come. "The crew have orders to wait offshore till I return – or till morning, and have been bribed, I think, sufficiently, even for Neapolitans. But we will never find the way in the dark. It is a lucky thing for us that the moon is full. I think we must risk waiting till it rises. We will rest for two hours or so, have something to eat, and start out when the moon is up. It is a fortunate thing," a considering glance took in the stables, now burning fiercely, "that your house is built of stone. I think we may do well enough yet. So, come, show me the way to your kitchen before I faint with hunger on your hands."

She could not help laughing. "Oh, John, I am *glad* to see you. And, do you know, I believe I am hungry too. I am afraid there is little enough to eat, though. I had nothing but cold macaroni for my luncheon."

He made an expressive face. "That will not do for me. But look," he reached down a huge side of smoked ham from the chimney, cut off two thick slices and told her to find him some eggs, while he got the fire going. "And now a bottle of wine," he said. "This is probably the one time in our lives we shall dine alone together. Let us enjoy it, Mandy."

"Oh, John." For a moment, she was close to tears, then with an effort imitated his briskness as she fetched her best glass and silver. They carried their steaming ham and eggs into the saloon and John insisted that she eat hers on the big sofa. "You will need all your strength before the night is over."

"I wish we could stay here and chance it."

"So do I, but you know it is impossible. Oh, Amanda," he had finished his meal now and came across to take away her plate. "Amanda, how could you do it?"

She made no pretence of misunderstanding. "John – I could not help it. Or thought I could not. If you had been nearer – but he saw to that. He sent you away on purpose, you know, and stopped your letters to me. You did write to me?" she asked pitifully, the tears once more near the surface.

"Of course I did. By every packet."

"I should have known. But I had none of them. Your aunt heard nothing either. It was as if the sea had opened and swallowed you. And he made me all kinds of promises . . . and mother was in debt . . . and we were turned out of the house. Oh, John, I was mad, I know, but, at the time, it seemed there was nothing else to do. I . . . I did not rightly know what I was doing."

He had stayed close and comfortingly beside her; now he settled on the arm of her sofa. "I understand," he said. "Or almost. You were a child, Amanda. It was a wicked thing."

"Yes. I did not know . . . my mother should have told me. But what is the use of blaming her? It was my fault, and I am paying for it."

"Is it very bad?"

"Oh, John." Suddenly, the long misery rose up in her and she turned, sobbing, into his arms.

"Amanda," he was holding her tightly now, "do not cry so. I cannot bear it."

She raised huge, tear-drenched eyes to his. "I . . . I cannot help it." She did not know how like she looked to the child he had teased, and, a little, bullied, and loved, so long ago. And, as for her, she had forgotten everything in the safety of his embrace.

He gave a little groan. "Amanda, my love, my darling." His lips found hers in a kiss that was salt with her tears. For a long, timeless moment he held her so, then, very gently, pushed her away and raised his head from hers. "Amanda, forgive me. I must have been out of my mind."

She pressed closer to him, smiling up through the veil of tears. "Then so am I. Oh, John, if this is madness, it is also the only happiness I shall ever have. Hold me, John, hold me tight." And then, hoping to prolong the moment's ecstasy: "How angry you were with me last time we met. I thought you would never forgive me."

"Forgive you! I shall never forgive myself for letting myself be gulled into leaving you alone, unprotected, a

84

helpless child, with no one to turn to but that harpy of a mother. Oh, forgive me, Amanda."

"I could forgive you anything," she said.

Outside, the thunder of the volcano was unabated, but they had forgotten it, forgotten everything in the intoxication of this meeting. Here, in this room full of flickering firelight, was their world – each other. He was down on the sofa beside her now, his arms close and warm around her, his hands urgent against her torn dress, his mouth speaking to hers. Here was home, here was happiness.

At last she lay there, utterly quiet, spent with ecstasy, in his arms. But now he raised his head to look at her strangely in the flickering light of the fire. "Amanda, I am so ashamed."

She smiled up at him. "Ashamed? So should I be, John, but I tell you, I am not." Relaxed, utterly content, she found the idea merely absurd. "Oh, John," she whispered, "I did not know it could be like this."

"Amanda." It was a groan.

"Do not sound so. At least I shall have this to remember when – oh, John, must I go back? Can you not take me away? Now, tonight?" She knew it for madness even as she spoke.

"You forget," his arms about her were infinitely gentle, "I am a poor man, Amanda. If I were only rich, I would beg you to flout the world for my sake and come away with me. Somewhere, I am sure, we could be happy together. But how can I ask it, when I have nothing to offer you but the pay of a second lieutenant?" In both their minds was the thought that even that would be jeopardized if he were to disgrace himself by running off with the wife of a married man, and a baronet at that. And she could not help knowing, reluctantly, in her heart, what it must cost him even to make the suggestion. All his life he had longed for a glorious career in the Navy and now with the outbreak of war, his chance had come. She could not ask him to give it up for her sake. For herself, after what she suffered with her husband the idea of penury and disgrace with him seemed like purest heaven. But for him it must mean the end of all his hopes. She could not ask it of him. Instead, she smiled up at him bravely. "At least we have had this," she said. "I know now that there is such a thing as happiness. Now kiss me, John, quickly, for the moon has risen."

# Chapter Six

Outside, strange moonlight mingled with the flickering light from the volcano and they were just able to find their way down the steep and dangerous path to the shore. The ash fell as thickly as ever, though the hail of red-hot stones had slackened a little. But it was a nightmare journey for all that, and left no breath for speech. Only once, when they stopped for a moment's rest, she caught, again, that strange look on his face. "Amanda," he said, "even if you can forgive me, I shall never forgive myself."

"But why, John? You must not say such things. I tell you, there is nothing to forgive." How could she explain? "I owe Lord Meynel nothing – less than nothing. He tricked me into marriage, used me brutally; left me here, for all he knew, to die. Why should we think of him? You look at me as if you thought I should feel guilty too, but I do not, John; I will not. This night has given me back my belief in happiness. I tell you, earlier today, when the eruption started, I wanted to die. If I had done so, it would have been as much my fault as my husband's. I knew what was happening; the servants told me; they would have helped me to safety. But I did not care enough to go. Now, that is all changed. Now, I know what life can be; I shall cling to it. It is not just death you have saved me from tonight, it is suicide."

"Amanda, you must not speak so." He sounded as much scandalized as sympathetic. "But, come, are you rested? We must not be lingering here. Nor will talking do any good. I shall not forgive myself – ever."

"Oh, John . . ." But he had turned away and started down the long, sloping path to the shore. She followed him in silence, the bright light of her happiness dimmed. Did he really mean that he could not forgive himself – or her?

But by now she was almost too tired for consecutive thought, all her energies concentrated on the steep and dangerous path. Only, at last, when they reached the shore, she caught his hand. "I love you, John. Let me say it, just once, before we part."

He bent over her. "And I you, Amanda. You know I always have." His lips were cold on hers. "But here comes my boat. We are safe. I could almost wish we were not." And he picked her up and walked out through the shallow water to meet the boat that was drawing reluctantly in to the shore. Once settled in it, with her head in his lap, Amanda fell into the deep sleep of total exhaustion, only having time, as she plunged into oblivion, to think what a waste it was of her precious minutes with John. She only woke with the shock of the boat's beaching. The moon was behind a cloud and it was quite dark now, with the rumbling of the volcano dimmer in the distance, but she was still comfortingly aware of John's nearness. "Where are we?" she asked.

"At Portici," he said. "I thought it best to take you on by carriage from here. We do not wish to cause more scandal than is necessary."

"Scandal?" She thought about it for a moment. "I suppose you are in the right of it. Should you, do you think, have left me to die rather than risking my precious reputation?"

"It is no laughing matter, Amanda." He helped her out of the boat. "And we must think seriously what we are to tell your husband."

"When he is sober enough to listen," said Amanda. Oddly enough, she found the idea of lying to her husband more unpleasant than the fact that she had already betrayed him.

To John's obvious relief, they found the carriage he had hired waiting for them in the crowded main street of the little town. The sailors he had left in charge of it told them they had had to guard it at pistol point from some of the panic-stricken refugees who filled the town. "It is as well you arrived when you did, sir, or there might have been trouble."

Amanda leaned back in her corner of the carriage with a sigh of relieved admiration. "What a great man you are, John," she said. "I love to hear you order them around. Would they really have risked their lives rather than disobey you?"

"I should hope so," he said calmly. "But do you feel strong enough to talk, Amanda, for we must be fixing upon our story."

"Oh," she said almost impatiently, "what is there to say, but that you came, and found me, and brought me safe away?"

"What a child you are, Amanda." He, too, sounded impatient. "Have you learned nothing in all these years? Do you not understand that the story of this night's adventures will be all over Naples tomorrow? My sailors will talk — they are only human, after all — and they cannot help but remember how long they had to wait for us. We must think of a story to account for the delay."

"I suppose we must." She made a face in the darkness. "I wish we could just tell the truth and be done with it."

"Amanda, be serious." He was angry now. "It is your reputation I am thinking of."

She had almost said, "And your own," but restrained herself in time. Of course he was right to wish to protect her from scandal — and right, too, to wish to avoid the inevitable repercussions such a scandal might have on his own career. She thought rapidly, then put up her hand to her head. "I have it," she said. "When you found me, I was unconscious from the blow I had received from a falling stone. Do not worry, I have the wound to prove it. It took you," incorrigibly she smiled to herself in the darkness, "some time to bring me to my senses. As soon as you had done so, we made our escape. It is but to add solicitude to your heroism."

"Do not tease me, Amanda. You must know that I have your best interests at heart."

"Of course you have, John. I beg you will not think

me ungrateful; it is just that compared to the things that have happened to me, reputation does not seem so very important."

"You are wrong, Amanda, and so you would find, were you to lose it. But your story should do well enough. Is your head truly hurt?"

"Why, yes, as a matter of fact, it hurts abominably, and I think, if you will excuse me," how absurdly formal, considering everything, she sounded, "I will try and rest a little."

"Do, Amanda." Solicitously, he put his arm around her and let her rest against him, his support as firm and impersonal as that of a sick nurse. He was not to know as he sat there in the darkness, of the hot, silent tears that pursued each other down her cheeks. To avoid further talk, which could only still further illuminate the abyss between them, she pretended sleep, and did not know how soon the pretence became reality.

When she awoke, it was daylight and the carriage was rattling through the outskirts of Naples. Her head ached worse than ever and she was stiff in every limb. She moved a little and John, who had been gazing out of the window, turned to her. "Awake at last? I was beginning to think I must rouse you." His voice was as she had always known it, deep, gentle and friendly. Surely she had imagined the chill in his tones last night. She had been overwrought, and no wonder.

She smiled up at him. "I have slept well," she said. "Thanks to you. And you – did you rest at all?"

"A little; it does not signify. There will be time to rest when I am back on the *Agamemnon*." His voice held longing, and a new thought struck her.

"John! I hope you have not been absent without leave – and on my account. I should never forgive myself."

"No, no, do not fret yourself about that. I had Captain Nelson's leave, though it is true [he coloured] that I had not expected the expedition to be of such long duration. But we are not to be thinking of that. I have been trying to decide how best to bring you home."

She smiled at him. "At least you bring me home alive. Surely that is enough."

"I hope so." He sounded doubtful. "But here, if I mistake not, we are. Good luck, Amanda, and God bless you."

"What?" She could not believe her ears. "But surely you will come in with me? My husband – Lord Meynel – will wish to thank you."

"At this hour? You forget. And, indeed, to tell truth, I devoutly hope that Lord Meynel is sound asleep in bed and need never know exactly when I brought you home."

"You wrong him by saying so." She had never thought to find herself defending her husband – and to John Purvis. "How can he help but be overjoyed to see me safe? Do come in, John, and let him thank you."

But his only answer was to jump down and help her out of the carriage. Finding herself, thus, all of a sudden on neutral, public ground, she stammered one more plea. "John, you cannot leave thus?"

"Lady Meynel," his address was a rebuke. "I must. I am only too happy to have been of some service to you. I will call, later, if I may, to make sure that you have suffered no ill effects from this exhausting night."

As he bent to kiss her hand she burst into almost hysterical laughter. "Oh, John," she could not help herself, "that is too rich. No ill effects! If you could but hear yourself."

But he was looking at her almost, she thought, with dislike and suddenly she, too, was aware of a hundred watching eyes.

"I . . . I cry your pardon," she stammered. "I must indeed be over-fatigued. I thank you a thousand times, Mr Purvis." And without another word or look she turned from him and almost ran into the house.

When she had thought of it on the drive from Portici, she had imagined herself returning to the house while the servants were still asleep, rousing the indolent night porter and reaching the safety of her room unobserved. The reality was quite otherwise. Despite the early hour, she found the entrance hall thronged with servants, most of whom had no business to be there. Worse still, their noisy exclamations of pleasure at her arrival were suddenly hushed by the appearance of Lord Meynel at the head of the stairs. He was in evening dress still, and his flushed face warned her that he had been drinking even more deeply than usual.

"Well," he stood for a moment looking down at her, one hand, for balance, on the banister at the head of the stair. "So my lady is returned from her romantic adventure. But where," he made a great parade of looking about the hall, "where is the squire of dames? Can it be that your gallant has not the courage to face me?"

"What can you mean?" Amanda drew her torn dress more closely around her shoulders, but faced him proudly enough. "If you are referring to Mr Purvis, I urged him to come in with me and give you the opportunity to thank him for saving my life, but he has affairs of his own to attend to. So, I take it, had you yesterday."

The taunt went home, his cheeks whitened around spots of scarlet. "So that is to be your line, is it? The negligent husband and the gallant lover."

The unfairness, and at the same time the truth of his accusation almost silenced her, but she was aware of the whispers of the servants behind her, who though they could not understand English must be drawing their own conclusions from the tone of the exchange. "This is neither the time nor the place, my lord," she managed a tone of calm certainty, "to be discussing my danger, or your cowardice. I am hurt, and very tired, and must rest. When I have slept, and seen the doctor, we will talk more of this, unless you wish to make me your apologies now."

"Apologies, you slut!" He followed it with worse words from his extensive vocabulary, but she was beyond caring.

She turned and gave her arm to her maid. "Help me to my bed, Rosa. I am hurt and exhausted. And as for you, my lord," she went on as she passed him at the head of the stairs, "I can only urge you to rest and recollect yourself, before you start a scandal that must harm you more than it does me." It was a mistake, and she knew it as soon as she had spoken. With another oath, he flung past her, down the stairs and out of the house.

Consoling herself with the thought that John must be well on his way out to the *Agamemnon* by now, she let the maid undress her, with many exclamations about what she had suffered, bathe her wounds and put her to bed. Then, at last, she slept the sleep of utter exhaustion

She was awakened, she did not know how much later, by sounds of commotion below stairs. Sunlight sifting through closed shutters told her that it was high morning now. She felt much better; the pain in her head had eased and her stiffness lessened. But what could be going on below? The servants, always noisy, were now screaming at the tops of their voices. As she sat up in bed and pulled on a négligé the door of her room was thrown open and Rosa appeared. "Thank God you are awake, Milady." Her Italian was even harder to follow than usual as she plunged, with many appeals to her patron saint, into her tale of disaster. Milord was below, wounded, probably dying. "The blood, milady, you never saw such blood."

Amanda did not wait to hear more, but thrust her feet into slippers, pushed past the hysterical girl and ran to the head of the stairs. An alarming sight met her eyes. Two strangers in naval uniform had apparently just carried Lord Meynel into the hall and laid him down on a low gilt sofa that stood near the entrance. Blood streamed over his face and stained the front of his cream-coloured brocade waistcoat. Running down the stairs, she saw that his eyes were closed, his limp posture that of unconsciousness.

"Lady Meynel?" The taller of the two strangers came to meet her and she saw now that he was wearing the uniform of a British naval lieutenant. "I am sorry to frighten you so." He took her hand, looking down at her with great kindness out of searching blue eyes. Under that piercing, yet benevolent gaze, she was miserably aware, as he went on speaking, of her dishevelled hair and frivolous négligé, and at once ashamed of herself for even thinking of such things.

But his next words were reassuring. "It is not, I promise you, so bad as it looks. Your husband is not wounded." He had continued to hold her hand, his warm pressure in itself a reassurance. Now he let it go. "But allow me to present myself: Lieutenant Medway of the *Agamemnon*, and very much at your service."

A civil automaton, she acknowledged his greeting while her mind raced wildly: The *Agamemnon*? A friend of John's? Then – where was John? What had happened? At the same time, another part of her brain was summing up this stranger; midnight blue eyes; hair darker than copper; and, despite the seaman's weatherbeaten tan, an indefinable something . . . She had learned fine distinctions at the court of Naples and found herself comparing Mr Medway's manner with John's . . . Could it be to John's disadvantage?

But she had been silent too long. She grasped at the most important thread of her ravelled thought: "Not wounded?" she asked. "But . . ."

"He has had, I fear, a seizure of some kind." His expression, now, was faintly quizzical. "And – his nose has bled."

"His nose?" For a moment, Amanda was horribly afraid that she was going to burst out laughing. "All that blood? But – he is unconscious."

"Yes; he fell as he fired."

"As he fired?" She was far from laughter now. "You mean – he has fought? But who? How?" In her heart, she knew the answer already.

"My friend, Mr Purvis." He paused. "I must in fairness to my friend tell you, Lady Meynel, that your husband thrust the quarrel upon him. No man could, in honour, have done more to avoid it than Mr Purvis. Your husband, I am afraid, was – not quite reasonable."

"He was drunk," said Amanda simply and found herself at once aware of his steady, intelligent regard.

"I am afraid so," his frankness matched hers. "But had, of course, been torn with anxiety for your ladyship."

"Oh," said Amanda faintly. "You know about that?"

"I imagine," he said dryly, "that everyone in Naples does. Your husband did not exactly make a secret of his feelings. I am glad to see you none the worse for your adventure," he ended formally.

"Oh, I am well enough . . . But, John – Mr Purvis – he did not come with you?"

Suddenly, strangely, he seemed to be looking at her with compassion. "I am afraid Mr Purvis is wounded," he said.

Her hand went to her heart. "John? Wounded? But you said . . ."

"Your husband fired as he fell. It was an unlucky shot for Mr Purvis, who is wounded in the right arm." His tone and phrasing cast grave doubts on Lord Meynel's marksmanship. "But it is nothing to signify," he went on bracingly, "a scratch – no more. *Agamemnon's* surgeon will be attending to it by now. Mr Purvis sent you his compliments – and apologies – and begged me to tell you that he did everything in his power to avoid this unlucky encounter. He deloped, you know."

"Deloped? You mean . . ."

"Fired into the air. The quarrel was none of his choosing, and so he wished the world to know."

"Oh." Monstrously, she found herself sorry to hear this. Surely, by deloping, John had tacitly admitted guilt. Besides, deep in her there was something that wished he had fired to kill. Shameful to think thus. She found herself colouring.

"I am sorry to be the bringer of such bad news." Once again she had the odd feeling that he saw much deeper than she liked into her heart – and, again, disconcertingly, was sorry for her. "Can I be of assistance to you in helping Lord Meynel to his chamber? You would best, I think, have a doctor to him forthwith."

"Yes . . . yes, of course." She turned and gave rapid orders to her servants. "You do not think it will do harm to move him?"

"I doubt it. He is not, after all, wounded. But, look, he is recovering consciousness." Their eyes met. "I think," he went on, "it would perhaps be best if he did not find me here. If you are sure you will be able to manage . . ."

"Of course . . . The servants will help me. Sir, I do not know how to thank you—"

"It is nothing. I am only glad to have been of some slight service to a fellow countrywoman." He bowed deeply and turned to go.

She could not help herself. She laid a restraining hand on his arm. "Give my compliments – and thanks, too," she hesitated, "to your friend. And . . . and look after him."

"I will. I promise you, it is nothing, the merest scratch." The blue eyes held hers for a moment of unspoken sympathy before he turned to the door. How much – she turned back to the sofa where her husband was now stirring and muttering to himself – how much did he know?

But this was no time to think of that. She told two of the footmen to carry Lord Meynel to his room and then got Rosa to help her get him out of his bloodstained clothes and into a nightshirt. He continued to mutter to himself, but, to her relief, did not completely recover consciousness. His nose had bled a little more when they moved him, but now that had stopped and he lay quiet and pale on his bed, apparently deep in sleep, until the doctor was announced.

Dr Anderson had been a ship's doctor before he discovered that there was a very much better living to be gained in tending the ailments of the British colony in Naples. His methods were rough and ready enough, but Amanda had considerable confidence in his sound sense. He did not disappoint her. "Well," he said at last, "no doubt about it; 'tis an apoplectic seisure of some kind. I warned him, last time we dined together, how it would be, if he did not have a care to himself. Your husband is not a young man, Lady Meynel. If he insists on behaving like one, he must take the consequences. A bottle of port a day is enough for any man, and so I told him. Who drinks more, lays up trouble for himself." He had been taking his patient's pulse as he spoke, now he let his hand fall back onto the bedclothes. "He has got off lightly enough this time, and should wake presently none the worse, but if he does not change his way of life somewhat, I'll not be answerable for the consequences another time. You must try and persuade him, Lady Meynel."

Amanda looked at him thoughtfully. "I will try," she said. Her tone, and his expression, agreed in doubt as to her success. "But, for the moment, what treatment do you recommend?"

"Why, nothing but rest in bed. If I was one of these Neapolitan quacks, I'd doubtless recommend viper broth or powdered snails, but I'll not even bleed him – he's bled enough, by the look of him. No, no, keep him in bed, my lady, make him happy at home, and try, as long as you can, to prevent him from going jauntering about the countryside with His Majesty King Nimrod, and he may live for years to come. In the meantime, I will just have a look at those wounds of yours. You have had, I understand, a narrow escape."

Amanda submitted willingly enough to his examination and the inevitable questions that accompanied it. Indeed, she was glad of the chance to give her side of the story to this sensible, gossiping old Scotsman who could, she well knew, prove a valuable ally in the storm of scandal that must follow her husband's duel with John Purvis.

"Hmmm," he said at last. "Your husband, it seems to me, is fortunate to have escaped with no worse than a nose bleed. Picking a quarrel with him seems an odd way to thank Mr Purvis for saving your life. You are old acquaintances, are you not?" The question was accompanied by so sharp a look from his faded blue eyes that she found herself helplessly colouring.

"Yes," she said calmly enough. "Mr Purvis and I were children together."

"Brother and sister, eh? And so he saves your life while your husband, if you'll excuse my saying so, Lady Meynel, is too far gone to care. Oh well, you can hardly blame Lord Meynel for being in a miff. No man likes to look a fool." He rose to take his leave. "I must be about my rounds. If you'll take my advice, you will be indisposed for a few days. That head wound of yours is cause enough. And

I, with your good leave, will tell your story. It will come best from me." He bowed over her hand: "I hope you will always consider me your friend," and took his leave.

Left alone with her snoring husband, Amanda had time, at last, to consider her position. It was not a pleasant one. She had never succeeded in finding any common ground with the ladies of the English community, being unable to meet them on any of their favourite subjects. She had no children; she knew nothing of London gossip, and found the local kind tedious, and she got on so well with her Neapolitan servants as to infuriate women whose favourite talking point was the faults of their own. Worst of all, she knew, had been her casual reception of the news, so kindly offered by a handful of poisoned tongues, of her husband's association with the Grassi. If she had screamed, or fainted, or best of all, asked their advice, her busy informers would have become her friends and champions. Her calm, her almost relieved acceptance of the situation had made them her enemies. And then, of course, there had been her friendship with Julia Vespucci, whom they considered as a renegade Englishwoman. There must, they had hinted to Amanda, be some reason for the way her English relatives ignored her existence. And, naturally, the reason must be to Julia's discredit? not theirs. Amanda had done herself more harm than she knew by the vehemence with which she defended her friend against this kind of slur.

She was well aware that in this crisis she could not expect the ladies of the English community to stand her friends. But did she care? Did it matter that she should be the subject of scandal? For herself, she decided, it did not. To be ostracized by the British colony, if it should come to that, could hardly add to the misery of her position. But then, there was John to be considered. For herself, she was beyond caring, but the idea that his career might be damaged was intolerable. And yet – what could she do? The answer was – nothing. Wise old Dr Anderson's words had conveyed a warning. Anything she did, must do more harm than good. She would take his advice, stay at home, and do nothing.

She discovered, that afternoon, an unexpected and powerful ally. Lady Hamilton came to call, and would not be denied. Finding Amanda reclining, convincingly, on a sofa, she looked at her with approval.

"Quite right, too," she said. "You look every inch the heroine. Dr Anderson has been telling me of your adventures, and I may say I have had a perfect paean of praise for your hero from my friend, Captain Nelson. Though I can tell you he is not best pleased with the upshot of the affair. 'One of my best men wounded – and in a duel of all absurdities.' I truly believe he would not have minded Mr Purvis's being killed, so long as it was by the enemy. But, tell me, my love, what in the world possessed your husband to call out the man who had saved your life? It looks, I must tell you, not at all the thing, and we must put our heads together as to what's best to do now. Dr Anderson says he told you to stay at home and play the wounded heroine for a few days, but I said that was nonsense. You must come out and fight for it, my love, if you wish to have a scrap of reputation left."

"But do you know," objected Amanda, "I am not sure that I greatly care."

"That, my dear," said this surprising champion, "is purest nonsense as none knows better than I. Besides, if you do not care for yourself, what of Mr Purvis? Ah," she saw Amanda's colour change, "do I have you there? Very well then, for his sake, I beg you will defy the old cats and accompany me to the breakfast Captain Nelson gives on board *Agamemnon* tomorrow. Sir William tells me I have made a conquest there – and one, he says, almost worthy of my charms. Captain Nelson is not a handsome man, it is true, nor gifted with much grace of manner, but there is something about him – he will live to be a great man, Sir William says. Indeed he told Sir William himself that if he lived he would be at the top of the tree, and Sir William believes him. Only to think, he has already persuaded my beloved Queen to send Lord Hood 6,000 troops for the defence of Toulon, and the King, too, is his very dear friend, has called him the Saviour of Italy, had him to dine and set him on his right hand. Oh, yes, he will go far, my little Captain Nelson – he stays with us, you know; Sir William bade me give him the apartments we had prepared for our own Prince Augustus. Tomorrow's entertainment on the *Agamemnon* is his compliment to me as his hostess. And you, my love, shall be of the party. Trust me, gossip's tongue was never stopped by hiding in corners. Attack, Captain Nelson says, is the best mode of defence, and we will prove him right tomorrow, you and I."

It seemed to Amanda that there was much good sense in what she said. And after all, who should know better how to deal with gossip than Lady Hamilton, who had had so much to contend with on her own account? And, of course, inclination took strong part with reason in Amanda's calculations. If she joined the party on the *Agamemnon*, she must see John, however publicly. This argument was irresistible.

Her only proviso, to herself as well as to Lady Hamilton, was that she could not go if her husband had not yet recovered consciousness. But towards evening, as she sat beside his bed, she noticed his breathing becoming less stertorous, his sleep more peaceful. At last he stirred, groaned, and opened his eyes.

"Oh," he said, "so you're there are you, playing the loving wife?"

"Yes," she replied stung by his tone, "though I think it more than you deserve."

He looked at her in feeble surprise. She had never spoken to him so before. "What? Saucy too? Where is your shame, my lady? Are you not aware that all Naples must be talking of you this morning?"

"Perfectly, my lord, and equally aware that it is your fault. But come, we must not be wrangling thus. You are not well. Dr Anderson says you must keep absolutely quiet for a few days. There will be time enough for discussion when you are better." She rose to leave him but he detained her with a feeble, dictatorial gesture.

"So you have been mewling to Dr Anderson and got him on your side, have you? I might have known it. Rest

100

and quiet indeed – and be the laughing stock of the city before you've done with me. I'll have none of it. Ring for my valet."

"I warn you, Dr Anderson said he'd not be answerable for the consequences if you refused to obey his orders."

"Oh he did, did he? And you think I will lie here at your mercy, while you spread who knows what slanders about me? If you'll not ring for Carter, I'll do it myself." And he made to get out of bed.

"Very well." She could see what the effort had cost him, and thought it would be best to let him prove to himself that he was not strong enough to get up. She rang the bell, and when Carter appeared, left him alone with his master. The result was as she had expected. Carter came hurrying to her room soon afterwards to announce in frightened tones that his lordship had fainted and had to be put back to bed. She sent the man for Dr Anderson and, when he came, explained to him what had happened. His report, at last, was reassuring. Lord Meynel's condition was no worse; he had merely taught himself a useful lesson. Taking his leave, the doctor looked at her out of wise and worldly eyes. "If I were you," he said, "I would put off, for the moment, any subjects of discussion that might," he paused, "disturb Lord Meynel. In fact," he had noticed her reaction, "I will go further and recommend that you do not see him for a day or two. Doctor's orders." He smiled at her and took his leave.

# Chapter Seven

The next day dawned brilliant with expectation, and Amanda, putting on her most becoming sprigged muslin for Captain Nelson's breakfast, found herself suddenly conscience-stricken. She was a wicked woman, unfaithful to her husband. She looked at her reflection in the glass: soft curls, large grey eyes, a touch of unwonted colour in the curved cheek. She did not look guilty. Her maid adjusted the angle of her Dunstable hat: "Milady is in admirable looks today."

It was true. She neither looked nor felt guilty. She ought to be ashamed of herself. "How is my lord this morning?" she asked.

The girl's eyes met hers in the glass. "Better, milady. He has threatened Carter with dismissal because he will not bring him champagne. But he says he will not get up today."

"Good. Has he asked for me?"

"Carter explained, milady, what the doctor had said." The girl coloured and Amanda was able to imagine, pretty accurately, what her husband's reaction must have been.

A page knocked at the door to announce that Lady Hamilton's carriage was below. "Excellent," said Amanda. "If my lord asks for me, tell him I am gone out with the Hamiltons." He could hardly object to that. It would be time enough, when he was better, to tell him where they had taken her. How strange it was, she told herself, shaking out her skirts and starting down the curving stairway, that the events of the last few days had so entirely freed her from fear of her husband.

Amanda had never been on board a British man-of-war

before and she refused to let the dubious glances of the other English ladies in Lady Hamilton's party dash her eager anticipation of a day's pleasure. Of course her companions were all agog with curiosity about her husband's duel. Answering their pointed and over-pressing enquiries about his health with an easy courtesy that surprised them, Amanda hugged her happiness to her. What did she care for their trouble-mongering? She was going to see John's ship. She was going to see John.

The Captain's gig awaited Lady Hamilton and her party at the mole and Amanda was delighted at once with its crew of red-faced, clean-shaven seamen in their smart blue jackets and wide, white duck trousers. The grinning sailor who helped her on board the boat was John's shipmate. Everything about the ship must be of interest to her, because of its association with John. The midshipman in charge, who amazed Lady Hamilton by his combination of youth and aplomb, might be one of John's protégés, and John himself had once worn this becoming dress uniform of blue tailcoat and white nankeen breeches.

When, at last, her turn came to be swung up onto the *Agamemnon'* deck in the bosun's chair, Amanda charmed everyone by her readiness to be pleased. The crew were drawn up to salute Lady Hamilton's party; the marine band played; the sun shone; surely this was a day for happiness?

Her eyes had gone at once to the little group of officers, led by Captain Nelson, who were already greeting Lady Hamilton. At first glance, Captain Nelson himself struck her as an insignificant little man, but, as Lady Hamilton had said, there was something arresting about him. Perhaps it was the penetrating eyes that looked out so keenly from under noble brows, or perhaps the resolute set of the mouth. And, though his bow might be awkward and his manner abrupt, his voice, as he greeted her, had a stirring resonance. But – she returned his greeting politely – her host was not Amanda's main concern. Furiously aware that she was blushing, she raised her eyes to glance past Captain Nelson for a quick anxious look at the group of

103

officers behind him. Yes, John was there, his arm in a sling, with Medway beside him. Could he not have seen her yet? All his attention was focused on Lady Hamilton, to whom Nelson was now presenting his officers.

As the introductions became more general, Amanda was aware of a stirring of interest among the other ladies of the party, a dangerous concentration of their glances upon her. Mr Medway was being presented to her now and bowed deeply over her hand, his dark blue eyes faintly quizzical as they met hers. Silent, he was waiting, she could see, for his cue from her.

"I have met Mr Medway," she said steadily. "I owe you my deepest thanks, sir, for your goodness to my husband."

"I believe I do not need to make Mr Purvis known to you," went on Captain Nelson, and Amanda was aware, once more, of that little female rustle of interest about her.

"No indeed," she said calmly. "Mr Purvis and I are old friends. I hope I see you better, sir."

He bowed deeply, but did not attempt to take her hand with his one good one. "Much better, I thank you." There was something chilling about the formality of his tone. Surely he could not be angry with her for coming?

But there was something else that she must say: the thing, indeed, that she had come for. "I owe you my life, Mr Purvis. My husband and I are deeply beholden to you." She had managed it, and was aware, once more, of a muted gasp from her companions.

"It was nothing." He turned from her to pay his respects to Lady Hamilton and she was left with a chill about her heart. He *was* angry. She felt her colour come and go, and felt, worse still, female, observant eyes upon her.

"Lady Meynel," Lieutenant Medway was beside her and had seen it all, "I beg you will do me the honour of letting me show you our *Agamemnon*."

She accepted the offer gratefully and found herself still more beholden to him when he led her, casually, a little way away from the rest of her party on the pretext of showing her the view of the shore from the windowed gallery of the Captain's cabin. Pretending to admire Captain Nelson's snug quarters with their private galley, candle lanterns and charcoal brazier, she had time to get herself in hand. She had been right to take Lady Hamilton's advice and come, she was sure of that, and John was wrong – foolishly wrong, to be angry. She must not let him spoil her gesture by what she could only consider his childish behaviour. She forced a smile in answer to a remark of Medway's. He smiled back at her. "That is better," he said. "Do you think you can face them again now?"

She looked up at him with quick gratitude, the colour high again in her expressive face. "Thanks to you," she said, "yes."

The sun shone, the ladies ran here and there about the ship, exclaiming in delight at the apple-pie order of everything, the decks scrubbed shining white and the equally scrubbed and shining faces of the sailors. For Amanda, it was all nightmare, but one that must be endured with a stretched and smiling face. John did not come near her; Lady Hamilton was entirely occupied with Captain Nelson; the other ladies whispered and watched her; only Lieutenant Medway remained faithful at her side. She found herself talking to him, almost frantically, of everything and nothing, and wondered, afterwards, how much, in fact, she had told him about herself. But at all costs she must make it appear that nothing was the matter, that John's neglect meant nothing to her. Deeply, silently grateful below her flow of chatter, she was aware how admirably Medway was playing her game. When a sudden encounter with John Purvis, who was squiring the two silliest young ladies of the English colony, dried her up in mid-sentence, Medway skilfully took over the burden of the conversation, weaving variations around a slight remark of her own about music. He, too, it seemed, was delighted with Mr Haydn's symphonies, though he admitted to preferring those of a student of Haydn's called Ludwig von Beethoven. He envied her the opportunities of life in Naples, the acclaimed, he said, musical centre

105

of Europe. If it had not been for the nagging misery of her heart, she would have enormously enjoyed this rare oasis of civilized conversation.

But it was with an anguish of relief that she heard, at last, Captain Nelson announce that he must hurry their departure. He had received news of French men-of-war with an English prize off Sardinia and must give chase at once.

She looked up at Medway. "You will fight them?"

"If we have the good luck to catch them." She had gone very white. "Do not fret yourself. I will have an eye to him."

Another rigidly formal bow from John, another kind one from Lieutenant Medway – it was all over, and they were being rowed back to shore in the Captain's gig, all awhisper with excitement at the news of the impending chase. Already, when they reached the shore they could see frenzied activity on board the *Agamemnon* and by the time Amanda reached the quiet of her room and hurried to the balcony, the ship was dwindling out to sea. John had left, angry with her. She had forgiven herself, that morning, too easily, had let herself slide into a deceptive dream of happiness. What was the use of her feeling so miraculously free of guilt if he felt it for both of them? She had forgiven herself, it seemed, more easily than he could forgive her.

But he would come round. Of course he would. It was impossible that the memory of those few hours together should not be as exquisite for him as it was for her. Nothing should make her regret it. Why should she, when she had already paid for it, so amply, in years of wretchedness? She owed her husband, she told herself again, nothing. If she had been in doubt before, his carelessness in the last few days, first of her life and then of her honour would have settled the question. Whatever happened, she could not feel guilt towards him.

In the meanwhile, she must see how he was. Tapping at the door of his room, she found him sitting up in bed, looking much better and displaying all the unreasonable irritability of a convalescent.

"So you are come at last," was his greeting. "I have been sending for you all morning."

"I am sorry," she said. "I had to go out. Besides, Dr Anderson thought you should rest."

"'I had to go out.'" She had always disliked, intensely, his attempt at a flutelike imitation of her voice. Then, in his own voice, harsh with anger: "Yes, you had to go running to the fleet, after your lover. I wish I had shot to kill."

She looked at him calmly. "Did you not? I had thought you merely missed your aim. It has not, I collect, occurred to you that you owe your own life to Mr Purvis's self-restraint. He is, they tell me, a dead shot. If he had not deloped, you would not be lying there grumbling at me. As for my visit to the fleet; Lady Hamilton advised me to accompany her. She thought it the best, indeed the only way to put a stop to the scandal your behaviour has caused. It was not, I can tell you, any great pleasure to me."

He laughed his disagreeable laugh. "I should rather think not," he said. "And serve you richly right. I tell you, you should be thanking heaven, on your knees, for the condition you are in. Were it not for that, I should send you home to your mother today. As it is, for my heir's sake, I suppose we must weather the gossip you have caused as best we may. Nothing must touch my son's position in the world. I tell you, you have much to be thankful for."

She had indeed. In the excitement of the last few days she had entirely forgotten the lie she had told him. If he had been looking at her as he spoke of her condition, he must have seen her start of surprise. As it was, she had, at least, a little time. If his belief that she was pregnant would ease them through the situation in which his madness had placed them, she must, for the moment, let him continue to think her so. For she was well aware that he did not really believe her to have been unfaithful to him. His wild accusations both of her and of John Purvis were merely the cover for his own sense of guilt because John had rescued her when he himself was too drunk to care. It was the irony of fate – and no comfort to her – that these wild accusations of his should, as a matter of fact, be well founded.

She might have time, she thought in the privacy of her room, but that was absolutely all she had. Sooner or later, she would have to tell her husband that she had been mistaken when she told him she was pregnant. Would he believe her in this new and different lie? She could only pray that he might, and decide that if he did not, life with him would be impossible and, at whatever cost, she must leave him.

In the meantime, he continued for a while an invalid. His second fainting fit had frightened him, and though he made a great display of grumbling at them, he was now prepared to obey Dr Anderson's orders. It would have been a peaceful time for Amanda if she had not been so distractedly worried about John. Surely he would write to her? Surely he must be aware, as she was, of the new bond, invisible, intangible, strong as iron, that stretched between them? His strange behaviour on the *Agamemnon* that day, though painful, had been understandable enough. Perhaps because of his own uncertain place in the world, he had always been more sensitive to its talk than she was. He had laughed and flirted with the other members of her party, she told herself, not because he wanted to, but simply to protect her – and, she sometimes found herself adding – himself. He would write to her, of course, to apologize, explain, admit, however tacitly, the new bond between them.

But the autumn weeks drew on and still no letter came. News of a kind she had, for Lady Hamilton now corresponded with Captain Nelson, who had made, it seemed, at their first meeting, an enormous impression both on her and on her husband. Whenever she heard from him, she made a point of calling to pass on the news of the *Agamemnon* to Amanda. From her, therefore Amanda learned, with bitter disappointment, that though the *Agamemnon* had failed to catch the French ships, she had gone on to Leghorn, not back to Naples. Now, surely, John would write to her, his own hope of a speedy meeting dashed like hers.

Instead, she learned from Lady Hamilton (surely Captain Nelson's most favoured correspondent?) that the *Agamemnon* had been in action against the French off Sardinia. "Poor Captain Nelson," cooed Lady Hamilton making a great business of putting up his letter, "only think of his being baulked of his prey by French reinforcements and after he had given chase to 5 of them, too, with only 345 men at quarters. But never fear, he got off safe enough, with no worse effects than some damage to his masts and rigging – and one man killed. No, no, my love, never look so pale at me – 'tis a mere seaman, no one we know. But what do you think of Nelson's heading straight back to Toulon, where he says he longs to see land service – instead of coming here for a refit? He is a perfect glutton for action, that little man, but one cannot help loving him for it. Sir William is more certain than ever, from the tone of his letters, that he will go far."

This was cold comfort to Amanda, who, while deeply grateful for the crumbs of news that Lady Hamilton doled out to her, still could not help feeling a growing discomfort at her attitude of complicity. Between them, implied the lighthearted beauty, they were fooling Lord Meynel to the top of his bent. It was impossible not to like the ebullient Lady Hamilton, not to be grateful for her consistent kindness, but Amanda could equally not help finding something at times distressingly vulgar in the tone of her conversation. Her grammatical slips were merely endearing, but her tone of understanding and perhaps patronizing sympathy for Amanda was all the harder to bear because she had to admit it was justified. She was never more out of charity with herself than after a visit from her benefactress.

That was a depressing autumn. Things were not going well at Toulon, while the news from England was increasingly gloomy. The Duke of York's expedition to Holland, which had begun with such high hopes, was dwindling into failure. At home, prices had risen and, in Parliament, the

Opposition talked increasingly of peace. Mrs Carteret's rare letters were one long string of grumbles about the discomforts of her life, and she seized upon the first disquieting rumour about Amanda that reached her as a pretext to suggest that she come out and join them. She had heard, she said, sad tales about her daughter's goings on in Naples – besides, poor dear Lord Meynel was ill. She must help her daughter (in whom she made it clear she had no confidence whatever) to nurse him. For once in their lives, Amanda and her husband found themselves in entire agreement over this letter. Mrs Carteret had written that she would be only too delighted to join them – provided they sent her the money for her expenses on the journey. Lord Meynel tossed the letter back to Amanda. "Write to her that there is no need for her to be troubling herself," he said. "Tell her I am better and can have an eye to you myself. It is your reputation, I know, that she cares about, rather than my health."

Amanda privately thought that all her mother cared about was a pretext to leave the wartime discomforts of England, and wrote her a kind, cool letter pointing out the hazards of such a journey. More important, she sent no money. Although she knew that her mother's sordid bargain with Lord Meynel had left her perfectly able to afford such a trip, she equally knew that Mrs Carteret was far too mean to pay for it out of her own funds. From her mother's presence, at least, at this crucial juncture of her life, she would be free.

That it was crucial, she increasingly recognized. As the weeks passed, and Lord Meynel slowly recovered his strength, his sniping rather increased in bitterness. He could not forgive her for the way he had failed her on that night of the eruption and his tone to her became daily more unpleasant. This was bad enough so long as he was confined to the house, but when he began to appear once more in public, things became worse. He seemed quite unable to control his speech and manner to her, and, as a result, the rumours about her which had died down in the course of the autumn, sprang up again a thousandfold.

Amanda did not need to hear the voices that whispered "no smoke without fire, my dear". It was almost comic, she thought, returning one night, late and miserable, from a reception at Lady Hamilton's, that it was her husband's very confidence in her virtue that made him feel so free to assail it. If he only knew . . .

Her maid was hovering about her anxiously. "Milady is tired. Let me get you to bed quickly. Indeed, madame, I do not like your looks."

Nor did Amanda like the way she felt. She was glad enough to let the girl undress her and put her to bed, and agreed readily to her suggestion that she break her usual vigorous habit and breakfast in bed next morning. But when the meal came, she could not eat it, and Rosa, returning to remove the tray, found her lying there, pale and spent, the coffee and rolls still untasted. She broke at once into the voluble chiding of a privileged servant, but Amanda interrupted her feebly. "I beg you will not, Rosa. I feel too sick to speak."

The girl looked at her with a sudden gleam. "Sick, milady? Now Januarius and all the saints be praised. And faint last night?" She began excitedly to count on her fingers. "If I am not far out in my calculations, we shall have a little lordship to celebrate, come next harvest."

It was a new, amazing and, instantly, terrifying idea to Amanda. "You really think . . ."

"Past question, milady. Sick this morning," she seemed to derive pleasure from enumerating the symptoms, "and faint last night, and somewhat freakish these last few days, if my lady will forgive my saying so. Beyond question it is all of a piece. What a happy man my lord will be. Why, my lady!"

For Amanda had dissolved into hysterical laughter. Why had she not understood sooner? Beyond question, as the girl said, she was pregnant. Lord Meynel was to get his wish and only she knew that he was not the father. Luckily, Rosa took her hysteria as merely a conclusive symptom of her state, and hovered about her with much sympathetic tut-tutting and administration of hartshorn and spirits of

111

vinegar, until Amanda was sufficiently recovered to ask to be left alone. "And not a word to anyone, mind." She had no particular hope to being obeyed, but gave the injunction more as a matter of form than otherwise. After all, her husband already knew – or thought he knew. She had but to keep silence and she and her child were safe. Or were they? For herself alone, she had hardly cared what her husband said about her, and perhaps, too, awareness of guilt had taken the fight out of her. But the child was another matter. At all costs he must be protected. For like the maid, she automatically assumed that the child would be a boy, the heir, if he acknowledged him, that Lord Meynel wanted.

Sunshine was pouring in at the window that led onto her balcony, and the lively sounds from the street below told her that the morning was far advanced. It was high time that she paid her husband her morning visit, for since his illness he usually stayed in bed till late afternoon. She rang for Rosa and dressed, still wracking her brain, as the girl chattered away, for expedients that might protect her child. Curiously enough, she hardly thought of John, the father.

Lord Meynel was sitting up in bed, propped against half a dozen pillows and surrounded with letters and papers. He greeted her with his usual scant courtesy and tossed her a letter. "Good news," he said. "Read that."

The letter was from his English lawyers, the good news, it seemed, that of the death of his elderly cousin, whose ailing son was not expected to live through the hazards of childhood. "The measles will carry him off, if the scarlet fever does not," said Lord Meynel with brutal cheerfulness.

"And you call that good news?"

"Why not? You surely do not expect me to mourn for my old dotard of a cousin, do you? Or for the puny child of his old age? It would be merest hypocrisy, which has never been one of my vices. Oh, we'll *wear* mourning, of course, and do all that's proper; the world shall not have that handle against us. You had best order your black today. I have known for years that this was likely to happen," he

112

went on. "Now, perhaps, you will understand why it is so essential that I should have an heir. All this property is subject to strict entail and I want no barren inheritance. And that reminds me," he looked at her sharply, "is it not time you sent for Dr Anderson on your own account? I am glad to see that you do not propose to make the absurd fuss and parade some women in your condition seem to think necessary, but the fact remains that my heir must have every proper consideration, before his birth as well as after."

Once again, Amanda found herself close to hysterical laughter. His heir – if he only knew. But she merely remarked, mildly, that she thought him right, and would send for Dr Anderson next day. What a desperate moment, she found herself thinking, this would have been for her yesterday.

But her husband had not done with her. "You had best look out your mourning at once," he said. "I shall accompany you to Lady Hamilton's concert tonight." And then, noting her look of surprise. "To wear mourning is quite hypocrisy enough: I do not propose to curtail my amusements because an old man I never liked has died, at last, in England. And, besides, it is time you and I made an appearance together. There must be no breath of scandal attached to my heir."

Amanda looked at him calmly. "I am glad you have thought of that," she said.

Perhaps, she thought that evening, as Rosa fastened the tiny buttons down the back of her black velvet dress, it would all work out for the best after all. Lord Meynel should have his heir and she what, she felt now, was the most she could hope for – a quiet life. The news of the poor old cousin's death, however regrettable in itself, had come, it must be admitted, at a most happy time for her. Of all his unregulated passions, that for money was perhaps Lord Meynel's most powerful. Surely the financial argument would silence his dangerous tongue?

She had reckoned without his friends, or rather, she had let herself hope that in the time that had passed since the duel, society would have found more fruitful and newer subjects for gossip. It was therefore, with a sinking heart that she saw that King Ferdinand had taken the whim of attending Lady Hamilton's concert in one of the transparent disguises that left him even freer than usual to indulge his freakish humour. When they arrived, he was singing a duet with Lady Hamilton that amply justified her tart (if confidential) comment that "he sings like a king".

When the song ended, the King came forward to greet Lord Meynel with an exaggeration of his usual boisterous manner. He had been away for a few weeks and had not seen him since the illness occasioned by that fatal duel. Now he plunged into an elaborate speech at once of condolence and of mockery. How wise, considering the delicate state of his health, Lord Meynel had been to avoid the risks that would have been attendant on rescuing his wife from Torre del Greco – how unfortunate that all his care for himself should have come to nothing as a result of that disastrous duel. Naturally, the King's companions followed his lead; the jokes at Lord Meynel's expense grew broader and broader, and even Amanda found herself sorry for her husband, condemned, out of respect for the King, to endure this merciless badinage. In vain did Lady Hamilton urge another song, the King was enjoying himself too much. He had already hinted that Lord Meynel's seizure during the duel had been merely a coward's pretence, now he returned to the even more fruitful subject of Amanda's plight at Torre del Greco. Watching the red spots of rage grow in her husband's cheeks, she risked an intervention: "My lord sent a servant for me," she said.

It was fatal. The King burst into a fit of laughter and said, through delighted guffaws, that milord was quite right: "Never risk the master's life when the man's will do as well."

It was the last straw. Lord Meynel turned to his wife, white now with anger, the red spots burning dangerously in their pallid background. "And what claim, pray, can you make to my consideration? I have no doubt you were only too delighted with your romantic," he paused, "rescuer."

114

There was a chilly little silence in the room, then several people spoke at once. Lady Hamilton, ever resourceful, insisted that Amanda sing to them, Sir William dragged the King off to show him his latest acquisition from the diggings at Herculaneum. Singing, half conscious of what she sang, Amanda could see her husband standing alone, conspicuously neglected. This time, it seemed, society had taken her side, but what of the next time?

She would have liked to leave when the song was over, but Lady Hamilton detained her. "Best see the evening through," she said, "if you do not wish to give the old cats another handle against you."

Amanda sighed. "As if they needed any more," she said.

"Truly, my dear creature," Lady Hamilton put a friendly hand on her arm, "it would be best if you could silence that husband of yours – or keep him at home until he returns to his senses. Shall I have Sir William speak to him?"

"It would do no good, I fear."

"So do I. Well, I will do one thing for you," said the beauty, "I will put him in a good humour again."

She was as good as her word. For the rest of the evening, she paid marked attention to Lord Meynel and it was almost comic, Amanda thought, to watch him expand and glow under these unwonted attentions from the entrancing Ambassadress. For Amanda, the evening passed slowly and painfully enough. There were plenty of kind friends to hint at the delicacy and discomfort of her position, disguising enjoyment as sympathy. If only Julia had been there . . . but Julia was still with her dangerous cousin in Syracuse.

At last, head throbbing with fatigue and heart sore and angry she found herself in the carriage with her husband for the short drive home. Pretending even more exhaustion that she felt, she hoped to delay until tomorrow the inevitable explanation between them. But he had moved from fury to an equally dangerous exhilaration. Lady Hamilton had been too successful.

He talked for a while about the Ambassadress's charm and vivacity – "Quite a contrast," he said at last, "to you, my virtuous wife." His tone made the epithet an insult.

Suddenly she could bear it no longer. "You do not deserve a virtuous wife," she turned on him. "I am glad you have not got one."

"You are glad?" It took him a minute to take it in. "You mean?"

"I mean that everything you have thought fit to say about me is true. The child I am carrying is not yours, my lord, and I thank God for it. My son will have a better father. And now, since you have made me tell you a truth I had thought to spare you, there is nothing left for us but to part. If you will give me the money to go home to my mother, I will thank you for it. If not, I must go as a petitioner to Lady Hamilton who will, I think, stand my friend."

"Part? You do not know what you are talking of. And as for the child, you are talking nonsense, merely to gall me. You know perfectly well you had told me of the child before any of this happened."

"I lied to you." She would not let him off now. "The child is John's."

"You are overwrought." They had reached their house. "You do not know what you are saying. We will talk more of this in the morning." And he made a great parade of sending a servant to fetch Rosa, telling her that her mistress was ill, and urging her to take the greatest possible care of her. Dazed with surprise, Amanda submitted willingly enough to the girl's ministrations. She had told her husband the bitter truth and the result was the greatest display of kindness and consideration that she had ever received from him. Was he quite mad, or was she?

In the morning, she began to understand. Her husband's valet knocked on her door soon after she had finished her breakfast with an enquiry after her health. When she felt strong enough, Lord Meynel would be glad of her company in his room. Remembering the curt and dictatorial messages of the past, Amanda felt as if she were in a dream. For once it seemed almost a pleasant one.

She found Lord Meynel apparently none the worse for

116

his agitating evening, and responded with guarded courtesy to his enquiries as to her own state of health. She was well enough, she said, but a little tired.

"Then you must rest," he said. "You have the health and strength of my heir to consider now." That was all. His tone, his look, challenged her to correct him.

For a moment, she was almost tempted to do so, but common sense prevailed. "Yes," she said with apparent meekness, "I will be careful. And so must you be."

Did he understand the warning? At the time, since he said nothing, she could not be sure, but, later, she knew that he had. For from that day forward, he played, in public at least, the part of the devoted husband and father-to-be. Financial considerations had triumphed, and John Purvis's child was assured of his position as Lord Meynel's heir. Suspecting that her husband had contrived to convince himself that the child was his own and what she had said designed merely to annoy him, Amanda decided to let well alone. She had made her confession, there was no need to harp on it.

# Chapter Eight

Amanda had not thought victory over her husband could be so easy or so complete. But from that night of her rebellion, he played, for all the world to see, the part of husband and expectant father. It did not surprise Neapolitan society that this involved, among other things, his setting up his good friend, the Grassi, in a snug little house on the outskirts of Naples. He made the necessary public appearances with his wife; nobody expected him to be much with her in private.

The result, for Amanda, was a time of astonished peace – insofar as peace was possible in those darkening winter months. For the year that had begun so well for the enemies of France was dwindling to its close in an atmosphere of apathy and apprehension. The Allied armies that had marched so confidently into France had retreated again with equal dispatch, while the Duke of York's expedition into the Low Countries had met with stalemate, or worse. News from France was erratic, and always bad. The unhappy Queen, Maria Carolina's sister, was reported to be a close prisoner exposed to every possible indignity; there were fears for her life itself. After the massacres of August and September, anything was possible.

Against such a background of international disaster, Amanda's private misery seemed small enough – but to her it was misery indeed. She had still had no word from John and as the slow days dragged by, his silence became more and more painful to her. Surely it would not have been too much of a risk to her reputation – or his, for him merely to write her one letter. She had been sure that he would write a line to apologize for the enforced coolness of their parting – but now she did not even know if his wound was healed. Sometimes, the temptation to write herself and enquire about this was almost too strong to be resisted, but when she sat down with pen and paper it always proved impossible. How should she begin? What, in the face of his chill silence, could she say? And always, over everything else, hung one burning question: what would he think when he learned that she was pregnant? And, linked with that, the other, even more crucial problem: would she tell him that she knew him to be the father?

It was a relief, because a distraction, when, just before Christmas, Julia Vespucci returned from Syracuse. Calling on Amanda on the day of her return, she looked pale and anxious. She had just, she explained, come from paying a visit of courtesy to the Hamiltons. "The news is bad, my love. Captain Nelson has written to them that it may be necessary to evacuate Toulon. There is some young Corsican with an unpronounceable name – Bonaparte or some such thing – who has so bedevilled them with his gunnery that they find their position untenable. I only wish our contingent were safe away." And to Amanda's amazement she went on to explain that her beloved cousin, Antonio Vespucci, had joined the Neapolitan contingent that had sailed under Prince Pignatelli to join in the Allied defence of Toulon. "You may well look astonished, my love," she went on. "I was like to sink when Antonio told me he was going, but – if he only comes home safe, I think it will be the best day's work he ever did for himself. The Queen, surely, must forget those young revolutionary fidgets of his when she sees him risking his life for the Allied cause. I hope to see him, at last, taking his proper place in society when he returns – if he only returns safe. But he is so rashly brave, so impulsive – Oh, Amanda, I wish he was safe home."

While sympathizing with Julia's anxiety for her cousin, Amanda could not help wondering at his political volte-face. She had always suspected that his Jacobinism went very much deeper with him than his cousin cared to admit. She had even, at times, found herself reluctantly compelled to respect him for the passion of his belief in the equality of man. Could the news of French atrocities really have changed him so? For Julia's sake, she hoped so.

Her own anxiety about the plight of Toulon was as great as her friend's. Greater, she told herself, for Julia, at least, could count on receiving early information of any disaster that might befall her cousin there. For Julia, in fact, no news must be good news. But Amanda went in daily terror of hearing of John Purvis's death by accident, or, worse still, of not hearing of it at all. Or, she asked herself, would that kind Mr Medway, who had been so good to her on the day of Captain Nelson's breakfast, perhaps contrive to let her know if John was wounded? Sometimes she thought he would, sometimes she doubted it. She was oddly haunted by the memory of the almost alarming degree of comprehension that had shone in those midnight blue eyes. How much had he seen? How much understood? And, understanding so much, feeling, it seemed, so kindly towards her, might he not stretch a point of etiquette for her sake? A more perfect gentleman, she ruefully confessed to herself, than John Purvis, might he not for that very reason feel himself less rigidly tramelled by convention?

For she found it increasingly hard, those wretched winter days, to forgive John Purvis for his failure to write to her. Tormented by his silence, how could she achieve the cheerful calm that Dr Anderson recommended for her child's sake. But then, of course, John did not know about the child. How should he? It was not fair to blame him for a silence that was undoubtedly dictated by his very anxiety for her. And yet, for all her reasonable arguments, it made her wretched. Her only crumb of comfort was the incorrigible hope that if Toulon was really evacuated Captain Nelson might bring his *Agamemnon* back to Naples, where he had been so warmly welcomed before. If only she could talk once more with John, even merely as friend to friend, she might contrive to be happy again, or at least at peace with herself. But as the long, newsless days dragged by, she found it increasingly difficult to believe that, even for her, no news must be good news. She could not eat, she could not sleep, and her eyes were huge and dark-ringed in her thin face. Dr Anderson tut-tutted and prescribed carriage exercise and laudanum drops. Lord Meynel suggested impatiently that if she could do nothing in town but peak and pule at him, she had best go back to Torre del Greco, where, he was told, their house was in good order again. This idea was intolerable to her. She hoped never to have to revisit the scene of such delusive happiness. And anyway, how could she bear to leave Naples, where, any morning, she might see *Agamemnon* sail safe to harbour?

Christmas passed, and still there was no news from Toulon. Luckily for Amanda, she was neither alone nor conspicuous in haunting the Ambassador's apartments for news. The shrunken English colony met there daily to compare rumours and contrast anxieties. At Court, too, the rejoicings over the recent birth of a daughter to the Queen were dimmed by anxiety both for the Neapolitan troops at Toulon and for the Queen of France. But, Amanda thought, the Neapolitans were strange people. Nothing, it seemed, could quench their social exuberance. Carnival began and no one would have thought, watching the antics of the masqueraders who thronged the streets, that many of them were in an agony of anxiety for sons or brothers.

"But my love," said Julia, to whom she remarked on this, "you do not understand. We do not dare to appear anxious, for fear we may be thought less than loyal." She looked around nervously. "The Queen, you know, has her informers everywhere. It is not safe to be heard expressing doubt as to the fate of our soldiers. There is many a mask down there in the Toledo that protects eyes red with tears. I only wish I had your excuse to stay at home."

She rose to go, but was interrupted by the bustling entry of Lord Meynel, who had not visited his wife for some days. He apologized, now, at some length, and, Amanda suspected, largely for Julia's benefit, over this neglect. "You have been moping alone here too long," he concluded, "it is no wonder you look so pale and lifeless, but I have news to rouse you. I am but now come from Caserta where the King is busy planning his

121

Carnival appearance. He has planned a most spectacular equipage for himself and you, my love, are to have the honour of appearing on it. But it is all the most profound secret as yet, and I must beg your discretion, Countess."

Julia took the hint and rose. "Of course, my lord, and I beg your indulgence if I take my leave."

He escorted her ceremoniously to the door, then returned, all eagerness, to his tale. "Well at least she took my hint. I cannot bear that Countess of yours, my dear, and nor, I tell you, can the Queen. But never mind your pouting: we have more interesting matters to talk of. We were but Johnny Newcomes at Carnival time last year – no wonder we played little part in it – but this year's is to be something quite other. Only to think of the King himself wishing us to appear with him! He is to drive a carriage decorated in the likeness of one of his men-of-war, dressed, himself, as Neptune, I think, or Triton, or one of those fishy deities. There is to be a band of music playing amidships, and a bevy of mermaids at the prow. And you, my dearest creature, are to be one of the mermaids."

"I? A mermaid? In my condition? My lord, you cannot be serious."

"A pox on your condition. I tell you, my lady, I am sick to death of it. Anyone would think you were the first woman to bear a child since the world began. I tell you flat, you either accept the King's flattering invitation, or retire on grounds of ill health to Torre del Greco, and stay there till my son is born. You may take your choice. I, for one, care not which you decide to do. There are other ladies who would be glad of the honours you take so glumly."

Her quiet time was over. This was a threat, and she recognized it as such. Cross him too far and he was capable of getting his Grassi to play the mermaid's part. Even in the lax court of Naples, this must cause a scandal too serious to be risked, for her child's sake even more than for her own.

It was odd, she thought later, as she and Rosa set to work to contrive her mermaid's costume, how the fact of the child growing within her conditioned her thinking and her actions. For him, anything was possible. It had not, somehow, occurred to her that it might be a girl she was carrying. For her son's sake, she felt she could bear anything.

Just the same, she detested every moment of that carnival appearance. She had never liked crowds, and was appalled to find herself, in her exiguous, if becoming, mermaid's costume, high up on the prow of King Ferdinand's 'ship' equally exposed to the painfully admiring glances and comments of the crowd, and to the hard and inedible sugarplums they delighted to throw at each other. She had, it was true, a tiny silver shield with which she was supposed to ward these off, but she also had a trident which she was supposed to wave in time to the music, and an extremely uncomfortable tail, which practically immobilized her. The sun shone too hot for the time of the year, the King's inevitable bodyguard of enthusiastic *lazzaroni* swarmed and stank around the carriage, Amanda's head swam and she fought desperately against an increasing dizziness. It would be intolerable to faint in this exposed position. Her husband, by a freak of the King's, had been costumed as a merman and had his place not far behind her on the deck; she turned and whispered a frantic appeal to him to change positions with her, but received a sullen refusal. He had been in the worst of tempers ever since the King's decision that he must play the part of a merman and not, as he had hoped, one of the tritons who were entertaining themselves, under the King's command, by sallies against other parties of masqueraders.

"A prize! A prize!" While the King and his party were out on one of these raids, a group of masks costumed as satyrs leaped on board the 'ship' and made as if to carry off its crew of mermaids. Screams of simulated alarm quickly became real as these attackers began unceremoniously to carry off their prey, and Amanda, struggling in the bearlike grip of an enormous man who stank of garlic and red wine knew a moment of terror before he let her go as suddenly as he had seized her. For a moment, she thought that her husband must have come to her rescue, then saw that he, like the invading satyrs, had hurried to the edge of the 'ship', ignoring the screams of the dishevelled mermaids. The crowds around the carriage had suddenly hushed: a messenger was pushing his way through in the direction of the palace. "News," the word passed from mouth to mouth, "news, at last, from Toulon."

"*Malora*." King Ferdinand had fought his way back to the carriage. "They would pick today for their bad news."

"Bad news?" asked Lord Meynel, oblivious even of his own absurd appearance.

"The worst, and from two directions at once. We have lost Toulon; our casualties are heavy – and Marie Antoinette is dead." He was struggling out of his toga and breastplate as he spoke. "I must get to the palace. The Queen," he sounded almost dignified, "the Queen will need me."

Taking their cue from him, the revellers, silent now, lost no time in throwing off their masks and hurrying towards the palace in the hope of more detailed news. Lord Meynel had contrived to throw off the disguise he had disliked so much and hurry after the King, without giving a thought to his wife, who was left, with her fellow mermaids, to find her own way home through the tawdry debris that was all that remained of the morning's carnival gaiety. Confetti, sugarplums and abandoned masks lay about underfoot, or were being hurriedly snatched up by the naked children of the *lazzaroni*. The crowds were gone; the sun was overcast; carnival was over.

Amanda reached home in a state of collapse, her fears for John almost lost in those for her child. Rosa exclaimed with dismay, put her to bed and sent for Dr Anderson. But he, when he arrived, was soothing. Her ladyship had been rash, it was true, but with luck and good management neither she nor the child need be any the worse. Once more, he prescribed rest and laudanum drops.

These, however, Amanda flatly refused to take, nor, she told Rosa, could she rest until she knew the worst of the news from Toulon. Luckily Rosa's protests and exhortations were cut short by the appearance of Julia Vespucci, who had come direct from Lady Hamilton's.

Amanda cut short Julia's exclamations of dismay at finding her in bed: "The news, my love, only tell me the news from Toulon."

Julia shook her head. "The worst, I fear. Sir William has had a letter from his friend Captain Nelson describing the horrors to which the unfortunate inhabitants of the town have been exposed. Thousands, he says, have been lost."

Amanda had gone very white. "His *Agamemnon*, then, took part in the evacuation?"

"No, no; the evacuation was conducted by Lord Hood. Captain Nelson wrote, I believe, from Leghorn, where he was getting provisions for the investment of Corsica. I believe the ships from Toulon were to rendezvous there . . . But, oh, my love, I have not told you the worst of all. Our Neapolitan troops have disgraced themselves. Imagine them panicking in the retreat and shooting at the crews of boats that had no room for them. And, worse still, it is said that they began the rout by quitting their posts without leave. And – there is no news, yet, of Antonio."

Amanda consoled her friend as best she might, feeling almost guilty at her own lightness of heart. How foolish she had been to be so frightened! And all the time the *Agamemnon* had not even been at Toulon. She would not torture herself so again. When Dr Anderson called next morning he was surprised and delighted at the improvement in her condition and indeed that day marked a turning point in her pregnancy. From then on, thought for the child came first, and she refused to let herself be agitated either by her husband's ill-treatment or by John's continued silence.

News of any kind came seldom and slowly. Early in February the Neapolitan contingent came limping home from Toulon, with the news that the British fleet had, as Captain Nelson predicted, made its rendezvous at Leghorn, while the *Agamemnon* was still at sea off Corsica. Antonio Vespucci was home at last, slightly wounded, and a hero. He had distinguished himself, it seemed, by rallying his panic-stricken men and had played a gallant part in covering the Allied retreat. For a while Julia's happiness was a pleasure to watch, as her cousin was fêted and she herself made much of for his sake. The Neapolitans had brought back with them 500 French royalist refugees from Toulon and she was helping her cousin to find them homes and work. A group of them were to be settled on her estates at Syracuse and she and Antonio went there for a few weeks at the end of February to arrange this.

When she returned, her face was pale, her happiness, somehow, dimmed. Anxiously probing, Amanda could not, for some time, find out what was the matter, but at last Julia came out with it. "I am anxious about my cousin," she said.

"Oh?" Amanda refrained from saying, "again?"

"Yes. I had so hoped, when he came back covered with glory, and was welcomed so enthusiastically that his troubles were all over. But – Amanda, I am afraid . . ."

"Afraid? What can you mean?"

"I do not know exactly what I do mean. But something is wrong, I am sure; gravely wrong. Antonio is different. You remember how gaily he used to talk about revolution and the rights of man, almost as if it was a game? Something that he and his friends at the university dreamed of, but did not expect? Now all that has changed. He does not talk revolution any more, but, Amanda, sometimes I think he is plotting it. There are two of the Frenchmen he brought back with him, who – oh, I expect I am talking nonsense, but sometimes I have wondered if they really are royalists. There is something very strange about them, and they are always with Antonio. Amanda, what do you think I should do?"

"Why, nothing," said Amanda with a conviction she was very far from feeling. "You are imagining things, my love, and straining at shadows." She only hoped she was right, and that Antonio was not dealing in dangerous matters, in which he might all too easily involve his devoted cousin. For there was a new tension about Naples these days. It was whispered that the Queen had a secret room at the palace, where, late at night, she interviewed spies drawn from all classes of society. Nobody knew who these were, and people looked askance at each other, and watched their speech. On the surface, everything was patriotism and fervour: the masquerade festivities of carnival had been replaced by a series of manoeuvres and sham sea-fights in the Bay of Naples. It was impossible to tell whether these were intended merely to display the fine new Neapolitan navy, of which the Queen was justly proud, or to intimidate any subversive elements of the population.

Uncertain whether the constant untraceable rumours of revolutionary activity were merely the results of the Queen's system of espionage, or the cause of it, Amanda took precautions of her own. Pretending to find the burden of her pregnancy heavier than it actually was, she made constant excuses to keep Julia with her, and finally prevailed upon her to come and stay. In this way, she hoped that whatever trouble lay ahead for Antonio, his cousin might escape any connection with it. Paying her an early call one morning, Lady Hamilton congratulated her on this manoeuvre: "The less she sees of that cousin of hers, the better." She would say no more, and left Amanda increasingly anxious on her friend's behalf.

A few days later, on a blustery March morning, Julia came tapping at her door before Rosa had even brought Amanda her breakfast. Pale and distraught, Julia explained that one of her cousin's servants had just been with her. Antonio had disappeared.

"Disappeared? What can you mean?"

"Why, just that. He has not been home all night."

Amanda could think of several possible – and harmless – explanations of this, but forebore to suggest them in face of her friend's obvious anxiety. And as the morning wore on, it became all too evident that Julia's fears had been well-grounded. Rumour upon rumour ran through the streets of Naples. During the night, the Queen's secret police had called at many a noble house and taken away a son or a nephew. Nobody knew where they were now; nobody dared ask. Then, after hours of agonized suspense, Luigi d' Medici, the chief of police, made an announcement. A dangerous plot against the very life of the sovereigns had been discovered and the guilty parties arrested. They were now in the subterranean prisons under the castle of Sant' Elmo, awaiting trial.

For Julia, the truth was even worse than she had feared. "I shall never see him again," she said. Comforting her, as best she might, Amanda thought it all too likely . . . Though whether this was really matter for regret seemed another question. But then she had never been able either to like Antonio Vespucci, or to understand his cousin's devotion to him.

The wheels of justice moved slowly. Disquieting rumours filtered out of Sant' Elmo about what the prisoners were suffering. Were they really chained in subterranean dungeons? Was there any truth in horrid stories of torture? Their families, terrified of involvement, tormented themselves in secret, and showed a frenzied gaiety, a fervid loyalty to the Queen in public. More than ever, these days, people eyed each other, wondering who among their friends spied for the Queen, and visited her, under cover of darkness, to report their doings. On the surface, society was more brilliant than ever. Lent was over, and a round of balls and breakfasts was hardly interrupted by another scare in May, when the *lazzaroni* got wind of what they thought to be a new Jacobin plot and surrounded the palace, vowing to defend their beloved King and his Queen to the death.

This time, the crowds thinned and vanished as illogically as they had gathered, but Amanda could not help a little apprehensive shiver as she saw their numbers and heard their hoarse, half-human shouting outside the Palace gates. Another time, they might not scatter so easily. But she was very large and, in the main, wonderfully placid by now, glad of her excuse to stay at home and keep Julia with her. The King had found himself a new butt and Lord Meynel was himself again and had, of course, long since tired of his self-imposed role of devoted father-to-be. Grateful for Julia's excusing presence, he absented himself at will on hunting expeditions, or, Amanda suspected, in pursuit of less mentionable game. Her life would have been entirely peaceful had it not been for her grinding anxiety about John Purvis. The *Agamemnon* was now taking part in the British attack on Corsica and reports kept reaching Naples about the enthusiasm with which Captain Nelson and his men had thrown themselves into the struggle. Characteristically, Nelson's own letters, as reported by Lady Hamilton, emphasized over and over again that if the island was finally wrested from the French, it would be no thanks to the army contingent, but entirely due to his efforts and those of his men.

When she learned that they were mounting a land attack on the French positions at Bastia, Amanda lost much of her recently acquired calm. At sea, she had begun to feel that John bore a charmed life, but on land . . . Anything might happen, and she would not know. Physical discomfort exacerbated her anxiety. Her time was near now and the hot weather she usually loved made her wretched. She could not eat, she could not sleep; worst of all, she could not tell anyone what was troubling her. For as the slow, hot days dragged by a new terror had arisen to plague her. It was nine months, now, since she had told Lord Meynel she was pregnant and he had bragged the news about to his cronies. Soon it would be nine months since the night when Vesuvius erupted, that ecstatic, disastrous night with John. Thanks to Lady Hamilton's resolute partisanship, the rumours caused by Lord Meynel's duel with John Purvis had largely died down, but – everyone knew how Lord Meynel had been incapacitated by it. Amanda knew well that the gossip about her was only dormant, not dead: if her child was to avoid the slur of illegitimacy, he had best make his appearance without delay.

Dr Anderson, paying one of his frequent visits to her, tut-tutted anxiously at sight of the dark circles under her eyes. On his way out, he had a word with Julia: "Lady Meynel is fretting about something," he said. "If it be possible, it should be stopped."

"Oh," said Julia. The two of them exchanged glances and said no more. Suspecting a great deal, neither of them knew anything. Amanda had kept her secret well.

129

Even in the new high-waisted dresses that were all the rage, and suited her condition so admirably, Amanda hardly felt like going out now, but urged Julia, every day, to go to Lady Hamilton's for news. There was ample pretext for anxiety: things were going badly on every front of the widespread war. The Duke of York had been badly beaten in Flanders, London had been swept by a spy scare and Mrs Carteret wrote fretfully that she expected nightly to be murdered in her bed. And, worst of all for Amanda, Nelson's last letter to Lady Hamilton had been full of complaints about the army's failure to co-operate with him that boded no good for the success of his mission.

So, sitting in her coolly shadowed drawing room one hot June morning, Amanda hardly knew where to turn among her anxieties. Dr Anderson's urgings that, for her child's sake, she must keep calm and cheerful seemed merely a mockery. There had been news, this morning, of despatches from Captain Nelson and Julia had agreed to make an early call on Lady Hamilton. She had been gone, it seemed, hours, and the longer she stayed, the more Amanda's anxiety increased. Was the news too bad to be told? Was Julia trying to decide how to break it?

Impatient and restless, she wandered out on to the hot balcony to look once more across the beautiful bay to where an English ship lay at anchor. Alas, she was a mere sloop and not even the eye of hope could mistake her for the *Agamemnon*. Just the same, Amanda stood there for a while, despite the fierce heat of the sun, dreaming of the day when an English ship would take her home. Then, sounds of bustle within brought her hurrying back into the drawing room. Julia must be returned. And, indeed, as she entered the shady room from the balcony, Julia appeared at the door, a tall figure behind her. Amanda's eyes, dazzled from sunshine, could only make out the characteristic blue and white of British naval uniform.

She started forward, hands outstretched: "John," then paused, confused, already aware of her mistake.

Julia spoke almost at the same moment: "There is news

at last, my love, and I have brought Captain Medway to tell it you."

"We have met before." Gallantly bowing over her hand, Captain Medway showed no sign of having heard her exclamation. "I trust I see you well – and that Lord Meynel is quite recovered."

"Well enough, I thank you." Amanda was furiously conscious of her overblown appearance, and of the absurdity of her error in taking Medway for John Purvis. He was half a head taller. What a fool he must think her, and how could she bear, in her present condition, to have him looking at her with those curiously disturbing, far too observant dark blue eyes? Furious with herself for her mistake, she was equally angry with Julia for having brought a stranger to intrude upon her at such a time. Indeed, Medway was worse than a stranger, since he had been so closely involved with the duel between her husband and John Purvis. And, inevitably, she was angriest of all with Medway for standing there and looking at her so kindly. She had always detested red-headed men . . . Her fan broke in her hands and she was aware, as a last straw, of a wave of colour flooding her face.

Medway said nothing, and she was angry with him even for that. It was Julia, at last, who broke the awkward little silence. "You do not ask us for the news. And it is of the best, I promise you, except that poor Captain Nelson is wounded, and like to lose the sight of an eye. But Calvi is ours, and with fewer casualties than were feared."

"I am glad to hear it," Amanda managed. Surely Julia would have told her at once if John had been hurt? Or would she? No doubt she had meant well in bringing Medway to see her, but how could she ask him, of all people, the questions that burned her throat? She must make a little conversation first and work around to it casually. "Captain Medway?" she asked. "I am to congratulate you, then, on a promotion?" She coloured again, aware that in striving for lightness, she had contrived to sound almost insultingly casual.

But his steady regard was as kind as ever. "Why, yes,

131

I thank you. The little *Melpomene* out there in the bay is mine now. And what I am sure will please you, my friend John Purvis has taken my place as *Agamemnon's* First Lieutenant – a place that he has richly deserved long since, and would have had, I am sure, save that he is sadly deficient in the all-important article of influence."

"Oh. He is not hurt then?" She should be grateful to Medway for introducing the subject.

"Not he! They say in the fleet that he bears a charmed life. He was close beside Captain Nelson when he was hit, and did not receive so much as a scratch. He is in admirable health and would, I am sure, have sent you his compliments, had he known I would be so fortunate as to see you, but, to tell truth, I came away in some haste."

"The news was certainly too good to be let hang in hand," intervened Julia, who was aware by now that the interview was not, somehow, going quite as she had intended. She filled another silence with an animated description of the advantages to be expected from the taking of Corsica.

Amanda continued angrily silent. She was certain that Captain Medway was trying to spare her the knowledge that John had not even troubled to send her a message. Of course he must have known his friend was coming to Naples with dispatches. Was this his care for her reputation at work again? And what would he think when Medway told him of her advanced pregnancy? Or would Medway? What did he think of her, as he stood there so tall, so silent and so odiously self-possessed? What was he thinking, now, as he described the situation in Corsica to Julia Vespucci and yet contrived, somehow, to keep those large thoughtful eyes fixed on herself? Was he sorry for her? It was, somehow, an intolerable thought. She broke into the conversation with a suddenness that, once again, verged on rudeness: "And Captain Nelson is wounded?" After what had passed, it was an absurd question, and she was angrier than ever with herself.

But Captain Medway answered her with his usual serious courtesy and described exactly how Nelson had been wounded by the ricochet of splinters and stones from a hit on the English battery. Was there, incorrigibly, a twinkle in those deep blue eyes as he laboriously, and for the second time, described exactly how it had happened? If there was, he was impossible. But he went on to describe the gallant part played by John Purvis in the action.

Oddly, Amanda found this hard to bear. "You are a good friend," she said at last. "To hear you speak of Mr Purvis's conduct, one can only wonder why he is not an admiral at least."

Aware once more of a false note, Julia again intervened: "Captain Medway is too modest to tell you of his own exploits," she said, "but I had the story of them from Sir William. Tell Lady Meynel how you won your promotion, Captain Medway."

He looked down at Amanda with those dark blue eyes that saw so much too much. "I will not fatigue Lady Meynel any further," he said, and she was suddenly, guiltily aware that she had not even asked him to be seated. "I have taken up too much of her time already." Still speaking to Julia, he yet contrived, without discourtesy, to be looking at Amanda. "I am sure she is wishing me back on the *Melpomene* – or further." His eyes laughed into hers. "May I give any message to Mr Purvis when we meet, Lady Meynel?"

His implied consideration for her condition was the last straw. "Anything that you think proper." Her voice sounded cross, even to her own ears. And, fatally, she went on: "Congratulate him, pray, from me, on having stepped, so successfully, into your shoes."

She regretted it the moment it was spoken. He looked down at her for a moment in silence. Then, "I will take pleasure in obeying your first commands," he said.

It was a direct rebuke, and, worst of all, she knew she had deserved it. She coloured and stood, in miserable silence, her eyes treacherously aswim with tears, as he kissed her hand and took his leave. At the last moment, "Take care of yourself, Lady Meynel." How kind his eyes still were, and how little she deserved his kindness.

He was gone. Julia was looking at her reproachfully. "Truly, Amanda, if it were not for your condition, I should be in a fair way to be angry with you. How could you use poor Captain Medway so ill?"

"A fiddle for my condition." Amanda burst into furious and uncontrollable tears.

Very early next morning, her son was born. He looked, to her relief, just like any other baby. Sometimes, in her moments of conscience-stricken depression, she had felt sure that he must be born with some stigma, proclaiming him a bastard for all the world to see. But there he was at last, vigorously squalling, with the full complement of fingers and toes and a wizened old man's face that suddenly reminded her of her husband's.


But as he grew and thrived she was privately able to reassure herself that her little Peter was indubitably John's child. Lord Meynel's son would never have been so amiable. Naturally, she kept this opinion to herself, and encouraged the nurses in their chorused comments on an imagined likeness to Lord Meynel. She never knew what her husband thought, but he kept to his side of their bargain and behaved as if the child were his. That is, he condescended, once, to have Peter shown to him, and after that complained bitterly if the nursery door should chance to be left open so that he could hear him crying. But then, luckily, little Peter hardly ever did cry.

He was indeed an admirable baby and Amanda found it more and more difficult to feel a proper regret for the moment of madness to which he owed his existence. Sometimes, superstitiously, she found herself wondering if the price of her wrongdoing was not yet to be paid, and as the long months of exile grew into years, she began to think she knew what it was to be. For still her only news of John Purvis was what she heard, accidentally, of Captain Nelson and the *Agamemnon*. Nelson now corresponded with both Sir William and his wife, and Lady Hamilton never missed an opportunity to tell Amanda of the *Agamemnon's* adventures. Sometimes, in reporting his latest brush with the French, Captain Nelson would refer in glowing terms to Captain Medway or Lieutenant Purvis and Lady Hamilton always made a point of passing on these remarks, as well as Captain Nelson's less favourable opinion of his higher command. For Nelson had never been happy since Admiral Hotham had replaced his friend Lord Hood as Commander-in-Chief in the Mediterranean. *'My disposition can't bear tame and slow measures,'* he wrote, when Admiral Hotham refused to pursue the flying French. *'Had I commanded,'* said Nelson, *'either the whole French fleet would have graced my triumph, or I should have been in a confounded scrape . . . Nothing can stop the courage of English seamen.'*

Amanda was always grateful for these crumbs of information about the fleet, but doubtful of the motive behind them. Did Lady Hamilton intend to comfort or to tease her? She could never be sure, but in fact the comfort of knowing that John was still alive, still on board the *Agamemnon*, far outweighed her embarrassment at the Ambassadress's free handling of the subject.

The thing she found so hard to bear was that no word ever came directly from John himself. At first, she had consoled herself with the thought that it was his solicitude on her account that prevented him from embarking on a correspondence with her immediately after the scandal in which they had been involved. But when months and then years slipped by and still she had no word from him, she began to fear that her husband's taunts might be well-grounded. John must scorn her for having yielded to him and was making it clear that he intended to have nothing more to do with her. It was a bitter thought, but what else could account for his not having even written to congratulate her on the birth of a child he must surely half suspect to be his?

If it had not been for little Peter those would have been wretched years for Amanda, but it was impossible to be quite in despair when every day was variegated by some new instance of his progress. Amanda had never known a baby well before, and scandalized friends and servants alike by the amount she insisted on doing, herself, for her son. Only Julia delighted her by agreeing that playing with little Peter was an infinitely more satisfying pastime than boring oneself at dress parties or going to concerts when the music was drowned with chatter. For Julia, who had begun by suffering acutely because her beloved cousin was immured in Sant' Elmo was now beginning, as the slow years passed and still there was no sign of his or his friends' release, to suffer because she did not suffer enough.

This did not surprise Amanda, who had always disliked Antonio Vespucci and suspected him of paying his court to his pretty cousin simply because she was the heiress to the family estates, but it would have been heartless to suggest this to Julia. She had been shaken enough by the discovery that his revolutionary sentiments were so much more than mere talk. It was impossible ever for her altogether to sympathize with someone who had planned the cold-blooded murder not only of the King and Queen, but of all their children as well. Besides, Julia like Amanda had heard enough stories, now, from the Neapolitans who had returned from Toulon, of the massacre with which the French revolutionaries had celebrated its recapture . . . But then, there were other stories, equally distressing, about the sufferings of the young aristocrats in Sant' Elmo . . . The world had gone mad, it seemed . . . Whichever way you looked, there was nothing but suffering and wickedness. The two girls tacitly agreed not to talk – to try not even to think of politics, and distracted themselves by vying with each other in their devotion to little Peter. Their other comfort was in the idea of England. There, Amanda had convinced Julia, was the happy place to live. There was a monarchy without tyranny, a liberty without license. If only they could get there . . . Julia had now come round to the idea that her best hope of happiness in life lay in reconciliation with her English relations and had swallowed her pride and written them a friendly letter with that end in view. For though she had been effectively cured of her republican leanings, she remained deeply suspect with the Neapolitan court. Her existence in Naples could never be anything but precarious, and Amanda, who knew that she had narrowly escaped arrest with her cousin and his friends, lived in constant dread that a new Jacobin alarm might send her too to prison.

But as the years passed and little Peter learned first to crawl and then to fall and then, at last, to walk, their chances of getting to England seemed increasingly slender. Julia had received no answer from her relations there and had turned bitterly against them – and England – as a result. And, besides, the news went from bad to worse. The young Lieutenant Bonaparte who had distinguished himself at Toulon had risen now to command the French army of Italy and lead it to victory there. In the north, the French had conquered Holland and Amanda's letters from her mother told of England trembling in fear of invasion. In Europe, morale dwindled and, one by one, the Allied powers began to make their peace with the all-conquering French. Even in Naples, there were rumours of peace feelers. Bonaparte's lightning campaign through the north of Italy had caused Neapolitan loyalists to shake in their shoes, while the Jacobin party – those of them who were not in prison – were coming more and more out in the open again. The English colony was swollen by a steady stream of refugees from the north of Italy, each with a new tale of French atrocity, or of young Bonaparte's diabolical skill as a general. Amanda, increasingly anxious for little Peter's safety, consoled herself with the thought that if Bonaparte should invade Naples, the English Navy was pledged to evacuate its British residents.

Calling, one hot September morning, at the Palazzo Sessa to make a formal enquiry after Lady Hamilton, who had been mildly indisposed for a few days, Amanda was surprised to be summoned upstairs to her presence. She found her reclining *à la* Recamier on a chaise longue, every inch the invalid, in a swansdown-trimmed négligé of a blue that matched her famous eyes. Greeting her, Amanda could not help a side-thought that if the lovely

Emma continued to indulge her passion for good food and champagne it would soon be impossible to describe her ample curves as anything but corpulent. The beautiful girl who had entranced her three years before was gradually disappearing under layer upon layer of fat.

But the charm was as compelling as ever, even if some of the beauty's mannerisms might seem a little girlish for her girth. She greeted Amanda with her usual endearing warmth: "You are come in the very nick of time," she went on. "I was boring myself to distraction here. Sir William is gone to Caserta, to pay his respects to His Majesty, my mother is busy about her housekeeping, and I have not had a soul to talk to this livelong day. But tell me, love, what is the news in town? I am got, you know, quite against my will, into politics and must have some news for the letter I should write to my adorable Queen. She sends, you know, daily, to ask after my health and is always eager for the latest news."

"Yes," said Amanda dryly, "I am sure she is. But surely no one is better informed than she about what goes on in her dominions."

"Oh, pshaw," said the beauty, "have you been listening to the gossip about my beloved Queen too? You will tell me next that you believe all the lies that wicked Frenchman told of her in his vile book. As for the talk of her *sala oscura* it is all malicious gossip, I promise you, arisen from the fact that she is gracious enough to see some of her closest friends, such as myself, with something less than the usual court ceremony. The rest is nothing but wicked slander by those filthy Jacobins."

"Well," said Amanda mildly, "most of them are in no case to slander anyone. They hardly have much opportunity in Sant' Elmo. But tell me," it was time to change this dangerous subject, "is there, do you think, any truth in the rumours that Naples is about to make peace with France?"

"Not the slightest, and you may tell the world that I, Emma Hamilton, said so. My adorable Queen would no more make her peace with that *canaille* than—" she paused, at a loss for a parallel and was saved, in mid-sentence, by the appearance of a page-boy with a letter on a silver salver. Lady Hamilton snatched it eagerly. "From the Queen herself," she said. "Now you will see. Excuse me, love, while I read it; Her Majesty's words are too precious to wait on mere chatter."

Amanda smiled and was silent. It was strange to think that this opulent creature who corresponded with a Queen had once been a servant-girl – and worse. It was a far cry from the days when Amy Lyon had been the prime attraction in Dr Graham's Temple of Hymen with its celestial Bed and Electrical Throne. Looking up suddenly, the beauty must have caught some betraying glint of expression in her guest's face, for though Lady Hamilton's grammar might still, sometimes, fail, her instinct for people seldom did.

"You are thinking me a strange correspondent for a Queen, are you not, love?" she said. "Well, it is true enough, but at least I am a more faithful one than most of the rascals and whores who surround my beloved Queen. All I wish is to serve her: after all, thanks to my dear Sir William, I have everything my heart could desire, and, of course, in serving her," her voice rose, "I serve my husband, and my country too. And now," with one of her lightning changes of mood to the practical, "you must excuse me, love. This is news of the highest importance. I must send at once to Sir William. But stay – I know you for discretion itself; I will not be so brutal as to keep the news from you – though it is bad enough in all conscience. See, Her Majesty encloses a letter from the King of Spain to his brother, her husband. Sir William will decipher it, but the Queen tells me enough . . . Spain is to join France and declare war on England: now England and Naples face the tyrant alone."

She had sprung up from her chaise longue, her indisposition forgotten, and now struck a heroic pose worthy of Britannia herself.

"Good God!" Amanda was appalled at this piece of news and could not, like Lady Hamilton, distract herself by dramatizing her own reaction to it. "Do you not think that now the Court of Naples will feel itself compelled to make peace with France?"

"Never," said Lady Hamilton. "I know my beloved Queen better than that. Do you not know of her vows of vengeance for her sister's death? Do you not know that she has her picture always beside her, with a cry for vengeance inscribed on it? No, no, she'll never make peace; she has told Sir William so a thousand times."

Amanda was not convinced, but thought it best to change the subject. "And how is Sir William?" she asked.

"Well enough," said the beauty carelessly. "He has never, you know, enjoyed robust health since his last illness. He told me then that he would surely have died if it had not been for my devoted nursing. But," she paused, "he is not so young as he was."

It was true. Amanda had noticed, of late, that the spry and gallant Ambassador was no longer so active as he had been. A yellowish tinge to his cheek, and an occasional tremor in the graceful hand hinted at the inevitable toll of years of hard living. Amanda was not the only one to wonder how the robust Ambassadress bore this diminution of vigour in her husband.

Once again, Lady Hamilton seemed to read her thoughts: "But fonder of me than ever," she went on. "And says I make all his happiness, as, indeed, he is mine."

Did it ring quite true? Amanda was not sure, then chid herself for reading the bitterness of her own marriage – also to a much older man – into Lady Hamilton's. In a lax and gossiping society, Lady Hamilton, for all her dubious past, had kept remarkably clear of scandal. Amanda certainly, she told herself, had no right to think ill of her. She rose to take her leave and readily gave the promise of deepest secrecy over the news that was demanded of her.

Events were to prove that Amanda had been right, and Lady Hamilton, for all her boasted intimacy with the Queen, wrong in her predictions. By November, Naples had made peace with France and this, combined with Spain's declaration of war compelled the British Navy to evacuate the Mediterranean. Those were bitter days for the British in Naples, and most particularly for Amanda. Once more, Jacobins and Frenchmen flaunted their uniform of short hair and scarlet waistcoats in the narrow Neapolitan streets and once more Amanda's nerves were all at a stretch for news of John. Captain Nelson was a full commodore now, and had shifted his broad pennant to the *Captain*, but he had taken several of his junior officers with him, John perhaps among them. Nelson was busy, much against his will, in the unhappy task of evacuating British troops and nationals from the Mediterranean. Obeying his orders, he wrote angrily: *'They at home do not know what this Fleet is capable of performing; anything and everything . . . I lament our present orders in sackcloth and ashes . . .'*

But the evacuation of the Mediterranean continued. Nelson, Amanda presently learned, had shifted his flag to *La Minerve* and was occupied with the evacuation of Elba. Surely he would come to Naples before he left the Mediterranean entirely? Even under the galling terms of the Neapolitan peace with France, four English men-of-war at a time were allowed to enter the famous bay.

Christmas came, and instead of *La Minerve*, the *Inconstant*, Captain Thomas Fremantle, sailed into the bay. He, too, had been busy with the evacuation of British nationals from the Italian cities threatened by the rapid advance of the French armies, and he brought with him an English family called Wynne, whom he had rescued first from Leghorn and then from Elba. Lady Hamilton, hurrying in from Caserta at the news of an English ship in harbour, soon called on Amanda with romantic news. Captain Fremantle and the Wynnes' daughter Betsy were to make a match of it, and she, of course, was to arrange it all. Prince Augustus would give the bride away; her beloved Queen would take care of the little difficulty arising from the fact of the bride's being a Roman Catholic. And Amanda must come to the ball with which she proposed to celebrate the wedding.

141

Amanda did so and was immensely taken with vivacious Betsy Wynne – or rather Fremantle, who seemed, however, incredibly young to be setting up housekeeping on a man-of-war. She admitted to nineteen, her new husband teased her with being at least three years older, but Amanda could hardly believe her even nineteen. As for Fremantle, he won her heart, without knowing it, by some warm words about John Purvis, who was, it seemed, still with Nelson. "A coming man, that Purvis," Fremantle had concluded, and been amazed at the warmth with which this pretty young Lady Meynel urged him and his bride to use her house as their own while they remained in Naples. It was a bitter disappointment to Amanda when the *Inconstant* sailed two days later. She had hoped for so much more news about John.

Betsy Fremantle and Amanda had struck up an immediate friendship, and agreed to correspond, but Betsy's rare letters, when they came, brought small cheer for Amanda. The little details of her life on board ship Amanda found hard to bear . . . So, if only things had been different, might she be living . . . It might be John who was giving up snuff for her sake, installing her harpsichord, or fitting out two little cabins for them below decks. And as Betsy's letters came from further away, Amanda's jealousy increased. She wrote from Gibraltar and then from off Cadiz, where the *Inconstant* had joined the British fleet under Sir John Jervis, who treated her, she said with his usual gallantry. There, too, they had met her husband's friend, Captain Nelson, now covered with glory by his independent action at the Battle of Cape St Vincent. Luckily, said Betsy, Sir John was a generous enough man so that he had taken no offence at having his orders disobeyed to such glorious effect. More important, to Amanda, than any of this was Betsy's comment on the officers who had accompanied Captain Nelson to dinner on the *Inconstant*. '*That friend of yours, Mr Purvis, was there, and in high favour, Fremantle says, with Captain Nelson for his behaviour at Cape St Vincent.*'

Her next letter told a very different story. It was ill-written, hurried and almost frantic. Her husband had been wounded. The *Inconstant*, had joined Nelson's *Theseus* for an attack on the island of Teneriffe. But for once Commodore Nelson's luck had failed him. He had been wounded in the arm at the very beginning of the attack, and might have been killed had it not been for the devotion of his stepson, Josiah Nisbet. He had lost his arm, and there was danger that Fremantle, also wounded, might lose his. And this time, in her distraction, Betsy Fremantle made no mention of Amanda's friend, Mr Purvis. If both the leaders of the expedition were wounded, what might not have happened to him?

It was lucky for Amanda, that distracted summer, that little Peter could walk and talk and get into a thousand scrapes to distract her and his honorary aunt Julia. Lord Meynel grumbled, when he was at home, about the attention the child received and talked of spared rods and spoiled children, but then he very seldom was at home these days, having settled down now, in half public domestic bliss, with his Grassi, who had presented him with two daughters in rapid succession. Condoled with by kind friends, Amanda put a brave face on this: "If the royal dukes can do it," she would say, "why not my husband?" This was unanswerable, but she found herself appallingly weary, these days, of Naples and its English colony. If only they could go home . . . She had tried to persuade her husband to accept Captain Fremantle's offer of a passage on the *Inconstant*, but he continued terrified of the sea voyage, and anyway proclaimed himself perfectly happy where he was. "What," he asked, "return to England and have to pay these new-fangled taxes they talk of, on powder, and income, and lord knows what else?"

Increasingly bad news from England merely confirmed his decision. To invasion terrors and commercial panic had been added the last horror of mutiny in the fleet. Reading of officers held at pistol point by their own men, Amanda feared once again for John Purvis . . . But Nelson, she reminded herself, had always been adored by his crews.

There would be no mutiny on any ship he commanded. And she heard, at long last, in the autumn of 1797, from Miss Purvis, who wrote in an old lady's hand so shaky as to be almost indecipherable. But John's name, with Miss Purvis's unmistakable slanting 'J' recurred several times and at last Amanda was able to make it all out. John had indeed been wounded in the attack on Teneriffe, but not seriously. Best of all, he had been commended for his part in the battle and was now at home in England recovering. *'I hope to see him promoted Captain before he is fit to sail again,'* wrote Miss Purvis. And then, significantly, *'Promotion comes quick these days.'* After this, the letter turned to indifferent subjects: the high cost of bread, the bad news from Ireland, bad news, indeed, from everywhere. Then, at the very end, closing with fondest love, Miss Purvis added a sentence worth all the rest of the letter to Amanda. *'I fear I am but a poor correspondent these days,'* she wrote. *'To tell truth, John put me in mind to write to you. He asks me to send you his kind regards, and tell you he hopes all goes well with you in Naples.'* They were hardly passionate words, and second-hand at that, but Amanda cried herself to sleep that night with the letter under her pillow. Had John forgiven her – and himself, at last? Might she, one day, be able to tell him that Peter was his child?

# Chapter Nine

"But I tell you, my love, it is true." Amanda had called, one fine May morning of 1798, at Julia Vespucci's house outside Naples and had found her friend busy with her embroidery among twisted olive trees on a terrace overlooking the blue waters of the bay. "I promise you, it is true," she said again. "Lady Hamilton told me at her *conversazzione* last night. The political prisoners are to be released without delay, your cousin among them. It is the French Minister, M. Garat's doing, of course, and the first good result of this wretched peace with France. Lady Hamilton says her adored Queen is not best pleased about it, but M. Garat has put such pressure on her and her Minister Acton that they could not help but yield."

"It seems too good to be true." Julia had jumped up in her excitement and was pacing about in the scanty shade of the trees. "After four years! But I do not wonder that the Queen thinks it time to make some concessions to France. They say Bonaparte has an army of 35,000 men ready to sail from Toulon. If that Captain Nelson Lady Hamilton is always talking of but relaxes his blockade of the port for a day, Bonaparte will be out to sea, and what more likely than that he will attack Naples? He must know perfectly well that the Queen and Acton are neutral in name only, and would seize any opportunity to strike at him."

"And why not?" asked Amanda. "Sometimes, Julia, you talk almost like a Frenchwoman. You know as well as I do how the French have treated the other Italian states. They came with loud talk of friendship, it is true, but it is the friendship of the wolf for the lamb. Look at Berthier's treatment of the Pope!"

"I know." Julia shook her head. "I fear even my cousin must be sadly disillusioned by now. But, come, if he is really to be released, after all these years, what are we doing lingering here? I must hurry into Naples to greet him, for he will be in need, I fear, of everything I can do for him."

"Yes," Amanda agreed gravely, "by all reports, their treatment in prison has been almost as bad as that meted out by the French to *their* prisoners. Queen Maria Carolina complains day and night of the torments her poor sister suffered – and then proves herself no better than Marie Antoinette's gaolers."

"Hush, my love." Julia looked nervously around the quiet garden. "That is dangerous talk, even for an English-woman." And then, having reassured herself that they could not be overheard, "But it is the truth, for all that. I tell you, I tremble as to what the effects of what he has suffered may not be on my cousin. When he was arrested, four years ago, he was an idealist, a dreamer . . . but now – who knows?"

Amanda, who had had her own doubts about Antonio Vespucci's idealism even four years before, took advantage of this opening to suggest to her friend that perhaps it might be best to await her cousin here, in the privacy of her country house. But Julia would not agree, pointing out, not unreasonably, that she could not even be sure that Antonio would come to her. "And if ever he was in need of a friend and kinswoman, surely it is now."

Amanda could only agree and compromise with her fears by insisting that Julia come back and stay with her, hoping that in this way she might protect her at once from her cousin's probable extremism and the Queen's suspicions. For though she had never felt herself to be particularly *persona grata* with Queen Maria Carolina, her husband was still on the best of terms with King Ferdinand, while she herself had a certain status as an Englishwoman and a protégée of Lady Hamilton's who continued to be the Queen's very dear friend. And though the Queen had been forced into peace with the French, everyone knew that in

146

her heart she hated them with an unreasoning passion. She might have consented to release the political prisoners of 1794, but that did not mean that she would look on them, or their friends, with any more favour. There was no doubt, these days, of the terror that underlay the shining surface of Neapolitan society. Reports of their conduct, and their friends', would doubtless be pouring, nightly, into the Queen's secret room, and any crisis might trigger off a new round of arrests. If she could help it, Amanda did not intend Julia to be among them.

Julia's cloak bag was soon packed, since she would only agree to a very short stay with Amanda, and the two girls set out in Amanda's coach for the steep, circuitous drive back into town. When they got there, they found the Chiaia even more crowded than usual with loiterers from every class of society and soon learned that twenty-five of the political prisoners had indeed been released – and had gone at once to the French Minister's house to thank him for his intervention on their behalf.

"Madness," said Amanda. "Nothing could more enrage the Queen against them. No, my love, I will not take you there. I have no wish to see you lodged in the Sant' Elmo in your cousin's place – though how long he will stay free seems to be highly questionable if this is how he conducts himself on his first day of liberty." And she told her coachman to drive them straight home, only compromising with Julia's anxiety by sending one of her running footmen to take a message to Antonio Vespucci at the French Minister's house. Even this, since the man was in Lord Meynel's conspicuous livery of scarlet and gold, was a sufficiently rash act, but at least it was better than having Julia go there herself.

To Amanda's relief, her husband was not at home when they got there, for she was very far from being sure how he would take this unexpected visit from Julia Vespucci. Insofar as he took any interest in politics, he tended to follow the most extreme line of the court, and had done his unsuccessful best to discourage his wife's friendship with Julia. It would be very much better, Amanda thought, if she could see him alone to break the news of this visit to him.

They had hardly taken off their bonnets, kissed little Peter, who welcomed his "Aunt Julia's" visit with delight, and settled her in her apartments, when a servant tapped on the door to announce Signor Vespucci. Hurrying downstairs, they found him pacing angrily up and down the great salon and even Amanda, who had expected the worst, was appalled at the change in him. He had been an elegantly slender, olive-skinned young man, always point-device in appearance and manner. Now he was gaunt and yellow, his clothes shabby and ill-fitting, his hair cut short in the unbecoming revolutionary style, his manner abrupt to the point of rudeness.

"So," he greeted his cousin, who was silent with shock at his appearance, "I have to come to seek you out, do I? Do you know, I had deluded myself that your carriage would be waiting for me when I escaped from that hell-hole. It was fortunate, was it not, that the French Minister had arranged conveyance for us. Am I to understand that you had forgotten all about your unlucky cousin? It was wise of you, if you had: association with me can do you nothing but harm."

"Oh, Tonio." Julia's voice was thick with tears. "How can you say such things? I did not know you were to be released until this morning, when Lady Meynel was so kind as to bring me the good news. I have been living, you must know, much in the country."

"Ho!" He took her up at once. "In seclusion, I take it! Ashamed, of course, of your gaolbird cousin. I should thank you, I suppose, for consenting to disgrace yourself by seeing me – and thank your English friend, too." He made Amanda an ironical bow.

Amanda looked him up and down. "We must make allowances, I know, for what you have suffered, signor, but you must realize that you can do yourself little good by treating your friends thus. Frankly, I am afraid you will find you have few enough of them."

"I ask your pardon, my lady." He looked at her with

a new respect. This was not the shy girl he remembered. "And yours, too, cousin. Forgive a man embittered by years of ill-treatment. But we'll not talk of that. I am not come here to trouble you with my miseries. Indeed, I have been so long out of the world I have quite forgot my manners. I cry your pardon, cousin, and yours, too, Lady Meynel."

"It is nothing." Amanda found his sudden attempt at charm even less attractive than his previous boorishness. "I am delighted to see you at liberty once more, and will be only too happy to serve you in any way I can. Your cousin is my dearest friend and I know how she has suffered during your—" she hesitated – "your absence."

"No need to mince words with me, Lady Meynel, it is late in the day to be sparing my feelings. Call it what it was, my imprisonment in that stinking dungeon under Sant' Elmo, fit rather for gallowsbirds than for me and my friends. But do not look so grave at me; I promised I would not weary you with a catalogue of my wrongs and now, I have done. Besides, I have a favour to ask of you and my cousin here. Will you take pity on a poor gaolbird and let me accompany you to the San Carlo tonight? 'Tis *Figaro*, I am told, and you'll not believe how I have longed to hear one of Herr Mozart's mellifluous airs these weary months. Besides, I wish to lose no time in showing society that I am not ashamed of what I have suffered."

"Go to the opera?" Amanda looked doubtfully at Julia. "To tell truth, I have not been this age." She did not at all like the idea of joining this dangerous young man in his first public appearance.

"All the more reason why you should come tonight," he said. "Come, Julia, help me to persuade your friend to allow me this small indulgence. I must not, I know, ask you to accompany me unchaperoned; my heart is set on making this appearance; and who else will give her countenance to one so recently disgraced?"

"Do let us go," said Julia. "You know, Amanda, you were saying, only the other day, that you had sadly missed the opera of late. And *Figaro* is, I know, a prime favourite of yours. And, as Antonio says, if I do not stand by him, who will?"

Amanda hesitated, was lost. "If my husband makes no objections," she said, knowing perfectly well that these days Lord Meynel neither knew nor cared how she spent her time.

But she dressed, that night, with deep misgivings, which were hardly alleviated by Julia's obvious upsurge of happiness. Still, Vespucci's appearance, when he called for them, was somewhat reassuring. She had hardly admitted to herself how anxious she was lest he should arrive in the scarlet waistcoat and newfangled trousers that had become the Jacobins' badge of defiance, and the sight of his impeccable evening dress did much to calm her fears. Appearances, in Naples, were too important to be neglected. But Vespucci had obviously taken great pains to change himself from the morning's wild young revolutionary into a young gentleman of fashion, point-device in his appearance, courteously gallant in his behaviour. She almost reproached herself for remaining quite unable to like him, but could not help feeling that this evening's gallantry was a deliberate attempt to make them forget his morning's rudeness. To her, his obsequious attentions were nothing but a wretched sham, but Julia's reaction was quite another matter. She positively bloomed with happiness as her cousin took her arm to lead her out to the carriage, and Amanda was more than ever convinced that if he should choose to ask her to marry him she would accept him on the spot.

It was a depressing thought, and her fears for her friend's happiness were considerably exacerbated by their reception at the Opera House. Even the sentry at the door seemed to her to look at them askance, and this impression was confirmed when they were settled in the box she had used so little of late. Normally, she would have expected her enjoyment of the music to be ruined by constant interruptions from a stream of gentlemen calling to pay their respects, for Neapolitan ladies held court in their opera boxes as if they were salons. But tonight they were left strictly to themselves and she was uncomfortably aware of critical glances from many of her acquaintances.

To her relief, the Royal Box was empty, since the King and Queen were on a hunting party at Portici, but she was soon uneasily aware that their little party was the object of considerable interest in the British Ambassador's box, which faced them across the theatre. Although they were deep enough to hold twelve people, the boxes at the San Carlo were so narrow that it was difficult to see to whom Lady Hamilton was talking with such animation. The famous beauty was seated at the front of her box, with her mother beside her and a crowd of gentlemen, as always, in attendance. She seemed to be paying particular attention to one of them, to whom Amanda was sure she had seen her pointing them out, but try as she would Amanda could not make out his face in the candle shadows of the box. Surely, though, he must be a stranger, perhaps a new addition to the now shrunken English community. And yet there was something familiar, yet strange about that tall and elegant figure with its unmistakable air of command. She was about to point him out to Julia, when he moved out of sight at the back of the box and another man took his place behind Lady Hamilton. Amanda's hands clutched convulsively at the front of her box. It was . . . could it be? It must be John. Yet how could it be? She had heard of no English ship's arrival. And, besides, surely he would have come first to her. Or would he? The question was a bitter one to her. And from then on she hardly heard the beautiful, familiar music of *Figaro*.

When the curtain fell at the end of the first act of the opera, and the audience's whispered conversation rose to a roar, Amanda shook out the folds of her dress and passed a reassuring hand over her ringlets. If it was John in Lady Hamilton's box, surely he would come to her now? But minutes passed and no one entered their box. Uneasily aware of Antonio Vespucci's inhibiting presence, Amanda was delighted when he rose to make his excuses: he must, he said, most reluctantly, leave them for a few moments. If it was indeed John in the Ambassador's box, surely this would be his cue to join them. But on the other hand, the opera was no place for two unescorted ladies. Amanda half hoped, half feared that Julia would object, as she well might, to her cousin's leaving them, but, as always, she was his willing slave, and Amanda did not feel she could do more than urge him not to be long gone and then, as if accidentally, move with Julia to the shadowy back of the box and hope that their solitary condition would not be too evident to the rest of the audience.

She was soon to regret letting Vespucci go. She noticed that young Canzano and the Princess Colonna's cousin, who had shared Vespucci's imprisonment and had, like him, made an elegant appearance tonight, had also vanished from their boxes, then the door of their own box was flung open to admit two portly gentlemen she had never seen before. They stood for a moment, swaying to and fro in the narrow entrance and, it seemed, urging each other forward. Then the shorter and plumper of the two spoke: "Two English ladies." His voice was slurred with drink.

"All by themselves," said the other.

"An insult to the flag," said the first.

"And to the holy name of British womanhood. We'll show these Neapolitan rascals we value our ladybirds as we should. But I forget my manners. Allow me to present my good friend, Mr Smith." His companion bowed solemnly, recovered his balance with an effort and in his turn presented his valued friend, Mr Jones. Then, looking round approvingly, he declared that this was something like, but as public as a goldfish bowl and, before Amanda could even protest, leaned forward and extinguished the candles that illuminated the box. Then, deliberately, he settled himself on one of the gilt chairs at the back of the box and pulled Amanda down on to his lap. "That's better," he said. "Pretty girls, shady corner, sweet music; what could a man ask more?"

Amanda, trying at once to free herself and to protest, was agonizingly aware of the difficulty of her position. To make an outcry was merely to precipitate the scandal she wished of all things to avoid, even more for Julia's sake than her own. But how else could she rid them of their persecutors who were much too far gone in drink for reason? She knew only too well what license Englishmen allowed themselves so far from home, and these were not even gentlemen. To appeal to them was useless. She fought, silently, desperately, and was aware, beside her, of Julia doing the same. But already a hot and sticky hand had found its way down the front of her dress, while another was lifting her chin towards her captor's face. She twisted her head from his grasp and bit his hand – hard. He gasped out an oath and let her go for a moment. She was facing him, hard-breathing across the narrow width of the box, when the door opened behind her.

For a moment, the silhouette of a tall man was outlined against the light outside. He stood thus, a moment, surveying the scene, before he spoke, in English: "You will forgive me, ladies, if I intrude, but are these gentlemen," he paused, "friends of yours?"

"They most certainly are not." In the half darkness Amanda was able to adjust her dress. "Your appearance is most timely. They have been—" she hesitated for the word.

"Molesting you?" He found it for her. "You will allow me the privilege of ridding you of them." And then, in a very different tone of voice, "Come, sirs, you have disgraced yourselves, and annoyed these ladies, enough. There is the door. You had best apologize before you leave us . . ."

It was almost comic, Amanda thought, to see how their tormentors wilted under his scorn. Muttering something about having mistaken the young ladies for friends of theirs, they were slinking out of the box, when the new arrival delivered his last command: "And send a servant to relight the candles, will you? Meanwhile," he turned his back on them before they were out of the box, "allow me, ladies, to introduce myself. I have, in fact, had the pleasure of meeting you both before, but can hardly expect you to do me the honour of recollecting me after so long, and," his voice laughed, "in the dark, too. We have been so long

153

absent from the Mediterranean that I can only hope you still remember Captain Medway who remains, always, your servant, Lady Meynel, and yours, too, Countess Vespucci, or, may I say, Cousin Julia?" And then aware, at once, of their starts of surprise and of how badly they needed a few moments of darkness and quiet in which to collect themselves, he went straight on, addressing himself, this time, to Julia Vespucci: "My cousin and my father send you their kindest compliments, cousin, and beg you will forgive our family for having been something of the longest in acknowledging your letter. Ah," he turned to the door, "light at last."

A little silence fell while a servant with a taper relit the candles. Amanda and Julia exchanged glances, at once relieved and reassuring: no irreparable damage had been done to the toilette of either in their late tussle. Amanda was pale, Julia flushed, that was all. Amanda spoke first: "You are doubly welcome, Captain Medway," she said. "It is not the first time you have come to my aid." But where was John? She would not let herself ask the question, but there was another. "Your cousin?" she asked. "The Countess Vespucci?"

"Why, yes. Shall I remark that it is a small world? I did not know of the relationship when I last had the good fortune to be in Naples, but, if I mistake not, the Countess's mother was my grandfather's cousin. I am sorry, cousin," he had Julia's hand now, "to find you consorting so publicly and so much to your own disadvantage with what I can only describe as the wrong side of your family. Lady Hamilton has sent me to you both with a message – you might call it a command. She begs you will join her in the Ambassador's box for the rest of the performance. You have done yourselves, she says, and, what is more important, the English here, enough harm already. I trust you will allow me to add my urgings to hers. You must be aware that this is no place for you to be unescorted."

Amanda laughed, her spirits miraculously restored by his arrival. "If we had not been," she said, "it has certainly been most sufficiently brought home to us. I do not know how to thank you, sir, for your timely intervention, but as to joining Lady Hamilton . . ." she hesitated.

"How can we?" said Julia. "If we abandon Antonio now, the whole purpose of our coming here with him is lost."

"Abandon him?" Medway looked pointedly round the box. "I should rather have thought he had abandoned you. Do you not realize, Countess that he and his friends are up to their old tricks of holding their revolutionary meetings while the opera is playing? He has used you, shamelessly, for his cover. But, come, the interval will end soon, and I would wish you to be seen safely established in Lady Hamilton's box before it does."

"You are very masterful, cousin, for a total stranger," said Julia.

"You have every right to reproach me." He had an arm of each, now, and was ushering them, with courteous firmness out through the door of the box. "My family has indeed been most remiss in its neglect of you, but that is all to be changed now, if you will forgive us the past and bear with us for the future. You must understand that when your very friendly letter reached him, my grandfather was a very old man indeed, too old, I fear, to change his ways. He told no one he had received it, and it was by purest luck that my cousin, his heir, found it among his papers after his death."

"Oh," she digested this. "He is dead then, the poor tyrannical old man?"

"Yes, and may the old quarrel die with him. My cousin has family cares that preoccupy him," his voice was cold, then warmed again, "but my father and mother send you their kindest love, and their earnest entreaty that you will lose no time in joining them in England."

"They are most kind," said Julia stiffly. "Ten years ago, when my mother died, their invitation would have been very welcome, but now," she said proudly, "now I am Neapolitan."

"You are likely to be a Neapolitan exile shortly," he told her. "Have you not heard the news? The French are out in the Mediterranean. Most likely they are headed for here."

155

"What!" Amanda turned to him in amazement. "But where is Nelson?"

"Collecting his scattered fleet to go in chase of the French. His flagship was dismantled and his squadron dispersed by the late storm, and Bonaparte, who has, one must confess, the devil's own luck, seized the opportunity to get out of Toulon. No one knows where he is now, but the best guess is that he is headed for here, to add Naples and Sicily to his conquest of the rest of Italy. I tell you, this is no time for English ladies to be seen hob-nobbing with his sympathizers."

"I am not English," said Julia mutinously, "I tell you, I am a Neapolitan through and through."

He made her a courtly bow. "You conceal it admirably. But here we are, and you had best prepare yourselves for a scold from Lady Hamilton." And he ushered them into the Ambassador's crowded box. Since the number of candles burning in a box indicated its owner's social position, this one was a blaze of light and Amanda was dazzled for a moment as she went forward to greet Lady Hamilton.

"There you are at last, Lady Meynel," said the beauty. "I am to scold you, Sir William says, but, first, here is an old friend of yours who much desires to be reacquainted with you." And then, over her shoulder, "I told you she would come, Captain Purvis."

And there he was, the beloved stranger, bending to kiss her hand as formally as if she had never lain in his arms. But, be reasonable, she told herself, what else could he do? She contrived to greet him, herself, with equal formality and congratulations on his new rank. Then, a safe subject, there came enquiries after Miss Purvis, whom he had seen just before he last left England. The stilted conversation limped on, while she studied him, covertly, from behind her fan. Handsomer than ever, he was taller, broader, filled out and grown up, a man. Now he was asking – how could he? – after Lord Meynel. Almost angry, she longed to shock him into closeness, to tell him, suddenly, of their child. Of course, she did no such thing, but listened politely as he spoke of the English mission in Naples: they needed food and water for Nelson's fleet which was mustering for the chase, and news, if possible, of Bonaparte's whereabouts. She listened and answered almost automatically, aware, as she did so, of the lively conversation still carrying on between Julia and Captain Medway. He was teasing her, with a cousin's warm familiarity, about her ignorance of England and things English, and promising himself the pleasure, as he said, of educating her, when he got her home.

"And how do you propose to do that?" asked Julia in the same rallying tone. Amanda had never seen her so lively.

"Why, what but carry you off on my ship if necessary – when we have dealt with this little matter of Bonaparte, of course. I hardly think you would relish a sea battle, cousin."

"On the contrary," said Julia, "I should like it of all things. But do you truly hope to catch Bonaparte?"

"Of course. We have had a setback, it is true, but Nelson is not the man to let himself be discouraged by that."

"Oh, Nelson, Nelson," exclaimed Julia, "You sailors are a little mad, I think, about him." She turned to Amanda. "Did you find him so awe-inspiring a figure, my love?"

"Why, no," said Amanda, "I thought him a little, posturing man, but then," for a moment she allowed herself to look at John, "I was somewhat preoccupied the day I met him."

Lady Hamilton had heard her. "Hush," she said. "You are talking treason – and, besides, the music is beginning and this is my favourite act."

They fell obediently silent and settled into their seats in the crowded box, the men standing at the back. Amanda was soon aware that in her sparring with her new found cousin, Julia had not forgotten her other one. Pretending to concentrate on the music, she nevertheless darted many an anxious glance about the auditorium. At last she let out a little sigh of relief. Following the direction of her eyes, Amanda saw that Antonio had reappeared with young Colonna in his family box. From then on, Julia seemed able to relax and enjoy the music, although Amanda personally had her doubts as to the wisdom of the two young revolutionaries appearing so publicly together.

Even Mozart could not make the rest of the evening anything but interminable to her. More than anything, she longed for a chance to speak alone to John. And yet, if by some improbable fluke such a chance should arise, what would she say? How could she, in face of his cold formality, tell him of their child? Better, perhaps, if the opportunity did not arise.

The box was hot and smelt of tallow and patchouli. Her head began to ache, the music washed over her unnoticed. Only the outburst of talk and applause at the end of the opera aroused her. Lady Hamilton had risen. She did not, she said intend to stay for the farce, but invited them all back to supper at the Embassy, she would sing them her favourite aria from the opera they had just seen and, Amanda knew, they would tell her how infinitely she excelled the diva they had just heard. But there was no avoiding it, and, indeed, for Julia's sake, she knew they must go.

It was cooler at the Embassy, and an ice and a glass of champagne helped to revive her, but still she found herself counting the minutes until she could politely leave. Perhaps this was partly because John had contrived to attach himself to Julia now, while she found herself being squired by Captain Medway. It was ungrateful of her, she felt, to pay him such scant attention, but her eyes could not help but follow John and Julia as they moved about the room. Besides, her headache was worse than ever. It was a relief to her when Lady Hamilton began to sing, and politeness allowed her to be silent. At the end of the song, Captain Medway touched her arm, and spoke under cover of the applause: "I hope we are not to have the famous attitudes too. Lady Meynel, I earnestly wish a word alone with you."

"With me? Alone?" She looked at him in surprise.

He laughed. "No need to look so alarmed. I am not going to make you a passionate declaration, though," he was leading her out onto the darkness of a balcony, "I should not be sorry to have the world think so."

158

She could not help laughing. "And what about me?" Fantastic, after all she had gone through, to be able to talk of reputation so lightly.

"Why, you would but be thought to be making a graceful concession to the customs of the country. But, seriously, Lady Meynel," they were alone now, "I have a favour to ask of you."

"I owe you much, Captain Medway. If it is something I can do, you may count on me."

"I thank you. Well then, first, a question you may not like. Your friend – my cousin – is she to be trusted?"

"Julia? To be trusted! What can you mean?"

"Why, just what I say." Impatiently: "Can I trust her or is she too deep embroiled with that cousin of hers?"

"That cousin," said Amanda sharply, "has been all the family she has had to bless herself with."

"You are a good friend." She sensed his smile in the darkness. "And I – or rather my family – stand rebuked. But my grandfather was an old man; I hope the Countess will find it in her heart to forgive him. And – you have not answered my question."

"I think you must put it more clearly first. I would trust Julia with my life – but I would not ask her to do anything that might hurt her cousin."

"Why, nor would I. I hope I have more sense than that. But you are in the right of it, Lady Meynel. I must first begin, must I not, by trusting you."

"It might save beating about the bush."

"Precisely. Well then," we are here, as you know, to negotiate for supplies of food and water for Nelson's fleet. Without them, we have no chance of catching Bonaparte since we shall have to return to Gibraltar in a few weeks' time, leaving him free to – I know not: take Naples, very likely." He sounded entirely unconcerned, and Amanda, thinking of her child, could have hit him. If he noticed her reaction, he did not show it, but continued in the same tone of calm reason: "Nelson is well aware of the difficult position in which the Neapolitan court must find itself. Under the terms of their treaty with France, they can only permit four British men-of-war at a time in any of their ports. However great their sympathy for us – and there is no doubt, at least, of the Queen's – they can hardly connive at so flagrant a violation of the treaty as would be involved in our fleet's coming here, to Naples for supplies. When they declare that to be impossible, we propose to suggest that it could be done as expeditiously – and with less publicity – at Syracuse."

"Ah." Amanda was beginning to see.

"Quite so. My cousin has vast estates, and, no doubt, vast influence there."

"I am no longer surprised," said Amanda dryly, "that your family has thought fit, at last, to forgive Julia her crime of being born. Tell me, did they take much persuading?"

"Now you are being too hard on me, Lady Meynel. You must believe that I have always hoped for a reconciliation with the countess. I admit that I found this a convenient occasion for persuading my parents to abandon what had never been a quarrel of their choosing. Patriotism, Lady Meynel, is a powerful argument."

"Quite so. But you still find yourself wondering just how powerful, under the circumstances, it might be with the countess."

"Yes." He was grateful for having his point so quickly taken. "What I should like," he went on, "would be an invitation to visit my new-found cousin on her estates. Once there, I could make the necessary arrangements, with her help, so that when our fleet arrived all would be ready for them. The less time, for all kinds of reasons, that our ships spend there, the better."

"It is a pity," said Amanda, "about Vespucci."

"The cousin? Yes, I for one, could wish him safely back in Sant' Elmo. Nelson would not thank me for a reception committee composed of the French fleet when he reached Syracuse. We wish to choose our own time and place for destroying them. You think she is bound to tell him?"

"Yes, and he is no fool."

"If it was a party? An impulsive invitation? Would you come too, Lady Meynel?"

She laughed. "Now you are going too fast for me, Captain Medway. I have a husband and child to consider."

"Bring them with you. The more, for our purposes, the better."

Again Amanda could not help laughing. "You had best get your hostess to invite you first. It is true," she added thoughtfully, "that Julia has been pressing me to visit her at Syracuse. It might do . . . she would have to invite Vespucci too, of course . . . She was thinking aloud. "I think it could be managed, if Julia would agree. As for trusting her with that secret, you may trust her absolutely. You had best ask her, had you not?"

"Thank you, Lady Meynel. I will." He bent to kiss her hand.

Back in the crowded rooms, they found John Purvis still at Julia's side, and Amanda, stifling a little quirk of jealousy, told herself that this was doubtless all part of the plan for the more convenient victualling of His Majesty's ships. What cold-blooded creatures these officers were. She watched with amusement tinged with irony as Medway and Purvis changed partners. Now John had her arm and was leading her to the refreshment room, while Medway squired Julia out to the cool balcony from which they had just come. Still, at last she was with John. She smiled up at him. "It has been a long time." It was the nearest she would come to a reproach.

"Too long." And this, it seemed, his nearest to an apology. "I do not need to ask you how you are: your looks tell their own story."

"Thank you." Conscious, still, of her nagging headache, she thought she would have liked to be asked how she felt. "And you – I am to congratulate you on your promotion." Suddenly, it seemed merely a parody of a conversation she had once had with Captain Medway. As he bowed his acknowledgments, she changed the conversation to an easier subject, though one that they had, perhaps, already exhausted: "Your aunt is well?" She had asked him before, but no matter.

"Yes." He handed her a glass of iced lemonade. "But older."

"So are we all."

"You do not show it."

"Thank you." Controlling her voice with an effort, she was seized with a desire to scream, to throw her lemonade at him, to do anything to put an end to this civil farce. Had she longed, all these years, for the happiness of a few minutes' talk with him, only to be mocked with these platitudes? It was perhaps as well that Lady Hamilton chose that moment to put an end to her party by the prima donna's simple expedient of proclaiming herself exhausted. As the guests began to take their leave, Captain Medway and Julia reappeared, and the invitations to stay at Syracuse were formally given and as formally accepted.

Amanda smiled at Captain Medway. "You are a skilled negotiator."

"I had good advice." He smiled back.

Obstinately, she dreamed that night of happiness. Surely, at Syracuse, there would be time for her and John to find each other again. No wonder if he had been shy and ill at ease at Lady Hamilton's, with all the gossiping world about them. Away there, in the quiet of Julia's estates, everything would be different.

But morning brought bitter disappointment. News of the arrival of the British ships had brought Lord Meynel hurrying from his other home to his wife, and he had not, it seemed, lacked kind friends on the way to tell him who were the ships' officers. He joined Amanda at her late breakfast with a face black as thunder. It was so long since he had taken the slightest interest in her activities that she had let herself dream her way into a fool's paradise. The awakening was unpleasant.

"Let you go making a public fool of yourself in Syracuse, with that Jacobin countess of yours, and the last man on earth you should even be seen talking to? I'll see you in hell first." He meant it.

She protested, but knew it to be useless. He proceeded to read her a lecture on evil associates, which came, she thought, somewhat comically from him. But he had his ammunition ready. The Queen, had dropped a hint, or the King had done so for her, she could not make out which. Their Majesties, it seemed, had had early information of the events of the night before, and had lost no time in acting on it.

Lord Meynel pounded the table. "I have told you before," he said, "but do not propose to have to do so again, that the Countess Vespucci is no friend for you. I am delighted to hear that she proposes leaving for Syracuse; she cannot go too soon for me. As for you, I'll hear no more about it. You have harmed yourself and me enough already by your association with known revolutionaries."

"But if she is to be taken up by her English family?" Amanda did not feel herself entitled to explain just what claim Julia was likely to have on English gratitude. That was not her secret.

"English family! Pah! A parcel of sugar bakers, no doubt, or tea merchants, at the best of it. No, no, I tell you, I have had enough. I am glad to hear your draggle-tailed countess is to leave for her estates, since it saves me the trouble of ordering her out of my house and will make it easier for you to cut the connection. As for your going with her; it is out of the question, and we will not discuss it further."

Nor would they. What was the use? With a hand that shook, Amanda poured her husband a cup of the black Indian tea he liked, and withdrew to warn Julia to keep away from the breakfast room. It was equally impossible not to explain what was the matter, and awkward to do so. But Julia was blessedly quick in the uptake. "I understand," she said. "I am only amazed at the speed and efficiency of Her Majesty's information service. Which of our dear friends at the opera do you think hurried off to her secret room to report on us? Do you wonder at my cousin's rebelling against so iniquitous a system?"

"But, my love." Amanda felt bound to put the protest. "Have you considered that it may be the very rebelliousness of your cousin and his friends that has brought about the

163

system? You yourself have told me what a liberal-minded ruler your Queen used to be before she was terrified by the fate of her sister and brother-in-law of France. In all honesty, can you blame her for wishing to avoid their fate?"

Julia sighed and shrugged. "In all honesty," she said, "no. I tell you, Amanda, I had never thought to see the day when I would gladly contemplate leaving my home and all my friends here, but I found myself tempted, last night, to tell that new cousin of mine that I would accept his offer to arrange my passage to England and throw myself on the mercy of my relatives there. I do not like the way things are going here."

Nor did Amanda. Not only unpleasant in itself, her husband's sudden and unwonted intervention in her life had been a rude reminder of the explosive forces underlying the gay surface of Neapolitan society. Once more, seizing what seemed a propitious moment, she urged that they go home to England, and once more he refused angrily even to consider the suggestion. When she pleaded the possible danger to little Peter if the French should indeed attack Naples, he turned on her roundly. "Do not try me too far, my lady. I treat your bastard as my son, for my own reasons, but do not delude yourself that I feel towards him as a son. My real children are here, in Naples, and I intend to stay with them. If it inconveniences you, I am glad." And then, attacking on another ground, "When, pray, does your revolutionary friend intend to relieve my house of her unwelcome presence?"

"If she heard you speak like that, she would leave today."

"Then I wish she had."

To Amanda's relief, he left it at that. The plans for a casual visit to Julia's Syracuse estates were going far from smoothly. To begin with, there was the miserable fact that Amanda herself could not go along to act as chaperone. In her own bitter disappointment she had not, at first, realized what a difficulty this would involve, but it was, of course, out of the question that Julia should entertain

164

two unmarried officers without the respectable presence of some married woman. She had no suitable relative among the Vespucci clan, and it was the resourceful Captain Medway who provided the solution. He had, it seemed, a family connection with a Lady Knight and her musical daughter Cornelia who had been residing in Naples since the French had taken Rome. He was sure he could persuade them to spend a free holiday in Syracuse, if his cousin would permit him to make the attempt.

Julia laughed and shrugged: "Of course," she said. "What a capable cousin you are, cousin. I cannot imagine how I have contrived to conduct my life so long without your help. Amanda, am I not fortunate?"

"You most certainly are." Amanda was digesting the bitter fact that Captain Medway had called upon them alone. Presenting his friend's apologies, he had said something not quite convincing about business at the Embassy. It was so unlike him to fail to convince, that Amanda had been certain that the apology was entirely of his own concoction. John had simply not wanted to come. It was a thought almost too painful to be born. Perhaps, after all, it was best that she did not accompany them to Syracuse. Why expose herself to further misery?

But later she rebuked herself for a fool. Of course John had not wanted to come. He was too sensitive to intrude in the house of the man with whom he had fought. She had been absurd ever to imagine that he might. But then, hope is absurd. Now, hers was all focused on seeing John once more before he sailed. For the Knights had accepted with enthusiasm and arrangements for the party to Syracuse were soon completed. Antonio Vespucci had refused his cousin's invitation in no uncertain terms. He was done, he had told her, with leading strings, and had affairs of his own to attend to in Naples.

Amanda had been amazed and delighted at the calm with which Julia accepted this rebuff. At long last, her cousin's hold over her seemed to have slackened. Was it, perhaps, as a result of the appearance of her other, English cousin? Amanda suspected so, and felt a curious

165

little twist of jealousy, of which she was instantly ashamed, at the prospect of happiness that seemed to be opening out before her friend.

Captain Medway was to escort Julia and the Knights on their journey to Syracuse, where John Purvis would join them with the fleet. Speed was essential; at any moment the French fleet might be sighted; Amanda helped Julia pack and dropped a few quiet tears among her shifts. John had sailed without coming to say goodbye.

# Chapter Ten

Days of tension and terror followed, with rumour and counter-rumour rife in the streets of Naples, and all eyes turned daily to the horizon whence Bonaparte's ships might come. The Jacobins watched with hope, and talked openly in the streets of the hour of delivery. At the opera, the French Minister's box was crowded with would-be revolutionaries, who risked the Queen's wrath in their confidence of approaching victory. And on the other side, Sir William Hamilton celebrated King George III's birthday on the fourth of June with a splendid dinner for the English colony and announced, amid frenzied applause, the imminent arrival of Sir Horatio Nelson for their defence . . . But the days passed and still the blue horizon was empty.

Then, gradually, news began to trickle through. Bonaparte had attacked, not Naples, but Malta, which he had taken. Then he had sailed again – no one knew whither. But at least it had clearly not been to Naples this time. And still the city waited, with Jacobins and loyalists living together in a state of uneasy truce. At last, Captain Troubridge sailed into the harbour one fine June morning with the news that Nelson was hove-to out in the bay. But he had come not to bring but to ask for news . . . And Sir William Hamilton had none to give him. The English fleet sailed away again without entering the harbour, to continue its search for the French. And in Naples, as one hot anxious day followed another, nerves frayed and tempers rose. For Amanda, general anxiety was exacerbated by a total absence of news from Syracuse. What was Julia doing?

June dragged into hotter July, and people who would

normally have retired to cool country or seaside villas still lingered on in Naples. Society was hectically gay. Open-air entertainments alternated with midnight dancing and Amanda had just driven back from a royal ball at the palace of Caserta one hot July morning when Julia was announced. She greeted her with enthusiasm and a flood of questions, which Julia, who was in excellent looks, countered with laughing denials. There was, she said, no news yet. Oh, yes, the fleet had indeed come to Syracuse for water and provisions, but they had been tired and jaded from an unsuccessful search for the French. They had just missed them at Malta and then hurried off to Alexandria, on a rumour that the French were headed for there – but had found no sign of them. Then, at last, lack of food and water had driven them back to Syracuse, where Captain Medway had had everything ready for them. "You never saw a man chafe so at inactivity. I think he would have gone mad if they had not arrived when they did . . ."

"He has sailed with them now?"

"Yes." She coloured. "And Captain Purvis too."

"Oh. You saw him then?"

"Of course. With Captain Medway, he was in charge of the operations at Syracuse. I never saw men work so hard. They were both my guests while the work lasted." She sounded oddly ill at ease.

"And where are they now?"

Julia shrugged. "God knows. Sir Horatio received information about the enemy, I believe, the day before they sailed again. But if Captain Medway and Captain Purvis knew what it was, they most certainly did not tell me. They sent," she paused, "they sent you their very kind regards." Then, on a totally different note. "Oh, Amanda, they may be dead by now."

Comforting her as best she might, Amanda had difficulty in restraining her own tears, all John's coldness forgotten in her anxiety for him. It was thin consolation, in the anxious days that followed, that the whole of Naples was in a state of similar tension. And Julia's manifest concern for the fate of her recent guests was a new source of wretchedness to

Amanda. At first, she had been relieved and delighted that Julia seemed at last to have got over her long passion for her dangerous cousin Vespucci, but as the days of shared anxiety passed, Amanda began to suspect that Vespucci's place in her affections had been taken by John Purvis. Torturing herself, night after hot night, as she lay on her bed or paced up and down her room, she weighed up every one of her friend's references to the two captains. She spoke more often of Captain Medway than she did of John Purvis. Surely this was a good sign? No – a bad one; she was doing her best to conceal her preference for John. But then, why should she conceal it? She knew him only as Amanda's childhood friend, of whom Lord Meynel had once been unreasonably jealous. And, indeed, what claim had Amanda on John? She was married, old, shelved . . . Julia was young, beautiful, rich – and free. And, angrily Amanda reminded herself, John's recent behaviour to her had hardly been that of someone who intended to devote the rest of his life to a hopeless passion. What more probable than that during his stay in Sicily he had fallen in love with his charming hostess – and she with him?

Those were hard days for Amanda. It was impossible to talk and think of anything but the fate of the English fleet, and yet the subject, as between her and Julia, became increasingly fraught with discomfort. More and more convinced that her friend was in love with her lover (and yet, what right had she to call him that?) Amanda sometimes wondered whether to challenge her with it, and, indeed, half suspected that Julia was only waiting a cue from her to pour it all out. But – it was too much. She could not trust herself in such a conversation. It was, she sadly admitted to herself, on the whole a relief that her husband's dislike of Julia continued, so that they were only able to meet in public places, where conversation, inevitably tended to confine itself to generalities.

One close September morning, Amanda accompanied Julia on a visit of duty to Cornelia Knight and her ailing mother. They found the two ladies in animated conversation on their balcony. Miss Knight was peering out to sea through a telescope. "The blue ensign," she exclaimed. "I am sure it is blue."

"Let me look," her mother almost snatched the instrument from her hand. "Excuse us, ladies," her greeting was of the most perfunctory. "There is a sloop this moment come into sight beyond Posilippo. We are convinced she is British. If only it is news of Nelson at last."

Time passed. Talk was limited to exclamation and conjecture as they passed the telescope about between them. At last there was no longer room for doubt. The sloop was indeed British, the burning question now what news she brought. A boat pulled out to her from the shore, and still Amanda and Julia lingered with the Knights, watching two officers on the deck who awaited its arrival. From their uniform, recognizable now through the telescope, it was evident that one was the commander of the sloop and the other a captain doubtless on his way home with dispatches. It meant news at last. By mutual consent, the four ladies made ready to go and call at the Embassy, where the officers must also be going. It was long past Amanda's dinner hour, but what of that? It had been, so far, impossible to distinguish the features of the two officers: either of them could be John. Impossible to go home . . .

Julia, she knew, had had an engagement with her singing master, but she, too, appeared to have no other thought but to hurry to the Embassy for news. News, of course, as they both made clear, not of individuals but of the fortunes of the fleet . . .

As usual, the streets were crowded with loiterers and Amanda found herself infuriated, as so often before, by the Neapolitan convention that ladies must always drive in their carriages, however short the distance. By walking, and using the steep lanes and flights of uneven steps with which the hillside city abounded, they could have reached the Embassy in ten minutes. But by the time her coachman had been aroused from his siesta and the carriage brought round for them and then made its tortuous way through the crowded streets, more than half an hour had passed.

170

The officers had reached the Embassy before them. All was bustle, confusion and delight. Most of the other members of the British community seemed to have got there already, and for a while Amanda and Julia, making their way as best they could through the crowded rooms, could only learn that there had been a glorious victory. Nelson's name was on every lip. He had achieved, it seemed, another masterpiece of daring strategy. But where – and at what cost?

The enthusiastic phrases came thick and fast: "Alexandria," "Aboukir Bay," "The Nile," "Complete destruction of the French fleet . . ." "Bonaparte cut off in Egypt . . ."

"And our casualties?" Amanda managed to interject a question.

"Oh, heavy, I have no doubt," said the turbaned dowager she had stopped in mid-exclamation. "Dear Sir Horatio is so daring; his casualties are always heavy."

If true, it was scarcely consoling. Amanda and Julia set themselves to work their way through the crowd to the further room where they might expect to find Lady Hamilton. Miss Knight and her mother, more philosophical because less intimately concerned, were soon left behind in the crowd, but Amanda presently contrived to peer round the shoulder of a massive blonde and so look from the doorway of the second apartment across the room to where Lady Hamilton was engaged in animated conversation with a tall British officer. Impossible to see his face as he inclined his head deferentially towards a stream of questions from the enthusiastic Ambassadress, but surely she knew those broad shoulders under irrepressible curling dark-red hair.

"It is Captain Medway," she told Julia. "Can Captain Purvis be with him? I do not see him."

"No doubt he is with Sir William," said Julia. "But we do not know that it is Mr Purvis."

Her doubt proved only too well-founded. A young lady beside her in the crowd turned to set her right: "No, no, it is Captain Capel who is come with Captain Medway: he is to go home with dispatches. Captain Medway prepares the reception of the fleet."

171

"Reception?"

"Yes, Nelson is coming. I heard Captain Medway telling Lady Hamilton and thought for a moment she must swoon with delight. But, look, Captain Medway is coming this way!"

And indeed, Medway had disengaged himself for a moment from the stream of talk that was pouring over him, seen Amanda and Julia and made his excuses to Lady Hamilton. The crowd, so impenetrable before, opened with sighs of admiration to let him through, and he made his way, with here a bow and there a greeting, to where Amanda and Julia stood. He took Amanda's hand. "I bring you good news," he said.

"A glorious victory," she said almost mechanically. "But," she was aware of Julia, tense at her side, "is the news all good?"

"Our casualties, I fear, have been heavy, but there are no friends of ours among them." He was speaking to Julia now, as he kissed her hand. "Though I fear you will have to condole with our friend Purvis when you next see him. By the most devilish bit of bad luck in the world, his ship ran aground as we sailed in to attack, and he could only look on and fret his heart out during the engagement. He will need," he smiled impartially at the two of them, "the very gentlest handling."

"Oh, poor John," Amanda could not help it. "But at least he is not hurt!" And then, conscience-stricken: "And nor are you, Captain Medway?"

"Not I!" He turned again to Julia: "I have a message for you from Sir Horatio, Countess. 'Tell her,' he said. 'that we owe our victory to her goodness.' He will tell you so himself, I hope, soon."

"He is really coming?" asked Julia.

"Yes, the fleet is to refit here. This news, I collect, will make an end of the farce of Neapolitan neutrality and they will show themselves the friends to Britain that they have always wished to be. Most of them."

"Yes." Julia looked thoughtful and Amanda knew that she must be wondering how her cousin would take this

172

news. For him, and for his friends this resounding defeat of the French must be the death knell of hope. But on the surface, everything was delight and enthusiasm. The *lazzaroni* shrieked their pleasure outside the palace, while inside it the hysterical Queen embraced her children with tears of joy, crying out on "brave Nelson, saviour of Italy," while even the King showed signs of relief and pleasure.

As for Lady Hamilton, she was in a seventh heaven, and drove about Naples with a bandeau on her hair reading *Nelson and Victory*. Her dress, she wrote to the hero of the Nile, was '*á la* Nelson; even my shawl is blue with gold anchors all over; my earrings are Nelson's anchor; in short, we are be-Nelsoned all over.' She was delirious, she said, with joy, and had fainted when she heard the glorious news. She was soon busy preparing for the hero's triumphal reception. The Embassy must be illuminated; the hero's initials, twined with a Maltese Cross must be erected at the door, there were wines and provisions to be laid in for the banquets she would give in his honour. '*My dear Lady Hamilton,*' he had written to her, '*you will soon be able to see the wreck of Horatio Nelson. May it count for a kindly judgment if scars are marks of honour.*' And Sir William, in his turn, congratulating their 'bosom friend' on his victory, wrote, 'Come here, for God's sake, my dear friend . . . Emma is looking out for the softest pillows to repose the few weary limbs you have left.' For the hero of the Nile, who had already lost an eye and an arm, had been wounded once again in this his most glorious victory. Thinking himself dying, he had thought of his wife, at home in England, but when he began to recover, he remembered Lady Hamilton.

Meanwhile, in Naples, everything was excitement and fireworks. The unmanageable *lazzaroni* had defaced the insignia outside the door of the French Embassy and there were rumours of secret moneys being given to them to encourage them in their loyalist enthusiasm. As for M. Sieyes, the French minister, he thought it best to stay indoors and even his wife and her pug hardly dared to appear on their balcony. Julia, paying an early call on

173

Amanda, reported that her cousin Antonio had left town. The Jacobins were keeping very quiet these days.

The general enthusiasm reached fever pitch when Nelson finally sailed into the harbour in his crippled *Vanguard* which had had to be towed for part of the journey from Aboukir Bay. The whole harbour was alive with small boats, and Sir William and Lady Hamilton were rowed out in their barge, accompanied by musucians who had been industriously learning to play 'Rule Britannia' and 'God Save the King', with an additional verse written by the talented Miss Knight:

> 'Join we great Nelson's name,
> First on the rolls of fame,
> Him let us sing.
> Spread we his praise around
> Honour of British ground
> Who made Nile's shores resound
> God save the King.'

Swung onto the decks of the Vanguard, Lady Hamilton took one look at her battered hero, exclaimed, "Oh God, is it possible?" and fainted into his remaining arm. But, as he afterwards wrote to his wife, '*Tears . . . soon set matters to rights.*' Then the King came alongside in the Royal Barge, with its vermilion pennant, wrung Nelson's hand and called him his deliverer and preserver. '*All Naples,*' said Nelson, '*calls me "Nostro Liberatore",*' and he went on to praise Lady Hamilton to his wife: '*I hope one day to have the pleasure of introducing you to Lady Hamilton. She is one of the very best women in the world . . . an honour to her sex and a proof that even reputation may be regained.*'

On shore, Nelson went once more to stay with his dear friends the Hamiltons. Since Naples was still, theoretically, at peace with France, he could not be entertained at the Palace, but Sir John Acton gave a splendid entertainment for him, and the Imperial Ambassador another one. Those were maddening days for Amanda. Her husband had taken a miff because they had not been invited to accompany the

Hamiltons on their barge to greet the hero of the Nile, and had therefore refused to hire a boat of his own and join the enthusiastic crowds in the bay. As a result, Amanda had had to watch the stirring events of the day from the distant viewpoint of her balcony. Worse still, Lord Meynel flatly refused to attend either Lord Acton's dinner or Count Francis Esterhazy's ball because they had only been invited in the second category of guests – these who were expected to arrive after dinner. "This is your fault," he raged at Amanda. "It is your known connection with those Jacobin Vespuccis that has cost us the invitation. I tell you flatly, if we are not good enough to dine with that jumped-up Admiral Nelson, we'll not give him the meeting at all."

Amanda's only consolation was that John Purvis's *Falcon* had still not joined the crowd of British shipping in the bay. She limped in at last on the morning of 29th September and Amanda, watching her glide into her place in the line of damaged ships, was able to cheer herself with the thought that she and her husband were among the 800 guests who were invited, that night, to sup with the Hamiltons and celebrate the birthday of the Hero of the Nile. Receiving the invitation, Lord Meynel had looked at it, at first, askance. "To supper?" he asked. "And doubtless, by then, the cream of the guests will have already departed?"

"No, no." Amanda had been to see Lady Hamilton that morning. "It is not so at all. Only 80 are asked to dine. We cannot possibly expect to be included among them – they are the cream of the diplomatic colony. But 1,800 are invited to the ball and only 800 to stay, afterwards, for supper. It is a signal honour Lady Hamilton has done us."

He grumbled, but was finally convinced on discovering that several of his hunting acquaintance were delighted to have been invited to the ball alone. "Very well," he yielded, as always, ungraciously. "Best find yourself something fit to wear – and not that red velvet you are so deuced fond of either. Red's a dangerous colour these days. Have you not something in blue and yellow?"

Amanda made a face. The colours of the Neapolitan

army were hardly becoming to her. In the end, she compromised by wearing a ball gown of blue satin and thinking, wistfully, as Rosa dressed her, of the dress of palest blue sprigged muslin with the frighteningly deep décolletage that she had worn to her first ball, so many years ago, in Rye. Then, John had danced with her and told her he loved her. Would he dance with her tonight? Would he let her at least try to comfort him for the bitter disappointment he must have suffered in missing the Battle of the Nile?

Lord Meynel was late, and she had been pacing her room, fully dressed, in an agony of impatience, for half an hour, before he came bustling in. "Well," he said, "are you actually ready? Wonders will never cease." He looked her over critically. "I suppose you will do." It was the nearest he had come to a compliment for years.

Arriving at the Palazzo Sessa, they found the ball already in full swing. Lady Hamilton had excelled herself, and, muttered Lord Meynel, probably gone some way towards bankrupting her husband, by her arrangements. The whole Embassy glittered, a fairyland of lights, and in the centre of the rooms stood a rostral column under a magnificent canopy with Nelson's name and those of his captains. Amanda, eagerly surveying the crowded rooms from the grand stairway as she came down after leaving her shawl, was able to make out the famous little Admiral talking to his hostess in one of the smaller salons. They were surrounded by a group of his officers. She rejoined her husband. "Should we not go and pay our respects to our hostess?" she asked.

"What? And find ourselves mixed up with all that naval riff-raff that surrounds her? I thank you, no. They are all a parcel of great heroes, I am sure, but they do not need me to tell them so. They will have had enough to toad-eating by this, I should think. I hope I am as glad of our victory as the next man, but I do not see why I should be pushing myself in where I am not wanted, to deliver congratulations to which nobody will listen. It is enough that I have come; I do not see why I should have to listen to Sir Horatio's bragging and Lady Hamilton's chatter as well."

Amanda was at once disappointed and relieved. She rather thought she had caught a glimpse of John Purvis in the group of officers that surrounded Sir Horatio and Lady Hamilton and felt that an encounter between him and Lord Meynel in his present surly mood had best be avoided. At any rate, she would much prefer not to be present at it. And she knew her husband well enough to be certain he would seize the first excuse to leave her. It was provided by Captain Medway who soon made his way through the crowded rooms to ask Amanda's hand for the next dance. Almost at the same moment, Julia Vespucci joined them, and Lord Meynel, with an expressive grimace for his wife, thereupon took his leave to make his way, she well knew, to the rooms where enormous sums would change hands over loo and faro. Amanda was frankly glad to see him go, but only wished his greeting to Captain Medway and to Julia had been less perfunctory. Still, she supposed she should be grateful it had been no worse. And at least, now he was gone, she was able to make the enquiries she longed to about the *Falcon*.

"In better shape than her captain," Medway understood her question, she thought, almost too well. "My poor friend Purvis cannot forgive himself for the mischance that deprived him of his share in the battle. He is taking it hard – too hard."

"Oh, dear," sighed Amanda. "He always did take things hard. I wish . . ." she paused. She had almost said she wished he would come to her for comfort. But why should he? And why did she find it so dangerously easy to confide in this tall stranger, whom she had met so few times and yet seemed to know so well?

He had turned to speak to Julia. "You must remind him, Countess, of the prodigies he performed in provisioning the ships. I know he means to thank you in person for all you did for us at Syracuse."

She did not seem to be listening to him. "Here he comes now," she said.

And indeed, Amanda, quickly turning, saw John making his way towards them as best he might through the now almost impassable crowds. Something drawn and closed about him touched her heart. Then he saw them and his face lit up. Her own heart leapt. Did the sight of her really make such a difference to him? But when he arrived he seemed to divide his attention with almost mathematical exactitude between her and Julia. Julia, of course, must, as Medway had said, be thanked for all she had done for the British fleet, though she laughed and made nothing of it. "It is too much honour to have played even so inconspicuous a part in such a glorious victory." Then she coloured and fell silent.

"In which I played none," John took her up on it. "I shall never forgive myself." He was speaking to them both, but Julia answered while Amanda was still beating her brain for words.

"You refine too much upon it," she said.

"Impossible! The greatest victory of the war, and I, for God's sake, helpless, watching it from a sandbank. I wonder I did not kill myself for very vexation."

"You must not say such things," Julia was beginning, when Medway took Amanda's hand.

"Our dance is forming," he said. And then, as he led her away. "It will do him good to talk of it, and he will do so more easily without me there for auditor."

She could not deny the truth of it, nor help a pang of incandescent rage as he placed her in the set that was forming down the centre of the room. John was miserable, and she could not be there to comfort him. But, surely, she told herself, her turn would come. In the meantime she exerted herself to be agreeable to Captain Medway insofar as the figure of the dance would permit. It was pleasant enough. She had always found him easy to talk to, but just the same it was with a curious pang that she saw John lead Julia out to join the last set as it formed up at the bottom of the room. It had not, apparently, taken her long to comfort him.

But Medway was asking her what she thought of their

hostess, and she replied with all the warmth she felt. "Lady Hamilton has been kindness itself to me," she said, "and to many others I could name. Perhaps, sometimes, her very kindness, her enthusiasm, carry her away . . . She is not always quite . . ." she paused, at a loss for words.

He had a wonderfully kind laugh. "You mean she cannot help it if she carries her enthusiasms, at times, almost to excess? I suppose I should ask your pardon for making such an enquiry, but to tell truth, she seems to have our Admiral well and truly in her toils. I shall be glad to see him put to sea again."

"You cannot think—" she broke off. "No, no, it is not possible. She is absolutely devoted to Sir William – you should have seen how she nursed him through his last illness."

"Precisely," he said. "She nurses Sir William." And then, in apparent irrelevance, "He has aged greatly since I saw him last."

"It has been an agitating summer."

"And Lady Hamilton thrives on agitation. Look at her."

It was true. Lady Hamilton, in white satin, diamonds in her clustering curls, her husband on one arm, her hero on the other, was a sight to catch all eyes. True, she was no longer young, nor slender. Her colour was probably not her own; her laugh was too loud for perfect good manners, her voice too ringing . . . But she was every inch the beauty still and there was tonight a something about her, a glamour . . . an illusion . . . What was it, Amanda wondered, happiness? triumph? Or, could it be – love?

"She is splendid," she said.

"Yes," he agreed. "She is splendid, but I wish she would leave our Admiral alone. Look at her."

She was taking her husband and her guest of honour to the room where supper was to be served and, Amanda saw, it was true that she was paying all her attention to Sir Horatio. Sir William, on her left arm, walked along almost like an automaton taking no part in her lively conversation with the great man. But then, Amanda told herself, she was quite right. Sir Horatio was her guest of honour.

As they watched, there was an interruption. A young man in captain's uniform darted forward and intercepted them. Amanda could not hear what he said, but there was no mistaking the fury of his look and gestures. Lady Hamilton went very red, and Sir Horatio very pale. Sir William looked about him a trifle vacantly, as if he could not quite understand what was going on, but Sir Horatio stepped forward between Lady Hamilton and the youth and spoke to him in his resonant voice. "Josiah," he said, "you are not yourself. You will apologize to Lady Hamilton and leave us."

"Apologize to Lady Hamilton!" There was a certain dignity about the young man, despite the fact that he was obviously much the worse for drink. "Apologize to a common whore! I'll do no such thing, sir, nor should you expect my mother's son to do so."

"Good God!" Medway had started forward from Amanda's side. "It is Josiah Nisbet, the Admiral's stepson. I was afraid of this. Will you forgive me?"

"Of course." But he had already gone. Watching, she saw him force his way with courteous insistence across the room towards the little crowd that had already formed round Lady Hamilton and her party. She could not see what happened next, but in a moment she saw Medway and another man escorting Josiah Nisbet towards the door.

"Well!" Julia joined her. "So much for our partners. I collect we are to wear the willow for the rest of the evening, you and I, unless we can make interest with Lady Hamilton for new partners, since ours have left us on her service."

"Oh!" Amanda digested this. "It was John Purvis, then, with Captain Medway. I could not see."

"Yes." Julia laughed. "Their devotion to their Admiral is truly touching. I wish he seemed to merit it more."

Amanda flared up, hardly realizing what a comfort it was to have a genuine pretext for anger with Julia. "Shame on you," she said. "I thought you had suffered enough, yourself, from gossip and slander not to join yourself with

180

the poisonous tongues that have nothing better to do than libel Lady Hamilton."

"Slander?" said Julia meditatively. "Libel? I wonder . . ."

Medway and Purvis did not return to the ball and Amanda, finding little pleasure in Julia's company, was merely relieved when her husband sought her out to suggest that they leave early. The Grassi was shortly to present him with another child, and Amanda could not help finding his anxiety on her account mildly, and yet bitterly touching. Now, having done his duty, as he saw it, by his wife and by the world, he escorted her home and left her at the door of their house with one of the token excuses he was used to make on these occasions. She took it in the spirit in which it was offered. What, after all, had she to complain of?

Captain Medway called next morning to apologize for leaving her so abruptly at the ball. "I hoped to return to you, but to tell truth Captain Nisbet was in no state to be left. He is not—" he paused. "Well, the less said, perhaps, the better." He turned the conversation to ask whether she had recovered from the fatigue of the evening before. "Though I need hardly ask, since I find you in such admirable looks, if I may be permitted to say so."

She laughed. "Certainly you may. I am always delighted to be told I look well, whether it is true or not. But tell me, what news from the fleet today?"

"Less than I could wish. I shall be glad when we are done with these jollifications and back at work again, and so, I am sure, will our Admiral. There is talk of an attack on Malta, and I can only hope it will be soon, for all our sakes. The refitting of the *Vanguard* goes on apace – at least our victory has given us carte blanche in the Neapolitan navy yards. And that reminds me that the *Falcon* sails today for Castellamare, where she is to refit. But perhaps John Purvis has been here already to take his leave of you?"

"No – no, he has not." Amanda was suddenly impatient for Medway to be gone. John might arrive any minute and how could she tell him how she felt for his bitter disappointment if Medway were present? But Medway seemed settled for a long visit, and they had to discuss the likelihood of Naples actually declaring war on France and the curiously inopportune arrival of the new French minister before he finally rose to take his leave. And, thought Amanda bitterly afterwards, she might just as well have enjoyed his sharp and entertaining comments on affairs, for John Purvis never appeared.

Worse still, Julia called later in the day and Amanda was disconcerted to learn, from an accidentally dropped word, that John had not been too busy to call on *her*. But then, of course, he had been her partner; he was compelled by convention to call on her. It was not very adequate comfort, and the visit did not prove a successful one, despite Julia's avowed intention of apologizing for her hasty words, the night before, about Amanda's friend, Lady Hamilton. "You were right, and I was wrong," she said handsomely. "I have suffered too much, myself, from the world's tongue. I should know better than to join in its backbiting. Forgive me, Amanda."

"Of course." But conversation languished. Amanda found it increasingly difficult, these days, to talk to Julia, and confined herself more and more to generalities. Once more, she found herself discussing the chances of war . . . the arrival of the French minister . . . It was a relief when Julia rose to take her leave.

The festivities continued, but behind the enthusiastic crowds, with their cries of "*nostro liberatore*," and "*viva* Nelson," things were moving fast in Naples. Inspired by Nelson's victory, and encouraged by the consequent disorganization of the French, the Queen longed to act against the enemy she loathed. Nelson, too, urged action. The French were just across the Neapolitan border, in Rome. "Boldest measures are safest," he urged, both in person and through Lady Hamilton, who acted more and more these days as British intermediary at the Palace. If Naples did not attack the French, urged Nelson, the French would pick their own moment to march on Naples.

The Queen's powerful nephew, the Emperor of Austria, was less encouraging. He urged his aunt to hold her hand until the French should justify her by attacking first. Then –

182

and not till then – Austria would march to her assistance. In the meantime, he sent her an Austrian General, Mack von Leiberick, to organize and lead her army. Under him, troops were raised and drilled at San Germano, and the Queen rode out in a blue hussar's uniform with gold fleur-de-lys and a white-plumed hat to review them, with Lady Hamilton, of course, in attendance. At her friend's invitation, Amanda went too, and was delighted with the spectacle of the high-spirited troops in their brilliant blue and yellow uniforms. Captain Medway was there, in attendance on Admiral Nelson, and joined her when the review was over and the party settled down to enjoy a characteristically lavish picnic meal of Lady Hamilton's planning. When she commented on the spirit of the troops he shook his head.

"Their spirit may be good enough," he said, "though I am not sure, even of that. Do you know what the King said to Sir William when he suggested dressing his troops in red so that they might resemble their English allies?"

"No?"

"'Dress them in red,' said King Ferdinand, 'dress them in yellow. They'll run away just the same.' And he should know, should he not?"

"I suppose so," Amanda said doubtfully. "But surely General Mack will drill some spirit into them."

"Mack! Why, the man cannot move without a whole wagon train of baggage. He's no more capable of leading an army than I am. I tell you, Nelson is not happy about this day's work. 'The fellow does not know his business,' he said to me. And it's true. Even I could see what a botch he made of it. And this at a review. What do you think will happen when he goes into action?"

"Oh, well." The sun was shining, Amanda was drinking champagne and refused to be depressed. "Perhaps it will not come to war after all."

"But it is settled. Did you not know? King Ferdinand is to lead his troops on Rome as a new Defender of the Faith – of all things. I only hope His Holiness the Pope is properly grateful to him, but I doubt he will be, for between you and me, I think King Nasone has an axe of his own to grind in this operation. He refused, you know, last year, to send the tribute Naples has always paid to the Pope. Now, maybe, he has an eye on a fine slice of Papal territory."

"Do you truly think so?"

"I should not be surprised. Do you know what Nelson calls Naples? '"A country of fiddlers, buffoons and—"' he paused, "excuse me."

She laughed. "No need to apologize. I had heard Lord Nelson's phrase. But he seems happy enough here, just the same."

"Yes, too happy. The best thing, to my mind, about the projected march on Rome is that the British Navy will have its part to play in support. I shall be glad to see Lord Nelson safe away from here." He coloured. "I should not have said that. Forgive me, and, I beg you, forget it."

"Of course." It was impossible to pretend not to understand him when she could see, as she sat, the little group of Lady Hamilton, her husband, and the new Baron of the Nile and of Burnham Thorpe in the County of Norfolk. Sir William was sitting, as he often did these days, gazing, rather vacantly into nothing, while his wife talked and laughed with their guest.

"It means nothing," said Amanda unhappily. "She is so kind, you see. You must admit she has nursed him back to health."

"And now destroys it again with her late nights and all these junketings. You do not understand, Lady Meynel. No one can, who has not seen him at sea, in his proper element. He is a great man, too great to waste himself in this kind of—" an expressive gesture finished the sentence.

"I am sorry you do not find it more entertaining." Amanda regretted the unkind words the moment they were spoken and would have made amends but they were interrupted by Lady Hamilton's secretary, Mr Smith, come to summon Amanda to join her friend for the long drive home. She held out her hand to Captain Medway. "Forgive me," she said.

"Of course. These are anxious times. I hope you will

remember that whatever happens, my friend Purvis and I are always yours to command."

"Thank you." It was Lord Meynel who spoke. He had spent his time so far with King Ferdinand, the new Defender of the Faith, and now greeted his wife with unusual courtesy. "I am glad to know we have such good friends," he went on. "Who knows? The time may come when we have need of them."

# Chapter Eleven

"They have marched at last!" Lady Hamilton had paid a morning call on Amanda to give her the news. "They left at dawn this morning. Is it not famous? I told my beloved Queen we should all be wearing the laurel soon. Her army, I am sure, is irresistible, and the French already confused and despondent since the news from Egypt. As for that devil, Bonaparte, he is safe out of the way, thanks to our gallant Lord Nelson."

"I hope you are right." Amanda could not help but remember Captain Medway's depressing words on the day of the review. "The French are good soldiers, they say."

"Pshaw," said Lady Hamilton. "A parcel of brutes and bullies. They have had it all their own way so far; let them but taste of defeat and it will be a different story. And they will find themselves awkwardly placed in Rome, with Lord Nelson at Leghorn, and Mack battering at their gates. And the Romans, of course, will rise against them. You must remember how they treated the French minister when he insulted their faith."

"Yes," said Amanda thoughtfully. "They tore him to pieces, did they not? Do you know, I cannot find that altogether admirable."

"You refine too much," said Lady Hamilton briskly. "The French are beneath our contempt and beyond our pity." She rose. The conversation had not, somehow, taken the turn she intended. "I am come to bid you attend the gala performance at the opera tonight. The Queen celebrates her husband's march on Rome. All loyal subjects of Their Majesties will attend."

"Quite so." Amanda would have been hard put to it to

explain her own irritation. "But, thank goodness, I am no subject of Naples. Still," she hurried on, aware of having gone too far, "I shall, of course, attend the performance. It was good of you to tell me of it. The Queen, then, has no anxiety for her husband?"

"Of course not. Why should she? He has marched at the head of one of the finest of armies, and attended by a general," she paused. It was obvious that she, too, must have heard Nelson's strictures on General Mack. "Of course, it will be child's play," she said, as much to reassure herself as Amanda.

"Indeed, I hope so. But I wish it did not rain so." Amanda looked out of the window to the bleak streets, deluged with December rain. "It is not good weather for a march," she said.

"It is nothing," said Lady Hamilton robustly. "Our noble troops will not care about a little rain."

"Our troops?" Amanda could not help the question. She had noticed before to what an extent Lady Hamilton now identified herself with the Neapolitan Queen. And then, regretting the question as she saw her friend's colour rise. "But tell me, are our ships sailed already?"

"Why, yes, I thought you would have known. They sailed at first light. Our house is but a sad place, I can tell you, without our noble guest. But it will not be long, I am sure, before he returns in glory."

She did not prove a lucky prophet. At first, it was true, the news both from Leghorn and from Rome was all of triumph, but still there were disquieting hints for those who could to read. It was true that the French had retreated from Rome and Mack's army had entered it in triumph. But Julia, whose cousin Antonio had, to her delight, marched with his regiment, called on Amanda full of gloomy forebodings. "I do not believe that it is as good as it sounds," she said. "Oh, it is true enough that King Ferdinand has been hailed as the deliverer of Rome and is now comfortably ensconced in his palace there and busy, I believe, in collecting loot, just like the French. But – I had a letter from my cousin today."

"Oh?"

"Yes. He writes, urgently, for all the dry clothing I can send. The march to Rome was a sadly mismanaged business, I fear. Do you know that there were no arrangements made for fording – or better still, bridging, the river Volturno? And what with that and the rain – you remember how it has rained – my cousin says they have lost as many men from sickness as if they had fought a full battle. I do not like to think what the consequences will be if the French should mount a counter-attack now."

But this, of course, was exactly what the wily French General Championnet had planned. He had merely retired to attack the better. A few days later, another gala performance at the opera was interrupted by the arrival of a terrified messenger who summoned the Queen out of the royal box. By morning, the news was all over Naples. The French had launched their attack and the Neapolitan army was in a full and disgraceful retreat which soon deteriorated into a rout. As for King Ferdinand, the Defender of the Faith had lost his nerve entirely, changed clothes with his valet and driven ignominiously home to Naples, babbling of defeat and disaster. He found his wife prostrate with terror and opium, alternating between hysterical tears and a sullen, drugged passivity. Their panic communicated itself to their subjects and wild rumours of despair and flight flew about the city.

Julia had hurried in from her country house at the first news of defeat. Arriving to visit Amanda, she reported that the *lazzaroni* were out in force at the palace gates, shouting defiance at the French and proclaiming their determination to defend their beloved King Nasone to the last drop of blood

"I would not be surprised if he was not even more afraid of them than of the French," she concluded.

"Perhaps he is. One could hardly blame him, indeed, seeing how volatile they are. Though their devotion to him seems genuine enough. Unlike that of the upper classes. Is it true, do you know, that part of the army's rout is due to the desertions of whole contingents to the French?"

Julia paled, and Amanda wished she had not spoken. "I

188

am afraid it is," she said. "I wish I would hear from my cousin."

"I am sure you will soon enough." Amanda affected a confidence she was far from feeling. "I am told that many officers have stood out in this shameful retreat for the gallantry with which they rallied their forces. It is not all disgrace and panic. Doubtless he is with one of the bands who are standing against the enemy. Think, after all, how he distinguished himself at Toulon."

"Yes." Julia sounded doubtful and Amanda could not blame her. When Antonio Vespucci had served at Toulon he had not endured the long ignominy of imprisonment.

They were interrupted by a servant who announced Lady Hamilton. She entered on a wave of patchouli and conscious heroism. "Thank God I have found you both," she began dramatically. "I have been all day at the Palace trying to cheer my beloved Queen. It would wring your hearts to see her. She goes from tears to prayers to cursing of those vile French. Weeps, throws her arms round her poor children, tears her hair with very anguish . . . oh it is a pitiful sight." She spoke with entire approval. Dramatically inclined herself, she was always ready to appreciate the dramatic in others. "As for the wretched King," she went on with unwonted frankness, "what do you think of his blaming all this disaster on his poor wife? He calls her the Austrian hen and talks of petticoat government – after all these years when she has managed his kingdom better than any man could." She noticed their shocked expressions and recollected herself. "Best forget I said that. But it would make you mad to see him turn on her after all she has done for him." She struck her Clytemnestra attitude for a moment, then relaxed into intimacy once more. "I am come to bid you make ready for flight," she said. "I think when Lord Nelson returns from Leghorn, as, please God, he must soon, we shall, between us, contrive to persuade Their Majesties that their best course lies in flight to their other capital of Palermo. Protected by our glorious fleet, they can then continue the war from Sicily."

"Flight?" For the life of her, Amanda could not help

189

sounding shocked. "But surely all is very far from lost. The French are not even over the border yet."

"True." Lady Hamilton had the grace to look embarrassed. "But I fear they soon will be. There have been too many traitors in our midst – and are still, I have no doubt. How can my adorable Queen risk her sister's appalling fate, for herself and for her children, when she cannot even count on the loyalty of her subjects."

"The *lazzaroni* are loyal enough," said Julia. "Did you not hear them shouting outside the palace?"

"Oh, the *lazzaroni*! A parcel of *canaille* like that." The French word came oddly from her lips. "There is no counting on them. No, no, take my word for it, Their Majesties will do their duty when Lord Nelson returns, and withdraw to carry on their fight against the French tyrants. Their preparations are already making, and I advise you to begin yours."

"They wait, then, for the English fleet?" asked Julia. "And what of the Neapolitan navy which has never, so far as I have heard, been found lacking in loyalty? Surely Prince Caracciolo could more properly convey Their Majesties in his *Sannite*?"

"Bah!" said Lady Hamilton. "Do you not know that the Neapolitan sailors are deserting like flies? It is doubtful whether poor Prince Caracciolo, who is loyal enough himself, I have no doubt, can collect enough of a crew to sail the *Sannite*. And who is to guarantee they do not mutiny on the voyage and deliver our beloved Majesties into the hands of the enemy?"

"Well," said Amanda reasonably. "Lord knows we have had mutiny enough in the English fleet."

"But never in the face of the enemy," said the Patroness of the Navy. "Our sailors may grumble now and then, and, indeed, Lord Nelson tells me that, truly, they have grievances enough, but show them the enemy and they'll not mutiny. I would not say so much for the Neapolitans."

There was too much truth in this for argument. Amanda turned to a question closer to her heart. "Are our ships expected soon?" she asked.

"Momently," said Lady Hamilton. "You must know that Lord Nelson, who thinks of everything, had already considered the possibility of a flight to Naples before this disaster. He will be back to save my beloved Queen, never fear for it." She did not need to add, "and to save me."

She was right. A group of English ships sailed into the harbour next day and Amanda, scanning them eagerly from her balcony, was delighted to make out the *Falcon* among them. Her refit must have been completed in time for her to join Lord Nelson at Leghorn.

Even Lord Meynel was glad to see the English ships. His fear of the sea had been swallowed up by his even greater terror of falling into the hands of the French, who were reported to be rapidly advancing on the city. News of Lord Nelson's arrival brought him hurrying home to Amanda. To her amazement, she found herself being greeted as his "dearest love". Answering him coolly, she waited for the explanation of this unwonted friendliness. It came soon enough: "I see the *Falcon* is in harbour," he said. "And Captain Medway's ship, too – the *Illustrious*, is it not?"

"I believe so."

He took a turn about the room. "Does our friend Purvis still command the *Falcon*?"

"I believe so," she said again.

"Good." He came to stand behind her. "You had better write to him at once – let me see – an invitation to dine tonight. And Medway too. They will be glad of some shore comfort, I have no doubt."

"They may be surprised at the invitation."

"Why should they? Everyone knows me, I hope, for a true friend of our glorious fleet. Write quickly, my dear." And then, at a tangent: "I have it on the best authority that the King and Queen plan to leave any day now for Sicily. It is being kept dark, of course, but I am told that the Queen and Lady Hamilton have been busy night after night, preparing the royal treasure for shipment. Sir William, too, has packed up those priceless, boring vases of his. I have no doubt that Lord Nelson will find shiproom for him and his precious wife, as well as for the King and Queen.

191

Their departure will be the signal for a general exodus, and devil take the hindmost. Or rather the French will, which comes to much the same thing. We had best make our arrangements betimes. And, after all, young Purvis owes me his start in the world."

Amanda could only gasp in silence at this piece of effrontery. Could her husband have forgotten the treachery of that "start in the world"? Had he contrived to convince himself that when he sent John Purvis to India he had acted from motives of pure philanthropy? He had at least the grace to show some slight embarrassment now, as he stood over her while, with some difficulty, she began to compose her two notes of invitation.

"Of course," he took a fidgety turn about the room. "As British subjects we are entitled to the protection of our fleet." He paused, it seemed, expectantly.

"Yes?" She made it a question.

"But, no doubt, they will be taking Neapolitans too. After all, if Lord Nelson is taking the Court . . ." once again he hesitated.

"I believe," said Amanda, "that the Queen is making a list of Neapolitans who should be given passage." She thought she could see where he was leading, and could hardly help feeling sorry for him.

"Amanda." He hardly ever used her first name these days. "I have not, perhaps, always been so good a husband to you as you might have wished." He paused a moment, hoping, perhaps, for some disclaimer, then continued. "Now is your chance to show yourself a better wife than I, perhaps, deserve. Will you persuade Captain Purvis to give passage to . . ." he could not get it out.

"To your other family?" She took pity on him and finished his sentence. "Willingly, my lord, but do not, I beg, be hoping too much from my influence with Captain Purvis."

"Oh?" He thought it over. Then, "In truth, I have heard some talk. Well, best ask that Countess friend of yours to give him the meeting here tonight, and if one of you fails to wheedle him, the other will doubtless succeed. I collect she, too, will be wanting to show the French a clean pair of heels – and the Neapolitans, too, unless she intends to throw in her lot with that treacherous cousin of hers."

"Vespucci? What has he done?" Amanda had dreaded this.

"Why, the news is all over town. I heard it on my way here. He has merely gone over to the French with all his men. If you are as fond of that dark-haired witch as you claim, you had best get her here quickly, out of the way of the Queen's vengeance. But send your letters first."

Ignoring him, Amanda rang for a servant and sent him off post haste with an urgent request that Julia come to her at once. That done, she finished and dispatched her letters to the two captains. Her husband heaved a sigh of relief when this was done, but still lingered, pacing about her room, fingering her embroidery frame and the book she had put down when he joined her. She looked up at him coolly. What was coming now?

"Amanda." Once again the unfamiliar, friendly address.
"Yes?"

"The Signora Grassi," he stopped for a moment, then went to it at a rush. "She lives outside the town."

"I know."

"She is afraid – the *lazzaroni* are out of hand – besides, it is on the French line of march. Amanda, there are the children to be considered."

"Yes." Amanda saw it all now. But they were interrupted by a servant who announced with the raised eyebrows of total comprehension that the Signora Grassi was below, asking for her ladyship. "She has all her family with her."

Amanda looked at her husband. Then, "Make them welcome," she said. "Take the children to my son's apartments and bring the Signora Grassi here to me."

Lord Meynel took her hand. "Amanda, I will never forget this."

She could not help a laugh. "I collect I shall not either."

Julia arrived a few minutes later to find the household in a state of chaos. Little Peter had roundly resented the intrusion of two small girls and a baby into his nursery, and both mothers had had to hurry to the scene of action to settle the resulting confusion. Ushered to the nursery by a footman who seemed to be having difficulty in suppressing amusement, Julia found Amanda comforting Peter on her knee, while the dark and buxom Signora Grassi tried in vain to stifle the wails of her three homesick and vociferous little girls. As for Lord Meynel, having gained his point, he had left the house hurriedly: "To learn the latest news."

He returned for dinner full of gloomy information. The *lazzaroni* still surrounded the palace and had actually torn to pieces a royal messenger under the misapprehension that he was a French spy. The King, helpless on his balcony, had had to watch his servant's horrible death.

"I do not think the royal family will linger here much longer after that," said Lord Meynel with the gloomy satisfaction of the bearer of ill tidings. And then, eagerly: "What news from the fleet?"

"None," said Amanda. "I have no doubt that Captain Purvis and Captain Medway have other things to think about than dinner engagements."

"That is all very well," said her husband. "But they might at least have done you the courtesy of sending an answer. Perhaps you should write to them that the Countess here is in danger." It was the first notice he had taken of Julia.

"Danger?" Amanda asked.

"Yes. The Court must have had the news of your cousin's defection by now, ma'am. You would be well advised not to quit this house . . . It is possible of course that they have other things than vengeance to think about, but – you know the Queen. It is not a chance that you would be wise to take. I hope, in the meantime, that you will treat my house as yours."

Amanda could hardly believe her ears. This from her husband who had treated Julia always as the most unwelcome of guests. It was a symptom of the terror that kept his hand now irresistibly shaking – and also, she told herself, with no pleasure – of the rumours he must have heard about Julia and John Purvis.

Lord Meynel had other things to think about. He looked

around as they sat down to a dinner as formal as if there was no talk of precipitate flight from Naples. "But where is the Signora Grassi?" he asked.

Amanda looked him in the eyes. "She dines in the nursery with the children, my lord."

"Oh." He considered a protest, thought better of it, and said nothing.

It was an awkward and anxious meal, its long silences broken by little spurts of abortive conversation, and they adjourned as soon as they possibly could for coffee in another room. And now, at last, a servant announced Captain Medway and Captain Purvis. Lord Meynel let out a little exclamation of pleasure, Julia coloured, Amanda paled. The two Captains were shown in and made their excuses for having failed to answer Amanda's invitation. "We have been—" as usual it was Captain Medway who took the lead, "we have had much to do, and indeed must not stay with you more than a moment." He was addressing Amanda, as his hostess, while Lord Meynel listened eagerly and Julia had drawn a little aside, Amanda noticed, to speak to John Purvis. Mechanically answering Medway, she tried in vain to hear what they were saying.

Then, in an instant, Captain Medway had her full attention and her husband's. "I am come to tell you," he said, "that preparations are making to evacuate the entire British community to Palermo. It will be my privilege, or my friend's, to take you and your family, Lady Meynel. Can you be ready to sail at short notice? We cannot leave before the Court, but must not risk being too long behind them."

"Of course," Amanda said. "I will begin packing at once." She was aware of her husband's eyes on her in mute appeal. "For how many will you have room?" she asked.

"As few as possible. I beg you will bring no unnecessary servants. The Countess, of course, will accompany you."

"Yes." This was more difficult than Amanda had expected, but she knew that she could hope for no help for her husband, who hung, almost pitifully on her words. "Captain Medway," she bolted into it. "I have a favour to ask you. Can you take Neapolitans?"

195

"Only with the Queen's permission. The Countess, of course, we consider as English."

Angrily, Amanda wished that if he would not help her with it, her husband would go away and leave her to make this difficult request without the added embarrassment of his presence. But, she supposed, he did not trust her. She was not even sure that she blamed him. Well, she had promised the poor desperate Grassi and taken her and her bastards under her roof. Besides, she found herself thinking, who was she to cast stones at bastards? "It is for a Neapolitan and her children that I must beg your protection," she said. "It is the Signora Grassi." She raised wide, frank eyes and looked full into Captain Medway's dark blue ones. "You may have heard of her – she is an opera singer of some repute, and," now at last she faltered, then went bravely on, "and a friend of my husband's. I beg you will make an exception for her."

Captain Medway was silent for a moment, looking from her to her husband, then back. Then, "It will be difficult," he said, "but since you ask it, Lady Meynel, I will do my possible. Could the Signora perhaps pass as your maid?"

Amanda laughed with a sudden break in the tension: "I do not think she will like it," she said, "but if it is that or being left behind, I am sure she will."

"Very well. I must ask you to be ready to leave at a moment's notice."

"Will it be soon?" asked Lord Meynel eagerly. "I have heard that the French are over the border already."

"Quite soon. We merely wait on the arrangements of the royal party."

Ignoring the contempt in his voice, Lord Meynel began to ply him with anxious questions about the voyage: how long would it take? did he expect the weather to be bad? Amanda seized the opportunity to drift, as if by accident, to the other side of the room where John Purvis and Julia were deep in what seemed to be an argument. John greeted her with a warmth that delighted her: "Amanda, you are the very person. I have been trying to persuade the Countess that she ought not to venture out again into the streets of

196

Naples; it is dangerous to her on too many counts. You must join your persuasions to mine."

Delighted equally with his use of her christian name, and with the attitude of almost elder brotherly bullying which he had taken up towards Julia, Amanda at once joined in the argument. "It is what I have been saying to her ever since she arrived," she said. "You must face the facts, Julia: your cousin's action has left you very dangerously placed."

"That is all very well," said Julia. "But are you seriously suggesting that I start out for Sicily merely in the clothes I stand up in?"

"I do not see why not," said Amanda. "It will make a change after the Signora Grassi." For the opera singer's arrival had been followed by that of a wagon piled high with all her domestic possessions.

John looked shocked. "The Signora Grassi?" he asked.

"Yes." Amanda wished now that she had not mentioned her. "She accompanies us. Captain Medway has just agreed to take her."

"Are you out of your mind, Lady Meynel? Do you not know what society will say?"

"Oh, society," she had not imagined it possible to feel so impatient with him. "I am sick of society. I wish we could flee it, along with the French."

He looked disapproving, said nothing, and shortly afterwards suggested to Captain Medway that they must take their leave. Amanda watched him go with mixed feelings. How little she seemed to know him these days. Had she changed so very much since those happy far-off childhood times, or had he? Or was it merely the strangeness of their circumstances that made them ill at ease with each other? If only she knew whether it would be on his ship, or on Captain Medway's, that they were to be given passage. Her husband passionately hoped that it would be on Medway's larger *Illustrious*, but Amanda could not quite stifle an old, old dream of sailing across the blue Mediterranean at John's side.

# Chapter Twelve

The anxious days passed, with society apparently as gay as ever. On the 21st of December the Turkish envoy Kelim Effendi gave a grand reception in honour of Lord Nelson to whom he had presented a diamond studded plume of triumph on behalf of his master, the Grand Signior. All the English colony were there to do their hero honour and Amanda, looking at Lady Hamilton as she laughed and talked with Lord Nelson and the dark Turk, found it hard to imagine that she had spent the last few days arranging for the secret flight of the Royal Family, and receiving consignment after consignment of the country's treasure from the panic-stricken Queen. But Lady Hamilton, she saw, was making her apologies now to the Turkish Envoy. Her husband was tired, she was every inch the devoted wife, she must take him home. Lord Nelson at once offered to accompany them, and as they made their way through the crowded rooms Lady Hamilton paused for a moment beside Amanda.

"Do not go to bed," she whispered. "It is tonight. We leave our carriage outside to disarm suspicion and I am away to my beloved Queen to help her in her hour of need. There is a secret passage which will take her safe to the harbour. When they are safe on board, it will be your turn. Mind you are ready." And then in a louder voice. "Yes, a most delightful party, but I must not be lingering here. Goodnight, my love, and be sure you call on me in the morning."

Looking around the room, Amanda saw that there was not an English officer left. She hurried to join her husband. "We had best be going home," she said.

He was about to protest – he had been playing cards, and winning – then caught her meaning, shrugged and rose. "If you insist," he said.

At home, Amanda sent a servant to rouse the Grassi while she hurried to Peter's room, woke him gently and dressed him in his warmest clothes. "It is an adventure," she explained, as he protested sleepily. "We are going sailing on a great ship."

"I would rather go back to bed." But he let her dress him and then fell asleep again on a pile of luggage. The Grassi had appeared by now, blear-eyed and bad-tempered and was angrily directing a stream of servants who rushed to and fro with more and still more pieces of baggage. She held her sleeping baby in her arms, and her two little girls clung to her skirts and wailed in unison.

Time passed. The clock struck one, then two . . . Lord Meynel paced the rooms restlessly, and the Grassi grew more and more impatient. "It is all a false alarm," she said at last. "I know it. That Lady Hamilton of yours has had a jest with you, Lady Meynel, and I, for one, mean to lose no more of my sleep." She turned on her heel and was about to sweep from the room when she was arrested by a knock on the door.

It was one of the midshipmen from the *Illustrious*. Grey with lack of sleep, he told Lord Meynel that his orders were to get him and his family on board at once. "The Royal party are safe on the *Vanguard*. We hope to sail at dawn. There is no time to be lost." Then he caught sight of the Grassi's enormous pile of baggage and looked grave. "We cannot possibly accommodate all that on the *Illustrious*," he said. "Captain Medway's orders were that we must allow as little baggage as possible. I am sorry, ma'am."

The Signora understood no English, but when Amanda explained the position to her she burst into loud hysterics. "It is my all," she screamed, "my little all. Without it, I cannot live, nor my children."

Lord Meynel who had been directing the servants hurried over to her. "My dear, what is the matter?"

199

An angry look told Amanda that whatever it might be, it was her fault.

The Grassi explained the situation in a torrent of eloquence freely illustrated with operatic gestures. But the midshipman was growing impatient. "I am sorry to seem to hurry you, sir," he said. "But my orders are to embark you without delay. You would not, I am sure, wish to be left behind."

Signora Grassi countered this reasonable appeal, when translated, by bursting into fresh floods of tragedienne's tears. Her children caught the infection and also started to scream, while little Peter clung to his mother's skirts and eyed them with a mixture of bafflement and disapproval. Lord Meynel now attempted to make his hysterical mistress see reason, but she was beyond it: her baggage contained all the costumes she had worn in all her various parts . . . it was her livelihood, her security for the future, her children's patrimony. Here a nasty look for Lord Meynel.

The midshipman intervened. "It might," he said, "be possible for me to arrange passage for you on one of the Portuguese ships in the harbour. They have, I believe, more room for baggage."

Amanda's heart sank at this suggestion, but Lord Meynel leaped at it. The result, after a great deal of confusion and rowing about in small boats in the harbour, was that they found themselves deposited, hugger mugger, among a crowd of panic-stricken Neapolitan refugees in the crowded main salon of a small Portuguese merchant vessel. The dirt and confusion were indescribable, and to make matters worse a group of Neapolitan ladies recognized Julia and began conversing about her in venomous whispers with much repetition of the words "traitress" and "Jacobin".

It was therefore with a sigh of heartfelt relief that Amanda saw Captain Medway enter the crowded cabin. He saw her at once, and moved aside a pair of screaming little Grassis to approach. "What madness is this?" he asked. "Do you prefer to travel in this misery?"

Amanda hurried to explain, and to thank him for all his

good intentions on their behalf. He listened with a gathering frown, but could say little of what he obviously thought, as Lord Meynel had now joined them, and insisted that they were very well were they were. The Grassi had established herself on top of her pile of baggage, in a corner of the crowded cabin and it was obvious that nothing would shift her. Captain Medway tried a last appeal. "I do not wish to criticize our gallant allies," he said, "but the Portuguese are not invariably the most experienced of sailors."

This went home. Lord Meynel blanched, and he hesitated for a moment, but a languishing look from the Grassi's big black eyes hardened his resolve. "We are very well off where we are," he said.

"I hope you are right." Medway sounded far from convinced. "But if you are contented with your quarters here, will you not allow me the pleasure of taking Lady Meynel and the Countess Vespucci on the *Illustrious*? I can promise you that they will be well cared for."

Amanda had never been so tempted. The idea of the order and cleanliness of a British man-of-war, the courteous consideration of officers and men . . . But her husband was pale already from anticipation of what he knew he must suffer on the voyage, and the Grassi was all too obviously going to be entirely occupied with her own sufferings and those of her disorderly children. "I cannot leave my husband," she said, "but, Captain Medway, try and persuade the Countess to go with you. I do not think this is the place for her." An expressive glance directed Medway's attention to the group of Neapolitan ladies, who had given up their whispering on his appearance, and now contented themselves with merely looking daggers at Julia.

Always quick he caught her meaning at once. "Yes," he said. "I see. And I have news which may still further complicate your position. We do not sail at once. I think you are right: the Countess will be better on a British ship."

Julia yielded reluctantly to his persuasions and Amanda's. It was obvious that she hated to abandon her friend in this miserable discomfort, but the argument that Amanda and her party might easily be involved in her own unpopularity proved conclusive. At last, with a sigh of relief heavily qualified with jealousy, Amanda saw her take her leave with Captain Medway and turned, herself, to making the best she could of their cramped and deplorable conditions. She missed Julia at every turn and found the Grassi a lamentable substitute, with her airs and graces, and her frank horror at the idea of anything like real work. It was Amanda who found them mattresses and arranged them in the most secluded corner of the big cabin that she could find. She was just wondering, in quiet desperation, whether there was any possibility of rigging up a blanket as some protection against the hostile glances of the Neapolitan ladies who resented equally her Englishness and the Grassi's dubious social position, when the English captain of the ship made a surprise appearance in the crowded and noisy room. At once, he was surrounded by voluble ladies begging, demanding, insisting on better accommodation. He merely shrugged his shoulders as he made his way to Amanda's corner. "Lady Meynel?" She had not been difficult to single out in this noisy crowd.

"Yes?"

"My friend Captain Medway has spoken to me about you. I have persuaded one of my officers to let you have his cabin. It will not be luxurious, but it will be better than this."

She thanked and followed him, aware of more hostile glances than ever, but unable to bring herself to care for them. The cabin to which he took her was surprisingly large and commodious but stank of rotten apples. It seemed like paradise to her, and almost the more so because it was quite obvious that it could only accommodate herself, her husband and little Peter. The Grassi and her dirty and undisciplined children would have to take their chance in the main cabin.

When she explained this to her husband, he frowned angrily and insisted, at first, that in that case he too would remain in the open cabin. She was beyond arguing: "Very well, if you prefer it." She returned to her haven and began throwing rotten apples out of the tiny porthole. As she did so, she saw that the *Vanguard* on which Nelson had embarked the Royal party was beginning to move out of the harbour. To her dismay, the other ships of the convoy showed no signs of following. It seemed that they were condemned to spend another night in the odorous discomfort of the beautiful bay.

But she was to be grateful for this. The wind had been steadily rising all day and towards evening blew a full gale so that even in the harbour their ship tossed uncomfortably and Lord Meynel soon came scratching at the door of her cabin, too ill to care how he abandoned his mistress to the taunts of her enemies.

He recovered somewhat in the morning, when the weather eased, and scouted Amanda's suggestion that they might do better to go ashore again and risk the fury of the mob rather than expose him to what they both knew he must suffer on the voyage. They were still discussing this when the question was settled by the ship's sailing. At first, this was pure relief. The wind was favourable, the air outside the harbour pure and refreshing, and they congratulated themselves on the prospect of a swift and easy voyage.

They had rejoiced too soon. They were hardly out of sight of the town when the wind began to rise again, and all that night the ship battled through a storm that seemed to Amanda to be more like the hurricanes of which, long ago, John had told her. The little ship creaked and groaned; sailors ran about frantically overhead; officers shouted orders in tones that suggested more and more of panic. But Amanda had no time to be afraid. Both her husband and Peter were violently sick and she had hardly turned from ministering to one of them before the other one was crying for her attention. Towards morning, the wind eased a little at last and she ventured out of the cabin for a moment to see if she could find some fresh water for little Peter, who had finally stopped being sick and was crying from thirst.

In the main cabin all was panic, filth and confusion, and she despaired of obtaining any help until she encountered an English-speaking officer whom she had met while accompanied by the Captain the day before. He paused a moment to tell her that the storm was abating rapidly, but that they had been blown far off their course so that there was no hope of reaching Palermo until some time the next day. Most important of all, he told a passing sailor to fetch her food and fresh water.

Returning with the man, she found little Peter crying fretfully on his mattress, then turned to the cabin's one bed where she had left her husband tossing and turning wretchedly in the grip of nausea. To her horror, she saw that he now lay still and silent among the filthy bedding. For a moment, she thought him dead, then felt for, and found a pulse, but one that seemed, even to her ignorance, to beat with an alarming fitfulness. He must have had another seizure while she was away. At this moment, the Portuguese sailor appeared with the provisions the officer had ordered. He spoke no English, she no Portuguese, but she managed, by frantic signs, to drew his attention to her husband's state. He approached the bed, shrugged, crossed himself, pantomimed that he would fetch help and left her.

An age passed. Lord Meynel did not move, and seeing that there was nothing she could do for him, Amanda concentrated on giving Peter a little to eat and drink and telling him a story till he fell into a child's exhausted sleep. Still her husband's condition had not changed, and still no one came. He might be dying, while she sat there doing nothing, but what could she do? She remembered, after his previous attack, that Dr Anderson had insisted he be moved as little as possible. Rest, he had said, was the best treatment . . . She remembered, too, that Dr Anderson had said he would not be answerable for the consequences of a second such seizure. What madness, now, it seemed for him to have risked this desperate voyage – and yet, what else could they have done?

His breathing was getting still more stertorous. Should

she risk leaving him alone and go and try to get help from the unfriendly women in the big cabin? Surely the Grassi would watch by his side while she went to the captain for help? She looked again at Peter, but he was fast asleep now. There was little fear of his waking while she was gone. She hurried through to the large cabin, only to find the Grassi stretched out, dead drunk on her mattress, her children wailing beside her. There was no help here.

Frantic now, she climbed the narrow companionway that led to the deck, and hurried forward to where the Captain was directing the rerigging of the sails. He turned to her impatiently at first, then remembered her and listened with sympathetic impassivity to her story. "I am sorry for you," he said at last. "And for Lord Meynel. Unfortunately, we have no doctor on board. We must just hope," his eyes met hers for a moment, "for the best."

Back in the hot and stinking cabin, nothing had changed. Peter was fast asleep, his arms thrown wide, his hair tumbled, his breathing even. He would be better when he waked. Lord Meynel, on the other hand, was breathing more heavily than ever; his pulse seemed more irregular; his face more congested. Amanda damped a cloth in her precious supply of drinking water and used it to cool his forehead. At least the Captain had promised her enough water and an occasional visit from the English-speaking officer.

The day dragged on. From time to time, a sympathetic, useless, sailor would look in at the door. Once, the Captain himself appeared, looked gloomily at Lord Meynel, muttered something apologetic to Amanda about being short of crew, and left. The wind was beginning to rise again; it would be another stormy night.

Towards evening, Peter woke up, fretful and hungry, and Amanda fed him the least unappetizing of the scraps of food she had been brought during the weary day, washed down with some wine and water. To her relief this had its effect and he fell asleep again before he had had time to feel the effects of the ship's renewed tossing. Lord Meynel, on the other hand, groaned and stirred as the rolling and an even more disturbing sideways motion of the ship recommenced. Presently he opened his eyes and amazed Amanda by trying to sit up. Hope stirred at once: it had not been another seizure after all; he was better.

"Amanda." She had hurried to his side. "I . . ." his voice was hardly audible, "I think I am dying."

"No, no, you are better." She spoke to encourage herself as much as him.

He had fallen back helplessly on the pillow. "I can feel it," he said. "Not much longer now, and I'm damned if I care. Only," he was speaking with more and more difficulty, "my will: damned unfair thing. Sorry, Amanda, been a bad enough husband to you already . . . and where is the bitch when I want her? Help nurse me? Not on your life!" And to Amanda's horror, he burst into a fit of feeble laughter, rolled over on his side, and died.

She had not known death would be so unmistakable. Automatically, she tidied the body and pulled a sheet over it so that Peter, if he waked, should not be frightened. Presently, she supposed, she would feel something. Just now, she was too tired even to think. It was nearly dark now, with the sudden darkness of the Mediterranean. The ship tossed and plunged; the sailors ran about overhead; it did not seem to be so bad a night as the one before. But now it did not matter . . . Peter stirred in his sleep and she covered him again, then, almost without thought, she lay down beside him on the mattress.

In the morning, a sailor knocked on the door, looked in and ran in panic to the Captain, shouting of three dead bodies. Roused by the Captain's arrival, Amanda was able to reassure him about herself and Peter. Appalled at having slept so quietly by her husband's dead body, she agreed almost automatically to the Captain's suggestion of an immediate burial at sea. What was the use of delay? Then, gradually rousing herself, she remembered the Signora Grassi. She must be told, and given the opportunity of attending the service and letting his children see the last of Lord Meynel. Inevitably, the task of breaking the news to the Grassi fell to her lot. She did it as gently as possible, and was equally amazed and appalled at her reaction. Always hysterical, the Grassi burst into a torrent of incoherent accusations, calling Amanda a murderer who had forced her husband to leave the safety of Naples, when she knew how desperately he suffered from seasickness, and even hinting at worse things. Amanda had been alone with her husband: who knew what might not have happened? And why had not, she, the Grassi, who loved him, been summoned.

This was too much for Amanda's patience. "I came to fetch you," she said coldly. "But you were dead drunk." For a moment she thought that the woman was actually going to strike her, but the Grassi, too, was aware of the crowd of interested observers. She contented herself with a furious tirade at what she called this libellous untruth, and with dark hints that justice would be done in the end.

The funeral service was brief and painful, with Lord Meynel's wife and his mistress on either side of the body, and his three illegitimate children howling with their mother. Amanda was later to learn that the fact that she had spared little Peter this scene was seized upon by the Grassi as still another instance of her heartlessness. For the moment, she was beyond noticing anything. The shock and exhaustion of the last few days had caught up with her at last and she collapsed on the deck as her husband's body was thrown into the sea.

When she came to herself, she was back in the cabin. Her first thought was of Peter: how could she have failed him so? She got feebly up off the cot where she had been lying and gave a shudder at the thought that only last night her husband had died there. But there would be time enough to think of him; at the moment she must find Peter. Groping her way up on deck, she felt as feeble as if she was recovering from a long illness. The day was fine, the sea calm, and Peter, looking extremely well and cheerful, was sitting on the deck learning knots from a bearded Portuguese sailor. The fact that they understood not a word of each other's language seemed not to trouble either of them in the least. A great load lifted from Amanda's heart;

207

at least he was none the worse for his experiences of the day before.

Seeing her, her friend the English-speaking officer came over and told her with rough kindliness not to trouble herself about the child; the crew had taken him to their hearts and would look after him. "You had best rest," he concluded, "and try to get your strength back. We reach Palermo tonight, and I am afraid that mad woman below intends to make trouble for you there."

And indeed when they anchored at last close to a group of English ships in Palermo harbour, the Grassi went ashore at once, vowing vengeance on the murderess of her beloved. Since there was, Amanda learned, only one inn in Palermo, she was afraid she must encounter the woman there, before her first passion had worn off, as she hoped it soon must, but to her surprised relief she learned that the Grassi, who had insisted in Naples that she was penniless, had lost no time in hiring an expensive villa near the harbour.

Amanda, on the other hand, found herself very uncomfortably situated. Her husband had brought little ready money with him for the voyage, fearing, quite reasonably, the chances of being robbed by the undisciplined Portuguese crew of their ship. He had relied on cashing at Palermo several bills he had recently received from England. The friendly captain had made no difficulty about handing over all her husband's effects to Amanda, and she had the bills – but they required his signature. Now she regretted with bitter anger the inroads the Grassi had made on their supply of ready money on the voyage. Until her husband's estate was settled, she was going to be very short of money indeed. Her first thought was that she must apply without delay to Sir William Hamilton for the help he was bound, as British representative, to give her. But the landlady of the little inn burst almost at the moment of greeting her, into a flood of semi-comprehensible talk about the hardships that the Royal party had suffered in their crossing from Naples. The poor Queen, it seemed, had staggered ashore, two days earlier, more dead than

208

alive, and one of the little princes, the woman rolled her eyes heavenwards, had actually died on the voyage, only imagine, in the arms of the angelic Englishwoman, the beautiful Lady Hamilton. And now, worst of all, nothing was ready for their Majesties, the Palace cold and damp – "Well, signora, no one knew they were coming!" The Queen was ill from her sufferings and Lady Hamilton and her husband were installed at the palace, helping to achieve some kind of order out of the royal chaos. As for the King, once more the landlady rolled her eyes, "What a man! Do you know, milady, he has brought a pack of hounds with him, and is taking off for the hunting already." It was impossible to tell whether she spoke with admiration or disapproval.

Still volubly talking, she showed Amanda to a little room on the first floor of the primitive little inn. Here was a view of the harbour and Amanda hurried to look out. She had not seen the *Illustrious* when they entered the harbour and now questioned the landlady about her. Oh yes, the woman obviously kept up with all the movements of shipping, the *Illustrious* had come in two days ago, but had sailed, almost at once, for Syracuse. Amanda's heart sank. Julia would undoubtedly have seized the chance to go home on her. There would be no hope of immediate help from her. She asked the landlady about the journey overland to Syracuse but her answer was far from encouraging. The road was bad and, worse still, infested with brigands. If the signora wished to visit her friend in Syracuse, she had much best wait a chance to go there by boat. In the meanwhile, the woman volunteered to see that a letter reached Julia as soon as possible. From her tone, Amanda rather suspected that she had connections among the banditti through whom this would be arranged. She sat down at once and wrote a brief note to Julia, explaining her predicament and begging her to come to her if she possibly could.

That done, Amanda let exhaustion have its way with her and retired to bed in the tiny room she shared with Peter. He had entirely recovered from his seasickness now and his constant company and frank enjoyment of every novelty were her greatest comfort. In Naples, he had been kept from her by crowds of servants, and though she had always longed to see more of him, she had never dared do so for fear of provoking some dangerous outburst from her husband. Lord Meynel had never taken any notice of the child, except to swear at him if he got in his way, and it was not surprising that Peter, after one casual enquiry, had taken no further notice of his absence. It was, Amanda supposed, a kind of a comfort.

For herself, she was amazed to find how much she missed her husband. He had often been cruel, and never been good to her, and yet, she supposed, she had got used to him. She missed him, now, in all kinds of little, curiously painful ways and equally found herself regretting various of her own uncontrollable outbursts of anger against him. What a sad life he had had . . . She thought, as she drifted towards sleep, of his last outburst about the Grassi. That side of his life had not, it seemed, been over-happy or successful either. And then, sleepily, she thought of the Grassi's threats to her and of her own uncertain future. Tomorrow there would be much to do . . . She thought of home, and then, inevitably, she thought of John Purvis. She had heard no news of the *Falcon* since she had left Naples, but surely there was a good chance that she, too, would soon put into Palermo harbour where the English fleet was keeping rendezvous. John must soon learn that she was a widow . . . It was not decent to be thinking these thoughts, so soon after her husband's death. She got up again and prowled about the room in the cold darkness. It was bitterly cold and she had piled all the spare covers she could obtain on little Peter's bed. Now, shivering and disgusted with herself, she crawled in beside him in his little cot and fell asleep at last, soothed by his warmth and quiet breathing.

# Chapter Thirteen

Amanda was roused, earlier than she expected next morning, by one of the inn servants, who announced that a gentleman was below, asking for her. Her heart leapt up. Surely the *Falcon* must have arrived, and this would be John? Not wishing to leave Peter alone, she took his hand and hurried down with him to the inn's one public room, only to find a total stranger awaiting her. A little, bald, sly-looking Sicilian, he addressed her in tolerably good English, and introduced himself as a lawyer, Pietronelli. She hardly had time to look her surprise and acknowledge his not over-courteous greeting when he went on. "I am come on behalf of the Signora Grassi," he said. "She demands her rights."

"Her rights? I do not understand you, sir."

He drew a piece of paper from his pocket, unfolded it with a deliberation intended to insult, and held it out so that she could see without touching it. "I have here," he said, "the last testament and will of his excellency the unfortunate, departed Lord Meynel. You will see that he leaves much of his estate and all his personal effects to his esteemed friend the Signora Grassi. She has sent me to take delivery of them on her behalf."

Cold with shock, Amanda was silent, rapidly reading the crabbed legal writing of the document, which he held, so insultingly, just out of her reach. What he said seemed true enough; rapidly scanning it, she saw the words '*all my personal effects*,' and '*Signora Grassi*'. More convincing still, she remembered that dying apology of her husband's: "My will," he had said, and "damned unfair thing". In her shock and exhaustion after his death she had forgotten all about it, but now she understood. He had let the Grassi persuade him into leaving her everything he could. Rapidly thinking, while she pretended to go on reading, she realized the full wretchedness of her situation. It was true that a large portion of Lord Meynel's estate, and all his expectations, were entailed on Peter. The child would not suffer seriously through this will. But what of the present? So far as she could see, it empowered the monstrous Grassi to take from her everything but her own personal effects and the child's. Useless to imagine that the Grassi, her implacable enemy, would insist on anything less than her full pound of flesh.

The lawyer lost no time in confirming this. "You will find it all quite in order," he said. "You doubtless recognize your husband's signature." And when she did not deny it. "I would urge you, Lady Meynel, for your own sake, and the child's, to lose no time in complying with the Signora's very reasonable request and handing over to her Lord Meynel's effects. You will save yourself," he allowed a little sinister pause, "much unpleasantness by doing so." He stood there, blandly, a little expectantly smiling, as if he thought she would simply hand over Lord Meynel's keys there and then.

She must play for time. "You will forgive me, sir," she said, "but you must realize that I can do nothing on the spot. I must consult . . ." she paused – who should she consult?

Again that smile. "I would not recommend," he said, "that you lose too much time in your consultations. My client is not," he paused for the best word, "a patient woman. She can do you much harm, if she wishes. It is not a pretty story, that of your husband's death."

To her horror, Peter, who had so far been at the window, absorbed by the view of this new city, chose this moment to come running back to her. "What's not a pretty story, Mama?" he asked. "Will you tell it me at bedtime?"

The lawyer saw his chance of tightening the pressure on her. "It is not a story for little boys," he said. "I think your mama would rather you did not hear it."

She was caught, and knew it. But, "Give me till tomorrow," she said. "I must make arrangements for the child and myself."

"Of course." He knew he had won. "Let us say that you will hand over Lord Meynel's effects to me at six o'clock tomorrow night? I am sure I can persuade my client, impatient though she is, to allow you that much latitude." He made it sound as if he was doing her an immense favour. "And here," he produced another document, "is a copy of Lord Meynel's will, which, no doubt, you will wish to peruse at your leisure."

She took it and dismissed him. "I will see you at six tomorrow, sir. Until then, I have much to do."

But what? Left alone, for a moment she despaired. But there was no time for despair. Peter was pulling at her hand. "What did he want, Mama? Why are you looking like that?" And then with a child's instinct to go straight to the point: "He was a horrid man, was he not?"

She answered him as best she might, smoothed the anxious frown from her face for his sake and told herself she should be grateful for the distraction he provided. She had no money for servants. Whatever she did in the next days, wherever she went, Peter would have to come with her. She began by ordering him a hearty breakfast and mechanically drinking coffee while she watched him eat it. He was hungry, and for a while his flow of questions stopped while he ate. She had been holding the paper the lawyer had given her and now smoothed it out on the table and deciphered the crabbed legal script. It was worse than she had imagined possible. Not only had Lord Meynel left all his personal effects to the Grassi, he had made considerable other bequests to her as well. To her, his wife, he had bequeathed out of his great wealth, an income of £1,000 a year – which would stop if she remarried. The residue of his personal estate was left to the Grassi, who would also receive Amanda's share, if she were to remarry. It was intolerable. The fact that Peter, as his heir, would automatically succeed to all the entailed estate was small consolation for the personal insult to herself.

"Mummy!" Peter had finished his breakfast. "Is that my father's will? Do you know, the servants here call me milord! Am I truly a lord like my father?" He jumped down from his chair and pranced across the room, singing gaily: "Milord, milord, Lord Meynel, Lord Meynel."

She could not blame him. Lord Meynel had never done anything to endear himself to him. Why should he mourn his death? But then, she could not blame her husband either. Why should he have gone out of his way for the bastard he had accepted as his heir? She ought, she supposed, to be grateful that at least this iniquitous will contained nothing that cast the slightest doubt on Peter's claim to the succession. In this, at least, her husband had kept his bargain with her.

But the fact remained that he had left her in desperate straits. Thanks to the Grassi's demands on board ship, the ready money they had brought away with them was almost exhausted. She could not cash her husband's bills without his signature, and his will made it impossible for any lawyer to stretch a point for her. Julia, she was sure, would come to her help as soon as she received the letter the landlady had sent off for her, but Syracuse was far off at the other side of the island. Allowing for the erratic brigand-post by which she had sent her letter, she must not expect her for a week or, very likely, considerably more. In the meanwhile, the Hamiltons were her only hope and she decided to go to them as soon as Peter had finished his breakfast. Surely, today, they would be well enough to see and advise her.

She was roused from these anxious thoughts by the stir of new arrivals to the little inn and in a moment Cornelia Knight and her mother entered the room, looking around them with a mixture of distaste and exhaustion. They greeted her warmly and plunged at once into an account of their sufferings on the crossing. First, it seemed, they had been accommodated in appalling conditions on a Portuguese boat, only to be rescued just before they sailed by "that charming Captain Purvis".

"Captain Purvis?" Amanda interrupted. "Is he here, then?"

"Why, yes," Miss Knight looked mildly affronted at this brutal cutting short of a story she had obviously looked forward to telling. "He reached Naples after the rest of the British ships had sailed and took pity on our plight. I believe he is with Sir William Hamilton now, giving him the latest news from Naples, which is of the very worst, I can tell you. What do you think of those fiends of *lazzaroni* sacking the Royal palace immediately after the King and Queen left it? Did you ever hear of anything so monstrous? We are lucky, I can tell you, to have escaped with our lives."

"No," said Amanda, and then, seeing Miss Knight's expression. "I mean yes. I beg your pardon, Miss Knight, I am somewhat preoccupied today." Absurdly, she remembered she had not told them her news. "My husband died on the way over."

Too human to help minding having their own story so effectively trumped, the Knights were also too kind-hearted not to react to Amanda's with warm sympathy and offers of help. They, too, were to stay, force perforce, in this deplorable inn, could they not, at least, look after little Peter for her? "I know you will not wish to leave him with these barbarous Sicilians, the best of whom seem little better than brigands, and you must have much to attend to?"

Amanda accepted the offer with a sigh of relief, and Peter was soon happily engaged in eating a second breakfast with Miss Knight and her mother, who, like him, found themselves famished after the ardours of their voyage. Amanda listened, in honour bound, to a brief résumé of these, then excused herself and hurried to the Hamiltons' villa. Her politeness to the Knights was rewarded. Owing to the delay it entailed, she encountered John Purvis just as he was leaving.

"Amanda!" His appalled glance reminded her at once of her dishevelled appearance. "What is the matter?"

"Everything. Oh, John, I am glad to see you. First, my husband is dead."

"Lord Meynel? Dead?" She could not interpret his expression. "But where is your black?"

"My—" for a moment she did not understand him. Then, horribly, helplessly, she burst into hysterical laughter. "My mourning, you mean? Oh, that is too rich! . . . Oh, John, that passes everything."

He took her arm. "Control yourself, Amanda. Remember where you are." And then, with a harassed look up and down the sun-drenched street, "Come, you are in no state to call on the Hamiltons." He led her, unresisting, grateful, indeed, even for the comforting firmness, the familiar disapproval of his tone, down the dusty street to where a handful of chairs and tables on the dirty pavement proclaimed a little house as some kind of café. Seating her, he ordered coffee. "You are overwrought, Amanda. When did you eat last?"

"Oh, John, what a comfort you are. Do you know, I do not remember."

He called to the black-garbed old woman who had taken his order and told her to bring food as well as coffee. Then he turned back to Amanda. "Tell me about it," he said.

At last, she was able to pour it all out. He frowned when she came to the Signora Grassi's behaviour on board ship. "I knew you were mad to befriend her," he said. "I only wish I had reached Naples sooner. I would not have allowed the absurdity of your taking passage on a Portuguese ship. It seems to me that if ever a man committed suicide, your husband did."

Amanda could not let this pass. "The Captain was kindness itself," she said. "And I do not see that a storm is any worse on a Portuguese ship than on a British one. I believe that Lord Nelson's *Vanguard* had a very much worse time of it than Prince Caracciolo's *Sannite*. But you were right about the Grassi. Wait till I tell you all." And she hurried on to tell him of the lawyer's visit to her.

His frown grew black and blacker. "Monstrous," he said at last. "You will fight the will, of course."

"I do not think so. What is the use? It is my husband's signature; he had the right to do what he wished with his own."

"And leave you penniless in a strange land? Nonsense.

No, no, this must be fought, Amanda, and fought now. If you give that dreadful woman the least trifle that belonged to Lord Meynel, she will have established the principle of her claim, and who can tell where it will end? You must fight her for the child's sake."

"John, I do not dare." She had spared herself the pain of telling him of the threats the lawyer had used to her, but now she saw that she must do so. She had not thought he could look angrier, but now learned her mistake.

"Madness," he said. "You should not have consented to the burial at sea. This has been an ill-managed business from start to finish, but you must not give way now. Give an inch to such threats, and there is no knowing what may happen. Tell that trickster of a lawyer that you must wait instructions from Lord Meynel's man of business in England before you take any action. He cannot possibly object to that, and nor should his client."

She noticed the change of mood, but did not comment on it. "And in the meanwhile?" How restful it was to be given orders.

"Go back to your hotel. I will see the Hamiltons on your behalf. It is not fitting that you should be running about the streets, with your husband hardly cold in his grave."

"Too cold, I am afraid, poor man." She could not help thinking of that bleak and watery funeral.

"Amanda, are you entirely heartless?" He rose and paid his account. "Let me escort you back to your inn."

"Do you think it right that I should be seen walking with a man, so soon after my husband's death?"

She had meant it in bitter jest, but to her amazement he took it seriously. "No, you are in the right of it; I should have thought of that myself. But nor should you be running about the town unescorted. Perhaps it will be best if you visit the Hamiltons as you had planned. It is only a few doors from here and I am sure Lady Hamilton will send you home in her carriage. Perhaps, too, she will be good enough to lend you at least a black shawl. You owe it to yourself, Amanda, to pay your husband the proper tribute of mourning."

She could not have imagined it possible to find herself so out of patience with him. Proper tribute of mourning, indeed. What had her husband deserved of her? But then, though she had told John the salient points of the will, she had not thought fit to mention the bequest to herself, with its insulting condition. He did not understand – of course he did not understand. How should he? In charity with him again, she walked meekly beside him to the Hamiltons' door, while he explained as much, she thought, to himself as to her, that it was better for her to have his escort than none.

To her relief, he did not suggest that he come in with her. He must return to the *Falcon*, which was under orders to be in readiness for immediate sailing. A thought struck her at once. "Is there any chance that you might be ordered to Syracuse?" she asked.

"Anything is possible. Why?"

She explained about her letter to Julia. "If you should go there, you would do me the greatest possible kindness by bringing her back with you. Or," another thought struck her – "Could you not take us there, Peter and me?"

"Without a chaperone? Impossible. Besides – you are dreaming as usual, Amanda. I have not even been ordered there."

She laughed. "Nor you have! I am afraid you must think me incorrigible, but I do so long to see Julia. I beg you will let me know if you should receive orders for Syracuse."

"You are as likely to hear of it as I am," he said. "Since you will doubtless meet Lord Nelson at the Hamiltons'."

"Oh? Does he stay with them?"

They were at the door now and he dropped her arm. "He lives with them."

There was something she neither liked nor understood about his tone She turned to face him. "He is fortunate," she said. "Lady Hamilton is the best friend, and the kindest woman that I know."

"You are a good friend." Once more she found herself disliking his tone. But the door behind her was opening. "Goodbye, Amanda. And, remember, whatever you do,

you must not yield an inch to that vile woman's claims."
He was waiting to see if she would be received and
it was, somehow, a relief, when the servant who had
opened the door said that Milady Hamilton was indeed
at home and ushered her inside. John was right, she told
herself, managing a smile of farewell, she was indeed an
incorrigible dreamer. She had hoped so much from this,
her first meeting with him since she had, so unexpectedly,
found herself free. By her very hopes, she had doomed
herself to disappointment. She would be more sensible in
future, and remember how much respect John had always
paid to the conventions.

For the time being it was pleasant to have the servant
come hurrying to usher her upstairs, and to receive Lady
Hamilton's enthusiastic greeting. Here was no lack of
sympathy, no lip-service paid to the conventions. With
her usual genius for going to the heart of the matter, Lady
Hamilton contrived at once to congratulate and to condole
with her on her loss. She had never pretended to like Lord
Meynel, or to think Amanda anything but unfortunate in
being married to him; she made no pretences now, but
kissed her warmly and made her feel at once liked and
understood. It was wonderfully pleasant, and she soon
found herself pouring out all her troubles. Lady Hamilton
frowned at the story of Pietronelli's threats, but sided, at
once, with John Purvis. "Of course you must not give way,"
she said. "As for money, you must not be troubling yourself
about that; Sir William, I know, will do everything that is
needful for you. He is out at the moment, but we will go
to him as soon as he returns." And she rang for a page
and told him to inform her the moment the Ambassador
returned from the Palace.

"Ah, my poor Queen," she exclaimed. "If you could but
see her sufferings, you would think your own troubles a
mere trifle. You have lost a husband, it is true, but hardly
one you will feel called upon to mourn for a day longer than
convention demands. She has lost a son – so promising a
prince that I wonder she has survived the blow. He died in
my arms, sobbing out his last breath while his poor mother

219

lay helpless in her cabin. I hope I shall never endure such another voyage. Even Sir William was overcome. Do you know that when I seized a moment's intermission from my labours in tending my poor beloved Queen and her unhappy family, I found him in our cabin, with a pistol to his brow. He would rather die, he told me, than hear the guggle-guggle of the water as the ship sank. 'Let us have no talk of sinking,' I cried. 'The hero of the Nile will not let us drown.'" And Lady Hamilton struck the heroic attitude with which, no doubt, she had comforted her despondent husband and cheered the hero of the Nile. "We landed more dead than alive," she went on. "And my poor Queen is still ill with the headache and the cold she caught on that dreadful voyage. And the Palace unheated, the children crying . . . It is a scene of such suffering that I am sure you would forget your own troubles in pity for theirs. Your child, after all, is well enough, is he not?" And then, in tones that carried complete conviction: "How I envy you that happiness. If Sir William and I only had a son – or a daughter, a little Emma, all my own. Nothing can take your Peter from you; you do not realize how fortunate you are."

With her usual instinctive understanding, she had hit on the one subject that was guaranteed to distract Amanda from her miseries and they talked for a while, comfortably, of little Peter, until a page announced that Sir William had returned home. To Amanda's relief, Lady Hamilton took the lead in describing to him the plight in which she found herself and he, too, urged that she must not yield to the lawyer's demands. "I will lose no time in writing to England on your behalf. In the meanwhile, you must let me be your banker."

She accepted gratefully and took her leave almost at once, shocked, though she concealed it as best she might, by the change in Sir William. The voyage that had killed her own husband had turned Lady Hamilton's into an old man. She could not help remembering John Purvis's tone when he told her that Lord Nelson now lived with the Hamiltons. It was, indeed, a curious ménage, but then, she told herself, Lady Hamilton could carry off stranger situations than this.

Back at the inn, she found Peter contentedly playing at jackstraws with Miss Knight and joined their game as the best means of concealing her own preoccupation. All her advisers had agreed that she must not yield to the Grassi's demands and yet all her own instincts told her that they were wrong. If only John would call, so that she could let him convince her all over again. And yet – would he be able to?

"Mama, you are not paying attention!" Peter's exclamation interrupted her train of thought and she did her best to pay full attention to the game until one of the inn's tatterdemalion servants announced that Signor Pietronelli was below, asking for her. Too late, now, for doubting. She went down to him and explained that on the advice of Sir William Hamilton she intended to await instructions from her husband's English men of business.

He listened to her impassively. Then: "You may be within your rights, Signora," he said. "I am only a poor Sicilian lawyer, and would not venture to question that, but I think you are foolish just the same. You will hear from me further." And he rose without more ado and took his leave

He left her a prey to every sort of anxiety. It had seemed reasonable enough when John and the Hamiltons had urged her to take a firm stand, but now she was very much less sure of the wisdom of it. The Grassi was a hysterical and stupid, and therefore a dangerous woman. Surely, it would have been better to have placated her, at whatever sacrifice of principle. After all, it was not as if she had any sentimental feeling about her husband's personal effects. Why not let his mistress have them, if it would give her any satisfaction? Whatever happened, Peter would have enough. For herself, she did not very much care.

It was bitterly cold. Snow lay on the flat roofs of the houses, and frost sparkled in the streets. Peter had outgrown his last winter's clothes and Amanda stayed indoors, cutting down a warm pelisse of her own to make

221

him an overcoat. She did not admit, even to herself, that she was also waiting for a visit from John Purvis who had left on a short cruise but should return any day. He did not come, but the Knights returned from a morning visit to Lady Hamilton with a budget of news. Lord Nelson had been there, loud in praise of his hostess's heroism on the unlucky voyage from Naples. He was full, too, of dark hints of treachery in Naples at the time of the embarkation. The Royal party, it seemed, had only by lucky chance escaped an ambush on their way to the harbour. "The Queen," said Cornelia Knight, "is mad with anger at the thought that someone of the chosen few to whom she gave warning of her impending escape must have betrayed her. I would not like to be in the traitor's shoes."

"No," said Amanda reasonably, "but then, no doubt they will have stayed in Naples and be busy in establishing this Parthenopean republic they talk of."

"Yes," said Miss Knight, "or in welcoming the French." She had seemed, Amanda thought, ill at ease since she had returned from Lady Hamilton and now seized a moment when Peter had run to fetch a toy from his own room. "I have bad news for you, my dear," she said.

"For me?"

"I am afraid so. The Grassi – you will forgive me for speaking of her? – has lost no time in finding herself a powerful protector here. There is talk in the town—" she paused.

"Yes?" Amanda told herself she was ready for anything.

"About Lord Meynel's death. I wish, for your sake, that he had not been buried at sea."

Amanda shivered. "But what else could I do?"

She could not sleep that night. This was the beginning of the Grassi's revenge. Who could tell where it would end? She tossed and turned on her hard pillow, listening to Peter's quiet breathing at the other side of the room, and tormenting herself with regrets that she had not yielded to all the Grassi's demands. Anything, surely, would be better than the campaign of slander she sensed to be beginning.

222

She must go to Sir William in the morning and ask him – or, perhaps more to the point – Lord Nelson, if they could not arrange a passage home for her and Peter.

She slept at last, restlessly, and was still only half awake when a servant announced that there was someone below asking for her. She jumped up, certain that this time it would be John, but when she had made a hurried toilet and run eagerly downstairs she found herself once again confronting a total stranger. He introduced himself, courteously, but with an odd note of formality, as Palermo's chief of police, and came at once to the point. Information, he said, had been laid against her in the matter of a serious crime – in short, of murder. He looked at her sharply. "You do not appear surprised, signora."

At all costs, she must keep her head. "Nor am I," she said, "since I had already heard rumours of this ridiculous charge against me and know its author. It is the Signora Grassi, is it not: my husband's mistress, and my enemy?"

"That does not necessarily make her charge untrue. You should be grateful to me, signora. I might have had you brought to me for questioning, but because you are English and," he bowed, "unfortunate, I have done you the courtesy of visiting you here. I strongly recommend that you answer my questions truthfully."

"But of course. I have nothing to hide."

"Good." He looked at her, she thought, quizzically. "Then you have nothing to fear." His tone changed. The preliminaries were now complete and the cross-examination would begin: "Your husband died on the voyage here from Naples?"

"Yes. He had always suffered gravely from seasickness. Only the extremity of the situation in Naples induced him to risk the crossing."

"To which you urged him."

"That is not true. I neither urged nor tried to dissuade him. It was a question on which he had to make up his mind for himself, and for us."

This won her an approving look. "Quite so. Your duty

was to stand by his decision, which, you say, you did not attempt to influence."

"Yes. The only pressure to which he was subjected was from the Signora Grassi herself. If it had not been for her, we would have travelled, perhaps more safely, in an English ship. Captain Medway, who arranged our departure, will confirm that."

"And where is this Captain Medway?"

"I do not know. He left before I arrived, for Syracuse."

He shrugged. "That is unfortunate. But to continue. Your husband became ill even before the ship sailed, did he not?"

"Yes. Whereupon I urged that we should go ashore and take our chance there. You perhaps do not know that some years ago he had an apoplectic seizure. His doctor had warned him that any strain might bring on another and fatal one. I was afraid of the consequences of prolonged seasickness."

"You seem to have been in all things a most considerate wife, signora." Was there irony in his bland tones? "And where is this doctor now, who advised against the risk of strain?"

"Dr Anderson? I do not know. He went home to England two years or so ago."

Once again the shrug and the phrase – apologetic? ironical? – "Most unfortunate." He returned to the attack. "So you stayed on board, and, having, by influence of some kind, managed to obtain a cabin of your own, refused to allow the Signora Grassi and her suffering children to share it with you."

"There was not room," said Amanda simply. "Nor do I admit the slightest obligation, save that of common charity, to the Signora Grassi. And besides—" she could not help it – "have you seen her suffering children?"

"We must keep to the point, signora. The fact remains, that by one means and another you ensured that you would be alone in the cabin with your husband, who was, by all reports, in the most helpless of conditions."

"I was not alone, sir. My son was with us. Do you

224

seriously imagine that, even if I had contemplated such a thing, I would have murdered my husband before the eyes of my child?"

"Ah yes." He went off at a tangent. "The child. There, surely, we come to the heart of the matter. I notice you say 'my child' not 'our child'." He paused, expectantly.

Amanda had been frightened before, now she was frozen with terror. "What difference does it make?" she asked.

"Perhaps the greatest; the difference of a motive for murder. The Signora Grassi has a strange tale to tell about that child. A tale, she says, that your husband, Lord Meynel himself told to her. A bastard, she says, foisted upon Lord Meynel as his heir, and accepted, unwillingly, by him. Suppose, signora, that your husband had changed his mind about that acceptance, had decided to secure a divorce for unfaithfulness and marry the Signora Grassi, thus making her children his heirs . . . would not that have been a powerful motive for murder?"

Ice-cold in the face of danger, Amanda's brain worked, just the same feverishly. She managed to look at the policeman with calm contempt. "You have met the Grassi," she said. "Can you seriously believe that an aristocrat like my husband could have contemplated marrying her? And, if he had, you must know as well as I do that her children would still be bastards, incapable of succeeding to his estates."

"The next one could have," he said imperturbably. "But we are wandering from the events of that unlucky voyage of yours. Your husband grew more and more seriously ill. You called on no one for help, but insisted on nursing him yourself."

"On the contrary," she said. "I went to the Captain for help. The Grassi, unfortunately, was too drunk to be appealed to."

"Oh," he looked at her strangely. "That is not what she told me."

"I do not expect it is. But any of the Neapolitan ladies with whom she was sharing the main cabin will confirm that I came to look for her, found her asleep, incapably

225

drunk, and left her. I did not have time to look for her again."

"But you appealed, you say, to the Captain?"

"Yes, and he did what he could for me. The ship was in disorder, you understand, after a night of storm, and, unluckily for us, there was no doctor on board. Inevitably, the responsibility for nursing my husband fell to me."

"And he died?"

"Yes. He died, if you wish to know, cursing the Grassi for her failure to come to him." She wondered if this was a mistake.

But he had taken another tack. "Whereupon, without reporting the matter to anyone, you went peacefully to bed and slept till morning. By which time all traces of – shall we say – suffocation would have vanished."

She could not think her case could look so black, but she would not show her terror. "Sir, I was exhausted: I had not slept for three nights."

"And in the morning," he went relentlessly on, "you gladly agreed to the Captain's suggestion of a burial at sea."

Now, hearteningly, she was angry. "I did not gladly agree, sir! I let the Captain have his way because it was his ship – and it did not seem to me to make much difference to my unfortunate husband whether he was buried in a strange sea or a strange land."

"Just the same," he said, "as things have worked out it was either very lucky for you—"

"Or very unlucky," she interrupted him. Suddenly anxiety for herself was lost in a more immediate one for Peter. She had left him, amazingly, still asleep. Soon he must wake and miss her. "Sir," she said, "I have answered your questions to the best of my ability. The captain of the ship, the ladies in the cabin, Captain Medway when he returns will all confirm my story. Now, I must leave you: I left my son alone."

At last he was looking at her with respect. "I will, naturally, talk to them all," he said. "For the moment, I must ask you not to leave Palermo."

226

"Where would I go?" she asked simply.

And, "You are a very brave woman, signora," was his odd reply.

She might be brave, but she was also terrified, and not for herself alone. Suppose she should be arrested, what would happen to Peter? Hurrying upstairs to find him, she cursed herself for having taken John's advice. If only she had given in to the Grassi's demands, she would have been spared all this. The accusation of murder was immediately terrifying, but not, she thought, ultimately so serious as the Grassi's revelations about little Peter. Any impartial investigation must, she told herself, clear her of suspicion about her husband's death, but the story about Peter's birth would not be so easily answered.

Reaching their room, she discovered new cause for alarm. Peter was not there. Visions of kidnapping darted through her overwrought brain, only to be dispelled by the sound of his loud, unmistakable joyous laugh from further down the corridor. He was sharing their breakfast with the Knights.

# Chapter Fourteen

For a few minutes Amanda sat on her bed, her head in her hands. She had been accused – officially accused – of murder. It might be only a matter of time before she was arrested. It was all very well to tell herself that in the end this charge would prove less serious than the slurs on Peter's legitimacy. For the moment, she was terrified by visions of Palermo's filthy gaol – and of Peter left alone, with only the Knights for his friends. But this was no time to sit and shake with fright. She jumped up, found a warm pelisse and followed the sound of Peter's glad laughter to the Knights' room. She could not explain, in front of Peter, what was the matter, but her white face and shaking hand told the Knights that the message which took her so suddenly to the Hamiltons must be urgent indeed. Of course they would look after Peter for her.

Soon she was outside, half running through the icy streets, but taking time, as she went, for one quick glance down to the harbour. No, neither the *Falcon* nor the *Illustrious* had tied up in the night. She paused for a moment as much in bitter disappointment as to get her breath. Captain Medway, she knew, if he would only return, would stand her friend and would be able to bear out much of her story of the events that led up to her husband's death. As for John – that was another matter. It was his advice – and, of course, the Hamiltons' – that had involved her in her present wretched situation. Would he be able to forgive her for the fact that he had advised her so unluckily? But there was more to it than that. What would he think when he heard the Grassi's accusations, which must doubtless already be all over the town? He knew, already, of the woman's wild accusations about Lord Meynel's death, but her other story, of Peter's illegitimacy must be news to him. Formidable news, since if Peter was a bastard, he must know that only he could be the father. How often, in the past, she had dreamed of his learning the truth about Peter's birth. But not like this, she told herself, shivering with shock as much as cold. How would he take it? What would he do? How strange it was, after all the years of loving John that now she understood him so little. He had seemed, at their last meeting, almost a stranger . . . And yet, of course, she loved him, had always loved him, always would . . . Shivering with cold, she was yet back in imagination in the moonlit garden of the George at Rye – or, again in moonlight, that night of the eruption: "Kiss me, John, for the moon has risen."

She shook herself. This was no time for dreaming. Time enough, when the immediate danger of arrest was past, to wonder how John would take this news. She hurried on to the Hamiltons' villa. Sir William would know what she must do . . . Lady Hamilton would cheer her as always by the ready warmth of her sympathy . . .

It was only as she reached the entrance of the Hamiltons' villa that she realized how early it was. Impossibly so for any kind of visit. She stood, for a moment, wondering what to do. Could she rouse the Hamiltons at this unfashionable hour? On the other hand, could she afford not to? At any moment, the Chief of Police might change his mind and issue a warrant for her arrest. Once again, visions of prison, and of Peter alone, rose to terrify her. She took a few hesitant steps towards the villa door, then paused, amazed, as sounds of music and merrymaking came out to greet her. The door of the house, she now saw, was not quite closed and, almost without thinking, she pushed it open and found herself in the wide, marble entrance hall of the villa. A door at the far end of the hall was also ajar and here, to her amazement, she saw lights still burning, despite the cold sunshine outside. It was from here, too, that the sounds of music and voices were coming. Lady Hamilton must still be entertaining her last night's guests.

No servants were about. Desperation drove Amanda on down the hall. Then she stopped in the doorway, amazed at what she saw. Shutters, closed against last night's cold now kept out the morning light. In its place, guttering candles burned low in a score of miscellaneous receptacles. The air was heavy with their odour and that of wine and a long night's revelry. Facing Amanda across a baize-covered table sat Lady Hamilton, cards in her hands, a little pile of gold beside her on the table, where also lay an overturned wine glass, its red wine seeping into the green cloth. Her face was flushed with wine and triumph, her short curls disordered, her breathing heavy as she threw her cards on the table, exclaiming, "My game, I think."

Beside her sat Lord Nelson, his face as pale as hers was flushed. Someone, at some point in the night, had crowned him with laurel and now the wreath had slipped, absurdly, down over his bad eye. He looked dizzy, Amanda thought, with fatigue and wine, and as she watched, his head nodded for a moment and slipped towards Lady Hamilton's shoulder. Looking up, she caught Amanda's eye for a moment, then, deliberately ignoring her, she put her arm around Lord Nelson to shake him gently awake. "Your deal, my lord."

Concentrated on the cards, the rest of the little group round the table seemed to notice nothing of this, but to Amanda, watching with the cold eye of sobriety, the little, intimate gesture proclaimed them lovers more clearly than any words could do. She turned and tiptoed quietly away down the hall. This was no moment to be troubling Lady Hamilton with her own affairs. But Sir William? He had not been among the group around the table. She paused for a long moment, hesitating by the open front door and as she did so a footman emerged sleepily from a door on her right. His wig was awry, his livery jacket unbuttoned, and he was stretching his way into wakefulness as he approached. She asked him, in her fluent Italian, for Sir William and he replied with an expressive shrug. They had put Milord to bed only an hour or so ago. No chance of his receiving her before evening. And now, from the

230

end of the hall came sounds of movement. The card party was breaking up at last. Intolerable, somehow, that the late revellers should find her here, apparently spying on them. Amanda muttered an incoherent apology for her early call and took her leave.

Outside, the frost-filled air was crisp and refreshing. She stood, for a few moments, taking deep breaths of it and wondering what to do next. Appeal for mercy to the Grassi? Impossible. And anyway, the Chief of Police had not seemed to her the kind of man who would be easily stopped. The Grassi had made her accusation, he would follow it up until he had proved it true or false. Therefore, an appeal to Pietronelli, the lawyer, would be equally useless, if it had not anyway seemed an impossible humiliation. But this was no time to be thinking of humiliation. Peter must be her main concern. What happened to herself was of only secondary importance.

And she had left him too long with the Knights. Bleakly surveying her own prospects, and his, she told herself that they were now her only friends – at least until Julia arrived. Impossible, after what she had seen today, to turn to Lady Hamilton for help, and almost equally difficult, although she was entitled to his aid, to go to Sir William. In all the bleak years of her marriage, she had never felt so lonely, nor so afraid. She had turned, at the thought of Peter, and was walking homewards, aware, as she went, that the sun was now high in the sky and had thawed the frost from roofs and balconies. It was more than time, she told herself bitterly, for Lady Hamilton's party to be breaking up. People were about in the streets at last, carriages passed, the lazy Sicilian day was beginning.

Conscious that in her distraction she had hurried out without paying more than the most perfunctory attention to her appearance, she hastened her step, only to be aware, as she did so, of hostile glances and a pointed finger from a carriage on the other side of the street. It contained a group of English young ladies whose "dearest Lady Meynel," she had been only yesterday. They had begged her to let them help her by taking charge, whenever it suited her, of "their darling little Peter". Today they were pointing her out to each other, but at the same time pretending, now that she had seen them, that they had never seen her in their lives before. The Grassi's story must be all over town already. How would the Knights take it? Only pride prevented her from running the last hundred yards to the inn.

To her deep and heartfelt relief, she found the Knights enthusiastically on her side. They had received, they told her, during her absence, a morning call from two busybody friends of theirs, who had done their best to persuade them to have nothing more to do with a probable murderess and her bastard son. Fortunately for Amanda, this attack, conducted, shamelessly, in the same room with Peter, had merely confirmed the Knights as her friends. "Do not worry," Cornelia concluded significantly. "I took care that Peter heard none of it. But, tell me, what do the Hamiltons advise?"

Amanda had had time now to think what she must say, and merely told the Knights that she had been unable to see either Sir William or Lady Hamilton. Miss Knight urged her to return as soon as she thought there was any hope of their receiving her, and she realized, however reluctantly, the sense of this. Inevitably, in this crisis, she must turn to Sir William for protection. Besides, she had had time to get over the first shock of the curiously disturbing scene she had witnessed. Who was she, she asked herself, to be casting stones at Lady Hamilton? She, too, had betrayed an elderly husband with a younger man. She had had more excuse perhaps – she shivered at recollection of Lord Meynel's cruelty. Sir William on the other hand had always seemed a perfect paragon of husbandly devotion – but, there was no getting away from it, he was a very old man these days and, increasingly, Lady Hamilton played rather the part of nurse than of wife. From sneering remarks of her own husband's, Amanda knew a good deal about Lady Hamilton's past history and knew, among other things, of the cold-blooded way in which her protector, Charles Greville, had sold her to his rich uncle, Sir William. All too well she remembered her husband's coarse jokes at Charles

232

Greville's expense. His idea, of course, had been that once safely equipped with a mistress, Sir William would never consider remarriage, and Greville's own position as his heir would be safe. But beautiful Emma had so wound her way not only into Sir William's affections but to those of Neapolitan society, and, it was said, even the Queen's, that Sir William had ended up by marrying her.

And had got a good bargain, Amanda told herself. In the loose Court of Naples, the new Lady Hamilton had been held up as a model of feminine propriety. Her affection for Sir William had been a byword; she had nursed him devotedly through his various illnesses and had infinitely strengthened his position as Ambassador by her friendship with the powerful Queen. But what of the other side of the picture? What had warm-hearted Emma Lyon got out of this marriage above her station? Money, of course, and social success; music lessons and the friendship of a Queen. But Amanda, aware of the great emptiness and longing in her own heart, had often wondered how warm-hearted Lady Hamilton bore her position as an old man's darling. Now, with Peter on her knee, she remembered how often and how wistfully Lady Hamilton had spoken of her own love for children. Sir William had given her neither the happiness of a true wife nor of a mother, and now, a very old man indeed, could he blame her if she focused her great capacity for hero-worship on England's hero?

Oddly, Amanda found herself ashamed, now, of her own intrusion on Lady Hamilton's private happiness, and, she feared, the look of shocked surprise with which she had greeted it. Of course she must go to the Ambassadress, who had always been the kindest of friends to her, and try to show her that even if she was bound to disapprove, she still understood . . . But Peter was tugging at her skirts.

"You finished my coat yesterday, Mama, you know you did, and you promised that today we would go out."

It was true that he had been confined too long indoors, and now the sun was shining. She exchanged an anxious glance with the Knights, then shrugged her shoulders. Whatever the risks of insult, or even of arrest, they could not stay mewed up in the inn for ever; she might just as well take the plunge and hope for the best.

"If anything should happen," said Lady Knight, "send for us. We will come at once, never fear."

Thanking her, Amanda fought back tears. If she should be arrested, they would be Peter's only friends. And then she told herself not to be absurd. She knew Lady Hamilton's kindness of heart too well to doubt for a moment that she would prove a most loving friend to Peter if the worst should happen. No doubt her first thought would be to treat Peter as the child she herself had always wanted. But even this idea had its horrors. Peter – to live in that curious *ménage à trois*? To see the nightly gambling and who knew what worse? It was one thing, a little guiltily, to feel herself sympathetic towards Lady Hamilton, quite another to imagine Peter exposed to such things.

It would not bear thinking of. She must not be arrested. Her thoughts had come full circle. Once again she found herself meditating some kind of appeal to the Chief of Police, and again decided against it. There was nothing she could do but wait. Determinedly cheerful, she took Peter to the terraced walk that led along the shore to the royal gardens and instituted a lively game of hide-and-seek among the statues of the Kings of Sicily that lined the coast walk. Luckily, the cold was still so intense that no one was about in the gardens, and she did not have the pain of concealing from Peter the fact, which she had already noticed, that the English colony in Sicily were going out of their way to ignore her.

"Mama," Peter's voice recalled her from her gloomy thoughts. "You are not even *trying* to find me!"

It was a relief to forget her troubles in concentration on the game. She had thought, in the shock and terror of the morning, that she would never be warm again, but now, as she chased Peter from one statue to the next, she felt life tingling once more through her body. Things could not possibly be as bad as she had been letting herself think. She had frightened herself into a nightmare, that was all.

234

She laughed and pounced on Peter, inadequately concealed behind the statue of King Frederick the Second, *Stupor Mundi*. The widow's cap she had bought had slipped back from her soft curls, and her flushed cheeks and soft, delighted laugh as she caught him in her arms made her seem rather another child than a widow in her weeds. For a moment, holding her child, panting in the bright, cold air, she was illogically, absurdly happy.

"Amanda!" John Purvis's unexpected voice brought her up short, but only for a moment. He was standing quite near, watching her as she hugged little Peter whose delighted laughter continued while hers suddenly stopped.

"Oh, John, I am so glad to see you." She hurried to him, Peter in one arm, the other held out in welcome.

"Amanda." He took her hand, but was looking, she thought, rather at Peter than at her. But now, he turned the full force of his eyes upon her. "Is it true?" he asked.

What was the use of beating about the bush. She looked up at him. "Yes."

"You should have told me."

"What was the use?" But Peter was pulling at her hand.

"Mama, it is your turn to hide."

John looked down at him with – what? Exasperation? A father's unexpected feeling for the son he did not know existed? Amanda could not be sure. Then he felt in his pocket. "You speak Italian no doubt?" It sounded as if he was addressing another man.

"Of course." Peter was jumping up and down with the cold.

"There is a man selling hot pasta at the entrance to the gardens. Run quick and buy us some." He held out a coin.

Amanda intervened. "John, he is too young." And then, to the child: "Peter, Mr Purvis and I must talk a while. Do you see how many times you can run up and down the walk before we have finished."

"Will I get a prize?"

"Of course."

He was off like a flash and they both looked after the small, active figure for a moment. Then, "Mine!" said John.

"Yes."

"You should have told me. If I had known, I would not have advised you as I did the other day."

"Oh." It was not surprising, somehow, that it should turn out to be all her fault. "But I did not, you see, know that my husband had told the Grassi. Our understanding was that no one should know." And then, "Well done. Now, again," as Peter came panting towards them, then turned back towards the far end of the walk.

"How did Lord Meynel know?"

"I told him."

His eyebrows rose. "*Told* him?"

"Yes – it is too long to explain now. But he agreed to acknowledge Peter as his heir, and, so far as I knew, never went back on his side of the bargain."

He did not ask her what her side of the bargain had been. "It is an unlucky business. The story is all over Palermo. I heard it almost the moment I landed."

She turned to look at the harbour. Something had been troubling her. "But where is the *Falcon?*"

"Outside the harbour," he shrugged it off. "I cannot stay more than an hour or so. I lose time now that I should be spending with Sir William. Amanda, we must announce our engagement without delay. Have I your permission to tell the Hamiltons?"

Her cheeks had been scarlet. Now they were white. "John, are you serious?"

"Never more so. It is the only way, as you must realize as well as I do. There is the child to be considered." And then, "Well done – once more," as Peter rushed towards them, catapulted into his mother's arms and then turned, puffing a little, away again.

What did she feel? What did she not feel? "You really wish it?"

"Of course," almost impatiently. "But it is not the time for wishing, it is a time for action." And then, breaking

236

off, "Sir William, the very person. I had been coming, this instant, to see you."

Sir William, wrapped to the very chin in furs, had been taking a brisk constitutional from his villa nearby. Now he paused, red-cheeked with exertion, to shake them both warmly by the hand. "Captain Purvis – and Lady Meynel – delightful. But let us not be lingering here. Come you in; Lady Hamilton will be delighted to see you."

"Three times!" Peter hurled himself on his mother. "And now I am 'sausted. Is it time to go home yet?"

"We are going to see Lady Hamilton," said Amanda. No time to wonder whether the beauty would be awake, or how she would receive her.

He greeted the news with delight, announcing that he had a friend in Lady Hamilton's kitchen. Amanda was used, by now, to her son's tendency to have friends in the most surprising places, and watched him scamper off to the back purlieus of the villa with a calm that she rather suspected of shocking John. But then, so much that she did these days seemed to shock him. What was the matter with her? And why was she not happier? At last, after all these years, he had asked her to marry him; the long loneliness was over; she must be happy.

But it was all so strange. Relieved that Sir William, who looked sadly aged and shaken, had buttonholed John and was lamenting the loss of his priceless antiques on the *Colossus*, she walked silently along beside them, telling herself that it was merely the abrupt manner of John's proposal that had disconcerted her. There would be time, later, for all that exquisite comparison of memories that makes up a happy courtship. Together, they would remember . . . What would they remember? Why was she so ill at ease?

They found Lady Hamilton singing "Banish sorrow, until tomorrow", to Lord Nelson in the room where, this morning, Amanda had seen her self-betrayed over the card table. Now all signs of the night's merrymaking had been cleared away, and the room smelt freshly of spices from the brazier Lady Hamilton had introduced to make up for its lack of a hearth. There was no doubt about it, Amanda told herself, the Ambassadress, or, perhaps, her mother, was an admirable housewife. And Lady Hamilton was in remarkable looks, considering that she had been up all night and could not have had more than a few daytime hours of sleep. She was wearing the white dress and blue sash that she particularly affected, and her manner, as she greeted her husband and his guests, was perfect. For a moment, Amanda found herself wondering if she could have imagined the significance of that early morning scene. Could she really have exchanged that strange look of total understanding with the hostess who now greeted her with such kindly condescension? But a glance at Lord Nelson told her that it had not been imagination. No adept in society, his burning, steady regard announced his devotion to Lady Hamilton for all the world to see. Surely, then, Sir William, who was no fool, must be aware of what was going on.

Listening as Sir William explained the circumstances of their meeting, Amanda realized that of course he knew it all, and, she thought, understood and forgave it all. Then what right had she even to imagine blame? Curiously relieved, she returned Lady Hamilton's kiss warmly, and knew, as she did so, that the incident was over, never to be referred to between them by even so much as a glance or an intonation.

And indeed Lady Hamilton made no mention of the morning's encounter. "My love, I have been longing to see you all day," she said. "Ever since I heard the shocking rumours that are going about the town. That witch of a Grassi should be burned at the stake."

This gave John Purvis the opening he had been waiting for. "It is monstrous, is it not?" he said. "But at least I am glad to say that I have prevailed upon Lady Meynel to give me the right and privilege of protecting her name. There can be, of course, no formal engagement until she is out of black gloves, but I would be most grateful if you, Sir William, and you, my lady, would make it known that I am ready and eager to defend

238

Lady Meynel's reputation in any manner that may be necessary."

"Oh?" To Amanda's own surprise, Lady Hamilton's look was one of purest amazement. "You mean that I am to congratulate you? What a delightful surprise, is it not, Sir William? But let us have no more duelling, Captain Purvis. I am convinced that you will do Lady Meynel's name more harm that way than good. If you will be ruled by me, both of you, you will leave all to time, the greatest salve I know for reputation. But in the meantime, you must indeed allow me to felicitate you on your happiness." Was there again that faint note of surprise?

Sir William too looked oddly, disturbingly doubtful. "It is delightful news indeed," he said rather to John than to her, "but you will forgive me, I know, if I suggest that this somewhat – well, to be frank, precipitate engagement may not give scandal even more material to feed upon?"

"I do not care," John said roundly. "Lady Meynel must be protected, and how else is it possible?"

"I am sure you are in the right of it," said Lady Hamilton with more warmth than conviction. "It is too romantic for words, and the greatest surprise. Why, I had been imagining . . ." she dwindled to a pause. Whatever she had been imagining they were not, it seemed, to be told of it.

Lord Nelson who had so far been a silent spectator of the scene now intervened to congratulate them both warmly. On this hint, John rose to take his leave. He must, he said, hurry back to his ship. "I will see you safe to your inn first, Amanda."

How delightful it was, she thought as they took their leave, to be taken care of again, to have John sending a servant to fetch little Peter from his friends in the kitchen and telling him, when he arrived, almost like a father, to clean the tomato paste from his face before he walked home with his mama. Using her own handkerchief on the stained little face, she was aware of a stiffening in the child. Of course, Peter knew nothing of the special relationship that had always existed between the three of them. What happiness it would be to tell him that he was,

239

at last, to have a father. Or would it? Peter was oddly silent as they walked home together and John, wisely, made no attempt to draw him into their conversation which was, inevitably, confined to indifferent subjects. To her relief, she learned that John's cruise was merely to be towards Malta and back. He hoped to return within the week. "The announcement of our engagement will surely protect you from that harpy for so long. When I return, we must turn, seriously, to making our plans. You will wish, of course, to return to your mother and be married from your home. I will write to my aunt and warn her to expect you as soon as I can arrange your passage home. Do you write to your mother to the same effect?"

She was amazed. "Go home before we marry? But, John, why?"

She was growing used to that impatient little frown of his. "You heard Sir William. We do not wish the world to be calling our marriage precipitate."

Peter tugged at her hand. "I'm cold, Mama." They had reached the inn.

"I must not linger." John bent over her hand. "Take care of yourself, Amanda. We will talk more of this when I return."

And he was walking quickly away towards the harbour. Was it like a dream or a nightmare? She was engaged to marry John and yet there had been neither kisses nor talk of love. Amanda shook herself and hurried Peter indoors. There would be time, presently, for that. She should be ashamed even to be thinking of it, with her husband hardly dead a week. Had she shocked John again by seeming to forget her recent widowhood. She sighed. Very likely she had . . . Would she ever learn to understand him?

# Chapter Fifteen

Amanda was soon to learn that Sir William had been nearer the mark than John Purvis in his estimate of the probable result of their announcing their engagement so soon after her husband's death. She had been aware of odd looks and curious whispers before, but now they were redoubled. The Hamiltons and the Knights remained her staunch friends, but no one else came near her. Worse still, little Peter came running to her, in floods of tears, one morning when he had been playing in the inn yard. "They say they won't play with me," he cried, "because I'm a . . ." to Amanda's relief, he had forgotten the word, but she could guess all too easily what it must have been. She consoled him as best she might, and decided that this was the moment to tell him her news, which, for some reason she did not herself understand, she had so far delayed in doing.

"Do not mind them!" she set him on her knee. "We shall be going home to England soon, and I expect they are jealous." She was beginning to think John had been right: the sooner they left Palermo the better. She hurried on, finding it curiously hard to tell her news. "And you are to have a brand new father, a ship's captain. What do you think of that?"

His face lit up. "Captain Medway! Oh, Mama, will he take me on a cruise? He said once that he would one day if I was a good boy. Shall we go home in his ship?"

She felt an unaccountable pang. "No, no, my love. It is not Captain Medway but Captain Purvis who has promised to look after us. But I am sure he will take you on a cruise if you ask him nicely."

The small face crumpled in disappointment. "But I do

241

not like Captain Purvis, Mama, he talks at me." And he got down from her lap and ran off with a sudden assumption of almost grown-up independence that brought a rush of tears to her eyes.

He would get over it, of course. She realized now, looking back, that when the two Captains had visited her, it had always been Medway who had paid attention to the child, and this had, in fact, sometimes made her wonder if John might suspect the relationship and be going out of his way to avoid drawing attention to it. And yet, often and anxiously as she had looked for a likeness to him in Peter, she had never been able to find one. It was lucky, of course; gossip would never have that to fasten on.

An endless-seeming, anxious week dragged by. Despite the continuing bitter cold, the pattern of Neapolitan social life had already begun to establish itself in Palermo. The Queen, it was true, still huddled wretchedly in her cold palace at Colli, seeing no one but Lady Hamilton, alone with memories of her dead son, but the King, who had brought his favourite pack of hounds with him, was out hunting every day. Lady Hamilton and Sir William entertained as usual, but Amanda was too conscious of scandal and its result in cold and hostile glances to venture into any general society. As much as possible, she kept Peter with her, to protect him from the careless cruelty of the other English children who had, of course, heard their parents talking about her. She had received another visit from the Chief of Police, which left her more frightened than ever. He had asked her the same questions all over again and had seemed surprised when her answers continued the same as before. Taking his leave, he had warned her, once again, that the case was far from being closed; she must not think of quitting Palermo.

Lady Hamilton, when Amanda paid her an early morning visit and told her this, was robustly comforting. "Nonsense," she said, "if the worst comes to the worst, Lord Nelson will get you and Peter on board one of his ships and home to England before the Chief of Police can so much as say 'boo' to you. Do not look so anxious. I have his promise for it."

Amanda thanked her with tears in her eyes. She was very far now from indulging in criticism of her hostess, whose kindness to her had been unfailing, and, equally important, understanding. Now, when a page announced a new group of guests, she let Amanda take her leave by another door. "What is the use of your letting yourself be troubled by these old cats? You will be safe from their claws soon enough. But – before you go, tell me, have you had any news of the Countess Vespucci?"

"Why, no!" Amanda found the question surprising. "Though I hope to see her any day. I wrote to her as soon as I reached here. I am sure she will come to me as soon as she gets my letter."

"Oh." Lady Hamilton considered it for a moment, then went on, once again surprisingly, "That is what I was afraid of. I think you had best write her again, my love, and tell her to stay where she is."

"But – why?"

Lady Hamilton put a finger to her lips. "Ask no questions," she said archly, "and you'll be told no lies. But do it, I beg of you, without delay. And now, I suppose, I must receive these good talkative ladies."

It was dismissal, and Amanda made her escape down a back stairway and hurried home, brooding in puzzlement about Lady Hamilton's last words. Why must she write Julia not to come?

She had left Peter with the Knights as usual and he ran out to meet her all agog with excitement. There was a ship, he said, heading for the harbour: "Perhaps it is the *Illustrious*, Mama, with Captain Medway and Aunt Julia!"

Too late, if so, to warn Julia not to come. But, surely, it was more likely to be the *Falcon*? John had promised to come back to her as soon as he could, and a whole week had passed since he had left. Yes, she was sure it would be the *Falcon*. And, because Peter disliked it so, she had left off her widow's cap this morning. John must not find

243

her thus. She hurried upstairs and put it on, straining her rebelliously curling hair away from her face and asking herself, as she did so, why her heart was so heavy.

Peter came dancing in to her. "I was right, Mama. It is the *Illustrious*. Now, perhaps, Captain Medway will take me for the cruise he promised."

Amanda hurried to the window. He was right. It was not the *Falcon* but the larger *Illustrious* that was making her graceful way into the harbour. She watched with a silent tremor. What on earth was the matter with her these days? Why did her hands tremble so as she fastened the cap to her soft hair? She had not been properly glad at the idea that John was coming to her. Now she was terrified and, absurdly, illogically, wretched at the thought of Captain Medway and, perhaps, Julia learning of her engagement.

"Look, Mama." Peter was beside her, watching too. "There *is* a lady on board. See, she is going over the side, now, in the bosun's chair. It must be Aunt Julia."

"Very likely." Amanda felt worse and worse. Increasingly, since she had become engaged to John, she had been troubled by thoughts of how Julia would take it. She had done her best to shake them off, telling herself that she must have imagined Julia's feeling for John just as she had his for her. But now, confronted with the imminent prospect of having to tell Julia her news; she found herself less sure, remembering many occasions when John and Julia had laughed and talked together and she had – yes, she had felt left out of it. But it was all imagination. It must be.

"It is Aunt Julia; I am sure of it," shouted Peter. "Look how lightly she jumped out of the chair. Mama, let us go down to the harbour and meet her. Please!"

She was not at all sure that she wished to hasten the moment of meeting, but Peter was set on going, and she was too delighted at his enthusiasm – for their near ostracism had been hard on him – to refuse. They were delayed, however, by Miss Knight, who came running to their room with a budget of bad news from Naples where, it seemed, the Jacobins were now in full control, had declared their Parthenopean Republic and were awaiting the arrival

244

of the French army with open arms. By the time Amanda had exclaimed suitably at this and found warm coats for herself and Peter, they were only able to greet Julia at the doorway of the inn.

She came hurrying to Amanda with open arms. "My dearest love, I came as soon as I could." They kissed, Julia all sympathy, Amanda aware of miserable restraint. "You must come home with me as soon as we can arrange it," Julia went on. "Captain Medway sends you his kindest regards and sympathy. He is gone to see Sir William and Lord Nelson, and hopes, if nothing else prevents, to be able to take us back to Syracuse. You will like it there," she bent to hug little Peter. "I have a garden that runs right down to the shore. As soon as this wretched winter is over you will be able to swim every day."

"May I really? Oh, Mama, may we go?" And then he remembered. "But Mama says we have to go back to England with Captain Purvis. I would much rather go with you, Aunt Julia." He turned from one to the other. "Mama, say we can go! I do not think I want Captain Purvis for a Daddy."

There was a little silence. Julia had turned dead white, while Amanda felt the slow tide of colour rise in her face.

Julia spoke first. "Captain Purvis?" she asked.

Nothing for it. "He has done me the honour of asking me to be his wife."

"I see." And then, mechanically, "I give you joy, Lady Meynel."

The use of her title cut deep. "Oh, Julia," Amanda exclaimed. "Do not be angry with me."

"Angry? Why should I be angry?"

Worse and worse. Amanda plunged on. "Oh, Julia, I have been so wretched. You do not know the half of it. Only think of that Grassi—" she paused, remembering the child. "Peter, my love, run and tell them in the kitchen that your Aunt Julia stays for dinner with us." She knew the fascination of the kitchen and Peter's friends there well enough to be sure that this would give them time

245

to talk freely. When he had run eagerly off she made a little business of leading Julia up to her room and seating her in the only comfortable chair. "You must be exhausted from your journey."

"No," Julia still spoke mechanically. "You know I am an admirable sailor."

Once again that wretched silence. Julia broke it. "You were speaking of the Grassi."

"Yes . . . Would you believe it, Julia, after all we did for her, she has accused me of murdering Lord Meynel."

"My love!" At last the barrier between them was down. "You cannot be serious?"

"Never more so. Lord Meynel had made a will, you see, leaving her all his personal property. A lawyer came, a horrid sly little man called Pietronelli, and told me to hand it over, or I would regret it. And truly, Julia, I wanted to, but John and the Hamiltons said I must not. So then she began to spread it everywhere that I had killed my poor husband – as if she knew anything about it," Amanda added with a flash of spirit, "seeing that she was dead drunk at the time. And – and, Julia, there is worse – or at least I think it worse. She is telling stories about Peter too. I think," something compelled her to say this, "I think it was when John heard of them that he felt he must ask me to marry him." Suddenly it was all dust and ashes. She burst into tears. "Oh, Julia, I am so miserable."

Julia was stroking her hair. "My poor love, what a wretched time you have had of it. But at least you have not been arrested."

"No, I told the Chief of Police everything, and I think he believed me, but still I do not know, from day to day, what will happen to me. And, worst of all, my engagement to John, which he hoped would stop the voice of scandal, has merely aggravated it."

"That does not altogether surprise me," said Julia dryly. "Oh, Amanda, I wish I had been here. But we must think what is best to do now. You say Captain Purvis wishes you to return to England?"

"Yes, he intends—" how hard, somehow, this was to

246

say. "He wishes we may be married from my mother's house."

"I see."

Julia sat for a few moments silent, staring out of the window. What exactly did she see? Amanda found herself stammering once more into speech. "I wish we may go soon," she said. "It is not so much for my sake – I can bear it – but for Peter's. Julia, the other children will not play with him: their mothers call them away . . ."

"I wish Captain Medway would come," said Julia. Once again, the silence drew out between them. The moment of intimacy had passed; there was too much between them that could not be said, that could hardly even be thought. When the silent tension became intolerable, Amanda plunged into an account of the news from Naples. Julia frowned anxiously. "I wish I knew where my cousin was," she said. "I have heard nothing from him since I left Naples."

It was a deep relief to both of them when one of the inn servants announced that Captain Medway was below, asking for them. They hurried down to the inn's one public room where they found him looking very grave indeed. As he greeted her with formal condolences that sounded unexpectedly stiff, Amanda's heart sank. He, too, was angry with her. But his first real words were for Julia. "I have bad news for you, Countess. You must lose no time in going back on board the *Illustrious*. The Queen had news this morning that your cousin is one of the leaders of the new Parthenopean Republic and is reported to be urging an immediate alliance with the French. Worse still, she suspects you of being in traitorous communication with him. It is not safe for you to be here."

"I? Traitorous! But what in the world am I supposed to have done?"

"Merely betrayed the detailed plans for the Queen's flight from Naples."

"Good God." Amanda now remembered the rumours she had heard of treachery concerning the Queen's escape. "Now I understand it all. I clean forgot to tell you, Julia, that Lady Hamilton told me, only this morning, that I must warn you not to come to Palermo. What's to do now?"

But Julia was not thinking of her own danger. "Oh my poor cousin," she said, "if he has truly thrown in his lot with the French, he is lost indeed."

"I am afraid so," said Captain Medway, "but it is of your safety that we must be thinking. Let me escort you back to the harbour. My gig is waiting there and will take you directly back on board the *Illustrious*. I cannot be answerable for your safety else."

She looked from one to the other. "It is worse even than I feared," she said. "But . . ."

He took her up impatiently. "This is no time for buts. I am your cousin and, I am much afraid, by this the head of your family." And then, as she looked her surprise, "Yes. My father is dead, and my cousin dying. Only a miracle, the doctors say, can save him. They have sent for me to come home. It is a bitter blow that I must leave the scene of active service at this time, but I see no alternative. My mother needs me, and there are other circumstances that make it imperative that I should return to England without delay. I have Lord Nelson's permission to take the *Illustrious* there for a refit. You will accompany me."

She looked up at him for a moment, half mutinous, half pleading. "What – with little more than the clothes I stand up in? But – what's that to the purpose! You think my danger truly so great?"

"I know it. Believe me, cousin, I would not urge you to leave your home if it were not necessary. A happier day may come, but at the moment you risk not merely liberty but life itself if you stay here. Indeed we have already lost more time than we should. Come." He took her arm, then turned back once more to Amanda. "And do you be packing, Lady Meynel. Sir William advises that you should come with me too. I will explain when I return for you, but first I must see the Countess safe to my gig. Her danger is too immediate for more talking."

He left Amanda with her head in a whirl. Mechanically beginning to collect her possessions and Peter's she tried at the same time to collect her wild and random thoughts. She was to go home at last. How often, how vainly she had dreamed of the day when she would sail out of the blue bay and home to England. To fog, perhaps, and cold, to the old uneasy relationship with her mother, but, at last and at least, to home, to the thousand familiar trifling things that made for security and, she was beginning to think, for happiness.

Happiness. She paused in her work and stood, for a moment, her arms full of Peter's nightshirts, to think that she had forgotten what happiness tasted like. She was engaged to John: she should be happy. She was going home: she should be happy. Or, was that the trouble? Captain Medway had spoken as if he meant to sail at once and this would almost certainly mean that she must begin the long voyage home without seeing John to say goodbye. Surely this was the reason for her unaccountable wretchedness. She dropped the nightshirts angrily into a trunk and a tear followed them. What in the world was the matter with her? She was actually relieved to be going without seeing John again. In fact, suddenly, incredibly, she found herself wishing that this chance to go home had presented itself before she had engaged herself to him.

She was being absurd. Returning with renewed vigour to her packing she told herself she was making emotional mountains out of molehills. Julia's reaction to the news of her engagement had been merely that of surprise. But what of Captain Medway, who must have heard of it, and yet had made no attempt to congratulate her? Instead, there had been something freezing in his cold courtesy to her, which had contrasted painfully with the dictatorial warmth with which he had treated Julia. Suddenly, ridiculously, Amanda found herself envying Julia that protective kindness. Medway had always been kind – quite wonderfully kind, it seemed now – to her in the past. Why was he so cold to her now? Could he have heard the rumours about her? Could he – horrible thought – could he believe them? And why did she care so much?

Her preparations were almost completed when she

was once more summoned downstairs and found Captain Medway awaiting her. "She is safe on board," he said. "Are you ready?"

"I can be in five mintes. But – do you mean I must come on board at once? Should I not say farewell to the Hamiltons who have been so good to me – and to the Knights?"

"No time for that. I did not wish to alarm you unnecessarily before, but the Hamiltons have information that a warrant will be signed, any moment now, for your arrest. The Grassi, it seems, has made powerful friends here in Palermo."

"Oh." He must have heard it all. No wonder he looked at her so gravely. "You have heard the stories then?"

"Of course. I was afraid your kindness to that woman would bring you no good, and yet," his tone warmed suddenly, "I could not help but admire you for it."

How different, how heart-warmingly different from John's reaction. She looked up at him, her eyes suddenly blurred with tears. "Thank you," she said. "I have asked myself so many times whether I should not have left her behind. But how could I?"

For the first time, he smiled at her, the dark blue eyes suddenly kind. "I know. For what it is worth, I think you were right."

"Oh, thank you." And then, with an effort that surprised her. "But you have not congratulated me on my engagement."

His eyes were cold again. "I see no cause."

Speechless with mortification, she ran upstairs and finished her packing in five frenzied minutes. Rejoining Captain Medway, she was relieved to find Peter with him. They were well embarked on a grave discussion of the course they would take for England. "You see, Mama," Peter interrupted himself to say triumphantly, "I was right and you were wrong. It *is* Captain Medway who is to take us home, and he says he will teach me navi – how to sail. Oh, Mama, I do wish—"

Terrified of what the wish might be, she interrupted him

with a perfect barrage of maternal command. By the time he was ready for the journey, he had quite forgotten what he wished. And by the time Amanda had paid what seemed to her the innkeeper's grossly exorbitant bill she found herself once more penniless, Sir William's loan exhausted. There was no doubt about it that the offer of accommodation on the *Illustrious* was providential for her, but, oh, how she wished it had been the *Falcon*. Or did she? She was not sure what she wished any longer – mainly, she thought, simply to be left alone. Worn out with all that she had been through, she could have asked nothing better than to be let sleep out the voyage home to England. But, instead, she must face Captain Medway's disapproval, and Julia's misery. It did not look to be an enjoyable voyage.

And yet, why should Captain Medway disapprove? Surely, he if no one else must know of her long love for John. Could he possibly be in love, himself, with Julia? Could he, by some fantastic stretch of devotion, resent the engagement on her account? It would be just like him, Amanda thought, and then, surprisingly, found herself making a rather painful comparison with John Purvis in this respect. There was certainly no doubt about Captain Medway's sympathetic attention to Julia, which was in marked contrast to his continued cool civility to herself. He was concentrating, now, on answering Peter's flood of questions about the voyage, leaving her to say her farewells to the Knights, who had luckily just returned. Thanking them warmly for all their kindness both to her and to Peter, Amanda found herself nevertheless listening with half her mind to the friendly talk that was going on at the other side of the room.

At last a sailor knocked at the door to announce that all Amanda's luggage was on board. It was time to go. The last farewells were soon said, with many hopeful promises of a happy reunion in England, and many messages left by Amanda for Lady Hamilton. Outside, the wind blew cold and Amanda's heart was oddly heavy as Captain Medway escorted them to his gig, with a flow of friendly talk for Peter and a continued grave, aloof courtesy to herself that she found increasingly hard to bear.

Piped on board with her captain, Amanda found that the *Illustrious* presented a marked contrast to the slovenly Portuguese ship on which they had come to Palermo. As for Peter, he had never been on board an English man-of-war before and was in a perfect seventh heaven of excitement, exclaiming at the decks, holystoned to brilliant whiteness, and at the sailors, agile as monkeys in the rigging: "Mama, may I try?"

Acknowledging Captain Medway's introduction of those of his officers who were on deck to greet him, Amanda found herself preoccupied with the question of their accommodation, and learned with deep, unspoken relief, that she and Peter were not, as she had feared, to share a cabin with Julia. Captain Medway, it seemed, had arranged otherwise.

He went further. "The Countess," he said, "is worn out with shock as much as with travelling. We had a rough voyage of it from Syracuse and she was in no state for the blow she received today." And then, as Amanda asked herself miserably what blow he meant, he went on. "She may be half English, but she has lived here all her life, and now leaves, at the shortest of notice, and with none of her possessions. It is no wonder that she finds herself indisposed. I have recommended that she keep her cabin for the rest of the day."

"Yes, poor Julia." Amanda now blamed herself bitterly for having thought of her own miseries to the exclusion of Julia's, and then blamed herself still more for feeling a spurt of resentment at Medway's consideration for Julia. He had wasted little enough sympathy on her, a widow of hardly more than a week, and a fugitive as well as Julia. But – poor Julia. "May I go to her?" she asked.

"Best not, I think. She is in no mood for company." His tone made it an order. "And, indeed, you, too, would be well advised to keep to your cabin until we sail, which I hope to do at dawn. There is no knowing when the warrant for your arrest will be issued, and though you

252

are, of course, safe on my ship, Sir William particularly asked me not to flaunt your presence here. We do not want to make an international incident of you."

"Indeed not. I will go below at once." Then a new thought struck her. "I am running away, am I not? I have been so busy that I had not properly realized it before, but everyone will think I have proved myself guilty by this retreat. Should I not stay and fight, for Peter's sake if not for my own?"

His voice was suddenly kind as he answered. "Do not be troubling yourself about that. Your flight will be a nine days' wonder: no more. After all, what more proper than that you should take the first opportunity of returning to England, circumstanced as you are? And as for the charges against you, Sir William will see that they are properly answered and your name cleared. I gave him my deposition for the Chief of Police when I was on shore, which should explode many of the slanders against you, and it is but a matter of time until the others are equally answered, but it is time that you will spend more happily, I hope, on board the *Illustrious* than in a Sicilian prison. Besides, there is the child to be considered. What would happen to him if you were to be arrested?"

"That is what has terrified me," she said. "I do not think I am usually cowardly for myself, but where Peter is concerned – that is another matter. He is all I have," she went on, and then thought how oddly this sounded in one who had just announced her engagement.

He did not seem to notice. "He is a fine boy and does you credit." His voice was warm with approval, then suddenly chilled to formality. "But I must excuse myself. There is much to do before we are ready to sail."

To Amanda's exacerbated nerves it seemed like the snub direct. She turned away to hide a sudden, absurd start of tears. What a wretched voyage this was going to be, with Captain Medway cold and Julia estranged. But it was still nothing, surely, to cry over. She called Peter from his enraptured study of a group of busy sailors and turned towards the companionway that led to their cabin.

Peter dragged back against her hand. "Sir! Sir!"

Captain Medway had moved away across the deck, but now looked back over his shoulder with the smile that so transformed his usually grave face. "Yes, Peter?"

"May I not stay on deck? How can I learn to be a sailor if I am to stay below with the women."

Amanda could not help a smile at this assumption of masculine equality, and Captain Medway laughed outright. "Very well," he said. "You shall stay with me. And the first time you get in my way, or ask questions when I am busy, you go below. Right?"

"Right, sir."

"Good." And then, to Amanda, "Do not trouble yourself about him. He will mind me."

She was sure of it. On his own ship, Medway was a formidable figure. She hurried down to her cabin, passing, almost on tiptoe, the door that she knew to be Julia's, and kept thought at bay by busying herself in making the tiny room in which she and Peter must live for the next weeks as comfortable as possible.

Peter came bouncing down at bedtime in tearing spirits. He had been all over the ship and made friends with the sailors. One was going to teach him how to tie knots – "He says that Portuguese told me all wrong, Mama. They do things quite otherwise in His Majesty's ships." They were certainly to sail in the morning, he told her, ate his share of the supper that had been brought, and fell fast asleep practically in mid-sentence. For Amanda, sleep came less easily, and when at last she did doze off it was into a succession of nightmares, the day's events transmuted into terror.

Inevitably, Peter waked her at first light. There were already signs of activity above them: shouted orders, the scurry of feet across the deck. Peter was struggling into his clothes. "Mama, I promised I would be up to see them weigh anchor!" And then, characteristically, a question: "Why do they weigh it, Mama?"

She had not the heart to forbid his watching the ship sail, but dared not let him go up alone. "Just a moment," she was quickly dressing. "I must take you up and find someone to look after you."

"Oh, Mama," but he recognized finality in her tones, and waited for her, jumping up and down with impatience.

They emerged, a few minutes later, into the hazy light of very early morning. Gazing across the harbour, Amanda saw that another ship had tied up during the night. Surely it was the *Falcon*? Her heart did something so complicated and uncomfortable that she had to stand still for a moment, holding on to a rope. Around them was highly organized chaos as barefoot sailors rushed hither and thither in response to shouted, incomprehensible orders. But Amanda paid no attention to them, straining her eyes in the morning mist. It was the *Falcon*. A new volley of orders warned her that they were to sail directly. It was not possible. To sail, without seeing John? But – did she want to see John? And if not, what was the matter with her?

"Lady Meynel!" Captain Medway's cool voice made her jump. "I thought you were to stay below decks till we had sailed."

She turned to face him, conscious that the harbour wind had whipped her curls about her cheeks, unaware of the becoming flush of colour that stained them. "I – I cry your pardon. Peter was longing to see the *Illustrious* sail. I meant but to find someone who would have an eye to him."

"I see." He smiled a kind greeting to Peter. "Well, it hardly signifies now, since we sail directly."

"But—" how could she say it, yet how could she not? "Is not that the *Falcon?*"

"Yes." For a moment she thought he would leave it at that. Then he relented and went on. "She came in last night. Captain Purvis, I am sorry to say, is wounded. He comes home with us."

"John! Wounded!" And she had not even thought to be anxious about him. "Not – not seriously?"

"No – in the arm. He says it is deuced inconvenient, no more. But it is his right arm; Lord Nelson has ordered him home."

She had been taking it in slowly. "You said – he sails with us?"

"Precisely. He is already on board. We shall be a merry party, shall we not?"

He was mocking her. She looked up at him, for a moment, in speechless reproach, and then turned, just before the tears filled her eyes, and almost ran back to her cabin. She would have given anything to be able to stay out the voyage there, but anxiety over Peter drove her back on deck soon after the *Illustrious* had cleared the harbour. The wind was fair, the day fine, and the chaos above-decks had calmed into order so that brown-faced, bare-footed sailors had time to grin at her and promise her "a right speedy voyage".

It could not be too speedy for her. The idea of the inevitable foursome over meals in the Captain's cabin appalled her. For Julia's behaviour since she had heard of her own engagement to John had convinced her that she must love him too. Poor Julia, she thought. Her position was worse even than her own, and wondered whether it had been broken to her yet that she was to have for ship companion not only the friend who had stolen the man she loved, but that man himself. Oh well, Amanda told herself bitterly, she could rely on Captain Medway to look after Julia's interests and make things as easy as possible for her.

She met the ship's doctor that afternoon and learned from him that the countess was still gravely indisposed. He had just seen her and had recommended, he said, that she keep her cabin for several more days, and had given the same simplifying verdict to John, whose wound had brought on a bout of fever.

"May I visit them?" asked Amanda.

He looked at her repressively. "The Countess wishes to see no one," he said, "and young ladies do not visit gentlemen in their cabins on board His Majesty's ships."

Feeling about Peter's age, she sought consolation in his company on deck and allowed him the promised treat of showing her all over the ship. Amazed and delighted at

256

the neatness and order of everything, in contrast to the dirty confusion of the Portuguese ship in which they had travelled from Naples, she won golden opinions from the crew – who were already Peter's firm friends – by her exclamations of pleased surprise. And, oh, what a pleasure it was, after all the years of exile, to be speaking English again as a matter of course. Peter had naturally grown up bilingual, with a strong tendency to break into Neapolitan slang, but now he was picking up the British kind, and she found herself unable to repress her laughter at his grave parroting of nautical phrases.

Altogether, they were surprisingly happy days that followed. Julia and John were still confined to their cabins, Amanda and Peter spent peaceful days on deck in a halcyon spell of mild winter sunshine. Gradually, as three peaceful days passed, Amanda began to feel safe again and, as she did so, to realize just how desperate and frightened she had been those last days in Palermo. Now it was all over. She had not been arrested: she had escaped; she was going home. Scandal, no doubt, would follow her, or even be there already to greet her, but scandal could be faced. Days in the fresh air meant nights of dreamless sleep; her cheeks were brown again, her hand no longer shook, and returning health brought with it a return of courage. Absurd to have been so frightened back in Palermo . . . But, no, she told herself, it had not been absurd, for there had been Peter to think of. What would have happened to him if she had been arrested?

Dinner was the only formidable time of her day, since then tradition demanded that she dress in her best and dine with Captain Medway in his cabin. To her deep relief, the other officers had been present on the first day, so that what she had dreaded as a private ordeal had proved a pleasant enough social occasion, with the young lieutenants vying with each other to entertain her. But next day, to her dismay, she found herself facing Medway alone across the diminished table. She still did not understand why he had been so angry with her in Palermo, but his fierce comment on her engagement echoed in her ears. He had always been so kind before, she had considered him so safe a friend, that this sudden change in him had been doubly painful. Aware of returning strength, and, with it a reassuring improvement in her looks which had been, those last few days in Palermo, positively haggard, she determined to take advantage of this opportunity to try and make him, once more, her friend. Finding him, on this occasion, himself preoccupied, she exerted herself to be entertaining, finding that many episodes of her stay in Palermo, however painful at the time, could now be relegated to their proper place as comic stories.

He listened, and laughed. At last, "I am glad you can find it entertaining," he said. "You did not at the time."

"No," she said frankly. "I was terrified."

"I do not blame you. I only wish . . ." He did not tell her what he wished, but changed the subject. "The doctor tells me that both our invalids are mending rapidly. A few more days will see them able to leave their cabins."

"Oh," she paused. "I am glad to hear it." She could not quite make herself sound glad. Did he intend it as a warning? A threat? If only she knew what he thought about it all.

To her relief, he changed the subject to that of the changes she would find in English life. London, he said, was as gay as ever, but there were rumblings of discontent, particularly in the north country. The long strain of war was beginning to make itself felt.

"Five years," she said thoughtfully. "It is a long time – and six since I have been home. But, of course, I hardly know London, nor do I intend to stay there. I mean to go straight to my mother."

He looked, she thought, approving. "You will be wise. Unless . . ." again he failed to finish his sentence, and again changed the subject, to query, in surprised tones, her statement that she hardly knew London. "I would have thought your husband . . ."

How long ago it all seemed. "He liked it well enough, but liked the country, I think, better. The only occasion when we stayed there for any length of time was at the

258

last, before we sailed." How she had suffered then, hoping each day, that John would arrive . . . and when he had, at last, come to her, he had been so angry . . . It was a very long time ago. Could anything ever be so painful again?

Two days later, she knew that it could. The peaceful interval of tête-à-tête dinners with Captain Medway was over. No longer could she sit across the table and let him lecture her, as he clearly liked doing, about politics and the inquities of Mr Fox. Julia and John were both better and made their first appearance, pale and drawn, for the Captain's dinner. Amanda would not have thought she could have greeted John's appearance with so little enthusiasm, but then he brought so many problems with him. His right arm was still in a sling, so he took her hand in his left, and bent low over it. Julia, equally pale and even more fine-drawn, received exactly the same greeting. In the background, very much in command, stood Captain Medway. Nobody said anything about the engagement, and yet she and John were meeting for the first time, publicly, as an affianced couple. But it was Medway's ship, if he did not mean to say anything, no one else would. It was a strange evening, with little sharp bursts of conversation, mainly between Medway and John Purvis, and long silences, when Amanda wracked her brains for an innocent subject and listened half-consciously to the thousand small noises of the working ship.

Julia was silent and grew, at last, so pale that Amanda rose. "You are exhausted, my love, let me take you to your cabin."

The two gentlemen bid them a courteous and, she thought, relieved goodnight, but when they reached Julia's cabin door, and Amanda would have come in and helped her exhausted friend to bed, Julia was firm. "I thank you," she said, "but I am best alone." It was gentle, firm, and final. Amanda had been put out of her life.

It was very early still, for Captain Medway dined at three. Restless and miserable, Amanda prowled about the confined space of her cabin, wishing she had Peter for company. But this was the time of day when he had what he called his navitation lessons from his friend the first mate. He would not come to her till bedtime. There was no protection from her thoughts. She loved Julia dearly and had made her desperately, perhaps incurably, unhappy. Or would Captain Medway's courteous attentions, which had been particularly noticeable at dinner, presently effect a cure? Would there be another engagement before they reached England? She ought to hope for it, but, oddly, could not. Wherever she looked, there was misery. John had made no move to see her alone and discuss their engagement. He had not even kissed her since he asked her to marry him. Worse still, she was not sure that she wanted him to. What a long, long time ago they seemed, those frenzied kisses at Torre del Greco, with the volcano thundering outside. Indeed it was so long ago that it seemed, now, like a dream – a dream of lost happiness.

If she could have, she would have paced the tiny room. Had she made a terrible mistake in engaging herself to John? Was that long love of hers nothing but a mirage? – a defence, perhaps, against the misery of life with her husband? And – more important still – what did he feel? Why had he treated her, this evening, so formally? Memory of the stilted wretchedness of that dinner was too much to be born. For Medway, too, who had seemed to warm towards her during their solitary dinners, had become once more the formal captain, keeping her at courteous arm's length while he plied Julia with every possible attention. Julia must eat a little of this and a little of that, she must take a glass of wine with him. Afterwards, "Your health, Lady Meynel," had been the most obvious of formalities. Oh, she was miserable – miserable. And she dared not even allow herself the relief of tears since Peter might come in and find her so.

Still, it was a relief when he came bouncing into the cabin, flushed and cheerful, to demand the story she always told him at bedtime, and it was faintly disconcerting when

260

he fell fast asleep half-way through. Once again, she was alone, bitterly, totally alone in the busy ship. The swift Mediterranean night had fallen while she was getting Peter ready for bed and she had been reading to him by the light of a swinging lantern. She sat for a while, hands loosely folded in her lap, probing for the causes of her misery. Everything was out of joint – but why?

She was roused by the sound of voices from the deck above. The night was still, and they came down to her clearly, above the soft innumerable creakings of the ship. The speakers must be standing almost immediately above her cabin window.

"I should not have come." It was Julia's voice.

"I had to see you." John Purvis. Amanda's hands clenched tight in her lap. There was nothing to do but listen.

"There was no need. I understood. I am come only to tell you how completely I understand it all."

"You cannot . . ." He broke off for a minute. "You must not think . . . Oh, Julia, pity me."

"Pity? Should I, do you think?"

"If you knew what I am suffering, you would. Tell me what else I could have done, finding her so beset?"

"You could have kept faith with me. Or were you just amusing yourself, that night in Naples?"

He gave a groan. "I cannot blame you if you do not forgive me. Julia, I shall never forgive myself. I should not have tried to snatch at happiness, and so involved you in my misery. I should have known that, whatever happened, I was morally committed to her."

"Because of the child?" Julia's voice shook on the question.

"I did not know then, about the child. Now, what else can I do? Oh, I am ashamed to be talking to you so, but I cannot face my life without your forgiveness, the knowledge of your pity, your understanding. I am bound to her by my own act, my own madness. There is no escape."

"No." Her voice was steady now. "There is no escape. I am sorry for us all, Mr Purvis. Now, goodbye."

261

"Julia!" There was the sound of movement, a little exclamation of protest from her, then silence as Amanda buried her head in the coverings of Peter's bed. It was lucky he slept so soundly, or her sobs would have roused him. At last, she was quiet, sitting there in the flickering light of the lantern, looking, dry-eyed, at the disaster she had made of her life. No wonder they had all been angry with her. How could she have been so wilfully blind? Looking back, the fact of John and Julia shouted from every meeting. She had seen it, herself, often enough, and refused to believe what she saw. Doubtless Captain Medway had been equally aware of it, had perhaps even been John's confidant. And still she had let John bind himself to her, out of pity . . . No, she caught herself up, it was worse than that. It had been out of a sense of obligation. She had been right in suspecting that he had never forgiven himself for that night at Torre del Greco. Now, he was taking his punishment.

No wonder he had never kissed her, nor spoken of love. No wonder he had avoided her. She was on her feet now, standing, looking at nothing, her hands clenched. Bolt upright there, under the swaying lamp, she knew she should be in despair. In fact, she was at once angry and relieved. She had lost her one, her only love, had lost John, for whom she had suffered so long. Her heart should be breaking. Well, maybe it was, but with rage at herself for having been such a fool. How long had she gone on dreaming of love, after the reality had faded? She was as bad as John; worse, because he had at least been honest with himself. He had felt morally bound by their night together, she had dreamed herself into a state of emotional purblindness because of it.

So far from loving John, just now she was not even sure that she liked him very much. No wonder Julia had looked so wretched . . . no wonder Captain Medway, looking on, had blamed her. But what now? The tiny cabin stifled her. As always, before anything else, there was Peter to be considered. John was his father. If she broke off her unlucky engagement as every instinct cried to do, she snatched from the child his chance to have both parents.

She stopped to look down at him, busily asleep in his cot. He had done well enough so far. Better no father than a reluctant one. Memories flooded in on her, of the times when she had thought John oddly careless about Peter. And as for the child, he made no secret of his preference for Captain Medway. Suddenly, unaccountably crimson, she remembered how Peter had jumped to the conclusion that Medway was to be his new father. No, to marry John for his sake was to indulge in just the kind of emotional self-delusion that had brought her where she was. The decision brought enormous relief. How odd not to have realized before that she did not in the least want to marry John.

Very well then. She sat down in the cabin's only chair. But how to break off the wretched engagement with a minimum of discomfort to everyone? She sat very late, until the light of the lantern burned dim, but climbed into bed at last with a smile on her lips, and slept the deep, unbroken sleep of relief.

# Chapter Sixteen

Amanda woke next morning to a novel and delightful feeling of self-confidence. All her life, it seemed to her now, she had been giving way to other people's plans for her, waiting on their decisions, accepting their advice. Her marriage had been her mother's doing, this new and wretched engagement, John's. Now, at last – and not before it was time – she was going to take charge of herself, and, of course, of Peter. If it led to disaster, well, at least it would be her own disaster.

The first thing was to break her engagement. But how? At all costs, she must give John no inkling that she had learned of his commitment to Julia. She must leave him free, not burdened with the old feeling of guilt towards herself; that was the least she could do for him. The idea of a letter was tempting, because it seemed easy, and as she ate her breakfast she sampled different phrases along with her coffee. But, no, somehow it would not do. There were too many chances of misunderstanding in a letter, and it seemed also dangerously deliberate. He would be bound to suspect that she, for her part, suspected something about him and Julia. No, it would have to be a quarrel and, it occurred to her, as public a quarrel as possible. It was not only John who must know himself free – the sooner Captain Medway and Julia knew it too, the better.

Very well – a quarrel then. Surely, considering the way John must feel towards her, it should be easy enough. The worst of it was that it meant biding her time. She must wait until the chance for getting into a convincing rage with John presented itself.

She was lucky – or perhaps the stretched state of all their

nerves made it inevitable. At all events, her opportunity came over dinner that same day. It had begun as a wretched meal, with Julia, who had stayed in her cabin all day, white and silent, and John saying little more. Amanda, convinced now that all this misery was her fault had exerted herself to talk about indifferent subjects and Captain Medway had seconded her admirably. But it is curiously difficult to carry on a tête-à-tête conversation with a silent audience of two. Subjects which should have lasted through the meal dwindled and died on their hands. The weather, that invariable British standby, led naturally to Captain Medway's hopes that they would reach Gibraltar next day, and this to the course of the war, about which he was discouraging. Peace, if it should come, could only be a shameful one; he hoped the Government at home would have the courage of its convictions, however heavy the odds seemed. Suddenly eloquent, he quoted Shakespeare: "'This England never did nor never shall Lie at the proud foot of the conqueror'," and Amanda's enthusiasm rose to match his. But still there was the mute burden of the others' silence, and now a midshipman came tapping at the door to whisper something to Medway who rose and excused himself. Left alone with her dismal companions, Amanda tried a new tack and talked of Palermo and then, by an almost inevitable transition, of the Hamiltons and their goodness to her. "I must write Lady Hamilton a note of thanks for all her kindness and send it back from Gibraltar," she said, as much to herself as to them.

It drew a surprising reaction from John, who had been drinking, she had noticed, rather heavily. "You will do no such thing," he said.

"I beg your pardon?" She did not believe she could have heard him correctly.

"I said, 'You will do no such thing.' It was well enough to associate with Lady Hamilton when you were in Naples, or in Sicily. Her position as wife to the Ambassador made it impossible to do otherwise. But remember, I beg, that though she may be the Ambassador's wife, she has not, in fact, been granted the rank of Ambassadress, nor did the Queen think fit to receive her upon the occasion of her marriage. It is a connection, Amanda, that can do you nothing but harm, and should be dropped without delay."

"Drop Lady Hamilton?" Amanda still could not believe her ears. "Have you taken leave of your senses, John?"

"Far from it, but I have often wondered the same thing about you. Associating with Lady Hamilton in public was one thing, granted, as I have said, the peculiar circumstances of her position, but to be running in and out of her house all day, and exposing your child, too, to the contamination of her presence was quite another pair of sleeves. I am surprised you would not have had more sense."

"Let me understand you correctly." She was dangerously, deliciously angry now. "So long as it was useful to me to be acquainted with Lady Hamilton, I was right to take advantage of the connection, provided, of course, that I took care to involve myself in it as little as possible, but now that Lady Hamilton can be of no further use to me I should drop her without delay."

He had the grace to look uncomfortable. "You do not understand, nor do I like to explain the matter further to you, and particularly," his glance wavered to Julia, "in the presence of a young lady. But surely you, as a married woman, must be aware that there is much in Lady Hamilton's past that makes her an unsuitable acquaintance for you." She was about to interrupt him, but he raised a monitory hand and went on. "But there is more. I am sorry to have to say it, but there is talk now, too much talk in the fleet about her relations with Lord Nelson. Why does he stay there in Palermo, gambling the nights away, risking health and reputation, but because she has ensnared him with her Circean charms?" He seemed, Amanda thought, to have forgotten the presence of the "young lady" now as he warmed to his theme. "As for Sir William, he is the butt of the fleet, for a compliant old fool. The three of them share expenses in that house of theirs; did you ever hear of anything so shameful? The money paid to Lord Nelson by a grateful nation for his victory is squandered on that trull.

266

Who wears the fur pelisse that the Grand Turk sent Lord Nelson for his services to humanity? Who postures about in the diamond plume that once adorned a monarch's brow? Who ministers to our Admiral's every vice and causes him to forget duty, honour, everything? Why Lady Hamilton, or should I say Amy Lyon, for that, I believe, is the name under which she once walked the streets."

Amanda had forgotten plans and policy now. She had not believed she could be so angry. "You are speaking of my friend," she said.

"Your friend! Your confidante, too, I have no doubt, and your adviser. I might have known it, with such an example . . ." he stopped, appalled, himself, at what he had said.

"Yes?" she was still dangerously quiet. "Do, pray, continue. With such an example, you were saying, it is no wonder if I have conducted myself with so little propriety." Her cheeks burned as she remembered that night at Torre del Greco, but consideration for Julia prevented her from saying more. "I wish you had given me a ring," she said instead.

"A ring?" His tone was a blend of irritation and surprise.

"An engagement ring." She felt herself cold white with anger. "So that I could take it off now, and throw it in your face."

The cabin door had opened while she was speaking and Captain Medway silent there, had heard every word she said. Now he advanced. "I am sorry to break up the party," he said, his ironical glance for Amanda alone, "but I fear I must order you to your cabins. We have run, I am sorry to say, into a fog. I shall feel safer if I know where you all are."

There was a little sigh in the cabin as the tension broke. They all rose.

"Amanda," said John.

She swept him a low curtsey. "I meant it," she said. "Every word of it. We will not discuss it further. Now I must go and write to my friend Lady Hamilton."

She found Peter fretting in idleness in their cabin.

Usually he would have still been up on deck at this time, but today darkness had fallen early. "There is going to be a regular snorter of a fog," he informed her, rolling over on his cot. "Mr Mansel says he does not wish to see me on deck till it clears. They will have enough to do without me getting in the way."

Amanda's heart sank at this confirmation of what Medway had said. They had spoken too soon at dinner when they congratulated themselves on the speed with which the voyage was being accomplished. And, indeed, two days of maddening inactivity followed as they lay almost becalmed in the unseasonable fog which seeped gradually through the ship, so that everything was damp, and grey, and gloomy. Only John and Julia were in tearing spirits, which they did their best to conceal when Amanda was about. As for Captain Medway, he seemed to be on deck twenty-four hours out of the twenty-four, peering ahead through the murky darkness. At least, Amanda congratulated herself, there was an end to the misery of the Captain's dinners. She and Peter ate and lived in their cabin, fending off boredom as best they might.

By the afternoon of the second day, Peter was so fractious from the long confinement that Amanda could bear it no longer. "Come," she said, "wrap up warmly and we will take a turn on the Captain's walk. I am sure Captain Medway will not mind it."

Peter was all enthusiasm at once. To be out in the fog turned it immediately from a dead bore to an exciting adventure . . . But Amanda, venturing out with him on to the damp and slippery deck, was not so sure. She had not expected quite so grey and strange a world. "One turn on the deck," she had a firm grip on Peter's hand. "And we will go down again. I do not think we should be here." It was with a mixture of fright and relief that she saw a tall figure loom out of the mist towards them.

"What are you doing here?" Captain Medway's voice was sharp.

"We could not bear it below decks any longer. I promised Peter one turn before he goes to bed."

"Very well," he took her arm. "But go carefully, the deck is slippery."

"Yes. I am glad you found us."

"You should not have come up without permission." It was hardly a rebuke. "I am gradually learning what a precipitate young lady you are. Is it true that you have broken your engagement?"

"Quite true." They were speaking low, and Peter was too busy making foghorn noises to hear them.

"I am glad to hear it."

She laughed. "You were very angry when you learned of it, I know. What a poor fool you must have thought me."

"I never took you for a fool, Lady Meynel. Impulsive, perhaps—" Suddenly his arm was iron against her side. "Hush!" And then, leaning beyond her to Peter. "In with you and down to your cabin. There is the door." Before she could protest, Peter was gone, implicitly obedient to the command in Medway's voice. Light had shone out for a moment from the entrance way and now the fog seemed thicker than ever. And, "Hush," again said Captain Medway.

Standing beside him in the darkness, intensely aware of the pressure of his arm on hers, she strained every sense to understand his sudden command. Then, she heard what he had, a disembodied voice from over the water shouting a command – in French. And now an officer materialized out of the fog beside them and there was a quick, whispered interchange of report and command before the man vanished as silently as he had come.

Medway bent towards her. "You, too, must go below," his voice just carried above the creaking of the ship.

"What is it?"

"It is lucky you are so adventurous a young lady." Was there the hint of a laugh in his voice? "We seem to be in the midst of the French fleet."

"Oh." She peered up at him through the fog. "How . . ." she searched for the right word. "How inconvenient."

"Is it not?" Now there was no mistaking the laughter in his voice. "Do you know; I hope we elude them. There is

269

something I would like to say to you, Lady Meynel." His hand on the doorway, he bent suddenly over her, kissed her hard on the lips, then pushed her through without another word and turned to hurry away through the darkness.

Below decks, all was activity – and whispers. The news that they were in the midst of the French fleet had travelled with amazing rapidity and the crew were hurrying to their action stations, showing every sign of enthusiasm at the idea of taking on the entire French fleet single-handed. Hurrying, herself, to her cabin, Amanda came suddenly on John Purvis and Julia at the doorway of Julia's. Fast in each other's arms, they sprang guiltily apart at sight of her, but she merely smiled at them and hurried on, absorbed in the tumult of her own thoughts. To her relief, Peter had gone, as bidden, to their cabin, and was kneeling on her bed, trying to see out through the murky darkness. He turned to her eagerly, "Is it truly the French? Will there be a battle?"

"I sincerely hope not." Like him, she spoke in a whisper.

"Oh, Mama," he was disgusted with her. "You cannot mean it."

"I most certainly do. I have no wish to be a dead heroine." She turned, as Julia entered the cabin, still crimson with the confusion of their recent encounter and obviously uncertain whether to refer to it or not.

"My love," Amanda held out welcoming hands. "I am so glad you are come. This child of mine is all agog for a battle, which, between you and me, is the last thing I want."

"Or I either," said Julia. "John Purvis is gone to offer his services to Captain Medway – and his wound is nothing like healed."

"Still," said Amanda reasonably, "you would not expect him to do anything else."

"Of course not." Still holding hands, they looked at each other searchingly for a few moments, then, silently, leaned forward and kissed.

"Mama," an eager whisper from Peter called them back to the window. "Look! A ship!"

For an instant, peering out through the murk, they saw a darker shape in the darkness, with here and there the fuzzy glow of lights, then, as quickly, it was gone. Julia's hand was cold in Amanda's. Had they been seen? If they had, the alternatives were death or capture, with death much the more likely. The silence drew out. Amanda was counting to herself, slowly. She reached a hundred . . . two hundred . . . her hand in Julia's relaxed. If they had been seen, they would surely have been blown out of the water by now.

Peter turned from the window in disgust. "A perfect target," he said. "And we let them go."

"Bloodthirsty little savage," said Julia. "What say you to a game of cards, my love?"

Half an hour later they were roused by a tap at the door. John Purvis looked in. "Have you seen—?" he began anxiously, and then, seeing Julia, "Oh, there you are, I was nearly distracted—"

Amanda smiled up at him from the improvised card table. "She is teaching my son to gamble," she said. "And being roundly beaten for her pains. But what's the news?"

"All's well." He closed the cabin door behind him. "Medway sent me to tell you that we are clear of the French and the wind is rising. We should be out of the fog in half an hour or so . . . and, with luck, at Gibraltar tomorrow."

"Excellent." Amanda was dealing. "Do you wish to cut in, Mr Purvis?" And then, casually, "What a fortunate thing the fog did not clear half an hour sooner."

"Yes, was it not?" He settled himself on the floor beside Julia. "May I really join you?"

"Do." She dealt him in. "It would be too tame, would it not, to go meekly to bed after being cheated of a glorious death. Peter here is quite inconsolable."

John's hand was just touching Julia's knee. "I can bear to be alive," he said.

Amanda smiled at them impartially. "So can I."

They played on until Peter fell asleep with his fair curls among his cards, but still Captain Medway did not join them. Amanda sighed and picked Peter up. "Well, time for bed, I suppose," she said.

"Yes." John rose and held out his good hand to Julia. "Come. I will see you to your cabin." And then, turning suddenly back to face Amanda, he took the plunge. "I have been trying to persuade the Countess to marry me at Gibraltar."

"So soon?" Amanda thought about it for a moment, then: "Do you know, I think it an excellent notion." She smiled at Julia. "Then you can chaperone me for the rest of the voyage, my love. It will make a change . . . But for the moment," she settled Peter on his bed, "I must wish you both joy and bid you goodnight."

She woke next morning to brilliant sunshine and the sounds and smells of harbour. The *Illustrious* was already tying up under the rock of Gibraltar. Peter, miraculously, was still asleep after his late night and she was able to lie for a little while, conscious that it was late, sorting over the memories of the night before, nibbling timidly at a brilliant new taste of happiness.

"Mama, did I dream it?" Peter sat suddenly bolt upright, wide awake.

"No, no, it was a real adventure. And now here we are safe and sound at Gibraltar."

"Gibraltar!" He was out of bed in a flash. "Can you see the Rock? May I feed the monkeys? When are we going ashore?" He was pulling on his clothes as he spoke and Amanda sighed and followed suit. The day had begun.

Julia joined them just as they were finishing their breakfast and told Amanda that Medway and Purvis had already gone ashore, Medway to report to the Governor and Purvis to arrange for a special licence for their marriage. "Do you think me mad, Amanda?"

"On the contrary, I think you very wise." Their eyes met for a long, silent interchange. "As for me," Amanda went bravely on, "I would not have thought it possible I could be so beyond permission foolish."

"You are sure?"

"Positive." Impossible to explain what blinding illumination had come with Medway's kiss. Was it only yesterday that she had congratulated herself on being independent of others?

Julia was looking at her closely. "Tell me . . ." and then, "no, I'll not ask it."

Amanda laughed. "Thank you, my love, for truly, I should not know what to answer." And then, to change the subject, "But, tell me, what do you propose to wear for this sudden wedding of yours."

They spent the rest of the morning in a happy inquisition into their respective wardrobes. Julia's, since she had intended only a brief stay at Palermo, was deplorably scanty, and she yielded without much persuasion to Amanda's urging that she accept a new dress of her own that she had been prevented, by her sudden plunge into mourning, from ever wearing.

"Though truly," said Julia, bending to admire her reflection in the glass that Amanda held for her, "I wonder that you persist in wearing black for Lord Meynel. After all, his will, if nothing else, must free you from all obligation to him."

Amanda had been thinking very much the same thing, but hardly liked to say that it had been John Purvis who had advised her mourning. So much of his advice had turned out badly, poor John . . . But Julia, she thought, would keep him straight. Once again, she turned the subject. "Perhaps I will allow myself my lavender coloured muslin for your wedding. That white becomes you to a marvel, my love. It would never have suited me."

Peter was tugging at her skirts. "Mama, they are coming back; the Captain's gig is coming! *Now* can we go ashore?"

"If Captain Medway permits." But she was eager enough to follow him as he ran up on deck to greet the two men. Time seemed to have stood still since Medway had kissed her. How much longer must she wait for a moment alone with him, when he could confirm what all her instincts told her, but her reason still feared to believe?

273

By the time Julia had been disrobed and clad once more in her demure travelling dress of plum-coloured sarsenet, the Captain's gig was alongside, and the two girls reached the deck to see Peter dancing excitedly round Captain Medway. "May we go ashore, my mama and I? May we? May we?"

"Gently, gently." Medway detached an eager little hand that had grabbed at his uniform. "Your mama and I have business to attend to. Later, we will arrange for you to go ashore and see the monkeys."

"Later! Later!" Peter stamped his foot in the bitter disappointment of childhood. "Always later. Why am I not to be obeyed? After all, I am a lord and you are only a sea captain."

"Peter!" Amanda wished the deck would open and swallow her.

But Medway was unruffled. "If you are a lord, my lord, you had best try to behave like one." And then, to Amanda, "Do not mind it too much. The child is spoiled; he needs a father." Their eyes met on it. And then, to Peter, who had burst into tears, aware of wickedness. "Never mind, Lord Meynel'. This once, I propose to indulge you." He summoned one of his midshipmen and instructed him to take Peter ashore, show him the monkeys, "And do not bring him back before dinner time."

The midshipman – who was quite young enough to want to see the monkeys too – grinned grateful comprehension, there was a volley of orders and before she had collected her wits sufficiently to protest, Amanda saw her gleeful son being rowed ashore in the Captain's gig.

"He will be quite safe," Medway forestalled her question. "And it is time you were relieved of him for a while. Besides, we have much to talk of, you and I." He took her arm. "Come."

Julia and John Purvis were talking animatedly on the other side of the deck. All around, and above them in the rigging, the multifarious business of the ship went on. Everyone was, apparently, occupied . . . And yet, Amanda felt herself suddenly the cynosure of all eyes.

She looked up at Medway. "Should I, perhaps, show a suitable reluctance?" she asked.

"I do not see why. We are grown people, you and I, and besides," he shut his cabin door behind them, "we have, as I told you, much to discuss. But first—" He took her in his arms.

At last, Amanda drew a little away and looked up at him. "I did not know it could be like that," she said tremulously.

"I think, my love, that there is a great deal that you do not know – and that it will be my pleasure to teach you. What a little idiot you have been, have you not?"

"I am glad you call it little! I think myself the greatest fool in christendom. What must you have thought of me?"

"Why, that it was time someone took you in hand. And that child of yours, too. 'I am Lord Meynel' indeed!" His hand, gentle among her curls took the sting out of it.

"Was it not dreadful? I was ready to sink. But – Captain Medway—" there was something she had to say, but how hard, how brutally hard it was.

"Yes?" And then, lifting her chin, "You could, you know, even go so far as to call me Charles."

"Charles?" She savoured it. "But, first, I must tell you . . . You may not—" How could she get it out? "You may not want me, after . . ."

"I find that hard to believe. You are not, I collect, aware of how badly I have wanted you, and for how long, while you were dreaming of this absurdity and that. I warn you, there is to be an end of dreaming now. I want a wife, not a dream castle princess."

"A wife?" How delicious the words tasted on her tongue. But still, she had not told him. She moved a little away from the magic of his touch. "Charles, do not look at me. It is about Peter—" once more she paused.

"A spoiled, delightful brat, and very like his mother. But that is not what you are trying to say, is it, my love. You are trying, I collect, to tell me that that deplorable Grassi was right and he is not, in fact, Lord Meynel. Is that it, my poor love?" And then, as she nodded her head, speechless with confusion, he pulled her gently to him. "I am glad you told me, but of course I have known it, always."

"Always?" She could not believe her ears.

"Well, shall we say, as long as you have. You forget that John Purvis was wounded and delirious in my care. You were much on his mind . . . Do not blame him, my love, he could not help himself."

"And still, you were so good to me, that time on the *Vanguard?*"

"I thought you magnificent," he said. "And have done so ever since. Yours has been no easy life, my dearest, but it shall be my study to make it otherwise in future. I cannot tell you how long I have longed to look after you."

"Have you really?" Gradually, ecstatically, she was letting the full tide of happiness sweep over her.

"Yes." He laughed. "And could have shaken you, often, when I saw you persisting in that childhood dream of yours about John Purvis, and he, poor man, doting all the time on the Countess."

"What a fool you must have thought me."

"No, just wilfully blind, and wonderfully loyal. You have my permission to be as loyal as you wish to me."

She smiled up at him. "Thank you. I will see what I can do. But what a charge we shall be upon you, Peter and I – well not Peter, who will be a rich man, but I must tell you that Lord Meynel's will . . ."

"Was a most iniquitous document," he cut her short. "I know that you lose your income if you remarry – and I am glad of it. We do not want Lord Meynel's money, you and I. Besides – if you had a father, he would be asking me if I could support you in any sort of comfort – and I should have to tell him, what you, my love, seem not somehow to have grasped, that I am a shockingly rich man myself. If you have been indulging in visions of love in a cottage – or a captain's cabin, for the matter of that, you had best disabuse yourself of them and resign yourself to a life of ignoble affluence."

"Truly?" She did not try to conceal her surprise. "But I thought—"

"I thought you did, and I am glad of it. One marriage for money is enough for any girl." And then as she was about to protest: "Forgive me, I should not have said that. John Purvis has told me how it was."

"John Purvis seems to have told you a great deal." She could not quite keep the irritation out of her voice.

"Yes, has he not?" He was laughing at her. "You have yet to learn, my love, that men are far worse gossips than women. But truly you must forgive John Purvis, for though I have told him nothing, I think he has known for a long time how it was with me."

She had been following another line of thought. "No wonder you were so angry with me in Palermo," she said.

"What? When I learned of your engaging yourself to John? I should rather think I was: I have never wanted to shake anyone so badly in my life. I think, if the child had not been there, I would have done so, and, I hope, shaken a little sense into you."

"Poor John," she said thoughtfully. "He thought himself, I collect, in some sort obliged to offer for me."

"Yes, and I have no doubt most devoutly hoped that you would have the sense to refuse him."

"You mean," she could not help laughing, "that it was all my fault?"

"Of course." He bent, quickly, to kiss her. "I was never more relieved in my life than when you came to your senses and cried off. I was beginning to fear that I should have to carry you off by main force, and beat some sense into you." And then, feeling her suddenly shrink in his arms. "Ah, my poor love, you have had enough of force, have you not? I promise you, it is all to be different now you are mine."

"No beatings? No shakings?" With an effort, she managed to keep it light.

"Nothing but love – for you and for that bad child of yours, whom I cannot help liking, and of whom I have no doubt we shall contrive to make a man, between us."

"Tell me I did right." What exquisite comfort there was in being able to ask the question.

"What? In letting Lord Meynel acknowledge him as his heir? I am sure you did, though I could wish you had told him the truth."

"But I did." She laughed. "So you did not know quite everything about me after all. Oh yes, Lord Meynel knew. I have no doubt that the Grassi – and his will – were his revenge. If I marry, I lose everything. And I have nothing of my own, you know. Nothing."

"I am glad of it. Do not look so anxious, my poor love. I truly think that I can contrive to keep you in muslins and laces – and, that reminds me, what do you propose to be married in?"

"Married?"

"Well, yes. That is what we are discussing, is it not?"

"Yes." How deliciously matter-of-fact it was. "But, surely, Lord Meynel . . ."

"I know. He has only just died, poor man, and it will show the most deplorable lack of taste in you to cast off your black gloves and marry me; but will it, truly, be any worse, in the eyes of the tattling world, than to sail home with me, unchaperoned, and unmarried?"

"But, surely, Julia?"

"She returns with John Purvis to Palermo. I told you we had much to talk of. While we were beating about in the fog, the *Centaur* got a march on us and arrived here before us, with news from Palermo."

"Oh?"

"Yes. Stirring news. Your enemy, the Grassi is revealed, at last, in her true colours. It was she, all the time, who was giving information to the French. The Countess is exonerated, and the Queen has actually written, urging her to return and let her forgive her for having unjustly suspected her."

Amanda laughed. "How like the Queen."

"Yes, but just the same it is a command that should be obeyed – if the Countess wished to keep her estates."

"And Captain Purvis?"

Medway looked at her very straight. "Urges that they return. You must remember, my love, that he is a poor man, and not judge him too harshly."

She sighed. "Oh, poor John. And to think that he found himself saddled, for a time, with me – and no money. No wonder he looked so sad and grey." She paused. "But what right have I to judge him?"

"None," he agreed cordially, "having conducted yourself, too, with a good deal less than perfect wisdom, or, to be precise, like the beloved little scatterbrain that you are. But let us suspend judgement, and rather put our heads together and think what is best for us to do." And then, seeing that she still looked grave, "Do not be worrying yourself about the Countess. He will make her a very good sort of a husband, I am sure, so long as she holds the purse strings."

"Oh, poor John," she said again.

"Precisely: poor John. But I am tired of the subject. It is of myself that I wish to talk. Amanda," somehow he had her hands in his, "do you not think that I have waited long enough for you? The world will gossip whatever we do. Give me the right to protect you. Marry me now, and let the conventions go hang."

She looked down at her black dress. "What a pleasure it would be. To tell truth, I feel nothing but a hypocrite in this black."

"And no wonder." He pulled her towards him. "I am glad you think it will be a pleasure. But not 'would be', Amanda, 'will be'. I applied for the licence this morning along with John Purvis. Shall we make a double wedding of it?" And then, holding her by the shoulders, "Amanda, what are you laughing at?"

"My dress," she managed. "I have just given my only white dress to Julia."

"How like a woman." She was not sure whether he meant the gift, or the remark. "But never mind, my love, I will find the wedding dress, if you will but find me the bride."

"You really want me?"

"Amanda!" He shook her, very gently. "I promised

279

not to beat you when we were married, but I do not remember giving any rash guarantees about what I should do beforehand. If you ask me that kind of foolish question again, I'll not be answerable for the consequences."

"You mean, the sooner I marry you, the safer I shall be?"

"Exactly."

"Oh well, in that case, I would be an idiot, would I not, to hesitate?" She laughed. "And as for the proprieties, it seems to me that I am too far gone in scandal, now, for it to make much difference what I do. The sooner Lady Meynel is lost in Mrs Medway, the better. But I fear you are getting but a sad bargain, Charles: a suspected murderess . . ."

"And the woman I have loved for six years, though, truly, when you persist in talking like such a ninny, I wonder why. Let me, I beg you, be the judge of what I want. And, as for scandal, I believe my name may, in some sort serve to frank yours. And that puts me in mind that there is something else I must break to you. It is not only that I find myself, all at once, quite deplorably affluent; there is more to it. You have not asked why I am going home in such haste."

"Why, no. I did not think it any of my affair."

"What an admirable wife you are going to be! But it is, as a matter of fact, very much your affair. I told you, in Palermo, that my father was dead and my cousin dying. My poor father; I wish I had seen more of him, these last years, and I wish still more that he had had the happiness of meeting you, Amanda. But he was an old man, and an ill one. His death is cause more for sorrow than surprise. But there were letters waiting for me at Gibraltar. My cousin, too, is dead. Poor Roderick, we never liked each other, he and I, but I must needs weep his death, though I have no doubt he hated me as he died, and though I am hard put to it to be grateful for the inheritance he leaves me. It means the end of my career, and, Amanda, I have loved the sea, almost as I love you, and you must be my consolation for leaving it. My dreams of glory are ended now; Lord Nelson must save the world without me – and, believe me, my love, he will. But, poor Roderick! He married at seventeen – to secure the succession, and I often thought, to spite me. And his wife has born him a daughter a year ever since – I do not precisely recollect whether the grand total is seven now, or eight. And now, poor man, he has caught the measles from his own children – and died of it. And before he had succeeded in doing worse than casting the family's affairs into a state of confusion from which my presence is necessary to extricate them. Had he lived, I have no doubt he would have played at ducks and drakes with the whole."

"I can see you find it difficult to regret him. But his poor wife, and all those little girls. What of them?"

"They are precisely why I must hurry home, and why – aside from various selfish motives of my own – I shall be particularly glad to have you at my side. Poor Lavinia is the merest nothing and has, as a matter of course, taken to her bed as a result of this disaster. I shall be surprised if the upbringing of her children does not fall to our lot. How will you like the managing of six spoiled little girls?"

"Or maybe seven? I shall like it above all things, and it should be the very thing for Peter, who has been an only child too long."

"Yes, well, I have other plans about that. I do not propose to have six daughters in succession, and so I warn you."

She coloured and laughed. "I can see you are going to be the most complete bully of a husband any wife was ever blessed with."

"Of course. What else? And I shall begin now. Come here, Amanda, I have not kissed you for five minutes."

"Much too long," she agreed, returning, shyness forgotten, to his arms. This was so natural, like breathing, or being alive . . .

The cabin door flew open. "Mama!" exclaimed Peter. And then, "Huzza, so it's really truly true."

"Quite true," said Medway composedly, his arm still firm around Amanda's waist. "I am to be your new papa, and I shall begin by asking what you are doing here, when

I sent you, but half an hour since, to see the monkeys with Mr Jesmond."

"I made him bring me back," said Peter simply. "Pray do not be angry with him, he really could not help himself, not after he had told me. I had to ask your pardon, you see." He was very red in the face.

"My pardon?"

"For what I said this morning. About being a lord. But truly I did not know. Nobody called you anything but Captain Medway . . ."

"It is a title that, frankly, I prefer."

To Amanda's relief, he was meeting the child on his own ground. But what on earth were they talking about?

"You prefer it? To being Earl of – oh, botheration, I have forgot it again. What are you Earl of, sir? And will you forgive me for what I said this morning?"

"Readily. Though I would rather have the apology addressed to Captain Medway than to the Earl of Canterbury."

Amanda pulled away to look at him. "Good God," she said. "An earl?"

"I am afraid so. Will you mind it very much?"

"Well," she smiled at them both, "I suppose I shall have to bear it."